VAMPIRE SCIENCE

JONATHAN BLUM & KATE ORMAN

BBC BOOKS

Published by BBC Books,
an imprint of BBC Worldwide Publishing
BBC Worldwide Ltd, Woodlands, 80 Wood Lane,
London W12 0TT

Reprinted 1997

First published 1997
Copyright © Jonathan Blum & Kate Orman 1997.
The moral right of the authors has been asserted.

Original series broadcast on the BBC
Format © BBC 1963
Doctor Who and TARDIS are trademarks of the BBC

ISBN 0 563 40566 X
Imaging by Black Sheep, copyright © BBC

Printed and bound in Great Britain by Mackays of Chatham
Cover printed by Belmont Press Ltd, Northampton

For the cast, crew and other hangers on who helped make *Time Rift* (especially AC Chapin, Amy Steele and Kris Kramer) – without whom none of this would've been. Just one more take, guys!

FIRST BITE

CHAPTER 1
SOMETHING WONDERFUL, SOMETHING HORRIBLE

San Francisco, 1976

The girl was headed for a fall.

Carolyn watched her from the next table, with the appalled fascination of someone watching a car hurtle over a cliff in slow motion. The girl was breaking all the unwritten rules of the bar. Making herself look like easy prey.

Bars like this one were supposed to be safe, a refuge from the testosterone-crazed macho men who were taking over the disco scene. But the people here could be just as predatory. One bite and away, and good luck on ever getting a phone call after the following morning.

So you learnt how to play the game, how not to come on too strong or too easy. How to use all the little tricks Carolyn had spent far too much time picking up.

Her usual method was to bring along a sketchpad, in an attempt to look like some kind of artist. Her drawings had always ended up turning back into doodles of aromatic hydrocarbons as the homework she kept trying to forget pushed its way back into her mind.

But tonight she just didn't feel like bothering. So she sat, and drank, and listened to the woman playing guitar on the small stage in the corner, and tried not to look too interested. Being obviously available meant you were obviously desperate.

But this girl, the one sitting at the next table, was just casually scoping out everyone in sight without a care in the world. She had an easy confidence, with none of the furtiveness or discomfort which so many of the other women wore around here, and eyes that knew a lot more than they were telling.

It was either the face of someone who was a master player in the singles scene – and she looked far too young to be that – or someone who had absolutely no idea of what she was getting into. Pretty soon someone would descend upon her, and the girl would end up being eaten alive.

Carolyn figured she'd better beat them to her.

She leaned back in her chair to get closer to the girl, then murmured in her ear. 'I wouldn't be quite so free with the eye contact, you know? The pick-up artists are out in force tonight.'

'I'd noticed,' the girl responded, giving Carolyn a sideways glance. She was a young blonde with unbelievably short hair and a wiry, athletic body. Unapologetically butch. She was at least a couple of years younger than Carolyn – nineteen, at the very most – but her face was already disconcertingly hard to read.

'Well if they give you any trouble, just call for me. I'm Carolyn. Carolyn McConnell.' She extended a hand, and the girl clasped it.

'Sam. Sam Jones. And yes, that is my real name.' She had a British accent, very cool and precise. This girl was giving nothing away. Clearly this was going to turn into one of those fascinating, frustrating conversational dances, where each person tried to keep themselves intriguingly mysterious. Well, it was working, Carolyn thought: Sam had already got her curious.

'You here by yourself?' she asked Sam.

'Nah, I'm with him,' she said, pointing over to the bar, where a long-haired guy who looked like Oscar Wilde was collecting their drinks. The guy was dressed flamboyantly even by Castro Street standards, in a long green velvet coat which looked like a leftover from the glory days of the Haight.

Carolyn looked him up and down. 'I take it he's not your boyfriend.'

The girl smirked. 'No way on Earth.' A good sign, thought Carolyn. 'We're on the road together. He's showing me the universe, you know? Excitement and adventure and all that. Letting me get some new experiences.' Sam met her eyes, and Carolyn saw a piercing seriousness there which left her wondering just how much this girl had experienced already.

'And so he brought you here?'

Sam grinned. 'Yeah. We're just waiting for something to happen.' Suddenly Sam wheeled around in her chair and fixed her with another one of those too-calm focused looks. 'Pop quiz, hotshot. What do you believe in?'

Carolyn stumbled. 'Huh? What do you mean?'

'Just that. What do you believe in?'

Well, this was a new approach. Carolyn stalled for time, trying to think of a suitably deep response that would hold this girl's interest. 'Well, uh, lots of things. I believe my biochem professor is genetically incapable of giving anyone an A.' Sam smiled close-lipped at that, but her gaze didn't waver. 'Well, I believe in God, I suppose. But I believe that's not enough, that we've got to work to fix the world ourselves. That sounds awfully vague... I don't know what else to say.'

'Put it another way. What do you dream about?'

That was easy. 'Finding a cure for cancer.' But then that wasn't quite true, was it? If she really believed in it, she'd be at home studying for that exam she'd written off. 'Except when I dream about chucking it all and just becoming a stagehand at some theatre.'

'And what are you doing about it?'

'Um. Studying, mostly. It's not much, sorry...'

'Don't apologise. What are you doing about it?'

Damn she was good. 'Learning. Taking classes.'

'What else?'

'Digging up articles. Finding people who know.'

'How far are you willing to go?'

'As far as I can,' Carolyn breathed.

Suddenly Sam sat back, a satisfied smile on her face. 'Not bad, not bad at all.'

Carolyn had the distinct feeling that something significant had just happened, but she had no idea what. Clearly Sam knew just what she was doing. God help anyone who fed her a bad pick-up line. 'And how about you? What do you believe in?'

Sam grinned, slowly, and spread her hands wide. 'Everything.'

Carolyn had no idea what to say to that.

'Sam,' the man in the velvet coat called out from near the door. His voice was firm and urgent. 'She's outside. I think she's going around the back.'

In an instant Sam was out of her seat and bolting for the exit. 'Nice talking to you.' Carolyn was left staring in confusion as the pair of them dashed out of the bar.

It took her just a moment to decide what to do. She had a quick word with Lyn at the bar, who let her slip through the kitchen to the back door. If Sam didn't want to be followed, she shouldn't have spent so much time trying to be fascinating.

There were two women in the alleyway, in a close embrace. The taller one was all but sweeping the shorter one off her feet. There was no sign of Sam or the man in the coat. Carolyn saw that an old Ford Torino was blocking one end of the alleyway – behind there might be a good place to watch whatever was going to happen. The tall woman was pulling the other woman's head back by her hair and there was blood running down the other woman's neck and the woman had her teeth in the other woman's throat.

Teeth in the other woman's throat.

Carolyn screamed.

The tall woman looked up, was looking straight at her. Was running straight at her. The bleeding woman fell in a heap, and the tall woman was reaching for Carolyn, and there wasn't even time to think that this wasn't happening, just time to grab the door handle and try to fumble the door back open before the tall woman's hand grabbed her shoulder and the nails dug in –

'Stop!'

The hand let go. Carolyn got the door open and was halfway inside before she even thought to look to see who had shouted.

The man in the velvet coat was stalking into the alleyway, his hand raised high, his eyes blazing. Carolyn got her first proper look at him. He was tall and slender, with long chestnut hair and green, green eyes.

Sam followed a pace behind him, cool and impassive, as if she did this every day. The tall woman stood frozen in a fighting crouch, hands raised like claws, her mouth a mess of blood and lipstick.

'Eva.' The woman started with fear. 'That's the name you're using this time, isn't it?' The man kept advancing on Eva, slower now, relentless. 'I knew you'd come back here. You never thought anyone would notice, did you?'

Carolyn couldn't take her eyes off him. His voice was low and strong, and it was holding Eva transfixed.

The woman bleeding on the pavement was stumbling halfway to her feet, was running, falling, crawling towards the door where Carolyn was standing. Using the distraction as a chance to escape. Carolyn thought she should be doing the same thing, but she couldn't move. And the wounded woman ploughed into her, was suddenly a dead weight in her arms, dragging her off her feet. Pinning her to the ground.

She could see the man circling around Eva, light but unshakable on his feet, somehow surrounding her all by himself. 'Your last victim wasn't quite dead. I found her where you dumped her body. Her name's Cheryl, did you know that?'

Eva hissed.

His eyes were locked on her, and his voice rasped with barely controlled fury. 'The hospital's keeping her under close observation, but they think she's going to live now. Disappointed, are you?'

Carolyn felt the blood running down her blouse. It was coming from the other woman's neck. She sat up against the wall, supporting the weight of the woman sprawled on top of her, and started pressing around the wound. Trying to control the bleeding, trying to hold the woman's life inside her body with the sheer force of her fingers.

The woman's skin was already clammy. Her chest was rising and falling under Carolyn's arm, short, shallow breaths. For God's sake, don't let her die.

Eva had fangs. She could see them now. She'd never spotted them all the times she'd seen her around the bar. Eva had fangs, and she was baring them at this skinny English guy in the Jane Austen costume.

Eva's muscles were tightening. Oh God, she could rip him in half. She could kill them all and he wasn't scared in the slightest. He just kept advancing on her, as if unshakable confidence and righteous rage would be enough to protect him.

7

And she was backing away from him.

His words were like a gale blowing in her face. 'You think you're strong, don't you? You think you're more than human. You think that gives you the right to do what you do to them.' He pulled off his coat and stood there braced for her. 'Why don't you try picking on someone who's less human than you are, mm?'

Carolyn held her breath.

Eva was going to spring. Was going to kill him.

For one moment, all Carolyn could hear was the bleeding woman's breath rasping in her ear.

Eva ran.

And the man was shouting at her as she bolted for the car down the alleyway, and Sam leapt away from the car as Eva snarled at her, and the man was still roaring at Eva as she threw the door open and started the motor. And Carolyn found her own voice, yelled for Lyn, for a doctor, for an ambulance. She heard footsteps and commotion starting up inside. Then the man was suddenly flattening himself against the wall of the alleyway, and the car's motor was revving, and the headlights stabbed at her, heading straight for her and the woman whose neck she was holding together. *Move*. She dragged the wounded woman over the door sill as the Ford's wheels crashed through where their legs had been.

There were voices surrounding them now, back inside the hallway. Experienced hands lifted the bleeding woman's weight off her, started asking questions she didn't know how to answer. None of them registered. As soon as she could move, while they were tending to the victim, Carolyn ran back out. She had to see what that man was doing.

He was standing on the street corner, still shouting and shaking his fist at Eva's tail lights. 'Come and have a go if you think yer hard enough!' he called after her.

Then, as soon as he knew she was gone, he turned around, his face breaking into a sudden broad grin. 'I was beginning to think she'd never take the hint.' It was a face full of experienced innocence, the look of someone who had seen the worst the world had to offer and walked through unscathed.

'Did you get it in place?' he asked Sam.

Sam nodded, her cheeks still flushed with excitement. 'Right in the wheel-well, like you said.'

'I didn't have a chance to plant the other one on her. But still, it's a start. Good job getting that woman to safety, by the way.' With a jolt Carolyn realised that he was talking to her. Before she could answer, he'd moved on. 'Sam, get the car. I'll distract the innocent bystanders for you.' And he and Sam were bustling off down the alleyway together, leaving her with a hundred questions getting lost somewhere between her brain and her lips.

'Hang on,' she yelled. Sam and the man stopped and spun around to face her.

Others were beginning to fill the alleyway. A siren howled in the distance, growing louder. The man's gaze was flicking anxiously around them, as if he were itching to run off, to catch up with the events he'd unleashed.

'What's this all about?' Carolyn yelled at him. That was all she could get out.

The man dithered for a few precious seconds. Then he stepped towards her, and now he was staring straight into her eyes, grasping her hand and pressing it first to the left side of his chest, then to the right.

'Yes, I'm not human, and yes, that was a vampire, and yes, you really have wandered into an ancient feud between my people and theirs, and now you can either stay here and tell people stories they'll never believe, or come with us and help us stop her from killing people. Excuse me.'

And she could feel an impossible double pulse through her fingertips, and a tingling chilliness to his skin, and she had no idea any more what other questions there were to ask. He was already dashing off down the alley, and she was still standing frozen with shock.

Sam grinned as she hurried after him. 'He's the Doctor,' she said. 'Deal with it.'

Two minutes later she was squeezed into the back seat of a battered maroon VW Beetle, pressed tightly against Sam and holding on for dear life as the Doctor sent them barrelling downhill.

Sam was laughing giddily and bouncing in her seat with each bump. All the sophistication she'd shown in the bar had vanished; she looked years younger, maybe only seventeen.

Carolyn knew how she felt – the last time she'd been on a ride like this, she'd been twelve years old and her big brother had been showing her what his new GTO could do. Under other circumstances she would have been enjoying this, but... no, wait, strike that. She was enjoying this.

The front seat of the Bug was filled with a pile of electronics, which hummed like a theremin. As they gained on Eva's car, the pitch it put out wobbled more and more. If they got too close, they slowed down. The Doctor – funny how she'd just accepted that that was his name – explained that they were letting Eva lead them to any other vampires in the area. His whole challenge to her had been a bit of misdirection, a chance for Sam to slip a tracking device on to Eva's car.

'We've got to find out what we're up against,' he said. 'This could be one lone vampire, or a coven, or a fully fledged army out to resurrect ancient demons and mythological horrors. That sort of thing.' He cocked his head as the hum suddenly dipped in pitch. He turned the car down a side street, and the pitch climbed back up again. 'My people, the Time Lords, have been on the lookout for descendants of the Great Vampires for millions of years, ever since the war we fought against them. If any evidence of one turns up, we're duty-bound to investigate.'

'It plays hell with holiday plans,' Sam threw in cheerfully. 'Not that we didn't need some excitement round here anyway. I can't believe people get nostalgic for this.'

Right, thought Carolyn. 'And so Eva ran off because she knew you were a, uh, a Time Lord?'

'Nah, she ran cause she's a bully at heart,' said Sam.

'The people who believe the most in the idea of the food chain are the ones who think they're at the top,' the Doctor said without taking his eyes off the road. 'Remind them they're not, and suddenly they're terrified.'

He grinned again, and somehow it all seemed perfectly reasonable.

'We do this sort of thing all the time,' said Sam. Suddenly she was sophisticated again.

'We?' asked the Doctor.

Sam made a face. 'All right, you do this all the time. I'm just a beginner.' She quickly sealed over the puncture in her façade, turning back to Carolyn with the confident eye contact she'd shown in the bar. 'But anyway, whether they're human or not, you can still confuse 'em. And if you can do that, you can win.'

'You're just doing that deliberately,' she told Sam.

'What?'

'Being weird.'

Sam smiled tightly. 'Gimme weird over boring any day.'

The electronic whine reached a peak, a high sustained vibrato. The Doctor pulled up on to a side street, behind a run-down apartment building, and nearly rear-ended the dingy brown Torino in its parking space.

He pulled over half a block farther on, parking in the shadows of an expired street lamp, and leapt out.

They were in the back end of the Tenderloin district. A few hundred feet straight up to their left were some of the biggest mansions and swankiest hotels in the city. Here, there were only seedy row houses, tall and narrow buildings with tall and narrow windows, their cracked gingerbreading making even the new buildings look old.

The tall and narrow Doctor led the way back towards the apartment building on the corner. Carolyn took up the rear, watching the pair of them. Sam was glancing warily left, right, up, down, over her shoulder, looking for trouble from any possible direction. Perhaps she should be doing the same, instead of staring at them, but she couldn't seem to take her eyes off the team of two.

At the corner, the Doctor pirouetted, taking a quick glance in every direction at once, and then hared up the steps to the set of mail slots in the wall. He scanned through them for a name.

'Forty-seven,' he called out. Again he turned on his heel and nearly ploughed into Carolyn. 'Ah, excuse me,' he said without missing a beat, and dashed through the door, heading for the stairs.

Sam had to work at being weird, thought Carolyn, but for the Doctor it just came naturally.

Carolyn ran up the three flights of stairs to apartment 47. It gave her a little bit of pride that she beat Sam to the top, even if Sam was less winded at the end.

The Doctor was already hard at work at the doorknob to Eva's apartment, pressing at it with his bare fingers. Carolyn kept glancing over her shoulder to see if they were being noticed. At least none of the residents were crazy enough to be out of doors at this hour. Then again, probably most of the residents were the kind of people you stayed indoors to avoid at this hour.

'If she's in there,' whispered Sam, 'what's the plan?'

The Doctor thought about it. A little voice in Carolyn's head asked why he was only just thinking about this now. 'We scare her out again,' he said. 'Make her keep running till she runs to the others.'

He held up a finger, asking them for quiet, then gave the side of the doorknob two sharp taps. Carolyn heard a click, and the knob turned freely in the Doctor's hand.

There was no way that could have possibly happened.

With a conjurer's flourish he pointed towards the doorknob. 'Are you ready?' She nodded, and before she had another moment to think about it he'd thrown the door open and she was dashing inside with them.

It was dark. The Doctor hit the light switch as he charged past. Carolyn looked around, expecting the vampire to leap out at them at any moment.

A sheet of plywood covered the only window. Sam kicked open the only other door, the bathroom.

'Not here,' said Sam.

'Just left. And in a hurry.' He indicated the open cabinet.

'Could be skipping town.'

Quick shake of his head. 'Left the car.'

'Did she?'

The Doctor stopped for half a second, thinking, then bolted back into the hallway. Carolyn and Sam caught up with him in time to see him thrust his head out of the nearest window. The Torino hadn't moved. 'Yes, she did.'

'Somewhere on foot, then.'

He nodded. 'Could be warning the others.'

'If there are others. She could just be feeding.'

The Doctor grimaced at that. 'Goodness knows where. Carolyn?'

Carolyn jumped again. She'd been trying to figure out how to squeeze a word in. It was almost like they could read each other's mind. (Hell, maybe they could!) 'I dunno,' she said. 'This isn't my neighbourhood.'

'It's all right, I understand.' He spun around and headed back into the apartment. 'She doesn't know we're here. She'll come back. Sam, watch the front entrance.'

'Right,' said Sam, and promptly climbed out of the window.

Carolyn almost ran to catch her before she realised Sam was sitting comfortably on the foot-wide windowsill, looking down on the doorway like a gargoyle on a cathedral roof.

'Are you crazy?' Carolyn said, 'She'll see you!'

Sam shook her head and grinned. 'Think about it. Where would you watch for her from?'

Carolyn blinked. 'Oh, I don't know. The stairwell, maybe the alleyway...'

'Yeah. And she'd watch for you there. Remember, she's rattled, she'll be being cautious. She'll be looking for people in every dark corner on the street or in the stairwell. And while she's doing that, do you think she'll think to look at a window ledge three storeys straight up?'

Put like that, it sounded like it made perfect sense. Carolyn tried not to think about what it meant about the situation she was in, that clinging to the outside of a building three storeys up was the sensible thing to do. 'OK.'

Sam nodded and pointed a 'gotcha' finger at her. 'That's why you don't do things the boring way. They're expecting it. If nothing else, you get the element of surprise.'

'Carolyn,' called the Doctor.

She turned to leave, but couldn't help looking at the three-storey drop below Sam's free-swinging feet. Sam didn't seem afraid of it in the slightest. 'Just hang on tight, all right?' she said, and ran to follow the Doctor.

'Here, give me a hand with this.' The Doctor was wrenching the piece of plywood away from the window. With her help, it came away easily, revealing the street-lamp glow from just below and a surprising amount of starshine from above.

The Doctor fished in one of his coat pockets and removed a huge ball of string. He turned it over and over, looking for the end. His hands were large, his fingers were long and slender. She found herself watching them in fascination as he teased out the end of the string. 'Now,' he said. 'We're going to rig up a little surprise for Eva. I'll need your help.'

'What do I do?'

'For a start,' he said, 'hold that cupboard door open.'

He attached the string to the inside doorknob, and walked backwards, carefully, towards the closet. He tied something inside, and then went to the kitchen, continuing to unwind the string.

OK. 'So what do you do when you're not hunting vampires?' she asked.

He shrugged. 'Whatever I want.' He looped one bit of the string around another. 'I can go anywhere, do anything, with anyone I want to.'

'What I wouldn't give for a life like yours.' Might as well start trying to broach the subject... 'And you just pick up people like Sam and have them travel with you?'

He nodded, intent on his work. 'I can always use another pair of hands. Would you hold this for a moment?'

Carolyn took the ball of string and stood there with her heart in her mouth, wondering if that was an offer. If it was, it certainly sounded like a better deal than the endless grind of classes and lab work and exams. Running off with a tall, dark, handsome, mysterious stranger and a young femme fatale – two for the price of one. Hey, she wasn't picky: she'd take either.

The Doctor had got a knife from the kitchen. He took the string from her, sliced through the strong stuff, and tied off the end. 'All right then, I do believe that's taken care of it.' By now the whole apartment was filled with string, crisscrossing around the ceiling in crazy patterns, tied to everything. The Doctor ran a critical eye over it, adjusting a knot here, moving a line of string an inch to the left here.

He was slowing down as she watched, all the mad energy disappearing back to wherever it came from. He beamed at Carolyn for a moment, then took a couple of steps towards the window and sprawled out in Eva's beanbag chair. He was just as completely relaxed as he'd been completely focused a moment ago.

He hadn't opened the door by magic, she suddenly realised. He'd picked it when they weren't looking. Sleight of hand. Show-off. 'I still don't believe you're a spaceman,' she said.

'Carotid pulse,' he said idly.

She knelt down next to the beanbag. 'Go on,' he said. She reached out and pressed her fingers against his throat, gently. He watched her, clear eyes in the dim light, his hair in disarray around his long face. She caught a faint scent, like sandalwood incense.

She felt her own eyes go wide as she felt the four-four time of his pulse under her fingertips. There was no way he could fake that.

'OK,' she said. 'So where are you from? Mars?'

'Much further away. A world you've never heard of. Gallifrey. But as the song puts it, I've been everywhere.'

He jumped up, and inched the plywood away from the window. The strings moved, and he gingerly pushed it away from the glass. The excitement was there all over again as he pointed out of the window.

'See that one?' he asked, tapping his finger on the glass. 'The red star, just to the right of the building across the street.' Carolyn looked, hoping she had the right one.

'On the fourth planet out from that star, there's a race of intelligent sea serpents who worship whales as gods. The whales on that planet aren't intelligent, of course, and the serpents know that, but they believe the whales are so enlightened that they don't need to be intelligent. Around that one' – he pointed again – 'there's a frozen world where an old enemy once stranded me. I had to build a fire to keep warm till I could be rescued, and I ended up throwing one of my favourite ties on the fire to keep it going. And around that sun' – he pointed at another star, directly overhead – 'there's an ice-cream shop where they kept me waiting an hour and a half for a chocolate milk shake. Can you believe it!'

Carolyn burst out laughing. 'No way.'

His eyes were utterly earnest. 'I mean it. The shop was mobbed. I tried to complain, but the man behind the counter was just swamped. "I've only got six hands!" he said...'

It suddenly occurred to her that she believed every word of it. Little green men had always seemed ludicrous, but somehow little green men serving milk shakes had a kind of a ring of truth to it.

Of course it made no sense, but the possibilities of how interesting nonsense could be were unfolding before her eyes.

She looked out of the window. 'This is what the sky had looked like when I was a kid,' she said.

'So,' asked the Doctor, 'what do you do?'

They'd been waiting for an hour. The Doctor was sitting on the floor, back against the wall, while she dozed in the beanbag. She'd heard him go out, speaking with Sam, low voices at the edge of her consciousness. When he'd got back, she was wide awake.

'Not much,' she said. 'Nothing that compares to fighting Daleks and stuff like that.'

'Oh, tell me anyway,' he said. 'I know all my stories – I'd rather hear yours.'

'All right... I'm a student. Undergrad at UCSF, majoring in biochem.'

'What for?'

'What?'

'Why do you want to learn that?'

Now she could see where Sam got it from. 'Well, I'm kind of

interested in cancer research,' she hedged. 'Not that I get to take any classes about it – they don't teach you any of the good stuff until they've spent a few years boring you with things that'll probably be irrelevant to whatever you go into anyway.'

'Oh,' he said, 'so you study it for fun then.'

'Hardly,' she snorted. 'Well, I suppose it's sort of a hobby, if you can call it that. I want to go into the theatre. Sad, isn't it? What a life.'

It was odd: he didn't nod or anything, he just kept acting interested. 'Tell me more about it. What have you found out lately?'

'Well, I haven't crashed any flitters on Mars recently.' No way will he ever want to have me run off with him and Sam now. 'I'm doing this research project on a new test for environmental carcinogens, using frame-shift mutations... I'm sorry, I'm boring you already.'

He waved that away. 'No, no, go on, it sounds fascinating!'

'Well, they just developed it. It's based on the principle that mutagens are also carcinogens.' He nodded enthusiastically. 'You start with a mutant strain of Salmonella that can't produce histidine, expose them to the chemical, and see if any colonies revert to wild type...' With a shock Carolyn realised he really was fascinated, his eyes as wide as a child's, being told a fairy story.

She laughed in disbelief. 'It's not that fascinating to *me*.'

'Oh? Why not?'

'I don't know.' After all, wasn't this what she wanted to do with her life?

He leaned forward and grasped her hand. His face was so alight she figured she could read by it. 'It always amazes me how everything fits together,' he said. 'All the patterns that people would never suspect are there just to look at them. The way that atoms make up a molecule, molecules make up a protein, proteins make up a cell, cells make up people, people make up worlds. The tiniest interactions of these obscure little unrelated parts can change everything on levels you'd never dream of.'

She nodded. 'Yeah. A tiny change in a person's genes, and they get cancer. Or blue eyes.'

'It's stunning, it's something I could never come up with in a million years.' He grinned suddenly. 'Why not get enthusiastic about it?'

'I dunno,' she said. 'You just don't get overjoyed about things like lipids.'

'A pharmacist on Lacaille 8760 once gave me a half-hour lecture about lipids. Did you know that if you suddenly lost all of your lipids, your cell membranes would disintegrate, and your whole body would melt into a puddle? Think about that – isn't it just bizarre?'

'Guess so,' she said, feeling the beginning of a smile. She hadn't thought about things like that for a long time.

'Go on. Please,' he asked.

And she realised, as she rambled on about the Ames test and base-pair substitution, that she really could remember feeling the way he did about it. It had taken high school and college to drum that enthusiasm out of her, to convince her it was a chore, obscure and anally retentive and dull.

She really was allowed to enjoy it. She'd forgotten what that felt like.

She found herself staring at his elven face with something close to awe. So what if maybe he'd picked the apartment lock before she'd got to look at it? So what if his saving her from Eva had been all bluster and psychology? That didn't change the effect he had on the world around him.

He was magic.

'We're on!' called Sam through the door.

'Ah!' The Doctor sprang to his feet and hurried towards the kitchen, out of sight of the front door. 'Time to come inside, Sam. Mind the tripwire. Tripstring.'

'Trip*strings*,' warned Carolyn, following him. She pressed herself against the kitchen wall between him and Sam, and waited.

The next ninety seconds were the longest of her life.

She couldn't make out the door in the darkness. All she could think about was how loud her breathing was and base-pair substitutions and the alleyway and Eva's hand grabbing her shoulder and the – Don't think about that. Think about the stars. Absolutely do not think about the fact that you've just broken into a killer's apartment with two complete strangers and she's about to walk back in through the door and you've got an exam tomorrow too –

Then Eva's key was rattle-scraping in the lock.

Eva pushed the door open, reaching for the light switch.

Her entire apartment collapsed on top of her.

The strings went berserk. Six of them were tied to the door, and as it closed behind her they pulled junk out of the closet and dragged furniture across the floor. Saucepans went flying out of the kitchen cupboards.

The vampire yelled. An ironing board fell on her. The Doctor was suddenly there among the flying junk, ducking as the saucepans swung back and forth on the ceiling. The plywood fell away from the window, and pale light filled the room.

Eva was half buried by a pile of junk. The worst of it was the desk, fallen across her legs. She was struggling to get up, the Doctor grabbing at her arms while she hissed at him and tried to bite him.

Sam ran over, tripping in the mess, and took hold of Eva's legs, pushing her down. Carolyn stayed pressed against the kitchen cupboard, staring at the vampire's furious face, wondering what to do. What should she do?

The Doctor was sitting astride Eva now, pinning her in place while Sam struggled to hold her kicking legs. He reached into his coat pocket and produced a stake from a croquet set, its end incongruously painted in multicoloured stripes. He placed the tip just over Eva's heart. The vampire froze.

'Now,' said the Doctor calmly, 'you're going to tell me all about the other vampires here. How many of you, where you came from, anything you think I might be interested in. And then, if you'll pardon the expression, you're going to take me to your leader.'

Carolyn couldn't take her eyes off the stake. The first hints of dawn were filling in the light from the window. As the sun rose, the spot where the beams hit the floor would keep moving.

Towards Eva. She still couldn't take her eyes off the stake. What was he going to do if she wouldn't talk?

'I'm waiting,' said the Doctor.

He had her pinned. She was struggling under him. Everything she'd ever been taught said that if you saw a man doing this to a woman you made a scene or grabbed your Mace or did something to stop it. But this was the woman who had tried to kill her, lying there mute and terrified.

'You're not just going to walk away from this one,' the Doctor said levelly.

'No,' Eva gasped.

'Whether you cooperate or not, either way it's over. No more killings. I can't let you kill anyone else.'

Eva was staring up at the Doctor, an animal look of hatred and fear on her face.

'At least I'm giving you a choice,' he said. Carolyn realised that his hands were shaking. 'That's more than you've given anyone.' He looked – he looked afraid, as though he was the one on the business end of the stake. 'Please. Talk to me.'

Eva's left hand shot up. Her fingers locked around the Doctor's hands, around the end of the stake.

Carolyn ran towards the Doctor, tried to pull Eva's hand away. He was straining against her. She could feel each bone in Eva's hand, the fingers tight, her strength overpowering them both.

'Sam,' cried the Doctor. 'Hide your eyes.'

The stake pushed down under her hand.

Something hit Carolyn in the eyes. She tried to blink it away, and Eva was screaming but only for a moment, and the Doctor yelled something she couldn't make out. She felt Eva's hand spasm, become rigid under hers, then suddenly brittle. She pulled it away from the Doctor, then realised it had crumbled like old paper between her fingers. It wasn't attached any more.

She opened her eyes. There was more blood on her blouse.

The Doctor was kneeling in the midst of a human-shaped pile of red-flecked grey ash, his head bowed. Bits of Eva's clothes were still visible among the powder.

Slowly he stood up, the horror on his face fading into a quiet, lost look. He made a dazed attempt at brushing the blood from his waistcoat, as he looked down at the chalky remains.

Carolyn wanted to hold him. She didn't want to touch him. She ran to the kitchen and started trying to wash the blood out of her clothes.

The sunrise was a pale yellow. Carolyn just stared through the window of the Bug as they drove back to her apartment near the campus. The sun was all she could focus on at the moment.

Sam was sitting next to her, her voice subdued. 'Look, it had to happen, you know that. Yeah, it was a mess, it was horrible, but we're talking about a vampire.'

Carolyn's hands wrung vaguely at her white blouse, stained pink, still wet. 'I've never had to deal with a vampire before.'

Sam grasped her hand. Carolyn stopped her wringing. 'Forget the unreal bits then. Just remember, that woman was a serial killer. A maniac.'

'I've never had to deal with a serial killer before either.'

Eva had dropped the Tupperware container she'd been carrying with her. Carolyn had picked it up, and found her fingers coated with the red residue which still coated the inside. Leftovers, she thought. Eva must have still been hungry, and come back to her apartment to grab a quick bite from her fridge.

God knew what the police were going to think.

'It had to happen eventually,' said Sam helplessly.

'It did not have to happen,' said the Doctor. His hands were grasping the wheel as tightly as they'd grasped the stake. 'There's got to be another way. Must be another way.' He went on mumbling under his breath, his brain churning onward, refusing to let go of the problem even for a moment.

She couldn't follow his hands. She'd been right there and she didn't know for sure what had happened. She hadn't been able to tell whether Eva had been pushing down on the stake and the Doctor desperately trying to hold it up, or the reverse.

Maybe he wanted it to be ambiguous, she thought for a moment. Sleight of hand.

'Carolyn, we're here,' he said. She looked up and saw her

21

building outside. He opened the driver's-side door and unfolded himself out of the car.

Sam leaned over and gave her a hug, a warm full-bodied one. 'Take care,' she said. When she let go, Sam looked just like she had before all this in the bar, the same unshaking direct gaze, the unflappable mask back in place. For a moment Carolyn wondered how she could look on everything that had happened and not be changed.

The Doctor opened the passenger door for her. 'Hell of a ride, wasn't it?' she said vaguely.

'So,' he said. 'Do you want us to wait for you?'

She shook her head. 'I can't. I gotta study. I have an exam in ...' She looked at her watch. 'Two hours. Maybe later? What are you going to do now?'

'There's not much else we can do. No leads, no sign that other vampires even exist. All we have left to do is check with the police and ask if the woman from the bar is all right.'

'I'll do that,' she said. 'I want to know.'

Her brain was still doing its best to keep it all from sinking in. All the images were blurring together now: kneeling beside the woman who'd tried to kill her and seeing the rage and fear in her eyes, and lying in an alleyway with her arms wrapped around a bleeding woman, trying to hold in her life with her bare hands. The Doctor, standing up for that woman's life with nothing but the force of his words and his wits, and the Doctor stabbing a piece of wood into a monster who screamed. Starscapes and blood spatters.

'How do I contact you?' she said. 'I mean, I guess you're not in the book...'

'Wait, wait, wait. How about this?' He reached into the Bug and rummaged around in the glove compartment. Finally he produced a stack of opaque white squares, twelve of them, each about four inches by four. 'If you ever run across any more vampires, just give us a call,' he explained as he handed them to her.

'How?' she asked.

'Oh, you'll know what to do,' he said, and headed back around the car.

She stood there, trying to ignore the inner voice that was nagging her that she'd made the wrong choice. She was alive and well and her world was still here. She'd go inside and get cleaned up and she'd be fine, even ready for the exam, just a bit fuzzy-headed from the unexpected all-nighter. That was all.

Maybe, when she was ready to remember it, she'd remember the magic. Maybe she might even get a little overjoyed about it.

'Wait,' she called. 'Maybe I can see you tomorrow?'

He grinned hugely. 'I've no idea. We don't even know if we'll be around tomorrow.'

And they weren't.

CHAPTER 2
VAMPIRES ARE REAL

San Francisco, 1997

Friday

Carolyn McConnell drove up to her house on Divisadero Street. She parked the car, turning the wheels against the kerb out of long habit, and sat in the silence for a moment. She was forty-one years old today.

Her mobile phone rang, startling her. She grabbed it out of the coat on the passenger seat. 'Hello?'

'It's James.'

'Hi honey, what's –'

'I'm in the house. I just saw a prowler – someone looking in at the window.' The outside lights snapped on suddenly.

Carolyn craned her neck. The house was one of dozens, narrow two-storey buildings stacked beside the sharply sloping street. White paint, beige curtains, young ivy. 'I don't see anyone,' she said.

'I think I frightened them off. Stay there, lock the doors – I'll be there in a minute.'

'Don't leave the front door unlocked!' she said.

A moment later, James stepped out of the front door, carefully closing it behind him. He held an umbrella as though it was a baseball bat, looking around. He ran down the steps and up to the car.

She wound down the window. 'That'll be handy,' she said, 'if you're attacked by a vicious squall.'

'I think the prowlers ran off,' said James. He leaned in and kissed her. He was five years her junior, short and muscular with dark hair and blue eyes. 'Happy birthday,' he said.

Inside, the house was full of candlelight. James had put a

couple of oil-burners on, filling their home with the scent of violets. 'Oh, James,' she said, putting down her bag and keys.

'Dinner is in the pipeline,' he said. 'I've fed Mina and the kittens. You put your feet up and watch the idiot box. I'll have everything ready in half an hour.'

'Yes, sir.' She kissed the top of his head.

She threw her coat over a chair and sank gratefully into the couch, grabbing the TV remote. 'How was your day?'

'Very ordinary. Dress rehearsal for the Scottish play, all going very well. And you?'

'Paperwork. We're about an inch from getting the grant for the retrovirus project.'

The news was just starting. Carolyn pushed her shoes off. She had closed her eyes, letting the anchorwoman's voice roll over her, when she heard it. The V-word.

'... coming up, Senator Daniel Ben-Zvi is murdered in his own front yard. Police are investigating a possible repeat of last year's Noe Valley vampire killings. Stay with us.'

Carolyn leapt across the living room and shoved a tape into the VCR. She reached up to the bookshelf and grabbed her scrapbooks.

When James came back in, she was deep in mid-rummage. 'What's up?' he said.

'Oh,' she said, thumbing the TV remote. 'It's you know what.'

'OK,' he said, sitting down next to her. 'What happened?'

She nodded at the television, eyes glued to the tube.

'... according to police, the senator was found in his front yard early this morning by a neighbour, dead from loss of blood. They are not ruling out a repeat of the Noe Valley vampire murders from last year.'

Carolyn said, 'Why don't they ever tell you anything more?'

A man in a police uniform appeared on the screen. Detective Greg Allinson, announced the caption. 'At this stage, we can't rule out the possibility that this is linked to the so-called vampire killings in Noe Valley last year.'

'Argh!' said Carolyn. At least she'd found the clippings she was looking for.

'Mi-Jung Kanaka, KKBE 7 nightly news,' said the reporter.

'What makes them think it was another one of those "vampires"?' said James.

'Probably a similar MO,' said Carolyn. She was running her thumbnail down a clipping, reading fast. 'That cult in Noe Valley attacked seven people and killed two. They cut open their victims' veins and drank their blood, and then left them for dead. The two murdered people bled to death before help could reach them.'

'Sick,' said James.

'Very sick.' She looked up, thinking. 'It's odd. Why make the connection to Noe Valley? If they had a suspect, someone seen lapping up the poor old guy's blood, it might make sense. But if someone opened up one of his veins, couldn't it just be an assassin? Or even suicide?'

'Maybe it was an animal,' said James. 'Like one of those squirrels that get hooked on crack.'

'Vampire crack squirrels?' said Carolyn. She started thumbing through her clippings.

'Maybe the police are sitting on the full details for the time being,' said James.

'Maybe.'

He took the scrapbook gently out of her hands, and leaned over her, pressing himself against her. 'Now, Doctor McConnell, it's your birthday today. Leave the detective work aside.'

He kissed her until she grabbed the hair at the back of his neck, pulling him in closer. 'That's better,' he gasped, when they came up for air.

A timer went off in the kitchen. 'The rice!' he exclaimed. 'Scuse me!'

She waited until he had been gone for fifteen seconds. Then she wound the tape back and watched the news item again.

And two blocks away, the Doctor walked up to Sam and said, 'We're early.'

Saturday

Carolyn and James both had to work. He headed to the theatre, and she drove her Lexus to the lab and fought with her paperwork backlog until lunchtime.

The news report was on her mind as she brown-bagged it. She turned her photo of James around. He smiled from beneath a cowboy hat, crouching next to Fortinbras, his golden Labrador. It had been Fort who'd brought them together, poor old thing.

James made jokes about her 'vampire thing', but he never laughed at her, bless him. She wasn't sure if he knew just how seriously she took it. She'd never told him about Eva. Not once in the eleven months they'd been together.

They'd met for the first time at behind-the-scenes drinks for the Bay Area Music in Theatre Society. James had been able to describe the lighting for every minute of *Rosencrantz and Guildenstern*, his hands swooping and weaving in description. Holding her rapt in a way that everyone else at the party had resolutely failed to do.

She had promptly forgotten his name, cursing herself the next morning. When the play opened she made a point of being there, scanning the program for his photo. 'James Court, Lighting Designer'. His face was so serious, peering intently out of the black-and-white photo, that she'd actually laughed out loud.

She'd met Andrew Chi Hun, the theatre's manager, about a dozen times. The elderly man recognised her, waving her backstage with a smile. Carolyn had found James there, sitting on a sandbag, looking even more serious than his photo. 'Someone ran over my dog,' he said, without preamble. He'd looked so miserable that she'd insisted on buying him a drink.

'I used to be in show business,' she told him in the bar.

'Really? What did you do?'

'Two years backstage and in the chorus. I gave it up and went back to finish my degree in biochemistry.'

'Biochemistry, wow.' He was genuinely impressed, it was sweet. 'What do you do?'

'I want to find a cure for cancer,' she told him.

It was the same answer she had given since she was twelve. 'What do you want to do when you grow up, Carolyn?' 'I want to find a cure for cancer.' The same answer she'd given Sam Jones twenty years ago. The answer that had haunted her while she was working tech or performing in bit parts.

She'd been up to her elbows in chemicals and cell cultures for twelve years. Now she oversaw the new generation of researchers, kids fresh out of college who were still keen enough to do the mind-numbing, badly paid, repetitive work. Because they were going to find a cure for cancer.

God knew, one of them probably was. Every day they used techniques that had been way out and experimental when she was working in the lab, and came up with new techniques of their own. She had to make sure the retrovirus project got funding. Lewis had been in here this morning, shouting at her over the desk about it. Fifteen years ago it would have been her doing the shouting.

That was more important than 'the vampire thing'. For the moment, anyway. Carolyn folded her lunch bag and slipped it into her handbag, picked up the sheaf of papers on her desk, and tried to focus on the latest round of grant requests.

Sam opened her eyes.

Sometimes she was still confused when she woke up in the TARDIS. Confused and excited at finding herself in the wrong bed, like waking up on the first day of a holiday. Sometimes a little disturbed, as though she was intruding. This room had belonged to another teenager, long ago.

But it was her room now. She and the Doctor had spent an afternoon furnishing it, pushing bits and pieces around the TARDIS corridors on huge trolleys, laughing, their sleeves rolled up.

There was a beautiful Victorian writing desk, right out of a BBC costume drama. The chair was an ergonomic design from the mid-2050s, all plastic and padding. There was a mammoth wardrobe with children's coloured stickers and peeling paint, a fourteenth-century Persian rug, and a four-poster bed.

Sam climbed out of the bed and opened the wardrobe. She

found a clean pair of jeans and a Greenpeace T-shirt with a cartoon radiation monster, and took them with her soap and toiletries bag to the bathroom.

The bathroom was never in quite the same place each day. Sam suspected this was the TARDIS's little joke: moving its internal architecture around was the ship's equivalent of giggling. The Doctor invariably spoke about his time-space vessel as though it – she – were alive.

Sam opened doors at random – study, blank wall, cupboard full of old cardboard boxes, staircase – until she found the bathroom. She grinned triumphantly at the sight of the giant brass-legged bath. Within five minutes she was submerged to her nose.

The TARDIS was a she. Was it just because she was a ship, or was there more to it than that?

Sam had never dared to ask the Doctor if he had a girlfriend. (Or a boyfriend, she admonished herself – don't jump to conclusions.) It was a part of his life he never talked about. Maybe, once upon a time, he'd even had a wife and kids. But it must have been a long time ago; the TARDIS was the closest thing he had to a girlfriend now.

And what about you, Sam Jones? Where do you fit in?

Sam dried herself and dressed, sitting on the edge of the bath while she tugged on her sneakers. They were her third pair since Coal Hill – she'd done an awful lot of running since she'd started this magic-carpet ride.

Last night she'd left the Doctor in the console room, fussing over the controls with a jar of wood polish. She had slipped out, as usual; for some reason it always made her feel strange to say, 'Goodnight, Doctor.'

Maybe it was because he didn't actually seem to sleep. Maybe it was because she was torn between wanting to call him 'Uncle' or something, and wanting to know his actual name so she could call him that. It was probably a Gallifreyan name that a mere human couldn't pronounce. She grinned. It was probably 'Fred'.

He was still in the console room, sitting in his armchair, reading an ancient issue of *Scientific American* through a pair of bifocals. His cravat was undone and he'd kicked his shoes off. The jar of polish was sitting on top of the console, abandoned, and a bunch of wires were hanging down from the destination monitor.

He sprang up when he saw her. 'Sam! Excellent! There's a great deal to do.'

She saw his clear blue eyes sparkle behind the lenses of his glasses.

'Good morning, Uncle Fred.' She grinned at his confusion. He tucked the spectacles away in his waistcoat pocket and snatched up his jacket. 'Today's the day.'

'Tomorrow's the day,' he repeated. 'It's Saturday. Local time is' – he produced his pocket watch – 'three p.m. I'm going out.' Before she could protest, he said, 'I need you to stay here and do some absolutely vital work.'

'This is about my age again, isn't it?' said Sam. 'Old enough to dodge Daleks, too young to go to a nightclub.'

'Sam, Sam, Sam –' He was struggling into his shoes.

'You know I'm not going to wander in there and start throwing back tequila slammers,' she insisted. 'You know you can trust me. Undo the laces first.'

'I do trust you,' said the Doctor, struggling with the knots in his shoelaces. 'But I also need you to do some legwork for me.' He wiggled his toes at her.

Sam laughed. 'Do you really need me to stay here?' He nodded. 'All right, then. You run along and enjoy yourself. But be back by midnight!'

The Doctor did up his cravat with an elegant, practised movement. 'Hopefully before then,' he said.

'Doctor,' said Sam, just as he was about to go through the door. 'What are you going to do?'

He turned back to look at her, hands clasped behind his back. 'Well,' he said. 'I'm going to do nothing.'

'I don't think I should talk to you,' said Mi-Jung. 'So I'm going to.'

'Right,' said Carolyn.

They were sitting at the reporter's desk, in the middle of an open office. Everyone seemed to be panicking, running around and shouting at one another, but Mi-Jung took no notice. Carolyn had the feeling it was normally like this here.

'The truth is,' said the reporter, 'I've been leaned on. I think. There was an army general here this morning. She held me up for an hour, asking questions. I was right there at the scene, before the ambulance even took that poor old man away.'

The army? 'Did she threaten you? Or tell you to keep your mouth shut, or anything?'

'Not quite.' Mi-Jung smiled, shaking her head. 'It was all to do with national security. She didn't ask us not to broadcast anything more, though, which is what I was expecting. She just wanted details about the murder.'

Carolyn took a mouthful of newsroom coffee. 'Couldn't she get that from the police? The hospital?'

'I think she'd already talked to them. She said she wanted "a fresh angle on the case".'

'What did you tell her?'

'The strange thing…' said Mi-Jung. 'I've seen six dead bodies in my time as a reporter. Senator Ben-Zvi was the sixth. Someone opened a vein in his leg, and he bled to death. But the strange thing was this. There was no blood on his clothes. There was no blood anywhere – not in the yard, not in the house. I checked with one of the police officers, Detective Allinson – he's in charge of the case. According to the paramedic, he couldn't have lost so much blood somewhere and then walked or dragged himself out to the yard. So the question is: where's the blood?'

Carolyn was hypnotised by the reporter's measured voice. 'OK,' she said. 'Where is it?'

Mi-Jung shrugged. 'Your guess is as good as mine.'

'Sucked out,' said Carolyn. 'Swallowed.'

The reporter nodded. 'That's what one of the policemen was saying. But the Noe Valley attacks were messy, and…they used knives.'

Carolyn put down the coffee cup. 'He was bitten,' she said.

'Yes, he was.'

'I knew it.'

'You did, huh?' said Mi-Jung. 'Listen, if you can add anything to the story…'

Carolyn blew out a breath. 'Not just yet. I might be able to, though. Listen, you've been incredibly helpful.'

'My pleasure. Watch out for that general. And give me a call if you've got any info.'

Somewhere in the Haight, there was a phone booth with a handwritten sign tied to the door with a piece of string. It said OUT OF ORDER, EXCEPT FOR EMERGENCIES. The message was repeated in three languages. A bundle of wires ran from the insides of the phone, down the pavement, around a lamppost and into the TARDIS door.

Sam sat in the TARDIS console room, with the San Francisco Yellow Pages and an antique phone. She sighed, drew a line through another hospital, and turned the page.

Sam sighed. She'd been sitting here for an hour, dialling number after number, asking the same strange questions over and over. The notepad beside her contained nothing but doodles.

She picked up the phone and checked her place in the phone book. By this point she had reached Shotwell Clinic, a small facility on the north side of the Mission District.

'Hi, this is Sam Jones, calling from San Francisco State,' she began for the umpteenth time. 'I'm working on a paper, and I'm making a few general inquiries about recent deaths by blood loss in the area…'

'Oh,' said the woman on the other end of the line, 'You want to talk to Doctor Shackle. Hold, please.'

Sam was then subjected to a full minute of a Muzak rendition of 'The Girl From Ipanema'. Had she finally hit paydirt? Come on, come on, answer!

Finally a man's voice came on the line. 'David Shackle.' She repeated her introductory spiel, and Shackle responded with a sardonic 'Ohhhhh. Well it's about time someone noticed.'

His voice was rounded, cultured, a tone which suggested that the voice's owner would much rather use it to read Shakespeare than waste it on mundane conversation. 'Let's make you an appointment for tomorrow morning. I've got some data I think you'll just love.'

For some reason, Detective Allinson wasn't laughing in her face.

Carolyn had stopped by the police station and asked to speak with him about the police investigation into the Ben-Zvi murder. She'd brought her scrapbooks, pointed out the couple of cases with a similar MO she'd found over the years, and waited for the snickers to start.

Instead, the silver-haired man started paging through her scrapbook, chewing on a toothpick with intense concentration. 'OK if I get someone to make photocopies of this?' he said.

'Sure,' she said. 'Anything, if it'll help.'

'Appreciate it,' he said. 'At this stage we can use every lead we can get. Can I get you some coffee?'

'Thanks,' said Carolyn. 'I'm fine.'

He nodded, and went back to her scrapbook.

Twenty years ago, she thought, I'd never have even thought of going to the cops. Now I'm just on the verge of asking one whether he believes in vampires, in real vampires.

How would he react? Throw her out? Nod and smile, uh-huh, sure there are vampires? Pull out a file fat with victims of the undead?

She was just about to ask him when the phone rang.

He picked it up, still reading through the scrapbook. 'Yeah? Yeah. Yeah. I'll be right out there.' He put the phone down. ''Scuse me for a minute, would you?'

Carolyn turned the scrapbook around, staring at a photo of two of the Noe Valley killers. She was making a bit of progress here. If there were vampires out there, the police were one step closer to believing it. She would definitely ask him. She could trust this guy.

She glanced out through the open office door.

Allinson was standing across the station, talking to a short, stocky black woman in an army uniform.

Carolyn almost jumped to her feet. The woman glanced in her direction. They'd be in here, any second.

She left her scrapbooks. She picked up her handbag and walked out through the office door. She kept walking, staring right ahead, heading for the station entrance. Nice, innocent woman, minding her own business.

She didn't start running until she got to the parking lot.

She made herself drive home slowly.

Carolyn sat at the lights, taking deep breaths. The face in the rear-view mirror frowned back at her. She'd driven around for a while at random, but if anyone was following her, she was damned if she could tell.

Now the adrenaline was wearing off, she was starting to wonder why she'd bolted. Maybe it was nothing. Maybe she'd stumbled over a military conspiracy to cover up the existence of vampires. Maybe the black woman was a friend of the senator's.

If only the Doctor was here. She remembered him challenging Eva in the alleyway. Facing her fangs and her glaring eyes, and laughing.

The car behind her tooted its horn. She pressed down on the accelerator, reluctantly. She didn't want to face James. She didn't want him involved in any of this.

Carolyn pulled up into the drive and pressed the garage remote. The door climbed ponderously upward and clanked to a halt. Her ears rang in the sudden silence as she looked around, up and down the dark street. Waiting for a face to appear at the window.

Never mind. She and James would have a quiet evening, maybe rent a movie, maybe just fool around. He would make her forget all about the day's hassles, the way he always did, and she would wake up in the morning knowing that everything was fine.

When she got in the door, there was a black woman in a smart green uniform sitting on her sofa, wearing a gun. She turned to look at Carolyn.

'Hi, honey,' said James, getting up and giving her a peck on the cheek.

'You let her in,' said Carolyn. 'Of course you let her in. How would you know –'

'Er,' said James. 'Carolyn, this is –'

'Brigadier-General Adrienne Kramer, United Nations Intelligence Taskforce,' said the woman. 'I believe we've got a friend in common.'

CHAPTER 3
NOW YOU SEE ME

Carolyn realised her mouth was hanging open. She shut it, firmly.

'Pleased to meet you,' she told Kramer, putting down her keys and bag. She plonked herself down on the sofa. 'Did you ask to see her ID?' she demanded.

James shrugged. 'No. But I don't think I could tell a real one from a fake.'

Kramer extracted a small leather wallet from her jacket pocket and passed it to Carolyn, who made a point of opening and looking at the card inside.

'Detective Allinson is wondering what happened to you,' said Kramer. Her voice sounded like someone tiptoeing across gravel.

'Why were you following me?' demanded Carolyn.

'I wasn't following you. You were next on my list, though.'

'Why?' said James. Carolyn was aware of his presence, just behind her shoulder.

'You've been looking for information about vampires. I want to know what your interest in my case is.'

'What case?'

'This case.' Kramer picked up her briefcase. Carolyn looked at it, bewildered. The general turned it around and snapped it open, then took out a folder and started to read. 'Cause of death: exsanguination. Wound possibly an animal bite. No blood found on the subject's clothes –'

'Daniel Ben-Zvi,' said Carolyn.

Kramer passed her the autopsy report. It was dated a week ago. The name at the top was Grant Oxwell.

'Now let me tell you what the report doesn't say,' said Kramer. 'First, Oxwell was found on the roof of a fish shop four blocks from Ben-Zvi's house, dressed in… a diving suit, with a note pinned to his back saying 'bite me'. Second, he was working for me.'

'For –' Carolyn looked at the ID again. 'UNIT?'

Kramer nodded. 'He was investigating the death of Gordon Pymble.'

'The diplomat?' said James.

'The United States ambassador to Buranda. You probably read about him in the papers last month.'

Carolyn nodded. 'I remember, he was murdered. But the papers didn't mention anything out of the ordinary.'

'Pymble had some pretty weird… tastes. He was found in the alley behind a nightclub with his pants around his ankles, a tangerine in his mouth, and bite marks on his right hip and left shoulder.'

Carolyn heard James breathing out hard through his nose, which was his way of politely not laughing. She said, 'So your agent was killed in a similar way.'

'Well, except for the tangerine,' deadpanned Kramer. 'Oxwell disappeared the day before I was going to debrief him. He was supposed to meet me at SFO. I spent a couple of days wondering where he'd got to; then he turned up on the roof. I think someone with a very sick sense of humour was trying to make a point.'

James said, 'I think I'd remember the tangerine.'

'The details were kept from the press,' said Kramer. 'Same with Oxwell. He didn't deserve that.'

'My God,' said Carolyn, 'Ben-Zvi was just the tip of the iceberg. How many of these killings have there been?' She looked at Kramer. 'That's why you're here, isn't it? You don't want some curious civilian poking around under the surface of your cover-up.' She couldn't help glancing at the gun on Kramer's hip. 'You're here to warn me off.'

Kramer gave her a withering glance over the top of her glasses. 'No, Doctor McConnell. I'm here to ask for your help.'

'Why me?' said Carolyn. 'You don't need an administrator: you need a forensic specialist or a doctor. Don't you have those in the army?'

'Yeah, I do. But you know the Doctor.'

38

'OK,' said James, 'so who is the Doctor?'

Carolyn looked up from her star map. 'Oh, he's just someone I worked with once…'

It was 1 a.m. They were sitting up on the roof of her house. James was trying to look at the moon through binoculars.

Kramer hadn't mentioned the Doctor again, sticking to the details of the killings. Carolyn had been bursting with questions, but James had insisted on staying until the general left, even though he was due at his premiere. He'd gotten back at midnight, with roses and champagne from Andrew Chi Hun.

'Do you want to try looking at Epsilon Lyrae?' she said. 'It's a double double star…'

'He must have been a hotshot,' said James, 'if you guys call him *the* Doctor.'

'It's right near Vega.' She tapped her finger on the star map. 'Look, you can see it even with the skyglow. Let's try the binoculars.'

'Do you suppose there's anyone up there – you know, out there?' He passed her the binocs.

Carolyn lifted them to her eyes. Epsilon Lyrae was a group of white spots, jumping in her field of view. 'I guess there must be,' she said.

'Kramer's probably got a satellite looking back at us,' James said. 'It's been there for months, beaming in through the bedroom window.'

Carolyn shuddered. 'Don't joke about it,' she said. 'For all we know, she did take a peek in our window.'

'Hadn't thought of that.' James put his arm around her, softly. 'I don't like thinking about my beloved in the company of the Men in Black.'

'You're telling me. She's probably got a file on us an inch thick.'

'She's got a deal with the BEMs. We'll be sitting here one night, and the biggest UFO in history will come right down on the house. Whoosh, we both get beamed up off of the roof, and carried off to Mars.'

'Where we have fascinating conversations with the prehistoric bacteria.'

'No, imagine it. Didn't you ever dream about that when you were a kid? Being carried off to some special world…'

She put the binoculars down. 'Oz?'

'Wonderland.'

'Terabithia.'

'Shangri-La.'

Carolyn said, 'Do you know how long it's been since we talked like this?'

They lay back on the roof, Carolyn resting her head on his shoulder. James said, 'Newsflash. Young rebels grow up into staid professionals. Film at eleven.'

Carolyn made a sad face. 'When did we get so settled?'

'Sometimes, lover, I think that's why you go looking for monsters.' James tucked an arm behind his head. 'The ordinary world isn't enough.'

'Fantasy worlds are just fine,' she said, 'until you meet your first dragon.'

'Kramer scares me more than any ol' vampire,' said James. 'She's real.'

Carolyn wondered how many stars there were up there. How many eyes were staring back at her, through alien binoculars…

James put on a terrible British accent. 'To Carolyn McConnell,' he intoned, 'he was always *the* Doctor.'

She laughed, and for a moment, she wanted to tell him everything.

Carolyn spent Sunday morning at the office again, finally finishing the grant applications. She'd arranged with Kramer to meet around lunchtime.

She hated keeping this a secret from James. They never kept secrets from each other.

No, that wasn't true, was it? Because she'd never told him about the Doctor.

She'd expected the general to turn up in uniform, but instead she was wearing a black pants suit. The briefcase was still by her side. 'Do you want some coffee?' Carolyn said, heading for the machine in the corner.

'No, thanks.' Carolyn poured herself a cup while Kramer opened her briefcase.

'Lieutenant Oxwell had been checking out some of Pymble's favourite haunts.' Kramer said, without preamble. She held the file in her hand, but she looked as though she knew it by heart. 'We can rule out a political motive, since Senator Ben-Zvi had no connections with Pymble.'

'How do you know?'

'Detective Allinson has been very cooperative.'

'I'll bet he has. Can I get copies of all of that stuff?'

Kramer looked at her. 'Not just yet, Doctor McConnell. Now, so far the only link between the diplomat and the senator is the murderer's MO. And this is the only connection between all three victims.'

She pushed a piece of paper across the desk. Carolyn picked it up. It was a photocopy of a San Francisco street map, with one corner circled in red, labelled THE OTHER PLACE in small, neat letters.

'That's the nightclub where Pymble was found. The killers wanted to make an example of him, presumably for political reasons. They wanted to make an example of Oxwell because he was investigating Pymble's death. But Ben-Zvi? The only connection is that he frequented the Other Place.'

'How do you know? Sorry, stupid question.'

'I found matchbooks on his mantelpiece, and the bartender recognised a photo,' said Kramer. 'If Ben-Zvi was killed for a reason, we don't know what it was. Plus there's the fact that his body was found in his own front yard. No "jokes". He's not an object lesson, he's just a corpse.'

'Maybe they were just in a hurry,' said Carolyn. 'Maybe he was on to them.'

'Them?'

'The vampires,' said Carolyn.

'Is that a professional opinion?'

'The sign on the door says "oncologist",' said Carolyn. 'Not "occultist".'

41

'I wish the Doctor was here,' both of them said at the same time. Their eyes met over the desk.

'We need to have a little talk,' said Kramer.

To get to the Shotwell Clinic, Sam had to descend almost to the lowest point of the valley below Bernal Heights. She looked at her tourist handbook while she idled at the lights. The North Mission district, despite decades of attempts at urban renewal, was still what was known as a 'declining' area, though as Sam inched through its streets she wondered what was left for it to decline to. She was surrounded by rundown warehouses, and blocks of flats which were barely distinguishable from the warehouses.

Once she left Route 101, she made sure the Bug's doors were locked, and then spent the rest of the trip feeling like a fish in a bowl. Every pair of eyes she passed on the street seemed to be making a threat or a suggestion.

The hospital itself was an unadorned brick building, tucked away on a side street about a mile from Mission Dolores. Sam left her rental car in the lot, wondering if the hub caps would still be on when she got back, and went inside.

The receptionist peered down at her in surprise. Sam had got into the habit of dressing old (though not as old as the Doctor, she thought): today she was wearing a tweed jacket and skirt. With her height, the right clothes and the right attitude, she could sometimes pass for twenty. A medical student doing interviews for her term paper.

The harried-looking woman at reception told her that Dr Shackle was in the emergency room, and he would be with her as soon as he got out. Sam settled down to leaf through a month-old *Time* magazine and contemplate the dingy yellow paint on the walls. Somewhere down the corridor, she caught the sound of shouting voices, and a gurney rattling through the hall at high speeds.

Finally a wiry-looking man crashed through the swing doors and headed straight for Sam's seat. He had a prematurely worn face, a carefully cultivated pair of dark circles under his eyes, and slick black hair that didn't quite reach his shoulders.

'All right, Maria,' he called out to the receptionist as he passed. 'Under no circumstances is anyone allowed to have a crisis for the next five minutes. I absolutely forbid it.' His entrance made, he collapsed into the chair nearest her, head thrown back, legs and arms flung outward in every conceivable direction.

'Doctor Shackle?' she asked. He grunted in the affirmative. 'I'm Sam Jones.'

He acknowledged her with a florid hand gesture. 'A pleasure to make your acquaintance, Ms Jones,' he said, and let his hand fall limply back to the armrest.

'Pleased to meet you too,' she replied, with infinitely less melodrama. She looked at him, sprawled in his seat. 'Is this a bad time?'

'Oh, no, it's no worse than any other round here. I'm just relishing the chance to sit still for a moment without the ceiling falling in or something.' He rubbed his eyes and sat up. 'It's non-stop, I tell you,' he pronounced. 'Non-stop.'

She grinned. 'I know the feeling. Anyway, on the phone you said you could help me with my research?'

'Indeed I can,' he declaimed, and shot a glare at the receptionist, who was hiding a giggle behind a copy of *People*. 'Let's go to my office – I've got all the files there.' He climbed to his feet and led Sam through the swing doors.

He took long loping strides down the corridor, scattering interns and nurses. Sam was forced into a stumbling half-run to keep up, while Shackle delivered a monologue about the surgery he'd just performed.

'Kid never had a chance. Someone shot him over something or other – one through the stomach, one through the lung, one through the family jewels.' His disgusted hand-wave almost caught Sam in the face. 'Another thirty-minute drama, over and done with. Ring down the curtain, send the players packing, et cetera et cetera.'

'Right,' said Sam, playing up to her role. He was so self-absorbed he hadn't even noticed her age or her accent; this was easy. 'I figure you get more of that in the Mission than we do in the Heights.'

'Naturally. It's the air up there, you see. It's so thin that all you rich people don't have the energy to run around shooting each other. Only when you get down in the valley does the air get thick enough to support some serious random violence.' Shackle looked over his shoulder at Sam, his face deadpan except for one half-raised eyebrow. 'I'm surprised you don't get the bends coming down here.'

Sam grinned despite herself. 'So the cure for street crime is oxygen deprivation. Cute.'

'Oh, it's not oxygen that's the problem, that's the point. Carbon dioxide is heavier than air, right?' Sam nodded. 'Ergo, all the crud you breathe out at the top of the hill, some poor shlub at the bottom of the hill breathes in. And all the extra toxins in their bloodstream makes folks down here cranky. It's the trickle-down theory of social unrest... Ah. My parlour, said the spider...'

'The first time I met the Doctor,' said Kramer, 'Washington DC was about to disappear down a time rift.'

'The first time I met him,' said Carolyn, as they passed a duck pond, 'he was making fun of a monster.'

'Uh-huh, that's him.' Kramer didn't smile, but Carolyn could hear the amusement in her voice. 'He's had a connection with UNIT for decades, on and off. Spent the last quarter of this century helping us fight off alien invasions.'

'What is UNIT, exactly? The Fortean branch of the military?'

'If you like. It's our job to keep the Earth safe from outside. And make sure nobody finds out about the aliens until we're all ready to handle it.'

'More cover-ups.'

'Who did you tell about the Doctor?'

'Well... nobody. But that's different from actively suppressing information.' Carolyn gave Kramer her best stern look. 'I find it kind of hard to believe that the Doctor would hang around with the army.'

'Why?'

'He just doesn't seem like that kind of guy...'

Kramer shrugged. 'You do whatever you have to to get the job done. Even play along with an alien who won't tell you what his clever plan is…'

'Are we talking about the same man? He's nothing like that.'

Kramer glanced at her. 'Try a physical description.'

'About yea high,' said Carolyn, holding her hand above her head. 'Looks like he's in his thirties. Brown hair and green eyes. English accent.'

Kramer shook her head. 'Must be a different regeneration. Try short and dark-haired, somewhere in his forties, with a Scottish accent. Irish, maybe.'

'Nope. The guy I met in seventy-six was nothing like that.'

'Sounds like you got a new guy. I'll have to add that to your file.'

'My file?' Carolyn shut her eyes. 'I knew it!'

'The incident was flagged "Possible Doctor Involvement". The file came up when I got HQ to do a search on you.'

For a moment, they stood together at the top of a hill, looking out across the city.

'If there are vampires…' Carolyn breathed.

'It's my job to identify and neutralise whatever threat they represent,' said Kramer. 'It's not your job, Doctor McConnell. I want your advice, but I don't need your direct involvement. Be sure you want to get mixed up in this.'

'It's a bit late now. But if you've got my file, why do you need me anyway? Doesn't the army have plenty of people?'

Kramer rolled her eyes in exasperation. 'You want to know what it's like trying to get the US military to cooperate with the UN? If they're not running the show, they don't want any part of it. If I even want to borrow a specialist from the army, I've got to fill out about three Michener novels' worth of paperwork. And don't even think about bringing in troops unless you've got hard evidence of an imminent threat to national security.' Carolyn nodded. 'So I like to bring in the occasional civilian adviser. Saves paperwork, stops the brass knowing what I'm up to… Besides, your average UFO hound knows more about what's going on than the desk jockeys in the Pentagon.' Kramer caught herself. 'Never mind,' she went on, 'that's all classified anyway. Now, we were saying?'

'All right,' said Carolyn. 'I'll give you whatever help I can. But I don't want James involved in any way, shape, or form.'

'No problem,' said Kramer. 'We'll keep him out of it.'

'The Other Place?' said James. 'Hey, I know the owner. Do you want me to ask him some questions?'

Carolyn looked at him, appalled. He always made her think of a big goofy dog when he hung over the back of the sofa like that. 'James, a man was killed right there!'

'Well, has the place shut down?'

'Well, I...' No, it hadn't. 'I don't think so…'

'So it can't be that dangerous. Not if you stay away from the tangerines.'

'Well, all right…' said Carolyn.

'What is going on, anyway?' said James.

'I don't know much more than you do,' said Carolyn, truthfully. At least, if you left out the Doctor. 'Ask the owner… How well do you know him?'

'He used to work in lighting, until he got bored and started up his own club. John Seavey. We worked together on a few productions. Pretty nice guy, very professional. I wonder what his light display is like…'

'James, I just don't want you to get mixed up in this.'

He shrugged. 'I'm not letting you get mixed up in it without a little support from your greatest fan.' He kissed her hand. 'I'll pop over to the club on my way home, and have a word with John. And then I'll treat you to lunch at Stromboli's, and we can decide where we're going from there.'

'I hate this,' said Carolyn again.

'I won't do anything illegal,' he said. 'Scout's honour.'

Shackle's office was a shambles, festooned with papers and milk crates full of bulging file folders.

Sam ran an eye over the scattered reference books, the stethoscope tossed over his desk chair, the balled-up turtleneck shoved on a shelf. All it needed was a couple of posters and a bulging laundry bag and it would look like her bedroom back home, in between clean-ups.

She squeezed herself on to a corner of the couch, avoiding disturbing the clutter spread across the rest of it, as he made a beeline for one particular pile of files in a corner.

'If you want exsanguinations,' he said, 'these should do you just fine for a start.' He grabbed ten inches' worth of manila folders off the pile and deposited them in her lap, then threw himself in his chair and leaned back to watch her reaction.

Sam glanced through the first bunch of folders. Each contained a photocopy of a death certificate, with notes scribbled by Shackle in the margins. 'Most of these look like natural causes.'

He gave her a look. 'Liver damage, alcoholism, probable ODs… Yeah, round here those count as natural causes,' he said.

'Lots of heart disease too,' she pointed out. 'Exposure, malnutrition…'

'Welcome to the bottom of the hill.'

Sam felt a familiar frown gathering on her forehead. Homeless dying on the streets; it was like London. 'OK,' she said, 'but blood loss?'

'It starts with this one.' He leaned forward and dug out one file from near the bottom. 'Old homeless guy found on his back in an alleyway. Natural causes, right?' She gave his look right back to him. 'No reason to pay any special attention. But on a visual exam, I noticed his back.'

He pointed at a black-and-white photo clipped to the death certificate, which showed a fairly hairy male back with a few scattered sores. 'No blotchiness. Now, I'm no forensic expert, but if he was on his back, the blood would have settled there after death. But there wasn't any discoloration. And when I opened him up, I checked his blood volume, and found out he was running on fumes.'

Sam looked at him. 'And there weren't any obvious wounds?'

'Oh, no obvious ones. A couple of small puncture wounds, partially healed, partway down his left side. No major blood vessels opened, no bloodstains left to draw attention. You'd think they were just ordinary bangs and scrapes to look at them.'

'So what did you do?'

'Do?' Shackle shrugged and spread his arms wide. He stood up and began to pace the room like an actor on a stage, waving the autopsy report around to illustrate his points. 'There wasn't anything to do. That man died because his liver was pickled – any doctor would tell you that. It's the only logical explanation. Because there's no way on Earth the man could have bled to death through a wound like that. Not without a suction pump pulling the blood out or something. And who would believe that?'

Sam reached up and caught his arm. 'You would,' she said, fixing him with her best penetrating stare.

Shackle's lip curled into half a smile. 'Good point.' He tossed the first file aside and went back to digging through the stack. 'But of course, I completely failed to mount a one-man crusade to bring an unknown wino's death to the public's attention. All I did was, the next time we got a DOA, I went looking.'

With a flourish he produced another file. Sam opened it, and found the paperwork for an old woman who had fallen down a flight of stairs. Clipped to the page was a close-up photo of a blotchy wrinkled neck, showing a cluster of bruises from the impact. Two large welts among them were set apart in a circle of red felt-tip.

Shackle leaned down and looked straight into Sam's eyes. 'And the next. And the next. And the next.'

Sam looked down at the ten-inch-deep stack of files, feeling the weight on her knees. It took her a while to think of what else to say. 'So all of these –'

'No, most of these. I haven't confirmed every one of them. Most of the other doctors didn't pay too much attention.'

'So some of them are from other hospitals?'

'Mm-hm, I asked them for any homeless or indigent deaths that fit my profile.'

'So you don't know if they –'

'No, but this stack is just the likely ones.'

Sam paused for a long moment. 'How many?'

'One hundred and ninety-three in six months.'

She shook her head. The number refused to sink into her skull. 'No, there can't possibly, someone would notice…'

'No one knows exactly how many homeless there are in the city. You can't count them – some are only on the street for a night, some for a month, some for years. *Street Sheet* is sold by over thirty thousand homeless people.' Shackle sat limply down on the edge of his chair. His voice was flat and dry, like that of a judge passing sentence. 'A couple of hundred isn't a drop in the bucket. Who cares?'

Sam looked down at the pile of folders in her lap, then up at Shackle. 'Well, now someone does.'

'No, you don't.' He sounded almost flippant. 'You care about whatever rich person just bought it the same way at the top of the hill. If that hadn't happened, you'd never have lowered yourself enough to come down here.'

Sam was furious to realise she was blushing. 'I came here to try to do something about it.'

'Oh don't get me wrong. I'm incredibly honoured that you've chosen to descend from on high and walk among us. But you wouldn't know how to handle things on the streets. It's a whole other world here.'

That did it. 'Oh, a whole other world?' she shot back, filling her voice with all the wide-eyed student enthusiasm she could muster. 'You mean with aliens and monsters and everything? Wow, San Francisco, the final frontier.'

She put a hand to her forehead, as if swooning before him. 'Oh, Doctor Shackle, I'm so glad I've got you as my native guide in the wilderness of 22nd Street.'

He started to protest, but she just stood up and calmly dropped the stack of files in his lap. She leaned over him as he sat blinking up at her. 'Look. The Doctor and I came here looking for this. Looking for vampires. We've done this before.'

'What?'

'We've got an actual investigation together, and we'd just love to have you help out. Of course, then you wouldn't be able to sit down here moaning about how nobody takes any notice of you.'

She thought about grabbing him by his tie, just to make her point, but that would be just a little too over the top. 'So, which will it be? Do you want in?'

'I –'

'Don't know what to say, do you?'

'Well, I, uh…'

'"Yes" would be perfect.'

'Um, yes!'

God, this was fun. No wonder the Doctor did it all the time. 'Oh, one more thing. If you think you can handle people round here better than me, then hey, who am I to argue? You can take care of that sort of stuff for us. But don't just assume I can't cope because I'm a kid. Because I can. Got that?'

He arched an eyebrow and threw her a salute. 'Yes, ma'am!'

As James set out from his work to the Other Place, he didn't notice the taxi behind him, its driver mildly excited to have been asked to 'Follow that car!'

The Doctor sat in the back of the taxi, his worried eyes fixed on James's station wagon. He couldn't do anything to stop what was going to happen. Not really. No, definitely not.

But he could watch. Perhaps he would learn something. Or perhaps he wouldn't. But someone ought to be there, even if only to witness it.

Carolyn was sitting under an umbrella out front of the Italian restaurant, people-watching. There was a matching umbrella in her mineral water. She took it out and twirled it in her fingers. Green paper and a toothpick. Fat men, skinny men, tall women, short women, walking by.

James was a quarter of an hour late. Hopefully that was a good sign – maybe he'd found out something really useful, something important. Either that, or he was stuck in traffic.

Gordon Pymble goes to the Other Place, and is murdered. Lieutenant Oxwell investigates Pymble's death, and is murdered. Daniel Ben-Zvi goes to the Other Place, and is murdered.

Things like this must happen all the time. There was a whole section of the United Nations devoted to it. It was Kramer's job, for goodness' sake. And no one ever knew about it. For all she knew, some of the people walking past were vampires, or Time

Lords, or bug-eyed monsters in disguise. For all she knew, all of them were.

The waiters were starting to give her funny looks. Or maybe she was just imagining it, embarrassed and conspicuous, sitting with one empty glass and one empty chair, slowly turning a paper umbrella in her hand.

Twenty minutes late. He should call, she thought irritably. She took out her phone and dialled James's number.

A waiter cruised up while she was listening to the *the mobile phone number you have dialled cannot be reached* message. She closed the phone with an angry snap and glowered at the street.

'Men,' sighed her waiter, picking up the empty glass.

If there are vampires, why isn't there more evidence? You'd think that blood-drained corpses would attract someone's attention.

Gordon Pymble goes to the Other Place, and is murdered. Lieutenant Oxwell investigates Pymble's death, and is murdered. Daniel Ben-Zvi goes to the Other Place, just before he's murdered. James Court –

Carolyn half stood, almost knocking her chair over.

'Are you all right, ma'am?' said the waiter, sailing back up.

She nodded, desperately, trying to find her phone again in her handbag. 'The check – I need the bill, please.'

'Yes, ma'am.'

She called the theatre. No answer. She tried his number again. And again. And again, after the waiter brought her the check and a concerned look, and again once more after another ten minutes, and then she knew that James wasn't going to make it.

CHAPTER 4
HOUSE CALL

Carolyn made it through the afternoon's paperwork by the simple method of pretending that nothing was wrong.

She phoned the theatre on her return to the lab, and again on her break, and got no answer in James's office. The stage manager said he hadn't come back after lunch.

On the way home she called the house over and over, getting more and more frustrated with the ever-so-cheerful voices on their answering machine. She rang the theatre again, the café again, then started working her way down the depressingly short list of friends of theirs whom they didn't work with. Everyone she got hold of sounded more concerned for her than for James, and she couldn't figure out why.

Finally she pulled up in front of their house – surprised that his car wasn't waiting there, despite everything – and went inside, feeling her body tightening all over.

He wasn't there. She had to do something. Something sensible. Feed Mina and the kittens, get dinner ready. After all, there wouldn't be dinner waiting. She climbed the steps into the kitchen and began rummaging through the cupboards. Her mind was flickering between studiously controlled concern and unreasoning irritation at James for pulling this disappearing act.

It was only when she opened the fridge and saw the only thing handy to eat was James's leftover rice and mushrooms that she found herself shaking uncontrollably.

For a long frozen moment she just stopped thinking. Her body was still moving, carrying her vaguely around the kitchen, looking for silverware. She couldn't think of anything more useful to do than set the table.

Finally, she put down the knife and fork and called General Kramer's number.

Kramer was an even bigger amount of no help. 'Carolyn, I'm

sorry. But what do you expect me to do? Conduct a house-to-house search of the city? Post a soldier on every street corner to ask people "Have you seen this man?"?'

Every word grated on her. Carolyn felt the urge to reach through the phone and grab Kramer by the throat. 'No,' she sighed, 'I guess not.'

'Well it's a good thing. With the budget cutbacks, we'd barely have enough men to cover a six-block radius anyway.' The voice at the other end of the line paused, awkwardly. 'I really am sorry. But you've got to keep calm, all right? I'll do everything I can. I'll start asking questions at the Other Place tonight.'

'No, wait, they'll get you too.' She was staring vaguely into space, her eyes not quite focusing on the casserole as it rotated in the microwave. 'My God. They got him in broad daylight.'

'Don't worry, I'll be subtle. I actually can manage that once in a while.'

'They got him,' Carolyn repeated, unhearing. She felt the cold spreading outward from her heart, as if it had just started pumping ice water.

'No. Carolyn, hold on a minute. If James were dead, we'd have found the body by now. The bastard wasn't exactly subtle about hiding Grant.' Kramer's voice burnt. 'We'll get him back alive. Just keep your grip, all right?'

Carolyn took a deep breath, then exhaled slowly. 'All right. So what do I do?'

'Just get some rest for now. Call me lunchtime tomorrow and we'll see what you can do then. OK?'

'OK.' The shivers had gone; now she didn't seem to feel a thing. Hold on. Get a grip. Get some dinner.

She went back to the fridge and dug out the leftovers. Then she busied herself at the microwave, holding the phone a little bit away from her ear, hearing the tinny little voice of the desk sergeant as he calmly asked her for details about a man who might be dead, a man whose Mickey Mouse coffee mug was still sitting in her sink waiting to be washed.

When the sergeant asked whether she and James had had any serious disagreements in the previous few days, she felt her throat lump up. She told him that with their schedules, they'd never had time for fights.

The sergeant was polite and noncommittally helpful, and assured her that everything possible would be done, and when she got off the phone Carolyn was sure there was no hope whatsoever.

Funny the things you notice. James's leftover rice in the casserole, looking like a culinary masterpiece. The unbelievably loud scrape of the kitchen chair across the floor. Funny the things you notice. The pile of lighting plans James had left scattered on his side of the table. The little sore grooves in her fingers, where the plastic ridges on the phone handset had cut into them. Funny the things you notice when there's nothing else left to think about.

Very quietly, Carolyn sat next to James's place at the table, eating the last of his food for him.

Midnight

Carolyn opened the chest in her bedroom and brought out the stack of white squares. She carried them down to the kitchen, pushed aside the stack of lighting plans on the table – James still hadn't put them away, she thought irritatedly before remembering – and laid the squares out. She stared at them for a long time.

What in hell was she supposed to do now?

She held one of the twelve squares in the palm of her hand. It did nothing. Her hand shook a bit as she held it, but then she realized she'd been trembling just as much before she'd picked it up.

In desperation she tried pushing the squares together on the table, making a rectangle of two rows of six, four rows of three, even one line of all twelve, but sliding them around did absolutely nothing.

Mina mewed at her curiously from her box. 'I have no idea,' she told the cat. 'It's like a jigsaw puzzle where all the pieces are the same.'

None of it made any sense. There had to be something she could do with these squares to make them contact the Doctor, but she couldn't even think about where to begin.

Maybe that was it. She took one square in each hand, closed her eyes, and thought at them. Once again, a miracle resolutely failed to happen. In the absence of any kind of telepathic instruction manual suddenly appearing in her head, she tried to come up with a message for the Doctor.

Dear Doctor, I… don't know… Even the effort of putting her thoughts into coherent words was too much. The sentences became a meaningless babble in her mind, a single sustained vibrating note of emotion. She was faintly conscious of her hands tightening convulsively around the two squares, the corners cutting into her palms. Her thoughts were lost under waves of panic, desperation, then despair, and finally the crushing realisation of just how silly it all was.

Eventually even that faded, leaving her mind empty of any feelings, of any ideas at all about what to do next. She just folded her hands together and leaned her face on them in despair.

The two squares in her hands stuck together at right angles to each other.

She felt a shiver run through her. Without opening her eyes, she reached for another square. She turned the two joined squares in her hand until she could fit in another square at right angles to the first two, and somehow now she could feel how if she turned it *that* way she could fit in another one at right angles to all three, and then another one, and another. The squares were coming together in her hand, to form a cube which had far too many faces to fit in three dimensions.

She didn't dare open her eyes, because somehow she knew that if her conscious mind tried to understand what was happening it would convince her that it was impossible, and right now she really needed it to be possible. Right now she needed to believe in magic.

She pressed the last face into place and felt the cube tingling between her fingertips.

'Send it.'

She jumped. Her eyes flew open. She couldn't look over her shoulder, out of fear that he might not actually be there. All she could do was stare in amazement at the faintly glowing impossible cube she'd somehow managed to put together.

'Go on, send it,' said the voice from behind her. 'Otherwise I won't receive it, so I won't have come here, and if there's one thing my life doesn't need it's another temporal paradox.'

She felt, rather than knew, what to do. The cube collapsed inward between her fingers and vanished into nothingness like a conjuring trick.

'Good.'

She took a deep shuddering breath and slowly turned around.

The Doctor was standing right behind her, his hand resting on her chair. He had that peaceful smile on his face. 'Hello, Carolyn.'

She hugged him and burst into tears.

CHAPTER 5
STAKE-OUT

Monday

Carolyn stood in the kitchen doorway and watched the Doctor cook breakfast.

He was in his shirtsleeves, wearing her apron. With one hand he scrambled eggs in one skillet, while with the other he deftly folded mushrooms and green peppers into an omelette. Every so often a hand flew over to flip a few of the pancakes browning on the griddle beside the stove, or leapt over to the cabinets to dig out a few more spices or jams for the collection he was amassing on the counter.

He moved with the grandiose energy of an orchestra conductor who was just getting to one of his favourite bits. Throughout it all he was singing, a long spiralling melody which jumped between scraps of Italian, snatches of what sounded like a bebop trumpet solo, and tongue-tripping percussion fills.

'What's that?' she asked.

'The rebirth aria from Paletti's *The Fourth Sister.* Don't worry if you don't recognise it: it won't be written for another few decades. Ya-te-de-dum…'

Carolyn smiled, bending to rub Mina between the ears. He'd even remembered to feed her, and now she was curled in her cardboard box, the kittens nuzzling her belly.

Somehow the sheer casualness with which he talked about future opera was incredibly reassuring. Nonsense like that was part of the Doctor's everyday world – if he could take that in his stride, he could handle anything San Francisco could throw at him.

Right on a cymbal-crash from the Doctor, two slices of cinnamon toast popped out of the toaster. He was already swinging around to scoop them up, and without missing a note he fed in two more slices of bread. Forget the conductor metaphor, Carolyn thought, he was playing every instrument in the orchestra at once single-handed, and getting away with it.

She started clearing away the things on the table. James's things. The impossible cube was sitting among the debris.

Last night, after she had 'sent' it, the Doctor had produced it from his pocket and told her he'd received it some time ago in his TARDIS. He'd said something about how the time displacement was a quirk of a hypercube's four-dimensional engineering. She figured it made sense as long as she didn't think about it too hard.

Then he'd tucked her into bed, saying three little words that made her heart leap for joy. *James is alive*.

As she turned the cube in her hands, this way and that way (and, without knowing quite how she did it, *that* way), she could catch glimpses in each of the plastic-metal faces of images contained inside: James's face, Ben-Zvi's corpse in the morgue. Her own face from last night, with her lost-looking eyes staring into the hypercube.

'Doctor,' she began, 'Um –'

'Oops, catch!' he shouted, aiming the cinnamon toast at her plate. Somehow she caught the slices.

Carolyn stared at the toast. She needed to say something profound, something about how grateful she was that he was here, how she felt as though a great weight had been lifted from her, that now she had magic with which to fight the monsters.

She said, 'You have cute eyebrows.'

He raised them at her, the pace of his frantic cooking slowing.

She put a hand on her face. 'That was not what I meant to say.'

'What did you mean to say?' He flipped a pancake and put down the spatula, looking at her.

'OK, you said James isn't dead. How do you know? Have you seen the future?'

'No.' The toast popped up behind him, unnoticed. 'But the vampires seized James as a warning – a warning to stop your investigation. The last time they gave such a warning, they killed Oxwell – but,' – he held up a hand to stop her from interrupting

– 'that time, they made sure Kramer found the body right away. If they were willing to, ah, annoy the military to that degree, they'd have no qualms at all about annoying you in the same way. But they haven't. Therefore, for some reason, they haven't killed James.'

That made about as much sense as that cube did, Carolyn thought. But she believed it.

'Therefore,' he said, folding the omelette, 'we should continue to investigate, until we provoke them into confronting us.'

'But that's insane,' said Carolyn. 'They'll kill him, what if they kill him anyway?'

'They won't.' He reached out suddenly, and took her hand in his. 'We will find James. And I promise I will do whatever is necessary to ensure his safety.'

'Thank you,' she whispered, giving his long fingers a squeeze. His skin was soft and cool. She wondered what his normal body temperature was.

Thank God he was here, she thought again. Everything was going to be all right. Everything was all right.

The Doctor spun around back to the stove. The pancakes were charring and the omelette had caught fire.

'So, I see his taste for younger women hasn't changed.'

Sam gave Kramer her best extra-polished freak-out-the-mundanes smile. 'Compared to him, we're all younger women.'

The general didn't even blink, turning back to the traffic. Damn, thought Sam. She'd been trying her best to rattle Kramer ever since she'd met her at the hotel.

The Doctor had sent her there, saying it was time to bring the general on board. She'd spotted Kramer in the hotel restaurant: a black woman in her fifties, built like a tank and twice as imposing, carving up her sausage-and-egg breakfast with ruthless military efficiency. She practically screamed authority figure, and right there and then Sam had decided to make bewildering Kramer her special project for the day.

So she had walked over to the soldier, out of the blue, and with no warning whatsoever said that the Doctor wanted to meet her.

And Kramer had just looked at her for a moment, raised an eyebrow, and asked, 'Which one?'

Now Adrienne Kramer was driving her to Carolyn's place in a government-issue Chevy Caprice, remaining completely unperturbed by anything Sam had been able to throw at her. 'So what's he up to these days?' she asked Sam. 'Still driving that ratty old police box on the wrong side of the spacelanes?'

'Hey, it's in better shape than this rent-a-wreck,' Sam said pointedly. 'Shouldn't you have a staff car or something? At least a driver?'

'Too showy,' Kramer said. 'The boys in the accounting office prefer subtle. Subtle is cheap.' She made a wry face and changed lanes to dodge a bicycle messenger. 'And besides, I was only supposed to be in town long enough to debrief Grant Oxwell. I figure you and the Doctor know about him too?' There was a note of resignation in her voice.

'We know everything Carolyn knows.' Sam looked coolly out of the window. 'She sent a message, and it told us where to find her, and you. We were supposed to arrive last night, but the Doctor got the landing date wrong.'

'That sounds about right,' said Kramer.

'Yeah. We got here three days early, so we've been investigating since then.' Sam filled her in briefly on what they'd discovered. 'We couldn't get in touch with you before now 'cause if Carolyn knew we were here, she might act differently, and then she might not send the message that got us here.' Sam tried to look inscrutably wise. 'Chronosynclastic retroactive continuity.'

'Uh-huh.' The gobbledegook slid right off Kramer without even leaving a mark. 'So all this time I've been chasing down dead ends and getting nowhere, he's been one step ahead? Typical. Absolutely typical.' She pulled a disbelieving face. 'You realise he's been working with us for about six or seven lifetimes now, and he still hasn't gotten his head around the idea of letting us know what he's up to? I dunno…' She shrugged and returned her attention to the road.

Six or seven lifetimes. Sam had the sinking feeling that this general, this woman in a suit, might actually know the Doctor better than she did. 'You've known him for that long?'

'Nah, I only know the older ones from the files. I met him once myself, back when he was in his previous regeneration. When he was that funny-looking little Scottish guy.'

Well, if she couldn't psych Kramer out, at least she could learn something from her. 'So what was he like?'

Kramer shifted in her seat. 'Let's just say we weren't exactly on the best of terms.'

'Oh.' Sam forgot to be sophisticated, and settled for just being puzzled. 'Why not?'

'Well, basically because he's a manipulative little weirdo who was always up to something behind my back,' Kramer said with a hint of a smile.

Sam blinked and shook her head. 'He's, er, changed. Quite a bit.'

'So I gather. I don't hold it against him. He always did what he did for the best of reasons. But it still annoyed the hell out of me, you know?' Kramer turned and looked at her. 'I figured I should put this all out in the open. I don't want you to feel like you're caught in the middle or anything.'

They pulled up outside Carolyn's house and walked up to the front door. Sam was surprised. 'You sound like you don't trust him.'

'I'd trust him with my life,' said Kramer. 'But he never invited me over for dinner, you know what I mean? We just saved the world and got on with it.' She turned the knob, found the door was unlocked, and stepped inside. 'And I don't think either of us was pushing to be any closer friends than that.'

'Adrienne!' The Doctor bounded into the foyer with a huge smile on his face, and before Kramer was even through the door he had grasped her hand in both of his. He shook it enthusiastically as she stood there with her mouth working up and down in confusion. 'It's been absolutely ages. So how's everything back in Washington? How are George and the little ones? Not that they're little any more, not by this point in time. Be sure to tell young Adam I said hello. I saw him at his university last year. Good job on handling that Brieri scouting party, by the way. Well, come on into the kitchen, there's pancakes and toast and eggs for everyone...'

Kramer looked like she'd just been hit in the face with a cream pie. She cast a bewildered glance over at Sam as the Doctor bundled them both into the kitchen. 'Get used to it,' Sam said with an evil grin.

Sam hadn't got any older.

Carolyn sat in her kitchen, looking at the impossibilities gathered around her table. The extraterrestrial was offering cinnamon toast to the commander of the secret military force, the vampire-hunting doctor – David Shackle, his name was – was wolfing down an omelette like it was his first decent meal in days, and across the table a seventeen-year-old who had been seventeen in 1976 was watching her with that same unflappable gaze.

When she'd seen Sam again, she'd completely frozen up. The Doctor had come to the rescue. When he'd realised that Carolyn hadn't known anything about his TARDIS, he'd been more than happy to explain at baffling length about the intricacies of space-time travel.

She looked back and forth between the Doctor and Kramer. Great, a general and a doctor. It was like she'd called in her parents. It made the leftover seventies-student part of her soul squirm to know that there was a member of the military-industrial complex sitting at her table, munching toast.

And across the table, Sam was still looking at her. *I didn't get old*, her face seemed to say. *When did you?*

The Doctor insisted they finish their breakfast and pack the dishwasher before they got to work.

Sam shut the door of the machine and thumbed a button. It immediately started a familiar humming noise that inescapably reminded her of home. She went out of the kitchen into the lounge, careful to avoid treading on the kittens. The Doctor and Kramer were peering at a map, watched by Carolyn and Dr Shackle.

'Our immediate objectives,' said the Doctor, 'are to rescue James, and to find out as much as we can about these vampires. We must avoid hasty actions, anything that will provoke the vampires into additional violence. Instead, we must provoke them into making contact with me. With us.'

'What's to find out about them?' asked Shackle.

'Practically everything,' said the Doctor. An exploring kitten tumbled down the sofa into his lap. He stroked it, absently. 'At the moment all we know about them is that they drink blood. For all we know, we could be dealing with ancient horrors from my people's mythology, human psychopaths, or the giant mosquitoes of Atraxi 3.'

Shackle snickered. The Doctor looked him straight in the eye and held his hands nearly a foot apart. Shackle stopped snickering.

'We need to know their numbers, their goals, and their abilities,' said Kramer.

The Doctor nodded. 'Different strains of vampires, different abilities,' he said. 'The curse manifests itself in many and various ways. All of the attacks so far have taken place at night, so we can assume they have an aversion to sunlight.' Another kitten had arrived, walking across his shoulders. 'The vampires of Time Lord legend had incredibly strong circulatory systems, allowing them to heal almost any wound – hence the traditional stake through the heart.'

'I thought the idea was to pin them to the earth,' said Carolyn.

'They can't heal a wound that has an inch-wide piece of wood through it,' said the Doctor. 'You've been reading.'

'As much as I could,' said Carolyn. 'Ever since 1976.'

'Be prepared to forget much of what you've read,' said the Doctor. 'Don't rely on it.' Carolyn nodded.

Kramer was drawing a plan of the nightclub, and the surrounding alleyways, on a sheet of typing paper. 'We're going to the Other Place on a stake-out.' She ignored Shackle's theatrical groan. 'There are two main entrances and exits. Outside' – she drew circles on the map – 'myself in the rear parking lot, Dr McConnell and Dr Shackle in the front parking lot. Inside the club, the Doctor.'

'And Sam,' said Sam.

'Sorry?' said Kramer.

'Inside the club, the Doctor and Sam.'

Kramer glanced at the Doctor, who looked vaguely bewildered. By now he had one kitten balancing on his head, two tussling in his lap, and one attempting to clamber up his waistcoat. He looked at Sam. She lifted her hands like paws, and panted.

'Sam Sam Sam Sam Sam.' He shook his head, carefully, and the kitten on top clung on for dear life. 'When are you going to learn not to pointlessly throw yourself in harm's way?'

'When you do. Look, I'm here to learn how to save the world, right? Well how'm I gonna learn how to do it if you don't give me the chance?'

'Oh God,' muttered Kramer. Sam saw how closely the general was watching him. 'Another one.'

'All right. On your head be it,' said the Doctor, removing the kitten. 'But remember, you did ask for it.' Sam grinned, and so did the Doctor, but Kramer's grim expression hadn't changed.

'So what precisely do we do?' Shackle wanted to know. 'Are you going to arm us with machine guns? Or squirt guns filled with holy water?'

'We watch,' said Kramer drily. 'We make a nuisance of ourselves by asking a lot of questions. If anyone suspicious notices and leaves, we follow them.'

'In the meantime, Dr Shackle,' said the Doctor, 'I want to take a look at your records of these killings.'

Shackle said, 'So we're going to defeat these supernatural monsters –'

'Not supernatural,' said the Doctor.

'– these night-stalking, blood-sucking creatures for whom there is no doubt a perfectly logical explanation, through a combination of medical research and patient observation?' He looked at Kramer. 'Couldn't you rustle up a few tanks, or something?'

'Rash action would be foolish,' said the Doctor sternly. 'If not fatal.' He finally managed to get up and head for the door. 'For now, patience is our weapon. You'll see, Dr Shackle. Tonight.'

He stopped for a moment, puzzled, then lifted the last of the curious kittens out of his coat pocket by the scruff of its neck. He presented it to Kramer, who looked at it in utter confusion, and made his exit.

'You know what the worst of it is?' Carolyn said to Sam as she scoured the kitchen, looking for her handbag. 'Now I've got to spend eight hours pretending none of this is going on. Forget with saving James, I have to spend all my energy trying to convince the Foundation to keep funding Lewis and Jeffries' viral research.'

'You could always call in sick,' Sam said.

Carolyn shook her head. 'This is important. Where is my purse?'

'Like getting James back isn't?' Sam caught her by the shoulder and grinned. 'C'mon. It's like me skiving off school to go to the gay rights march. This is big, it's once in a lifetime, you can let the ordinary work wait for a bit, y'know?'

Carolyn felt a surge of irritation. 'Don't want me being so boring and grown-up, huh?'

'Well, no, I mean –'

'Look. There are about four hundred people who are alive today because they're on drugs that my team helped develop,' Carolyn said crabbily. 'This matters. I'm not just going to blow it off, even today.'

Sam made a face. 'Well, fine, then.' She turned and headed for the door, muttering under her breath. 'It's like asking my mum to come to a Palm Sunday march.'

That stung. Carolyn spun around and snapped at her. 'At least your mom would have some sense of responsibility. I wonder what your parents would think if they knew about you running around hunting vampires?'

Sam snorted. 'Probably they'd think they were having acid flashbacks.'

Carolyn couldn't help but burst out laughing. Sam grinned with her, but as she watched the grin turned sour. 'You really want to know?' Sam said. 'I don't think they'd give a damn. They're past caring 'bout what I'm up to. They were children of the sixties, you know?'

Children of the sixties, Carolyn thought. *I'm* a child of the sixties.

Sam went on. 'Anything I could come up with to rebel against them, they'd been there, done that, smoked it. About the only thing I could do to really outrage them is become a major drug addict, or join the Conservative Party, and they know I'm not out to screw up my life like that.'

Suddenly Sam seemed normal, a teenager whose parents drove her berserk. 'They still think they care, but only about the little things. Vanilla things. Forget big issues like nuclear weapons or stopping genocide, they're too much to handle. Mum and Dad're never gonna get involved in anything bigger than cleaning up the park down the street. Or some kid's social worker problems. Or –'

'Or cancer research?' Carolyn asked levelly.

Sam checked herself. 'Nah, not the same thing. You could still change the world with that some day. But you gotta remember not to pass up the chance to do something really big, you know?'

'You make it sound simple,' said Carolyn, brushing in irritation at her eyes. 'Like there's not someone who's going to try to kill you if you get in their way.'

Sam shrugged and put her hands in her pockets. 'That's cause they're not gonna get to.'

Carolyn was aghast to realise that she was crying. 'Where's my damn purse,' she said angrily. 'I hate it when I can't find something I need!'

The Doctor breezed out of the living room, handed Carolyn her purse, and kept going, on his way to the kitchen.

Carolyn gripped it between her hands. 'James will be OK, won't he?' she asked Sam.

'Course he will,' Sam said with a grin. 'He always gets 'em back all right. He's the Doctor.'

Night

Kramer in her Chevy, tucked away between the dumpsters in the back alleyway, a cell phone pressed to her ear. 'Right. Now, if I tell you to watch someone, you might have to follow them, but that's not too likely. Otherwise just sit back and report anything that looks suspicious. Over.'

Shackle and Carolyn in Carolyn's Lexus, parked in plain sight across from the sunken entrance to the club. 'Oh, what a demanding and challenging use of our time.' Kramer imagined Shackle with the phone, his seat tilted all the way back, his feet up on the dashboard.

'That's 'cause you're the civilians. Over.'

'Oh, fine. Treat us like second-class citizens because we don't have a uniform.'

'You don't have any experience at this sort of thing. Over.'

'We don't even get a code name or anything, do we?' Shackle asked.

'This is serious. Over.'

'So am I. I feel very strongly about this,' Shackle said.

Kramer sighed. 'All right, then. Aardvark to Smartass One, Aardvark to Smartass One, I need an immediate arc-light on my ten-twenty and a C-4 with a side order of fries. Now, if you're quite finished? Over.'

It was her own fault for working with civilians, thought Kramer. One of the advantages of dealing with the regular army was that they never felt the need to waste time taking the piss.

The Doctor headed straight for the bar. The crowd, dancers and talkers, seemed to part easily around him. Sam followed in his wake.

He found them a couple of seats at the bar. Sam was grinning. 'What is it?' he asked.

'It's the bartender,' Sam said, glancing at the other end of the bar. 'She's dressed as Death from the *Sandman* comics.'

'All part of the friendly atmosphere,' said the Doctor.

Sam looked around. There were huge blow-ups of Giger paintings around the walls. A giant video screen was showing *Nosferatu*, black-and-white images flickering behind the dancers.

Everyone was wearing black, looking deadly serious. Some of the costumes were stunning, lots of period stuff and velvet. The conversations were full of knowing smiles and raised eyebrows. They were going to have a hell of a time spotting a real vampire when everyone in sight was trying to drop unsubtle hints that they were secretly one of them. They all wanted to make sure no one could miss the hint that they were part of this special world, that they knew mysteries beyond the world of everyday mortals.

Sam hoped that wasn't how she sounded.

The Doctor craned his neck, trying to catch Death's attention. The bartender meandered over in response to his little hand waves and nods. Sam caught the Doctor's look, and they both got to their feet.

'Yeah?' said Death.

'Ah, yes,' said the Doctor. 'Could I speak to the manager, please?' he asked.

Death looked at him. 'Is there a problem?'

'Not yet,' Sam threw in, and grinned. She moved down the bar, so the woman was forced to swivel to look at both of them.

'We're concerned about the hygienic conditions in this place,' said the Doctor. 'We've heard reports of large numbers of the undead frequenting this establishment, and I'm sure you're aware of the contamination problems that could cause.'

Sam nodded professionally. 'Especially when serving food on the premises.'

'Oh yes,' said the Doctor without missing a beat. 'All sorts of possible health-code violations.'

'Look, who are you?' snapped Death.

'Health inspectors,' said Sam from over her shoulder. The bartender had to twist around to look at her.

'Yes,' added the Doctor, making her twist back. 'Department of Necrological Affairs.' Sam flipped open her wallet and gave the bartender a half-second glance at an official-looking card. It was the Altairian driver's licence the Doctor had helped her get, tucked in front of her forged ID.

'We're here to ensure that you're in compliance with all federal regulations on vampires,' said the Doctor. 'We hear you've got quite a few as customers.'

'Possibly even staff.'

'Oh yes. The Internal Revenue Service frowns on income earned after death, you know.'

'So. You can either tell us what we need to know, or we'll have to start testing your staff for proof of continued existence.'

'We'd have to close down your kitchen.'

'Major disruption. We don't want that, do we?'

'Oh no.'

'Now wait – you can't just –' began Death.

'Think we should check her life signs, Doctor?' asked Sam. He nodded, his face a perfect expression of grave concern.

'Wait – look – I'll just go get Mr Seavey, all right?' said Death, and hurried off before things got any weirder.

'And they say beating Death is tough,' said Sam. She and the Doctor looked at each other, saw the same gleam in each other's eyes, and it was all Sam could to do keep from high-fiving him.

Sam pulled a bowl towards her and started on the pretzels while they waited, remembering the time she'd seen the three football players pummelling that new kid behind the school – she could have charged in swinging, and maybe given the kid a chance to get away while she got battered in his place, but it was so much more satisfying to just trip the school fire alarm, and thus send hordes of teachers and other witnesses hurrying out of the building.

'If you can't convince them, confuse them,' she said.

'Harry S Truman,' said the Doctor. She looked at him in bewilderment, and he took one of her pretzels.

'That's the problem,' said Shackle. He was finishing the last of his Big Mac. 'At the medical centre, death isn't something you can win against. Some people die, some people don't, but death is still around no matter what. It's like the sound of traffic in the distance.'

'I don't know how you can keep going,' Carolyn said. 'If that's what it's like being on the front lines all the time…'

'It takes a lot of strength. You need the focus, on every bit of good you manage to do, and the determination to keep going, even when you know you can't do it all. And the pretentious platitudes, don't forget the pretentious platitudes.' He gave a shrug, a very tiny one this time. 'Look, don't ask me, I don't know how I do it. There just doesn't seem to be any better option.'

'I know the feeling.' Carolyn let out a faint smile. 'It's like me the other night, after James disappeared. All you know to do is keep going. When you can't keep going, you don't for a while… and then you keep going again.'

Shackle looked faintly amazed that someone had actually understood something he'd said. Then he smiled slightly, a small but genuine smile. 'Sounds easy, doesn't it?'

'Ask Sam. She sure seems to think it's easy.'

'Sam Jones,' sighed Shackle, 'doesn't need to worry about holding down a sixty-hour-a-week job on top of everything else. Of course they can deal with their world. They don't have to deal with our world at the same time.'

'I dunno,' said Carolyn. 'If this is what their world is like, I could deal with a bit more of mine right now.' Now the initial adrenalin rush had faded, it was becoming all too clear that saving the world meant sitting in a car eating cheap fast food. It didn't seem fair, somehow.

'I wonder how they cope with the background noise,' she said.

Shackle shrugged broadly. 'It's beyond me,' he said. 'Got any more fries?'

'Hey, look,' said Reaper.

Shredder leaned over the railing, following Reaper's gaze. They were twins, both short and black, wearing matching battered leather jackets. They'd been hanging around all evening, waiting for something to happen.

'That must be the guy the bartender was talking about,' said Shredder.

'Nice threads.'

'Nice girl.'

'Look,' said Reaper. The man and the girl talked for a few moments, surrounded by dancers. Then they split up.

The girl started to dance, a little awkwardly at first, then more confidently as she found the beat. The man was swallowed by the crowd.

'I've got an idea,' said Shredder.

'We'll get into trouble,' said Reaper.

'Yeah.'

Seavey's office was a tiny room down a brick hallway lit by a naked light bulb. It was jammed with filing cabinets and cardboard boxes.

Seavey himself was old and balding and rude in a very quiet way. He led them from the bar, wordlessly, and lit a cigarette the instant they crammed into the tiny room. There were no chairs. The Doctor waved away the smoke.

'Vampires, Mr Seavey,' he said. The man didn't react, dragging on his cigarette. 'I have no doubts that you know that they're here. What I don't know is whether they've threatened you, or whether they're paying you to turn a blind eye to their activities.'

'Do you have any idea how crazy you sound?'

'Which is more insane, Mr Seavey – believing in blood-drinking killers, or inviting them into one's nightclub?'

'I don't believe in vampires,' said Seavey slowly. 'But an awful lot of the people out there do.' He waved his cigarette in the general direction of the dance floor. 'Some of them even want to be vampires. Some of them even think they are vampires. Why shouldn't they have their fantasy?'

'Fantasy is one thing,' said the Doctor. 'Murders and kidnapping are another.'

'You've got to look at this from a business point of view,' said Seavey. 'If there were real vampires coming to my club, I wouldn't want to discourage them. They'd be just the sort of thing that would interest my clientele. But that wouldn't make me responsible for their behaviour.'

'You know more than you're telling us, Mr Seavey.'

'What's that supposed to mean?'

'We need to contact them,' insisted the Doctor. 'Talk to them. I think you can help us.'

'I don't think I can,' said Seavey. 'You're welcome to stay. Maybe you can find these "vampires" for yourselves. Have a drink, have a dance. If there's any trouble, I'll bar you from the premises. Understood?'

'There's already been trouble,' said the Doctor quietly. 'Never mind, Mr Seavey. We'll have to manage without your help.'

Shackle was dozing, a magazine forgotten in his lap. He looked as though he hadn't slept for days.

On a normal night, a real night, Carolyn and James would be in the kitchen together right now, banging elbows as they worked to throw together something simple and tasty.

It was moments like that which she was missing these last couple of days, she thought. The momentary squeezes when they passed each other in front of the stove. The impromptu neck massages as she hunched over her paperwork, the kisses she stole at his drafting table. All the little touches which framed and fleshed out a day.

She sat back. Shackle said, 'The hell with this,' and opened the car door.

As ordered, Sam spent the time waiting for the Doctor to come back ingratiating herself with various groups of clubbers, and asking a few terse and cryptic questions about James and vampires.

'Excuse me, um, could we ask a favour of you?' The question came from one of two black guys in matching studded outfits who had come up to her. They looked like twins or clones or something. On her personal vamp scale, they rated about a six each, but their prominently displayed fangs looked distinctly plastic.

'Yeah, what is it?' she asked guardedly. She ran through the strategies she'd adopted while they were investigating in 1976. If they pull something on you or ask you to leave, make a scene, they're less likely to shoot or knife you in front of a hundred witnesses.

'A friend of ours has been worshipping you from afar,' said the one on the left. 'He's at our table, trying to work up the courage to ask you to dance, but he's too shy – could you do him a favour?'

Dance floor: open space, plenty of witnesses, lots of places to run to. Lots of people she hadn't talked to yet either. And she might as well have a little fun along with everything else going on tonight. 'Aw, how sweet,' she said. 'Bring him on.'

Carolyn fumbled with the mobile phone. 'Uh, General Kramer?' she said. 'Dr Shackle just got out of the car.'

'What's he up to?'

'I don't know. Maybe he has to go to the bathroom,' said Carolyn. 'He's heading for the main entrance.'

'I'll be there in sixty seconds,' said Kramer. 'Keep an eye on him, but don't go into the nightclub.'

Carolyn got out, locking the car door. The mobile phone went into her jacket pocket. Dr Shackle was talking to someone at the nightclub's entrance. The bouncer, maybe?

She glanced around, heading a bit closer. Shackle walked up to someone else. 'Excuse me,' he said. 'Have you seen any vampires around here?'

The woman laughed at him. 'I have now.'

Carolyn almost laughed. What's tall, pale, gaunt, and wanders about at night looking like a maniac?

She was about to walk up to him and suggest they get back in the car when he suddenly strode off, heading for the corner of the building.

She pulled out the mobile phone. 'It's me again,' she told Kramer. 'He's just wandering around talking to people. Is that all right?'

'Stay there,' Kramer's voice crackled in her ear. 'I'm just coming into the parking lot. I'll have a little word with Dr Shackle.'

Carolyn closed the mobile phone, heard Shackle shout, and broke into a run.

She was puffing as she rounded the corner. There were a couple of guys. One of them had grabbed Shackle and the other one was hitting him over the head.

'Oh my God!' she shouted. 'He's being mugged!'

The muggers stopped and looked at her. Shackle crumpled in the arms of the larger one, while the smaller one came towards Carolyn, taking a knife out of his pocket.

Abruptly, the man turned and ran. His friend dropped Shackle and joined him. Carolyn stared after them.

She turned around. Kramer was standing behind her, brandishing the largest handgun she had ever seen.

Shackle groaned. Carolyn and Kramer swore, simultaneously, and ran to help him up.

This was how she liked it, loud and hard and unrestrained, the music pounding through her brain till she couldn't tell if she was moving to the beat or the beat itself was vibrating her. All she felt was the *thump thump thump* echoing through her ribcage, bass and pulse merging into one sound.

The guys' friend was still there, dancing vaguely at her with an angular lack of grace that suggested he'd been dead since the days of the Funky Chicken. If he was a vampire, they'd have no problem – all Kramer would need to do was lean on this guy's shoulder and he'd crumple into a pile of bones. He had the wasted skinhead look and sunken eyes of a junior Nosferatu, but Sam had seen that look too many times in daylight to figure it was blood this guy was on.

The Doctor would be back in a moment. 'Look, I gotta go talk to some people,' she shouted at the guy over the *thump thump*. He stared blankly at her. Clearly the words hadn't made it across the few feet of noise between her and him. He stepped in closer to her, and she said 'I said, I gotta go talk –'

And *thump thump* he leaned in close to grab a kiss and she stepped away *thump* his hand grabbed the back of her head and pulled *thump* all she could see was his ear because his mouth was *thump* and she could barely hear her own scream under the music and the *thump thump* of her heart in full fight-or-flight

kick the back of his knee the way the self-defence course taught *thump* he's falling but he's not letting go, fingers wrapped around the sides of her ribcage like claws *thump* she's falling with his teeth still locked in her throat

thump the back of her head on the dance floor and him falling across her, fingernails stabbing into her back as she fell on them and

thump the waves of realisation beginning to

thump spread throughout the crowd that

thump hey waitaminnit something's wrong there and
thump that's real blood and
thump the two guys pulling the vampire the *vampire* off *her*
throat and disappearing as the crowd surged around her and her
throat was still flowing and her

thump

thump

The music stopped.

The Doctor walked back up the narrow hallway, deep in thought.
He plucked out the mobile phone and switched it back on.
Kramer ought to know about what Seavey had said. He started to
dial the number, when the music shut off suddenly, leaving his
ears ringing. He saw –

Sam was lying on the dance floor, surrounded by people, all
staring down at her. Someone was screaming.

The Doctor's hearts turned to ice. He bolted forward, shoving
his way through the crowd.

There was a vicious wound in her neck, bleeding all over the
floor. He cradled her head in his lap, snatching out a handkerchief
and pressing hard against the wound to staunch the flow.

'Happened…?' whispered Sam. The pain hadn't hit her yet. 'Did
I fall down?'

'Shh, Sam, close your eyes,' he said. He brushed his fingers
through her short hair, watching as she lost consciousness again.

'I called an ambulance.' The Doctor looked up, half blinded by
the ringing in his ears. It was the bartender. 'Jesus, poor kid. Did
anyone see who did it?'

'I know who did it,' said the Doctor, as Sam's blood soaked over
his hand and the ringing finally stopped.

'No answer,' said Kramer, putting away her mobile phone. 'Get
him back to the car, I'm going inside.'

Carolyn was supporting a dazed Shackle, who was holding a

hand to his bleeding scalp. She started walking him back to the safety – please, God, let it be safety – of the Lexus. Curious eyes followed them, and Kramer, as she ran for the entrance.

Carolyn realised she had started to cry.

Everything wasn't all right.

CHAPTER 6
FEAR OF FALLING

Tuesday

12:17 a.m.

It was the first time she'd ever been in an ambulance. Isolated details kept engraving themselves on her brain – she found herself fascinated by the metal ribbing of the ceiling. She tried lifting her head to get a better view, but then the pain dug its fingernails into her throat and she fell back.

The Doctor sat beside her, holding her hand, occasionally casting an odd glance at one of the paramedics. Each time she breathed, the dressing they'd applied to her neck shifted slightly, sending more pain rasping across her nerves. The wound was a deafening drone of sensation, drowning out her thoughts.

One of the paramedics shone a light in her eyes, murmured, 'Mild concussion, probably from banging her head.' That's cool, she thought, so I've got an excuse for feeling like this.

12:43 a.m.

She couldn't see or feel what they were doing to her neck. The anaesthetic had blotted out all feeling down there. The emergency room doctor was crouching over her – she could see the concentration on his face – but there wasn't even a sense of tugging as he pulled the thick black thread through the holes in her throat. It was like the part of her where the bite was didn't even exist.

1:09 a.m.

She presented her arm to the nurse, and noticed with a sense of disconnection that he'd stuck a needle in it. It seemed kind of odd that, if she'd already lost a lot of blood, they'd be taking any more out. The Doctor had a quick low word with the nurse, and exited with the blood sample and the saliva traces they'd swabbed off her neck earlier.

Oh, of course. It was to check to see if she was going to turn into a vampire.

1:13 a.m.

'Oh, Sam,' said the Doctor. 'I really don't know.'

She held on to him. She wanted to cry, but she was terrified she'd rip the stitches.

3:08 a.m.

The Doctor paced back and forth at the foot of her bed, his face furious with concentration. Someone had arranged a private room. Kramer and a dazed Carolyn were there too, trying to stay out of his erratic path.

The little part of her mind that wasn't drifting kept fixing itself firmly on odd details, studying the precise shape of the metal bed railing or the way the wallpaper pattern formed faces.

The Doctor was muttering, a little too loudly to be talking to himself, a little too fast to be talking to anyone else. His words came in short fluttering bursts. 'Got to think, got to plan. Figure them out. Know your enemy. What do they want?' His hands flew about in random distracted gestures. 'They've been killing the homeless. Trying to be subtle. Trying to keep a low profile?'

'Tangerine,' put in Kramer.

'True.' The Doctor didn't miss a beat. 'They kill Pymble. They kill Oxwell. Something's changing. They're not worried about being noticed now. What brought that on? Then they don't kill James. As far as we know.' Carolyn blanched, putting a hand to her throat. The Doctor was too busy rushing onward with his words. 'And now Sam. Got to be a reason. There must be a reason.' He put his hands to his temples. 'Why? Why why why why why?'

'Revenge?' asked Kramer.

'Yeah, for 1976,' added Carolyn. 'They could have found out you killed Eva.'

The Doctor shook his head violently. 'No no no, if they wanted me they could have got me the day that James disappeared. If they've decided to start being spectacular then why haven't they killed James? We've got to find that out. Was he a warning? Was Sam a warning? It doesn't make sense. There's something we're missing...'

He kept going on, the words sounding farther and farther away. The alert part of her mind held on to one thought and rolled it over and over. He never told me what he did while they were kidnapping James.

3:37 a.m.

The painkiller was wearing off, and the hurt was beginning to buzz around the edges of her awareness again. She felt too drained to pay much attention to it; even with the local anaesthetic, her brain had still been convinced the pain was there. It was getting hard to remember what it felt like not to hurt.

Shackle had joined them, his head cocked slightly to emphasise the bandage on his temple. 'The police said absolutely nothing of any use whatsoever. They figure it was just a random mugging. How about you?' He turned to the Doctor. 'Do you think it was connected to the vampires?'

'No, I think that was just you being an idiot,' the Doctor said. 'What on Earth got into you?'

'Oh, just that I really didn't care,' Shackle declared with a grandiose handwave. 'Death has long since ceased to hold any terrors for me.'

'Oh, really,' said the Doctor.

'It's like fear of falling. If you've got that fear, you stay away from cliff edges. If you don't, then you walk on the edge just like you're anyplace else. It's no risk if you don't care what happens.' He paused to take a breath and make sure they were all still listening. 'At least being bitten by a vampire would be a novel way to die.'

'Well then, Dr Shackle,' said the Doctor, 'while you await your tragic demise, you can continue to make yourself useful. Adrienne, could I have that blood sample of Sam's?'

Kramer looked around for the vial, bewildered. 'Never mind,' said the Doctor. 'I think I've found it.' He reached behind Shackle's ear and produced the vial, making him jump. 'Now,' he went on, 'if you could somehow avoid plummeting into the abyss for these next few hours, we could use someone to analyse whether there's any trace of vampiric elements in this blood. Assuming of course that the crushing burden of existence doesn't sap your will to live between now and then –'

Shackle grabbed the vial from him. 'Oh, it's funny to you, isn't it?' he spat. 'It's a joke when someone doesn't feel happy and joyful and glad to be alive. You know what it's like to really know that it doesn't make a bit of difference to the world whether you live or die?'

'You actually mean that,' said Carolyn.

'Of course I mean it,' snapped Shackle. 'After a few years, after a few thousand trivial deaths from gunfire or starvation, you realise you can't make a difference. You just can't.' His words began to trail off in defeat. 'It's like trying to beat back the ocean. Eventually it's just going to roll over you. I'm just going to be stabbed by a patient or catch AIDS during an operation or die in some filthy Third World hospital, still thinking I can hold back death…'

No one knew how to respond to his outburst. Sam knew there had to be an answer to it, something that made it all make sense, but the pain and dizziness were coming back and she couldn't get the words out even if she knew them.

She felt as if she was falling.

The Doctor came up to him, took the vial from Shackle and weighed it in his hand. 'I've died for enough pointless reasons in my time,' he said. A flicker of confusion crossed Shackle's face, but the Doctor didn't give him any time to think about it. 'I've left a lot of things undone. But in the end it doesn't matter whether you won all the battles. All that matters is the trying.' He held up the vial, offering it to him. 'Do you still want to try this?'

Shackle shrugged limply. 'Might as well…' He took the tiny vial of blood gingerly and held it at arm's length.

'All right, then. Look for any deviation from the human,' said the Doctor.

'I've got a friend who can PCR up some DNA samples and do you a gel electrophoresis,' said Shackle.

'That sounds adequate,' said the Doctor. 'Carolyn, could you do the same on those saliva traces? You might spot some characteristic elements if you…'

The words blurred again.

4:27 a.m.

They crept out while she was asleep. Afterwards she had a vague fuzzy memory of trying to drag herself out of bed while she was alone, trying, running just on groggy rage.

They couldn't stop her. Not her, Sam Jones, the girl who'd climbed on to a roof to spraypaint ANOREXICS DIE FOR BUSINESS £££ on to a lingerie billboard, who'd Taken Back The Night and formed the school Amnesty chapter. No way was she going to sit back and let psychos like the one who'd bitten her (who'd *bitten* her) go unchallenged (he'd sunk his teeth into her), she'd always fought and won and never even had to blink (he'd sunk his teeth into her and there hadn't been a thing she could do to stop him)…

She tried to turn her head, and her certainty snapped in a spike of pain.

4:39 a.m.

'Sam. You awake?'

General Kramer was leaning over her, her face pensive. From this close, Sam could see the worry lines around her eyes.

'Yeah.' Her voice was just a breath, it hurt less that way.

'I just wanted to talk to you for a minute.' Kramer pulled the chair up close to the head of the bed. 'By morning you're gonna want to get right back up and into things. They always do… I just want you to know, no one'll think you let us down if you take it easy for a while.'

''Cept me.'

'I mean it,' Kramer said quietly. 'It's not gonna get any easier from here on out. You know how they always say, "Don't worry, it's just a flesh wound"? Well, this is a flesh wound.'

Sam had to swallow again. It wasn't getting better.

Kramer looked her gently in the eye. 'The next time we meet the vampires, it's gonna be nasty. You've got to know you could get banged up worse.'

'I'm with the Doctor… I should be… used to…' She couldn't get the whole sentence out right then. It wasn't that the words were catching in her throat: it felt as if her throat was catching in her throat.

Kramer sighed. 'Yeah.' She turned away, shaking her head slowly. Her shoulders were slumped with exhaustion, with defeat.

'What?' Sam whispered.

'They all go through this,' Kramer said, and rested her head on her hand. 'Every single one we know of who travelled with him. You all figure it's worth getting hell bashed out of you, when you're with him. Because it's for a good cause. Because it's right.'

'It is,' Sam said simply. It was hard to sound convincing when her throat hurt so much.

Kramer shook her head sharply, suddenly. 'It's stupid, that's what it is. He takes so many foolish risks with people like you. Just ordinary people, who don't have the training to wander around in war zones. You're seventeen. That's not what you should be doing yet. He could get the job done so much better if he'd work with the professionals, instead of putting people like you in danger.'

So this was what had really brought Kramer in here. 'Don't want to just sit back.'

'I know, I know. But you don't have to do it all yourself either. We know what we're doing. Honest.'

'So does he.'

A shadow passed across Kramer's face. 'Yeah.' Her voice got very soft, and very serious. 'Yeah, he knows exactly what he's doing. But do you know what he's doing?'

'Whad'ya mean?'

'You trust him. You'd follow him off the ends of the earth, you know? But does he really tell you what he's up to?'

'Yeah.' A pause. 'Think so...' The general's words were beginning to worm their way into her brain.

Kramer leaned in close. Her eyes were lost in the shadow from the bedside lamp. 'I didn't want to make trouble, but I figure I should tell you this. The last time I met the Doctor, he had another girl about your age travelling with him. Her name was Ace. And you wouldn't believe the stunts he pulled on her.' There was a cold anger in her words. 'All sorts of head games and things going on behind her back. Some I saw, the rest she told me about later. You may think you know him, but he's done a lot more things than you think.'

'Wouldn't do that. He's not like that.'

Kramer's face didn't move. 'The thing is, it was all for her own good. Everything he did was for the best of motives. But they were his motives, not hers.'

Now everything was hurting. There had to be something she could hold on to to make the pain go away. 'Wasn't him. You met the one before him, you said.'

Kramer shrugged slowly and shook her head. 'Now, I don't pretend that I understand this regeneration thing. But he says that no matter what, he's still the Doctor. And I believe that, even when that means something bad as well as good.' The general got up and walked slowly away towards the foot of the bed.

Sam wanted to sleep. She wanted to sleep it all away, and wake up yesterday with none of this having happened.

Kramer stood and waited for her to say something. When she didn't, she went on stumbling for words. 'I just want you to know, you've got a choice. You don't have to go with him. UNIT's full of people who've done time with the Doctor, and now they're doing things that matter right here on Earth. At least, the ones who made it back home did. Now, it's not as showy as running around the universe... but you've got a better chance of seeing eighteen.'

Sam met those words with dull eyes. 'Is it just 'cause I'm a kid?' she muttered.

'Yeah, 'cause you're a kid,' said Kramer with a slight sigh of frustration. ''Cause you're a kid who's out there fighting for things. My daughter, Louisa, she's about your age, and if she would get off her butt and do half the things you've done, I'd be so damn proud of her I couldn't even speak.' One corner of her mouth curled into a smile. 'I just want you to get to live long enough to do a little more.'

Sam watched Adrienne Kramer walk slowly to the door. She looked old, Sam realised, old in a way she'd only ever seen the Doctor look before. 'Think about it,' Kramer said, and closed the door behind her, leaving Sam in darkness.

7:08 a.m.

The Doctor was sitting there when she woke up. He looked as if he'd been up all night, a crumpled magazine forgotten in his lap. 'Hello, Sam.'

The pain wasn't as bad. Probably her nerves were too tired to fire any more. Her head was filled with spinning fragments of thoughts, the remains of everything that had been running through her head all night.

He handed her a paper cup of water. When she drank, it felt like gulping needles. He watched her throat as she swallowed, and then gave a reassuring grin. 'Well, no obvious leaks.' She smiled; at least that didn't hurt.

'Any news?' she asked.

'About what?'

'About me.'

He shook his head. 'Shackle's taken the blood to the lab. They're waiting to see if anything developed. Sam... I'm sorry.'

'Yeah,' she said.

He sat there for a moment, his face blank, at a loss for what to say next. 'Well,' he came up with, 'you should be out of here by evening. Either way. You're free to get right back into the swing of things.' He looked a little closer at her expression. 'Or not. It's up to you.'

'Does this happen all the time?' she asked shakily.

'Outbreaks of vampirism?'

'No. Your friends getting… hurt like this.'

For a moment he looked like a lost little boy. 'Sometimes,' he said. 'It's been much more dangerous these past few years.'

Sam closed her eyes. After a moment she heard him shift, picking up his magazine.

Of course she'd always won all her battles – the ones she fought were always the easy ones. Even that mess with the drug-runners in the school had had a sense of unreality about it… It had never seemed like she could really get killed, knife wound in the stomach, blood pouring out of a hole in her neck. So of course it was easy for her to run off with the Doctor and be a daring student radical cyberpunk traveller saving the universe. After all, there wasn't any way she would ever really get hurt.

Somewhere women were standing in front of tanks and bulldozers, breaking chimpanzees out of research labs and strong-arming their way through protesters at abortion clinics. But not in her world, not in Shoreditch 1997, where stakes didn't get any higher than the playground. Even when she'd spraypainted the billboard, that was just to convince Elizabeth Elwell that she was ballsy enough to do it.

She'd looked over the edge, Elizabeth grinning up at her from the street, and she hadn't believed for a moment that she might fall.

'Hey wait,' she said, opening her eyes. 'The pain's gone.'

He grinned. 'Good, it worked.' She looked confused, and he repeated the action of handing her the cup of water. This time, he did it slowly, and she could see how he'd produced a small blue tablet from between his fingers and dropped it into the water behind his hand. It dissolved in a fraction of a second.

She shrank slightly away. 'What was it?'

'Oh, it's just a little something from the TARDIS.' He smiled at his own cleverness.

For her own good, she thought. It's always for their own good.

'Why'd you change your mind?'

He blinked. 'What do you mean?'

'Why'd you let me go with you this time, into the nightclub?'

He look surprised. 'You insisted.'

When next she spoke, her voice was very small. 'You didn't want to teach me a lesson?'

He sat there with his mouth open. Slowly she saw his face crumple, twisted with the horrible realisation that she doubted him enough to ask.

'Oh Sam. Sam, I would never let them hurt...' He trailed off, realising he couldn't say that any more. 'I won't let them hurt you again,' he said quietly.

He leaned over the hospital bed and hugged her, awkwardly. He felt disjointed, like a loose collection of arms and legs without much to hold them together.

'We'll find them.' He met her eyes with utter, childlike seriousness. 'We'll find them, and you and I will stop them.'

'Yeah,' she said listlessly.

Tuesday morning.

Carolyn woke up five minutes before the alarm went off, discovered herself alone in her bed, and decided it would be all right if she had a little cry.

When the alarm began to shriek in her ear she dutifully got up, switched it off, and stumbled into the shower. By the time she got downstairs she looked ready to tackle a day of meetings.

The Doctor had returned from the hospital at some ungodly hour to infest her kitchen once more. Breakfast was more downbeat this time, just oatmeal and muesli, eggs and toast, fruit juice and coffee. He gave her a hopeful smile, hanging the apron over the back of a chair.

She sat down. 'This is terrible,' she said. 'You've gone to all this trouble and I'm not really hungry...'

'Breakfast is the most important meal of the day,' he admonished her. She smiled weakly and broke off the corner of a slice of toast. 'Besides, you're under enormous stress and don't appear to have slept a wink.'

'I slept some,' she said, around a mouthful.

'And you've been crying,' he said. 'Are you quite certain you're ready to go to work?'

She swallowed. 'I'm needed,' she said. He nodded, but his eyes didn't lose their concern. 'How's Sam?'

'Sleeping. She'll be all right.' He suddenly ran both hands back through his hair, looking like a cartoon mad composer. 'I only just realised. You thought that once I arrived, everything would be all right again, didn't you?'

Carolyn forced back the tears. She nodded, unable to speak.

'It often seems as though I only make things worse. My meddling does tend to force the crisis... When we arrived I immediately set out to see you, but when I looked in the window and saw James, I knew we were too early.' He smiled and put a glass of orange juice in front of her. 'My prescription. I think I gave him quite a start.'

Realisation. 'The prowler. That was you.'

'I expect it was.'

She just stared at him. The implications began to unfold. 'You were here all along. You could have warned us –'

'Carolyn, it doesn't work like that –'

'You could have stopped it all. You could have gone to the club and stopped them from taking James.'

'You have to understand. I went there but I couldn't stop it.'

She couldn't have heard right. 'What did you say?'

'Er, that I went to the Other Place to see what happened when James disappeared. I thought I could learn something, perhaps see who –'

'You were right there?' Carolyn felt a hollow space opening up inside her. 'My God, you could have saved him and you just sat there...'

The Doctor made calming motions with his hands. 'Hold on, hold on, hold on....'

Her throat tightened. Somehow she said, 'You were the only one I was sure of in all this, and you could have made everything all right, and you didn't.'

'You've got to understand, Carolyn. The laws of time. Causality loops. Temporal paradoxes. If I kept James from being kidnapped, you'd never send the message that got me there, so I wouldn't be there to keep James from being kidnapped. I couldn't do anything about it.' His eyes pleaded. 'Please understand.'

'I believe you,' she said.

'You do?'

'I have to,' she said hoarsely. 'Otherwise there's nothing left to believe in.'

'Besides,' the Doctor raced on, 'he didn't stop anyway.'

She blinked. 'What?'

'Oh, I was waiting in a cab outside to follow him when he left the building. But he didn't get in his car: he went off down the alleyway around the back of the building. I got out of the cab and went after him, but I'd lost him.'

Carolyn shook her head, feeling bewildered and strangely relieved. 'You said he didn't stop.'

'Well, I did yell for him, but he didn't answer...'

'You were going to save him.'

'Well,' he said modestly.

She felt herself bubbling over with inexplicable joy and even more confusion. 'But what about the laws of time? Temporal paradoxes? Everything you were just talking about?'

'Yes, er...' He shrugged and grinned. 'I thought it wouldn't hurt to try.'

'This is very serious,' said the Doctor.

Kramer sat down on Carolyn's sofa. 'I worked that out after the first corpse.'

'No, you don't understand,' insisted the Doctor. 'This could be more serious than either of us guessed.'

'How many of them?' said Kramer. 'How many troops do I need to call in?'

'That's just it,' said the Doctor. 'None – for the moment. We have to be very careful, Adrienne.'

'Careful means having adequate resources to deal with the problem. Right now we have a handful of frightened civilians, and us.'

The Doctor sat down on the sofa opposite her, gesturing with both hands. 'If the vampires believe that they're under attack, they'll come to precisely the same conclusion. Only fourteen of us, they'll think. We need reinforcements.'

'They'll call in all their little vampire friends?'

'No. They'll start recruiting.'

Kramer took off her glasses.

'Turning people, turning them into vampires. And those vampires will create more vampires, and so on exponentially – until they have their army, and hundreds, perhaps thousands of innocent people have been changed!'

She thought hard for a minute. 'Wait. You said fourteen. How do you know?'

'It's the traditional number, according to the myths. One more life – if you can call it that – than a Time Lord. Our peoples were enemies before *Australopithecus* roamed the plains of Africa.'

'I suppose one city can only support so many vampires,' said Kramer, 'depending on how often they need to feed…'

'Only one Vampire survived that terrible conflict. But he spread the curse to other species… the War destroyed a dozen inhabited worlds as the Time Lords tried to wipe out every last trace of their enemies.'

'And they failed.'

'We failed. Adrienne, it's my responsibility as a Time Lord to deal with these vampires.'

'You mean to kill them,' said Kramer.

The Doctor took a deep breath. 'Yes. If it comes to that. I must make sure they don't turn or kill any more human beings.'

'If it comes to that?' said Kramer. 'Doctor, they drink human blood. That's how they survive, isn't it? What can we do besides killing them?'

He put his hands on his face. 'I don't know.' He looked up at her. 'But I do know that's the easy solution. It was easy for me to kill Lord Zarn's followers, I didn't know myself well enough at the time to know that's not what I do. But it shouldn't be that easy!'

'Lord Zarn,' said Kramer, completely deadpan.

The Doctor went on regardless. 'And I do know that if we let the situation escalate, even more innocent lives will be lost.' He leapt up and started pacing again. 'It's up to us to contain it. Find some way of defeating –'

'Killing.'

'– the vampires with a minimum of fuss.'

'What you're describing is a surgical strike,' said Kramer. 'We find the vampires' base, send in a small commando unit, and wipe them out before they have a chance to respond.'

'No no no no no. It won't be that simple. They won't have put all of their eggs in one basket. We don't know enough about them! What are their plans, what is their strength, why here, why now? What is their nature, where did they come from, how do they create new vampires?'

'You don't even know that?'

'I don't even know that. Different vampires, different rules.' He sat down, and took her hands in his, suddenly, startling her. 'Adrienne, you must listen to me. Start a war now, and it could expand to engulf the Earth – and beyond. I am not exaggerating when I tell you now that whatever you decide could have consequences for the cosmos.'

He stared at her with his intense eyes. And she wondered why he really didn't want her to bring in troops.

When Shackle's shift finally ended, he drove the few blocks back to Angel Labs. He'd checked on Sam's blood samples during his lunch break, but there weren't any results yet. Besides, stopping by at night would give him a chance to talk to Joanna Harris.

She was, as always, bent over a microscope in a back room. She'd pulled her mass of curly brownish hair back into something approximating a ponytail, but the first strands were already falling forward to obscure her face. He remembered having at least one conversation with her when he'd never got to see her face, just the mass of hair and the microscope.

'Hi, David,' she said without looking up. 'Want a moan about life, or just the test results?'

'Why settle for just one?' he asked. 'But first things first. Have you finished checking the sample yet?'

'Mm-hm. I got to it as soon as I got on shift.'

'And?'

She looked up at him and raised an eyebrow. 'It's blood.'

'Yes, thank you,' he said. 'Any abnormalities, foreign presences, depleted cell counts, anything?'

'No, no, no, and no. If this patient were any more utterly average, they'd have two point four kids and a Chevrolet.' She shrugged and brushed the stray hairs out of her eyes. He liked getting to see her face; there was something about the pallid, exhausted med-student look which suited her. 'It would have helped if you'd given us something specific to look for.'

He sighed. 'I'm not at liberty to say.'

'Ah,' she said dismissively. 'Somehow that doesn't surprise me.'

'I mean it. You don't think I'm melodramatic, do you?'

'Painfully so,' she snorted.

He had to admire the way she could deflate him so quickly. 'So the subject is perfectly healthy?'

Again with the raised eyebrow. 'Your patient? Or the meaninglessness of life?'

Sam watched the Doctor as he listened to the voice on the phone. His back was to her, so she couldn't read his expression.

Then he hung up, swung around, threw his arms wide, and let out a joyous 'Ha-haa!' which shook the ceiling tiles. Beaming, he dashed over to Sam's bed and wrapped her in a gigantic hug. 'There's not a trace of any infection in any of your samples. You're going to be fine, Sam. Better than fine! You're going to be wonderful!'

She didn't feel wonderful.

Shackle poured himself a cup of coffee in the lab staff lounge. He offered Harris one, but she declined, and after looking at the thin brew he wasn't even sure why he'd wanted some in the first place. He lay down on the couch and curled up into a large and awkward ball.

'This is different from the usual, isn't it?' Harris asked. 'All those samples you've asked us to run, looking for a common factor...'

'Aah, sort of,' he mumbled into the couch cushions. 'Different part of the same investigation.'

'You never did tell me what that was all about.'

'It's nothing important.' As he said it, he realised how much he believed it at the moment. 'It's just a little thing. Not worth getting yourself killed for.'

She shrugged. 'What is?' she asked rhetorically.

'Good point…'

He lay there for a moment. It would be very easy just to sleep, but for some reason he felt like that would be giving up too easily. Something was still nagging at him, saying that there should be a better answer to Harris's question than he'd given, that he really did believe in more than that.

'I was talking to someone earlier,' he said, 'who said that as long as you were doing the right thing, it doesn't really matter whether you made a huge difference or not when you die. That it really is the thought that counts.'

She just looked at him. 'And you believe that?'

He had to admit he almost had, at least up until this moment. 'Well, it would be nice to.'

She shrugged and sat down next to him. 'Me, I think dead is dead. Doesn't matter what you die for, you end up the same way no matter what.' Good old Joanna. No false illusions of nobility, no cheerful platitudes, just good old-fashioned grim truth.

It felt easier to sleep now, after her words. The secondary results could wait. He might as well take the rest of the night off. And the day off. Let the crusade go on without him.

Unless the monsters came to him. Came here.

He said, 'Maybe it matters who else you take with you. Who else gets killed because of you.' Like, perhaps, a somewhat frowzy med student working nights to make it through school, who's left alone with a blood sample which a group of ruthless killers would be quite happy to get ahold of.

She shrugged. 'If someone gives their life for you, that's their decision.'

'That's not what I mean…'

'Well what do you mean?'

He shrugged, sleepily. 'Don't know. Listen, I've got to get some sleep. If you give me a room here to crash in for a few hours, I can give you a ride home.'

'Well, that's original,' she said.

'No, it's not like that at all,' Shackle stumbled. 'It's just... well, you know what this neighbourhood's like. With you on the late shift, and heading home alone... I'd hate to think of you getting hurt.'

She shrugged and gave a wry grin. 'Don't worry. If med school hasn't killed me, what can?'

CHAPTER 7
SLAKE

'Lord, what fools these mortals be.

'Cast your eyes over them... weak, spineless creatures, slaves to their bodies, and to the morals their world imposes on them. Too squeamish to explore the depths of true pleasure. But we... We partake of the greatest of the forbidden delights. The drinking of blood. The taking of life.

'To us their taboos, their prohibitions, are an illusion. Nothing exists except the Will.' He paused to emphasise the capital letter. 'The Self, and the Not-Self upon which it acts. Desire... and the object of desire. The appetite, and its satisfaction.'

He stared piercingly into the eyes of the audience of young mortals gathered at his feet. 'I am Slake. I live for no reason other than my own desires. This, and this alone, is the real purity.'

He held the pose, looking over the collection of Goths and grungeheads gazing up at him, and waited for them to speak.

'Yes, thank you, Edwin, we'll let you know,' Abner said wearily from across the room.

Slake glowered at him. His audience shifted, turning to see who the heckler at the table in the corner was. Great. He had to say something fast, or lose their attention to Abner. 'We, the denizens of the night, have freed ourselves from the chains of a mortal existence –'

'Well, except for sleep,' Abner put in. 'We just work the nightshift instead of the day. Oh, and except for having to eat. We haven't quite got past that bit either...'

'As I was saying,' Slake snapped, 'we have freed ourselves from the chains of the society of mortals. We refuse to be bound by their straitjacket of morality. We know no good, no evil, no restrictions, no limitations...'

'No sense of humour,' Abner put in.

'We are beyond doubt, beyond fear –'

'Beyond melodrama?'

Any poise Slake had left vanished. 'Oh ha ha, very funny. Any closer to graduating yet, Abner?' His knot of onlookers were beginning to chat among themselves, no longer listening to him. This could not happen, he would not let himself be upstaged again. He made one more bid to grab their attention back. 'This is the truth of existence. There are men and supermen, and we are the transcendent ones. We terrify the mortals because we refuse to play by their rules.' His voice grew louder, more ringing. 'We are the darkness outside their gates, the world they flee from because they are so cringingly afraid. And we rule that world!'

'Oh yeah,' said Abner. 'You bad, you know it.' The words sounded so wonderfully incongruous in Abner's crisp British accent that the assorted hangers-on completely lost it.

Slake wheeled and stalked towards Abner Miller's table. He noticed that the onlookers had given up paying any attention to either of them: they were scattering back through the rest of the club. Fine. Filthy bunch of shallow mortal poseurs, they were, with no patience to pay attention to the real greatness in their midst.

Abner stood as he approached, and gave him one of his ever-so-dignified Victorian half-bows of greeting. He was a tall thin man, with the narrow face and permanent squint of someone who had spent far too much time reading in dim light.

'You bastard,' Slake snapped. 'Do you have to do this every time?'

Abner looked down his nose at him. 'You keep drawing the crowds, Edwin, and I'll keep driving 'em away.'

'Jealous little turd.' Slake paced the scrap of ground in front of Abner's table, in the hope that some of the nearby clubbers would notice that the scene was still unfolding. 'You just can't stand it if anyone gets to be the centre of attention, you know?'

Abner looked unimpressed. 'It's hardly my fault you keep feeding me so many straight lines.'

Slake struggled to come up with a comeback. 'Oh, sure. The deep truths of existence, it's all just another straight line to you, huh?' He glared at Abner, wondering for a moment what the table would look like if he bashed Abner's head to a pulp on it.

He'd been having thoughts like that for about twenty years now.

'Surely you don't think they believe in you, do you? They don't even think you believe all the things you're going on about.' Slake just stood there and smouldered as Abner went on. 'They think we're a couple of role-players with particularly good fake fangs. They just look up to you because they think you're better at the pose than they are.'

Slake shook his head smugly. 'It's 'cause I know what it's all about. We represent everything they admire.'

Abner rolled his eyes. Slake loathed him with immeasurable passion every time he did that. 'Look, we're all selfish gits, Slake, but at least we don't try to pretend we mean anything. We don't make a bloody religion out of it.'

'That's your problem,' said Slake. 'No convictions. You don't try to stand for anything.' He readied himself to deliver the killing blow, the line he'd been waiting for ages to work into a conversation. 'Face it, Abner, when it comes to being a vampire... you've got no soul.'

'Oh please.' Abner turned away disdainfully.

'Gotcha.'

'Give it a rest. You don't stand for anything more than any street ruffian with a knife does. You just use prettier words than they do.'

No sense of poetry at all, Slake thought. Of all the people I could be sharing eternity with, I have to get stuck with a goddamn Victorian accountant.

Abner stopped, and made a big show of finally turning back to tell him something. Of course, thought Slake, this was what he'd come there for in the first place. 'Oh, by the way. McConnell's out in the front room.'

Slake grinned slowly. 'Some people just won't take a hint.'

'And she's with the man who saw your friends' little stunt last night.'

Slake fell silent. Abner turned and walked away, shaking his head. 'If you're going to deal with them, deal with them, but try not to make any more of a mess of it than you have already.'

Carolyn sat opposite the Doctor, nursing a latte and glancing around the nightclub, nervously.

It was still the early evening; the real crowds wouldn't arrive until later. But the Doctor had declared that he was going to stay there until the vampires came to him. 'And they will come,' he had insisted.

A waiter put the Doctor's salad down in front of him. The Doctor smiled up at the woman and asked Carolyn, 'Are you sure you won't have anything?'

Carolyn shook her head. 'I'm not hungry,' she mumbled.

'Have you eaten anything at all today?'

'Quit it. If I can't eat, I can't eat, all right? There are snakes in my stomach and my scalp feels like it's on fire. I can't stop thinking about the last time I saw James, how I should have said something to stop him from coming here. Being all concerned and considerate isn't going to make these feelings stop. Please just stop pestering me.'

He looked stricken. She pushed her face into her hands. 'Jesus,' she said, forcing herself to take a deep breath. 'I'm sorry. I didn't mean to snap.'

When she looked up again, there was someone else sitting at their table.

It took her about three seconds to realise that it was a life-size, honest-to-God, not-an-incredible-simulation-but-the-real-thing vampire.

He was like something out of a Hammer film. Pale, tall, gaunt, dressed all in black, with a little gold earring – an inverted crucifix? – nestled in his awry black hair. He wore one of those shirts with frilly cuffs. When he smiled, you could see that he had fangs. And he was smiling.

'You must be Carolyn,' he said. He took her hand in his, so suddenly that she couldn't stop him. 'Charmed,' he said, and kissed her fingers. His skin was like ice.

She snatched her hand away. 'Where's James?' She forced herself to say it. 'Is he – is he still alive?'

'And scared to bits.' The vampire sat back in his chair. He had put a tall tumbler of red wine on the table between them. 'He sends his regards. He's told me all about you.'

Carolyn wanted to slap him. Actually, no, she wanted to deck him. She gripped the edge of the table and looked at the Doctor.

Who, to her astonishment, was calmly eating his salad, as though nothing was happening.

The vampire seemed a bit perplexed as well. 'Call me Slake,' he told them both, raising a plucked eyebrow at the Time Lord, who continued to ignore him. 'Mr Court will remain our guest for some time,' he went on, turning the tumbler in his long fingers, 'in an effort to discourage your inquiries.'

Carolyn couldn't take her eyes off the tumbler. 'You mustn't hurt him,' she told Slake. 'You mustn't frighten him.'

'Or you'll do what, Dr McConnell?' The vampire was amused. He leaned across the table, suddenly, and his eyes were pale and the light glinted off his upper canines. 'There's only one cure for this condition. But how do you kill someone who's dead?'

'You wouldn't need a hostage if you weren't frightened,' Carolyn managed, 'if you didn't need something. What do you want? What would you take in exchange for James?' She thought, frantically. 'I can get you all the plasma you want from the blood bank –'

Slake burst out laughing. 'Darling, we could always take a pint out of him if we're that desperate. Or from you. Or from anyone we choose. Don't imagine you have any power over us. Don't imagine you can bargain with us. We're the ones who make the decisions and the demands. Do you understand?'

'Are you quite finished?'

Carolyn and Slake both turned to the Doctor. He punctured the last cherry tomato with his fork, chewed thoughtfully, and swallowed it.

'Now it's your turn to listen,' he told Slake. The vampire raised his eyebrow again. 'I'm a Time Lord,' said the Doctor. 'From the planet Gallifrey in the constellation of Kasterborous.'

Slake gaped at him, showing his fangs.

'Moreover,' said the Doctor, carefully pushing his salad bowl into the centre of the table, 'I'm a former President of the High Council of the Time Lords, Keeper of the Legacy of Rassilon, Defender of the Laws of Time and Protector of Gallifrey. I'm called the Bringer of Darkness, the Oncoming Storm, and the

Evergreen Man. My people fought yours ten million years ago. We annihilated every vampire in existence – with a few skulking, terrified exceptions who crawled away to spread their curse elsewhere.'

He stood up, looming over Slake. 'I personally dispatched the King of the Great Vampires. If you harm James Court in any way, I will hunt down every last one of your pitiful band of bloodsuckers and see that each of you is destroyed. Permanently. Is that clear?'

Slake didn't say anything, staring up at the ancient enemy.

'In the meantime,' the Doctor continued, 'I suggest your leader and myself meet to discuss how we're going to manage this muddled little situation. So, if you could just drag your dreary little melodramatic self back to your master, and pass on my message...'

For a moment, Carolyn thought the Doctor was going to pat Slake on the head.

Instead, the Time Lord took her hand. 'Come on, Dr McConnell,' he said. 'We have more important things to do.'

She stood up, and Slake was gawping up at them, and suddenly she felt a hot flush of pride. She let the Doctor lead her out of the nightclub, her head held high, and neither of them looked back.

The human was in the middle of the stage, swearing and trying to fight off Rusty and Shredder.

Abner stalked up and cuffed them around the ears until they quit. Shredder snarled and stalked out. Rusty muttered, 'Aw, what's your problem?' slinking downstage and sitting down. His long legs dangled over the edge of the stage.

'Who said you could play with him?' said Abner. He reached to help the panting human to his feet, but the man scooted backward, glowering, and hauled himself up.

'Who got staked and left you in charge?' complained the gangly redhead. 'Harris gives the orders.'

'That's right,' said Abner. 'And Harris said we keep this one alive.'

'We weren't gonna kill him,' said Rusty. 'We were just having a little fun.'

'Don't you have something better to do?'

'Yeah,' said Rusty, jumping down from the stage. 'I gotta go clean my room now, Mom.'

Abner looked at the human, who was hugging himself, looking at the stage in disgust. 'What was your name again?' he said.

'Court,' said the man.

'Are you all right, Mr Court?'

'Oh,' said the human, 'I'm just fine. All systems go.' He looked up suddenly, at the rigging. The house lights were on, but the stage area was mostly in darkness. 'What do you – people – want? Why are you keeping me here?'

Abner glanced at his watch: midnight. 'You're supposed to be safely locked up in the basement,' he said. 'Let's get you back down there before Miss Harris finds out you're up here.'

'Too late!'

The voice echoed down the empty theatre. Mr Court and Abner looked up.

She was walking down the central aisle. Mr Court stared at her – a plump woman with mousy hair, deceptively ordinary in appearance. 'Rusty has just been explaining to me why our guest isn't where he ought to be.'

'Good evening, Miss Harris,' said Abner, adjusting his spectacles.

She nodded at him, jumping easily up on to the stage. 'I've sent Rusty to grab whoever's around. Bring out some chairs, OK?'

Abner nodded.

Slake nearly ran him down, emerging from stage right. 'Harris!' Slake shouted. His voice boomed. Miss Harris turned to look at him, calmly.

Slake looked back and forth between Miss Harris and the human. 'I think we may have a problem,' he said.

The vampires sat in a circle on the stage. The younger ones slouched in their chairs, or fidgeted. The older ones sat rock-still, utterly focused.

Slake had sent Reaper to lock James back up. The human had been unimpressed by Reaper's hissing and looming. Was captivity starting to unhinge the man's mind? When they'd first snatched him, he'd screamed and struggled like an animal caught in a trap, his mind unable to deal with the reality of it. Now he almost seemed disdainful.

There might be something useful in that, thought Slake.

'So who was this man?' said Harris.

Slake said, 'He said he was a Time Lord.'

'*Shītan*,' said Harris.

The vampires murmured, looking at her. Slake went on, 'I know the name. But there are… gaps in my knowledge.'

'You're never admitting there's something you don't know?' said Abner. Harris silenced him with a look.

'I thought they were just stories,' said Reaper.

Harris took a deep breath and said, 'We should have talked to you youngsters about this a long time ago. It's just that it didn't seem very likely that the Time Lords were still around, that they'd bother with Earth…'

'Have they come to destroy us?' said Gregorio.

She frowned. 'The legends talk about whole worlds being destroyed. If it is the Time Lords, they're being unusually subtle… but who knows what's changed in those millions of years? Maybe there are fewer of them. Maybe they've sent an agent to assess the situation.'

'Perhaps he was just taking advantage of the legends,' suggested Gregorio, stroking his peppered beard. 'Using them to put the fear of Rassilon into young Slake.'

'And the rest of us,' said Harris.

'You should have warned us,' said Slake. 'But you've got to keep your little secrets.' The younger vampires murmured their agreement.

'Slake, it was supposed to be when dinosaurs roamed the damn Earth. No one's even sure if the Time Lords were real.'

'Well, this one is.'

'Don't you talk back to me,' Harris snapped. 'If you young idiots hadn't been running amok, you wouldn't have attracted the attention you have.' Slake turned in his chair, sulking.

'What are you going to do?' asked Abner.

Harris considered, fingers gripping her hair as though she was trying to tug it out by the roots. At last she said, 'There's nothing for it. I'll have to meet with him.' She looked at Slake. 'But on our territory, and on our terms. He's to come here, unarmed and alone, and we'll talk about how we're going to handle this mess.'

'And if he is a Time Lord?' said Gregorio.

'Then I won't throw him to the youngsters,' said Harris. 'Otherwise…'

Slake looked around in irritation as the rest of the younger vampires grinned and giggled. Harris had overcome the generation gap, once again, by offering them some sport. They were pathetic.

But not as pathetic as the oldsters, sitting in judgment on them, giving orders and tedious advice. Curtailing the freedom they had literally bought with their lives.

If this Doctor was a Time Lord, then he ought to be killed. No games, no negotiations. It was so obvious they couldn't even see it.

He looked up at Harris, who was murmuring to Gregorio. One of these days, she was going to get them all killed.

She caught him staring. 'Get out,' she said, 'and give him the message. And make sure he comes here.'

Slake got up, forcing down his anger.

'Alone, Slake. Just you and him.'

Slake gave her a mock bow and stormed out.

Slake's apartment was in the lower basement, deep beneath the theatre. They'd been altering and adding to the building since they'd bought it after 1906. A century's worth of bric-a-brac and graffiti had accumulated in that maze beneath the stage and seats, much of it left by the upstarts.

Slake remembered the first day he'd seen his new home. Harris had led him through the corridors with their brick walls and their dust. 'Get a phonograph,' she'd told him. 'It's been too quiet here for too long.'

It had cost two interior decorators their lives to remake the filthy, insect-infested room. Since then he hadn't changed it, except to add a bookshelf for his Nietzsche collection.

He locked all four locks and strode across the living room to the bathroom. There were more locks on the bathroom door.

Slake paused, glancing up at the topmost hinge. It had nearly been forced loose. He'd have to get Rusty to take a look at it.

He undid the locks and opened the door.

James Court was sitting in the dry bathtub, his knees pulled up to his chest. It took him a moment to look up, as though he didn't want to see who was there, didn't want to know what was going to happen next.

'Hungry?' said Slake.

'Yeah,' the human said.

'I'm sure you are,' said Slake. 'Do try to resist taking bites out of the soap.'

Court looked at him with dull eyes. The human had at least taken advantage of his prison, and kept himself clean. But he didn't look as though he had slept since they brought him here.

'What the hell do you want?' said Court.

Slake closed the toilet seat and sat down on it, crossing his legs. The human wasn't being impertinent, not even brave: he just wanted to be left alone.

'Your friends haven't taken the hint,' said Slake. 'In fact, they've made something of a nuisance of themselves. So in perhaps twelve hours, Mr Court, you'll either be free or dead.'

'Good,' said James.

'It's a fifty-fifty chance,' said Slake. 'I thought I might offer you a third alternative.'

James sat on the sofa in Slake's living room.

The vampire had changed his clothes. It had taken him four minutes and thirty-seven seconds. In that time James had discovered that two of the four door locks required a key to open from the inside, and that there was nothing in the fridge.

Slake drifted back into the living room, wearing a scarlet dressing-gown. James found himself horribly fascinated by the vampire's naked feet. They looked like something dead from the bottom of a pond.

Slake didn't even bother to watch him. He yawned and

stretched and sat down on an easy chair, stretching out his long legs with those jellyfish feet at the ends.

James wondered what would happen if he attacked him. The vampire would probably snap him in half. He still had bruises from Sunday.

The vampire.

For two days he'd made himself think of them as the kidnappers, the Goths, sometimes the weirdos.

Slake yawned again. The fluorescent light glinted off his Goddam *fangs*.

'All right,' he said. 'What's this third alternative?'

'I turn you,' said Slake. James raised an eyebrow. 'Into a vampire,' said Slake in disgust.

James stared at him. 'No.'

'I could use another follower,' said Slake, 'and it guarantees you won't be killed.' James shook his head. 'Think about it seriously,' said Slake. 'Don't let your initial revulsion and your programmed scruples stand between you and life. Eternal life, Mr Court.' The vampire's pale eyes brushed over him. 'I could force you, but unwilling vampires have an unfortunate tendency to go sunbathing, the first chance they get.'

'I don't want to be here any more,' said James.

'Oh please. Don't beg. It's tedious.'

'You don't get it. I don't want to be in this Goddam apartment surrounded by you and your horror-movie buddies. I want to be back in the world I was living in two days ago.' James took a deep breath. 'Or nowhere.'

Slake gave him an angry look, those pointed teeth appearing again over his lip. 'I offer you eternity,' he said, 'and you want to go back to lighting direction.'

'And the horse you rode in on,' said James.

'Do you know, Mr Court,' said Slake, 'given the choice, I think I'd kill you. You refuse to be cowed.' He raised a pale finger. 'And it's not even a show of false courage. I can't tell you how uncommon – and how irksome – that is. I'd take you at your word and rip your throat out. Probably in the bathroom – these carpets are the very devil to clean.'

James didn't even bother to look at him..

'But it's not my decision to make, Mr Court. Fifty-fifty. Enjoy your potentially final day.'

Carolyn was woken at 4 a.m. by the shouting from downstairs. She lay there, listening, for a while. It reminded her of scared nights in Riverside, a little girl listening to her parents' angry voices through the Iowa silence. They had almost never fought, and every time they did, she was convinced they were going to get a divorce and therefore the world was about to end.

When she couldn't get back to sleep, she dragged on her dressing-gown and padded out on to the landing.

'I simply can't believe you went ahead!' the Doctor said, exasperated. 'Didn't I make it clear how the vampires might respond?'

'As crystal,' said Kramer. She didn't really shout, but even raising her voice was like shouting. 'Take it easy, Doctor. My people aren't even in the city: they're quartered at the Coast Guard station on Yerba Buena. Fifteen minutes away.'

Carolyn sat down on the stairs, unnoticed by either of them.

'And what if the vampires discover them?'

'Why should they?'

The Doctor shook his head and paced the room. 'Superior fire power is not the answer to this.'

'I just want my people within arm's reach,' said Kramer. 'If things do blow up.'

'It shouldn't come to that,' said the Doctor. 'When I talk to them –'

'When you talk to them?'

'Ah,' said the Doctor. 'I was coming to that.' Kramer waited. 'I've asked for a summit with their leader.'

'When did this happen? Of course, while you were out at dinner,' said Kramer. 'I can't believe you went ahead and did that without consulting me.'

'I wanted to negotiate with them there and then,' he admitted. 'But the vampire we spoke to was just an underling.' He glanced at his watch. 'I'm hoping to hear from them tonight.'

'And if you don't?'

'Oh,' he said quietly, 'I doubt they'll be able to resist. Not if they remember who they are.'

Carolyn realised her head was pressing against the railing. She had almost fallen asleep again. They hadn't seen her. She picked herself up and tiptoed back up the stairs, closing her bedroom door behind her.

The vampire from the nightclub was waiting for her.

He was just an outline, barely visible against the streetlight coming through the curtains. The open curtains.

She leaned back against the door, fumbling for the knob. She didn't seem to be able to move properly. She wondered if she was dreaming him.

He crossed the room to her, fast, grabbing the doorknob. This is it, she thought.

He hissed, 'Tell him the old Orpheum Theater, at Ellis and Fillmore, before dawn. And tell him to come alone. Alone, do you understand?'

She nodded.

He went back out through the window. She half expected him to turn into a bat and fly out. Instead, he walked out on to the roof, and she almost laughed when she saw him climbing down the garden ladder James had left propped up against the wall.

She wondered if he would show up in a mirror.

She went downstairs to deliver Slake's message to the Doctor.

CHAPTER 8
BLOODFASTING

'Are you out of your tiny little mind?' said Kramer.

'It's a trap, it's got to be a trap,' said Carolyn.

Sam said nothing, and just looked at the Doctor with huge frightened eyes.

'Give me until dawn,' said the Doctor. 'If I'm not out by then, Adrienne, you can hack and slash to your heart's content. But don't get your hopes up.'

He plucked the car keys from Sam's ear and dropped them in her lap. She just kept watching him, hunched over, trying to fold her body even more inside herself. He tried a reassuring grin. 'I'll be back soon.'

He got out of the car and strolled over to the steps, taking a moment to admire the worn marble edifice of the Orpheum. The abandoned theatre stood alone amid the squat housing projects, as if the whole building had been thrown off the top of the hill to land in a much less fashionable neighbourhood. He looked up the broad flight of steps towards the main entrance at the top, and started to climb.

Something was very wrong. Sam should have been demanding to go along, bursting with energy, suggesting that they rappel down from the roof or something just for novelty's sake. If the fight really had gone out of her, then she needed help, the kind of help he had no idea how to give.

That bite had gone a lot deeper than he had thought.

He looked around and realised that he'd already reached the top of the steps.

The vampires were waiting for him as he passed through the door. There were two of them, young-looking twins with sunken eyes, who sullenly closed the door behind him and left him in darkness.

It took him a few moments to adjust his eyes. A human

wouldn't have been able to make out anything in the blackness, but for him the trickle of moonlight through the windows was enough. He could see all the way to the high vaulted ceiling of the theatre lobby, and the dangling cable which had once held a chandelier, and focus clearly enough to make out the flaking paint on the water-stained walls.

Immersing him in darkness was an attempt to make it clear he was in their territory. Elementary intimidation, he thought.

'You, behind me,' he said, hearing a satisfying thump as the vampire sneaking up on him almost tripped over, 'Go and tell your masters I'm ready for them.'

'One thing at a time,' hissed one of the others. The three circled him, getting his measure.

'If you're going to kill me,' said the Doctor quietly, 'I suggest you start now. These things take a long time, and you'll want to have a good start before the others come in after me.'

He looked coolly at each of them as they shifted uneasily. 'I came here to talk. If you're not interested in listening, then I don't see why we should waste any time on formalities.'

The vampires stepped in close. One reached out a hand and took hold of his sleeve.

He didn't flinch as they touched him, cold fingers pulling off his frock coat. He obligingly raised his arms, trying not to think of all the potentially useful objects in the pockets, beyond his reach now.

When they had finished, he stood there in his shirtsleeves and waistcoat, feeling the utter lack of a breeze in the dead building.

They led him down the hall, ignoring the doorways to the balconies, preferring the grand staircase down to the orchestra seats. On the stairs they flanked him like bodyguards, blocking any escape. As they descended below the angle of the windows, they left the last bits of moonlight behind, and he found himself in unrelieved blackness. His eyes adjusted again, more slowly this time.

The stairs ended in a set of doors. Two of his guards pushed them open. Beyond it stood a fourth one, an older man with a beard and the piercing eyes of a fundamentalist minister. Those eyes swept over the Doctor, and then he was reaching into the Doctor's pockets and removing everything he found. Among the clutter was a telescoping silver rod with a metal ring-tip. The vampire held it up, raising an eyebrow.

The Doctor took it from him. 'Sonic screwdriver,' he explained. 'Don't worry, it's not as though it's an electric crucifix or anything.' The vampire, unimpressed, plucked it from the Doctor's hand.

He started to dig through the Doctor's waistcoat pockets as well, then grew impatient and motioned for the Doctor to remove it. He casually laid the waistcoat across the top of the pile of his possessions one of the young vampires was now struggling to carry. Now he'd given up every last thing he'd brought with him. The old man led them onward, and he followed, unafraid.

Another doorway, leading into the auditorium itself, and another vampire waiting beyond it. This one was a thin narrow-faced one, who simply looked him in the eye and reached for his neck.

With bony fingers he removed the Doctor's cravat and opened his collar, leaving his throat bare and vulnerable.

The Doctor didn't so much as blink.

The five vampires formed up around him and led him onward into the theatre. They were descending still farther, down the long sloping aisle towards the stage.

Ahead was candlelight.

The main stage was lit only by an assortment of wax candles and lanterns, which threw huge shadows in all directions. On it stood seven men in dark clothing, including the one he'd spoken to in the restaurant, arrayed around a short brown-haired woman who sat on a folding chair as though it was a throne.

'It's about time,' the Doctor said. 'I was afraid I'd run out of clothing before I got to you.'

The handcuffs were hurting James's wrists. He kept reminding himself of that.

They hadn't said anything. They'd dragged him up here on to the stage and chained him to the lowest overhead pipe of the side lighting rig. Then they'd just left him there in the wings, and waited in utter silence at centre stage.

So far he'd been able to squeeze out of his mind all the horror-movie possibilities of why they wanted him there, just by thinking about how much his wrists hurt.

And now the newcomer was emerging from the darkness towards them, with five vampires surrounding him like an honour guard. He looked more like James thought a vampire should look: old-fashioned clothes and a sense of ancient grandeur. As he climbed up to the stage, James saw the vampires surrounding Harris tightening up, shifting their balance slightly. At least he wasn't alone – even they were all a bit scared of this one.

Except Slake. 'Welcome,' he said, striking a dramatic half-lit pose, 'to the Opera… of Doom.'

'Oh, give it a rest,' said the newcomer. He stalked past Slake and stood in front of Harris's chair. He looked down at her, showing a complete lack of patience with the ceremonial atmosphere. 'You know what I'm here for.'

'For James?' she asked.

'Yes,' he said coldly, and James felt his insides twist into a knot. 'And to give you my terms.'

Harris didn't even blink. 'Which are?'

He shook his head. 'James first. I want to see him.'

She nodded, stood, and began to lead the newcomer across the stage to him. The other dozen vampires followed en masse. Once the scattering of candles was behind them, all he could see of them was their silhouettes, closing in.

The newcomer paced up to him. His gaze swept over James, and then he reached for James's neck. James flinched at his touch; it was cool, nearly as chilly as the other vampires'. Surprisingly gently, he turned James's head, searching for any evidence of bite marks on his neck. He's inspecting the merchandise, James thought giddily. He felt his whole body tightening up, trying to shrink away from the man, to force itself between the bricks of the wall at his back.

'What do you want me for?' he whimpered.

The man looked up at him. He had bright, clear, blue-grey eyes, which James could see somehow even in the darkness. 'Carolyn's outside,' he said gently. 'Don't worry, we'll get you out of here soon.'

And the man was stepping away from him, back into the midst of the vampires, and they were shifting distrustfully away from him. He moved lightly on his feet, looking around the circle forming around him, meeting all their gazes without a sign of fear.

He wasn't one of them, James realised. He was something else.

When Harris stepped into the circle with him, a head shorter and dressed in jeans and a grungy sweater, he knew he was watching a meeting of equals.

'So,' she said.

'We haven't been introduced. I'm called the Doctor.'

The Doctor, thought James. It's *him*.

'Joanna Harris. You said you had something to tell us?'

'First things first,' said the Doctor. His eyes swept over the assembled figures. 'I want to know which one of you attacked my companion, Sam.'

The others shifted and shuffled. Harris looked down at her feet. 'I had nothing to do with that. No one's claimed responsibility for it.'

'I see,' the Doctor said coldly. He paced in front of them like a policeman viewing a line-up. 'So. None of you are willing to own up to it, are you? To grabbing a girl in front of everyone and ripping her throat open?'

He rounded on a pair of young black men, who hung their heads to avoid meeting his eyes. 'You were the ones who introduced her to him. But none of you fit the description Sam gave.' His words were coming out faster and faster. 'Only thirteen of you here. One missing. Where is he? Well? Where is he?'

'He couldn't have done it,' stated Harris, in a tone which killed the subject dead. 'Look. Let's deal with the important stuff first.'

'I am,' said the Doctor with great dignity. 'Oh, very well.' He turned to address the others. While Harris stood like a waxwork, he paced madly about the circle, meeting each vampire's eyes in turn. There was more motion in his body than in all of theirs put together. 'Here's what you're going to do. First, you release James unharmed. Then, you gather yourselves together and leave this city. Go out into the desert somewhere. No more feeding on humans. Go back to mutilating cattle or whatever else you do. This ends here.'

'Or what?' Harris asked bluntly.

'Or I destroy you.' It was a plain statement of fact. 'I've already dealt with one of your number, twenty years ago –'

'Eva?' Abner exclaimed. James could feel the waves of shock and anger sweep through the vampires in the circle. Gradually it began to tighten around the Doctor. It took glares from both the Doctor and Harris to hold them in check.

The Doctor raised both his hands, as if to hold off the vampires. He didn't seem to have anticipated the strength of their response. 'The military are already moving into position to hunt you down. If I don't come back they will attack this place in force. Are you ready for a war?'

'Looks like we'll have to be,' said Slake, and he gleefully bared his fangs.

The Doctor sighed furiously and put his hands to his temples. 'No no no no no. That's not why I'm here at all. If I wanted a war, do you think I would be standing here talking to you? I've only held the military off so I could have a chance to make you this offer.'

'Let 'em come,' proclaimed Slake. 'We're survivors, you know that? They won't be able to lay a finger on us. We'll outlive you all…'

'Slake,' snapped Harris.

The Doctor matched Slake's manic grin. 'Oh yes, you've done such a wonderful job so far. Hiding like rats in a cellar. If this is your idea of eternal life, you're welcome to it…'

James felt a sudden urge to burst out giggling. It was the sheer theatricality of it all, being played out on the old Orpheum stage. Slake strutting, and the Doctor matching his pose, each playing to the audience like two old rival stars struggling to upstage each other. Jockeying for the most dramatic position in the low-angle candlelight. Hell, he could have designed the lighting for this scene, though he would never have dared make it quite so Gothic.

Slake was looking at him. 'Shut up,' he said, breaking formation. James realised he had begun to laugh uncontrollably. 'Why are we even wasting our time on these mortals? It's like having a discussion with a side of meat. Let's just –'

'Right, that's it,' sighed Harris, and grabbed Slake by the throat. His mouth gaped open; he couldn't even get a squeak of protest out. 'Will you just shut up already?' she snapped, and pushed him aside. He landed in a heap at the Doctor's feet. 'Sorry about that,' she told the Doctor as she plopped back down on her folding chair. 'If he gets into one of his Lestat moods he'll go on all day.'

The Doctor relaxed his stance and actually grinned. 'Well, now that we've got that out of the way,' he said casually as he stepped over Slake, 'maybe we can get back to some real business?' He sat down on the stage next to her chair, and let his legs swing freely over the edge.

James watched in astonishment, drawing deep breaths, the wave of hysterical laughter over. While Slake slunk away to lick his wounds, disappearing back into the circle of vampires to hide his loss of face, the Doctor had shifted gears in an instant. It was as if Harris, by treating all the theatrical trappings with such disrespect, had freed him not to bother with his own pose.

'OK,' said Harris. 'So tell me why I should listen to you.'

'It would be a shame if such a long life were suddenly snuffed out,' said the Doctor. 'If the soldiers attack, you won't stand a chance.'

Harris shrugged. 'Depends how many losses the soldiers'll accept.'

'Oh, quite a lot,' the Doctor said offhandedly. Both of them had people ready to die on their command – on their advice even, thought James. Even without the theatricality, the power was unmistakable.

The Doctor went on. 'And then there are my people. If I let them know you're here, not only will you never have existed, but probably neither will a large chunk of the population of San Francisco.' He looked at her with ever-so-sincere eyes. 'When it comes to dealing with the spawn of the Great Vampires, they like to err on the side of thoroughness.'

Harris looked thoughtful. 'These, I take it, are the Time Lords,' she said in perfect deadpan.

Time Lords, thought James. Oh boy.

'You make it sound like it's hard to believe,' the Doctor pouted.

'Just a bit. I mean, you expect me to buy that you're some kind of mythical creature?'

'Joanna,' he pointed out, 'You're a vampire.'

Touché. 'Yes, but at least I'd heard of them before I became one. The Time Lords are harder to buy into. The only reason I've even heard of you people is because I spent two hundred years as a librarian. I mean, why didn't you just say you were Osiris, or the archangel Gabriel?'

'You guessed,' the Doctor said, and stuck his lower lip out in a schoolboy expression of dismay. Harris raised an eyebrow, and James forgot to breathe. Then the Doctor grinned and winked, and James decided he would count that as a joke.

The Doctor unfolded himself and stood up. 'The fact remains,' he went on, 'that I am a Time Lord, and we swore an oath to Rassilon to destroy you.'

James felt the hysterical laughter beginning to well up inside him again. It was the utter sincerity with which the Doctor said something like that, and that he so clearly believed it, and most of all that he was making James believe it too.

'And yet you want to give us a chance to save our lives.' Harris spread her hands mockingly. 'Out of the goodness of your heart.'

'Hearts, actually. And yes.' He looked defiantly out at the circle around him. 'Do you find that hard to believe? That someone would care more about saving lives than ending them?'

'And the ancient oath to Rassilon?'

'Oh, oaths to Rassilon, proclamations of Rassilon, if you could only imagine how much I've had it up to here with the This, That, and the Other of Rassilon…'

'But why save our lives, specifically?' threw in Abner from the circle. 'After all, aren't we what you're supposed to be saving people from?'

'Because war is boring. It's all people telling other people what to do.' The Doctor was rattling off his words, as if trying to get them all past the audience before they could have a chance to think about them. 'Because hunting and killing people is what you spend your time doing, and I just don't want to. Because I don't see why I should have to be burdened by my past – how many reasons do you need, really?'

James just let the words wash over him, the silent laughter still shaking his body like dry heaves. He'd spent enough of his time at work figuring out how to convince people that the impossible was real, how to highlight a hastily assembled collection of feathers and muslin so that the audience wholeheartedly believed an angel was descending from the rigging.

But all the miracles melted away when you brought the house lights up. None of these people were real. What was real, what really mattered, was going home and cooking dinner with Carolyn, and wrapping his arms around her.

Slake said, 'You keep us fed, make it so we don't waste away from malnutrition on calves' blood, and then we can talk about morality.'

'Ah, very Brecht,' muttered the Doctor. 'Look, I'm a scientist. It should be easy to come up with a food substitute, end your dependence on human blood…'

'Will you listen to that,' Slake sneered to the crowd. 'He wants to cure us.'

'If you've got something else to feed on, then I don't have to waste my time wiping you out while I've got much better things to do.' He turned on his heel, speaking to the entire circle. 'So you'll have to give up all the night-stalking and random murders, but that'll give you plenty of free time to find something more interesting to do. Well? What do you think?'

'Sure,' said Harris. The Doctor blinked. 'I've been working on a substitute for years. It's been slow going, doing it all on my own. None of this lot have bothered to learn a bit about science.'

'She's trying to go against our nature,' protested Slake.

'Look, Slake,' Harris sighed, 'if someone hadn't started hunting the Remembered, we wouldn't have got noticed in the first place, and you wouldn't need to back off.'

'So we're agreed then,' said the Doctor, his voice tinged with disbelief. 'We're actually agreed?'

'Not quite,' said Harris. 'I'd like a few assurances of my own.'

'Of course. What did you have in mind?'

'Not in front of everybody.'

'James first, then.'

James didn't dare to believe they were letting him go. Rusty and Spike were reaching up over his head, sliding his handcuff chain off the overhead pipe, his arms suddenly falling like dead weights before he remembered to support them himself. They manhandled him towards the steps and down, barely giving him a moment to look back.

The Doctor was still in the pool of dim light on the stage, the other vampires closing in around him. Their shadows were falling across his face. 'Go on, James,' he called out. 'Get out of here and go to Carolyn. She needs you.'

Suits me fine, he thought as he bolted for the door. If you did all this to get me out of here, hey, who am I to argue? You're the star of this show – I'm just a bit player. Hell, I'm a backstage guy. Your drama can keep on running without me, just get me out of here.

Exit, downstage left, he thought, and felt the laughter swamp him again.

'The rest of you, you can go.' Harris waved offhandedly at the remaining vampires in the circle. 'I'm going to make sure we can trust him.'

'And if it turns out you can't?' asked Gregorio.

Harris shrugged. 'Then you've got real problems. If he's out to stab us in the back, then the army's probably about to raid the place. So I want you away from here, all right? Go already.'

The others turned and filed down the steps, disappearing into the darkness of the theatre. Shredder took a moment to push the Doctor's possessions back into his hands, then followed them. The Time Lord tugged on his waistcoat and frock coat.

Harris started blowing out the assorted candles. The Doctor watched her like a statue in the last of the light.

She took his hand and led him down the stairs, into the orchestra pit. Part of the back wall of the pit had been torn out, revealing a tunnel mouth that smelled of damp soil.

He stopped at the entrance and put a hand over hers. She looked down at the gentle touch, surprised. 'What's waiting for me in there?' he asked.

She looked straight at him. 'You said you wanted a peaceful solution. To get it, you'll have to trust me.'

'True,' he said, and walked into the dark.

The hallway was pitch-black. James fell against one wall and felt his way along until he collided with a door. He pounded on it, panicked, until he realised it wasn't locked. He wrenched it open and stumbled out into the night.

There was a street light right above him. He blinked, looking around. Carolyn was waiting, the Doctor had said. Well, where was she?

He realised he had walked out into the middle of the road. He kept walking, feeling his body picking up speed, breaking into a sweat, breaking into a run, getting away from the theatre before clawed hands could reach out and drag him back in.

Someone gripped his arm. He slapped at the hand in panic, jumping backward, trying to grab the fingers and pry them loose.

It was Carolyn.

He stopped, standing completely still, his hand closed desperately over hers.

'James,' she said.

The laugh came back, full and unstoppable. She took him in her arms, and he laughed until he thought he was going to throw up.

The tunnel led to another, and then another.

Harris was oppressively silent. The Doctor felt a momentary urge to whistle, but decided there wasn't any real point in antagonising her. 'So, how far have you got on the food substitute? I'd love to know what you've discovered so far.'

Harris shook her head firmly. 'Not till after I know you're not going to kill me.'

'And how are you going to manage that?' Harris didn't respond, and the Doctor let out a sigh. 'Look. You've got to trust me enough to make me trust you, so that I'm willing to do what you want to make you trust me.'

'What?'

'Oh, there are lots more questions where those came from,' he said, doing up his waistcoat buttons. 'Why kill Pymble and Oxwell? Why terrorise James? Why tear into Sam in front of dozens of witnesses? Why all the killings and the terror and the brutality?' He grabbed her by the shoulders and stared right into her eyes. 'What's it all *for*?'

There was fury in his words, and also an honest bewilderment.

'You're really asking,' Harris said, taken aback. 'You really don't see it.'

'Of course not. What could justify this?'

'It's because they're bored,' she said.

The Doctor stared at her in disbelief.

'Slake, and the younger ones. Like Shredder and Reaper and Elvis and Spike.' She drenched the nicknames with contempt. 'Mostly the ones we turned after what happened in fifty-six. They're at the age now where it's suddenly beginning to sink in that this is all there is to their life.'

'Such as it is.'

'They killed the diplomat just to show off. Forget hunting the Forgotten in the barrio: they had to be flashy and go after people who'd be missed. They were basically daring the police and the military to come after us.'

'You'd think being dead would have cured their death wish,' the Doctor muttered. He found his cravat in a pocket and slung it around his neck.

'So I told them no more killings. And then when someone else came around asking questions at the club, they panicked. I came out of my lab one night and found they'd kidnapped the guy and locked him in Slake's bathroom. Idiots. Couldn't have drawn more attention to themselves if they'd tried.'

'And then why Sam?' he asked.

She shrugged. 'That was probably someone's little joke.'

'How in the world can anyone be bored enough to enjoy something like that?' The Doctor shook his head and strode onward down the tunnel. 'What piece of their mind has to be missing to make terrorising someone sound like fun?'

'Don't ask me. I haven't been bored since they developed the Internet,' she said.

Joanna's lab was deep beneath the theatre. No one else came here, not even Gregorio.

A puff of cold air burst out as she opened the door. 'Close it,' she told the Doctor, as she stepped inside. 'This is a C1 lab.'

'Containment 1? For genetic research?'

'I have another lab elsewhere for the more hazardous experiments,' she said. 'This is where I do the bulk of my work.'

She switched on the light. The Doctor looked around. It was a large lab for one person, wide and long, with two benches and plenty of cupboards. Doors in the opposite wall led to the cold and hot rooms.

Joanna took her notebook out of a bench drawer as the Doctor eyed a blood culture, rocking gently on an agitator.

'All right,' he said. 'What exactly do you propose?'

'A bloodfasting,' she said. 'A physical and psychic link between us.'

The Doctor looked at her. In this light, his eyes looked yellowish-green, almost like a cat's. 'Tell me more,' he said.

'The bloodfasting has been used through the centuries by vampires as a way of avoiding conflict,' Joanna said. 'Once the link is forged, the participants are vulnerable to one another's injuries.'

'If I die, you die?'

'And vice versa.' She reached into the bench drawer and took out a scalpel, a syringe, and two measuring columns. 'The risks are serious. As far as I know, this has only been done between vampires, never between a vampire and a mortal. Either of us could die. You could be turned.'

'Is it reversible?'

'I don't have any data.'

He came over to the bench, standing on the opposite side. 'You sound as though you want me to refuse.'

'The bloodfasting is a token of trust,' she said, 'and much more than a token. There will have to be complete honesty between us.'

He nodded. 'All right. Let's try it. I think it's our best chance.'

Joanna wrote the date in her notebook. 'If you would prefer not be bitten, use this.' She pushed the syringe across the bench. 'There's a bottle of alcohol and some sterile swabs in the lower left drawer.'

'How much?' the Doctor asked.

'I'll need more of yours than you'll need of mine,' said Joanna. 'Let's say ten millilitres from you, five from me.'

The Doctor fished out the swabs while she unwrapped the scalpel. Expertly, she sliced open the vein in the crook of her right arm, and crouched behind the bench, her eyes level with the mark on the beaker.

He watched her for a few moments. Then he rolled up his sleeve, broke open a swab, and sterilised his arm.

Her blood had reached the five-millilitre mark. She stood up, and sucked and licked the wound until it closed.

The Doctor broke the disposable syringe out of its packet. He drew his blood slowly and gently. When he was done, he emptied the syringe into the second column, holding his arm up while the pinprick healed. She passed him a sticking plaster.

'All right,' he said.

'All right,' she said.

They looked each other in the eyes, swapping the blood samples.

Joanna drank hers carefully, tasting. It was similar to human blood, but with hints of dozens of additional components... warm and orange-red.

The Doctor picked up the column, considering the mouthful of dark-coloured blood at the bottom. He closed his eyes and drank it in a gulp.

They put the beakers down on the bench between them.

'Now what?' asked the Doctor. Joanna didn't answer, making notes.

She felt the first ripple a moment later, a distant movement at the back of her mind. It reminded her of the sensation of not quite being able to remember a word.

She looked up at the Doctor. He had turned quite pale, and was leaning against the bench, his palms pressed flat against its surface.

He looked up at her. Their eyes locked.

He was old. He was older than she was. A thousand years of experiences and times and places were looking back at her.

He was absolutely convinced that he had just made a terrible mistake. That this was a trap. At any moment, she would grab him and tear the life out of him.

He turned and tried to run for the door, but instead found himself colliding with another bench, holding on to it for support.

The inside of Joanna's mind was filled with ripples, like water in rain. She walked around the bench, pausing to put the scalpel and syringe into the biohazard container, and strode over to him.

He held on to the bench, face turned away. Where she felt ripples, the distant murmuring of his mind, he felt waves, overwhelming, drowning. She saw cold sweat start from his forehead.

He fell, suddenly, collapsing to his knees, as the stream of thoughts between them turned into a torrent. She knelt beside him, turning him so she could see his face. His teeth were clenched, his eyes tightly closed. He raised a hand, weakly, trying to keep her away.

He was falling inside. Falling into somewhere deep and dark. He would die rather than let her make him a vampire.

'No,' she said.

She put her hands on either side of his face. 'No. You're not turning.' He grabbed at her wrists. 'This is not turning. This is the fasting. Stay with me.'

She pushed his hands against his chest. 'Feel that?' The steady double-thump, constant rhythm under the chaos. 'Focus on that.'

Slowly, he came back. The torrent settled, became a steady stream between them. Joanna saw Metebelis and Androzani and Yemaya before the link subsided and stabilised.

She realised she was holding him, surprised by the slightness of his body, his head pressed to her shoulder. And she knew that if anyone would be able to kill her, after all these centuries, he would be the one.

'Doctor!'

Sam hurled herself out of the car and ran through the half-light towards him, ignoring Carolyn's protests. He had come out of one of the theatre's side doors, taken a few steps, and fallen to his knees.

She reached him in a moment, hearing the others running up behind her. 'What is it?' she asked him, trying to help him to his feet. 'Oh my God, what did they do?'

He didn't answer, looking around in bewilderment. Sam literally felt herself go cold with fear.

'Oh God,' said Carolyn, 'they must have bitten him.'

'Get,' said the Doctor. 'Get away.'

'Come on,' said Sam. 'Let's get him out of here.'

Objects were just starting to take on colour. The street lights went out as the three of them half walked, half carried the Doctor. Sam put a hand to his forehead. He was icy cold.

He started struggling when they were halfway to the car. 'Away,' he gasped. 'I have to get away.'

'Don't worry, Doctor,' said Sam. 'We'll get you out of here.'

He tried to pull free. James fell against the car. Sam and Carolyn grabbed for the Doctor. 'You don't understand,' he moaned. 'Something terrible's going to happen, it's going to happen, I have to get away, something terrible –'

The Doctor did something Sam had never seen before. He screamed.

She stumbled back from him in shock. He threw his arms in front of his eyes, desperate.

The sun came up.

SECOND BITE

CHAPTER 9
HURT/CHOCOLATE

Wednesday

James was watching the Doctor sleep.

They were taking turns to watch over him. He hadn't regained consciousness since they'd dragged him into the car.

James had expected the sunlight to kill the man. The way he'd panicked when the dawn came up...What happened to the powerful creature he'd watched confront the vampires?

Now there was a pale stranger in the guest bedroom, wavy brown-gold hair spreading on the pillow. His hands were clasped above the blanket, rising and falling slowly, very slowly, in time with his breathing. The morning light barely filtered through the curtains, closed tight, just in case.

James wondered what he had expected to see, when the sun came up over Ellis Street. Smoke pouring from the Doctor's coat? Flames in his hair? Or just a slow fading into nothing? What kind of special effect would be right for a vampire's death?

They'd raced back home, flying over the mountainous San Francisco streets, and he'd helped the general drag the Doctor out of the back seat. Then Kramer had simply hefted the slight body in her arms and carried him into the house.

She'd unbuttoned his shirt while they watched, turning his head from side to side. James remembered the Doctor doing the same to him. Looking for bite marks. There weren't any. Kramer kept unbuttoning, checking his chest, then his wrists. She kept rolling, until she found the sticking plaster over the vein in his left arm. She looked up at Sam, who shook her head, her arms folded tightly. Blood sample? Injection? They didn't know. They didn't know what was wrong with him.

After they'd taken care of the Doctor, Carolyn had made a tremendous fuss over James, making him sandwiches and soup and putting him to bed, snuggling up to him. Holding on to him as though if she loosened her grip he might suddenly fly away. He'd slept for – he looked at his watch – three hours. When he'd woken up, she wasn't in the bed. He'd found her in here, sitting by the Doctor's bed.

So now it was James's turn.

Kramer had wanted to send over a military doctor and some variety of shrink for James, but James had just shaken his head, his mouth full of mushroom and Swiss on rye. He felt fine. Dog-tired, bruised, starving, and distant, but fine. He didn't want debriefing. He wanted to be back in his lover's house, at home. He was fine.

The Doctor was not fine.

James looked up. Carolyn was in the doorway.

She came and knelt beside the rocking chair and put her arms around him. After a moment he hugged her back.

'It's so good to have you home,' she whispered.

He pushed his face into her hair. She smelled wonderful, human. 'I can't believe it,' he said.

'I know. Vampires. Real vampires.'

'No,' he said. 'I've spent the last three days making myself believe in them.' He looked around the room, at the frilly curtains, the vanity, the giant plush bear sitting in the corner. 'None of this seems real.'

She just held him tighter. 'What did they do to him?' he said softly.

Carolyn's head turned, resting on his shoulder. 'We're not going to know until he wakes up and tells us. All we do know is that they didn't bite him. He's not turning into a vampire.'

James glanced at the Doctor. No sign of change, no sign of anything except his slow breathing. 'Do we know for sure that it's the bite that changes people?'

'I hadn't thought about it,' she whispered.

'In the *Dracula* play, it was drinking the vampire's blood that did it… They wanted me to become one of them. He wanted me to. Slake.'

'Oh God. I know the one you mean.'

'I told him where to go.'

'Good for you,' said Sam, from the doorway.

She tried to smile, but there was a bandage across her throat. Instead she swallowed, uncomfortably. 'Why don't you two go upstairs,' she whispered, 'I'll look after him for a bit.'

'What's Kramer up to?' Carolyn wanted to know.

'She's gone,' said Sam. 'She said she was going to round up her troops, drive over to the theatre, and stake every vampire she could find.'

The Doctor stirred in his deep sleep, but didn't wake.

Joanna dreamed.

Carolyn sat down on the sofa and put her head in her hands.

'OK,' said James. 'We're getting out of here. Pack a suitcase.'

She looked up in astonishment. 'What?'

'We can go stay with my brother in LA. He's always pestering us to visit – this'll make him happy.'

'We can't just walk out!' Carolyn looked as though she had twice as many grey hairs. 'We're involved.'

'No, we're not. We're innocent bystanders. Let's get out of here while we can.'

'You don't understand,' said Carolyn. 'I asked them for help!'

'Who are they, anyway?' he said. 'The Doctor and Sam?' She looked at him, trying to decide whether he'd believe her. 'Go on,' he said. 'I just spent two days in a vampire's bathtub.'

'The Doctor's from another planet,' said Carolyn. 'Sam travels with him through time. When you went missing, I sent them a message.'

'You did what?'

'I met them back in seventy-six.'

James sat down on the other sofa. 'And were there vampires back then, too?'

'Yes,' said Carolyn.

'Why didn't you tell me?'

She just looked at him.

'All right, I'd have laughed my head off. I'm not laughing now. We're leaving.'

'Look,' she said, putting a hand on his knee. 'You've been through so much…'

'Damn right I have. I'm not going through any more.'

Carolyn furiously stage-whispered, 'The man who saved your life is lying up there, cold as a rock, and we don't even know whether he's going to live or die, and poor little Sam nearly got her throat ripped out trying to find you!'

James sat back on the sofa. 'Jesus,' he said.

'You didn't know,' said Carolyn. She raked at her hair, agitated. 'I'd better fill you in on everything that's been happening.'

'I think you'd better,' he said.

'And then?'

'And then we're leaving,' he said. 'Maybe.'

Sam jerked awake. She'd nodded off in the rocking chair.

The Doctor was the same as before.

She wanted to shout and scream and pull his hair and hit him until he woke up. Instead, she leaned back in the rocking chair. The ache in her neck wasn't as bad as it had been yesterday. Whatever had been in that little blue pill was doing the trick.

James and Carolyn were arguing in the lounge, keeping their voices quiet. She couldn't make out what they were saying.

Sam looked at her watch. It was past eleven. Kramer would be on her way.

'This city hates me.'

The Doctor's eyes were open, staring up at the ceiling.

'Are you all right?' asked Sam.

'Better,' he breathed. He sat up, frowning as he looked around. Sam sat beside him on the bed and took his hand. He startled. 'Have I been asleep all day? What time is it?'

'Eleven,' she said. There was a cold lump of worry in her stomach. 'Are you sure you're all right? Look at me, Doctor.'

'Put the light on, would you?' he asked.

Sam felt all the little hairs on her arms stand up. She waved a hand in front of his face. He didn't blink.

'Doctor,' she said, 'the light is on.'

He nodded, frowning, blank eyes searching in the direction of her voice. 'An unexpected side effect,' he said.

'Oh God,' said Sam. 'A side effect?' *You'd follow him off the ends of the earth, you know. But does he really tell you what he's up to?* 'Of what?'

'An arrangement I made with the leader of the vampires.'

'Slake?'

'No no. Slake is a minor player, much as he would like to think otherwise.' The Doctor was blinking, slowly looking around the room, as if trying to penetrate the blackness. 'Joanna. Joanna Harris.'

'What did she do to you?'

'She didn't do anything to me. Goodness, I'm peckish. We came to an arrangement. It's called a bloodfasting.'

'What?'

'Bloodfasting. It's a sort of psychic link between two vampires.'

'That's daft,' insisted Sam. 'You're not a vampire.'

'Of course not. But we decided to try it. If anything happens to me, you see, it happens to Harris as well. So it's a stalemate for the time being.' He gripped her hand, as though making sure of where she was. 'I didn't expect this.'

'Blind date,' said Sam.

'Is James all right?'

'He's just fine. He's upstairs with Carolyn. We're all fine.'

'And General Kramer?'

'She's –' Sam realised her fingernails were pressing into the Doctor's hand. She let go and reached for the box on the end of the bed. 'Do you want a chocolate?' she said.

'Yes please.'

Sam struggled with the wrapper. The Doctor said, 'I keep thinking I can see something, just out of the corner of my eye. Which direction is the light coming from?'

'To your left,' said Sam, ripping the shrink-wrap open with her teeth. 'From the window, mostly.'

He nodded. 'The agreement has gained us a little time. Joanna will make sure the vampires reduce the number of people they're killing.'

'But they won't stop.'

'They can't,' said the Doctor. 'Is there a Turkish Delight?'

'Let's see… How are we going to stop them for good?'

'Joanna is a scientist. She believes she's found the key to freeing the vampires from their need to drink human blood.'

'What?' Sam took his hand and put the chocolate in his palm.

'Think about it, Sam. No one would have to die, not even the vampires.'

'But they're –'

'Monsters?'

'Murderers! Some of them maybe hundreds of times over!'

'True,' said the Doctor, around the chocolate.

Sam looked at him. His eyes were empty, reflecting nothing. 'I think we should stake the lot of them,' she said. He blinked, surprised. 'I really do.'

'It may come to that in the end,' he said. 'But in the meantime, there are two good reasons not to attempt it.'

Uh-oh, thought Sam. 'What are they?'

'One,' said the Doctor, holding his hand up in front of his face and waving it, 'the vampires don't all stay in the one place. Those who survive an attack will simply convert more humans to replace their fallen friends. I think I can see a bit! And two, whatever happens to me happens to Harris.'

She jumped up. 'And whatever happens to Harris happens to you!'

'Sam,' he said, squinting up at her, 'I think you'd better tell me what Kramer is doing.'

There was a trick with the accelerator that stopped you from flying over the tops of the San Francisco hills or from rolling backwards down them. Sam hadn't found it. So she kept the pedal jammed down, as the Bug roared over the hills and careered down them, skidding across the flat interruptions of cross streets, narrowly avoiding cars and tourists.

'Woo hoo! Kojak!' she shouted, as they crashed down again. The Doctor clung on to the strap next to his seat. Sam wasn't sure whether it was the bloodfasting or her driving that made him look so pale. 'So what exactly did you and Harris do?' she shouted, over the sound of the motor. 'She didn't bite you.'

'Not to put too fine a point on it,' shouted the Doctor, 'we drank each other's blood.'

Sam suddenly remembered the sticking plaster on the Doctor's arm. 'But why would it make you go blind? And why were you so scared of sunrise?'

'Was I? I'm afraid it's all a bit foggy…'

'I thought you were turning into a vampire.' It hit her. '*You* thought you were turning into a vampire.'

'It must have been the psychic link with Joanna,' he said. 'There can't be anything that terrifies a vampire more than the sunrise.'

'Can you read her thoughts?' said Sam. 'That could be useful.'

'Alas,' he said, 'if I could read her mind, she could read my mind. Stalemate again. No, the connection is deeper. Subconscious.'

'So you don't know what she's doing right now.'

'Sleeping,' said the Doctor. 'Helpless. The sun is up. How much further?'

'Almost there. Sh– I mean, gosh, there's a barrier up. A whole lot of barriers. I don't think I'll crash it, I can see men with guns.'

The Bug slowed to a surprisingly gentle stop. Sam leapt out and dashed round to the Doctor's side, helping him out.

'Can you see Kramer?' he asked, leaning against the car.

'Do vampires sleep with their eyes closed?' said Sam suddenly.

He looked at her. 'Oh, of course!' he said. 'Why didn't I think of that?'

Something shifted in his eyes, something so subtle she saw it only because she was looking hard. His eyes focused on her face, and he grinned, squinting. 'Goodness,' he said, 'it's bright out here.'

He turned to look at Ellis Street. The whole block was closed off, military vehicles parked behind the barricades. 'Goodness,' he said again.

'Do you think they'll let us in?' said Sam, following as he strode off towards the barriers.

'They'll have to,' said the Doctor. He stepped between two barricades. Sam nearly bumped into him as he stopped suddenly. A man holding a rifle scowled at him.

Kramer had sent the troops on ahead, telling them to wait until she got there before they did anything. They'd been issued with SE-4 standard issue anti-vampire kits, with extra stakes just in case.

She was driving there in a jeep, keeping in touch by RT. Ellis Street was dead quiet. With any luck, the vampires would be asleep. If the Doctor was right, daylight would knock them cold, or fry them, or both.

It didn't matter if they were asleep or awake. They were trapped, outnumbered and outgunned. It would be a surgical strike. End of problem. Or at least major reduction in problem.

Two soldiers moved a barricade aside to let her into the street. She slowed, saluting as she drove past.

The Doctor ran out in front of the car.

Kramer slammed on the brakes, feeling the whole vehicle rise and thump to a stop, a foot from him. Another private was running up, dragging Sam along by the wrist, trying to catch up with him.

'Adrienne!' the Doctor shouted, over the engine. He looked terrible, pale and wild. 'You have to stop this at once!'

Deep beneath the theatre, on a canvas hammock nailed up between two walls, Joanna Harris was having the worst nightmare she had had in nine hundred years.

The hammock began to swing, moving softly as she struggled, her head tossing. She had to wake up. She couldn't wake up: it was the middle of the day. Somewhere above her, the noon was waiting to take her life. The noon, and more.

They talked in the back of a personnel vehicle. Around them, Kramer could feel her troops getting restless, picking up the uncertainty she was broadcasting.

The Doctor was sitting on the bench, leaning against the wall, his eyes closed. 'I'm linked to the leader of the vampires.'

'You're what!'

'We came to an arrangement. We're joined, psychically and physically.'

'If she dies, you die?' said Kramer.

'That's why we had to stop you,' said Sam.

136

'I don't believe this!' said Kramer.

'It's true, I'm afraid.' A shudder ran through the Doctor's frame. 'She's restless. I think she can perceive what's going on around me.'

Kramer looked at him, aghast. 'She can see through your eyes?'

'No, no. But she knew she was in danger the moment Sam told me what you were doing.' He opened his eyes, staring at the general. 'She's dreaming about us. She's terrified.'

'My God,' said Kramer. 'So this is what you were up to, all along. Making an – alliance? – with them. Closing off my options until I have to do things your way.'

'I'm sorry, Adrienne.'

'Sorry! I could shoot you myself! At least that'd take out their leader.' Sam gave her a startled look. Poor kid, caught between the two of them. 'Relax, Sam, I'm joking. Doctor, do you have any idea how frustrating it is to be jerked around by your schemes? Why do you have to go jump in the deep end, without even telling me where the pool is?'

The Doctor shook his head. 'Joanna suggested the bloodfasting. I had to agree, to save James. And to give us the time to find a real solution. Something better than genocide.'

Whether that was true or not didn't change the current situation. Kramer sighed, heavily. 'I'll pull the troops out. What choice do I have?'

'Surely we can do better,' breathed the Doctor. 'Surely you and I can find a better answer.'

In her hammock, Joanna was tossing and turning.

'We can,' she murmured. 'We can. We must!'

Kramer drove them back in her jeep, scowling all the way. One of her soldiers followed in the VW. Sam sat in the back seat with the Doctor. He didn't talk, staring at the back of the seat.

'Doctor?' Sam ventured.

He turned to look at her, slowly. 'Sorry,' he said. 'It's a bit hard to focus. It's like someone shouting in one ear while you listen to Billie Holliday with the other.' He shook his head, sharply, as though something were loose inside it. 'I haven't quite puzzled out how to manage this.'

For a moment, she could almost believe that he really had just walked into the vampires' lair without any plan, ready to deal with whatever came his way.

Kramer grated, 'Now what?'

Sam looked up. They were pulling up to Carolyn's house. James and Carolyn were in the front yard, arguing.

Sam and Kramer sat still, watching them, embarrassed. The Doctor got out of the car and walked up to them.

James backed off, suddenly, staring at the Doctor. Sam wound down the window to hear what they were saying.

'Carolyn says you're not –' he stammered.

'I'm not,' said the Doctor. 'But don't let that frighten you.'

'Human,' James managed to get out. 'I'm not frightened. But I'm not staying. And Carolyn's coming with me.'

'James,' said Carolyn, 'for God's sake, he saved your life.'

'I'm only – human. We both are. Come on.'

He held out his hand to her. She stood perfectly still, like someone on a cliff edge.

'You know where I'll be,' said James thinly. 'Call me when you want out.'

Carolyn watched him go, watched him walk down the sloping pavement with his back to her. He looked around for a moment, as though bewildered that his car wasn't there. Then he kept walking, heading for a bus stop, just heading away.

'I don't believe it,' whispered Sam.

'Too much, too fast,' said Kramer. 'I lose more officers that way.'

CHAPTER 10
TWICE SHY

'This is bad. This is very bad.'

Carolyn watched the Doctor, silently, feeling drained by comparison. He was a whirlwind in her kitchen, occasionally carrying dishes to the sink and dishwasher but mainly moving just for the sake of moving. 'This is precisely what I hoped to prevent.'

Kramer stood in the doorway, keeping out of his path. 'So this bloodfasting is backfiring? Your peace process is shot?'

The Doctor shook his head, sending his curls flying in all directions. 'No no no. I thought getting James home would take the strain off him and Carolyn. But James has been so shaken by the whole matter that it's only driven them apart…'

'Excuse me?' asked Kramer. 'Could we stick to the matter at hand?'

The Doctor held up his two hands, quite a distance apart, and looked from one to the other. 'Which hand?' he asked, and veered off in another new direction, towards the kitchen table. Towards Carolyn, as she finished off her mug of microwaved soup. 'Carolyn, can I get you anything?'

'Uh-huh,' she said quietly, and handed him the mug. 'Seconds.' He nodded and bustled off back towards the microwave.

Carolyn sat back and let the action keep swirling on around her. She had given up trying to fit the meals into breakfast-lunch-dinner pigeonholes; she couldn't see her life falling back into such an orderly structure, not for a long time to come now.

She'd given up trying to go to work. It had seemed so important yesterday to keep one foot in the world she knew, to keep working on everything she'd wanted to achieve here. Now James had gone and it was 5 p.m. and she'd grabbed seven hours' sleep in the past forty-eight-plus and there was no wake-up breakfast lunch dinner bedtime any more only sleep when it was possible and food when it was possible without the rhythm of an everyday daytime life. Days felt much more fluid this way. Maybe this was what it was like to time travel.

'Doctor,' said Kramer. 'The vampires.'

'Are under control for the moment. Joanna's collecting her notes on vampire biology, or thanatology, or whatever word there is for what keeps them unalive and kicking. You're looking pale, Sam.'

'I'm fine,' Sam said flatly. She was sitting on a stool in the corner, watching the Doctor's bustling from a distance. 'I'm better than fine. I'm wonderful, remember?'

The Doctor's face puppydogged. 'Oh Sam.' He actually stopped moving and put an arm around her shoulders. She clung to him like he was the most important thing alive. He ruffled her hair and held on to her for thirty straight seconds, until the microwave beeped. 'Soup,' he cried, and scampered back across the kitchen.

Before the expression on Sam's face had time to harden back into annoyance, he'd completed a dash from microwave to cupboard and back to her. She watched in awe as he somehow managed to stir the soup on the counter with one arm while hugging Sam with the other. Maybe this was something else you learnt to do by time travelling – not deal with things in a single straight line, but care about everything at once.

'Focus too much on one part of the problem,' the Doctor was saying, 'and we forget about the more important things we should really be dealing with. With which we really should be dealing. What kind of person actually sits down and decides that no one should be allowed to end a sentence with a preposition? Not even decide what ideas you should or shouldn't talk about, but to actually make rules about what order to put your words in… It's such an amazing kind of petty tyranny. Amazing.' He let go of Sam and crossed to the table, to present the mug of soup to Carolyn. She felt like giving him a round of applause.

'All right. At the risk of being disgustingly linear,' said Kramer, 'what's our next move?'

'Well, until I meet with Harris and the others again, there's nothing any of us could do.' A thought stopped him in his tracks for a bare moment. 'It would be a good idea to become nocturnal, though. From now on, all the action will be taking place at night. You've been working awfully hard, Adrienne. Take a little time off, have a good meal. Get some sleep.'

Kramer shrugged. 'OK. Sure.' She flipped open her mobile phone. 'Captain Groenewegen? I need six hours' sleep immediately. Get it for me, on the double. That's an order.' She snapped the phone shut, cutting off the astonished stammering from the earpiece, and eyed the Doctor. 'There. Satisfied?'

The Doctor did a double-take, stared at Kramer with eyes and mouth wide, and then exploded into uncontrolled laughter. He nearly bent double under its force.

Carolyn stared at him in disbelief as the sound rolled on and on. She saw Sam's scowl slowly crack under the waves of laughter, until finally Sam just pointed at the Doctor – who was stumbling across the kitchen and leaning on the counter to keep from falling over – and burst out laughing herself. And then Carolyn realised she was laughing too, and while she wasn't sure at what, she didn't quite mind.

Kramer stood gaping at him. 'What? What?' she insisted. 'It wasn't that funny.' The Doctor's laughter kept bubbling out regardless. Kramer shook her head in bewilderment. 'Was it?'

Finally she gave up and smiled as well.

'It's sacrilege!' said Slake.

'Bloody one-track mind, that's your problem,' said Abner. 'I've been having my worst semester in a decade, and you don't hear me going on about it like that.'

None of the others in the TV cave paid them any attention, aside from Spike who was watching them and filing his nails. The rest lay sprawled on the worn couches and boulders around the tiny twelve-inch TV, letting the late-afternoon reruns fill the hours between waking up and nightfall. Only the youngsters were up at this hour; the mustydusties probably wouldn't show their faces till seven or eight. Which of course had been the whole point of his bringing it up now, thought Slake, but were they interested in listening? Nooooo.

'Didn't any of you see what happened last night?' Slake

shouted at the room. 'This Doctor told Harris that we'd have to stop hunting, and Harris just – said – OK! It's fine by her! It fits right into her plans anyway, doesn't it? Now we've got to do things her way. Got to go against our nature.'

'Edwin, we're vampires,' threw in Abner. 'We're unnatural by definition.'

'I dunno,' said Spike, filing. 'What can we really do about it?'

'We can tell Harris to go bite herself,' Slake called out, trying to make the others hear him over the television. 'Why the hell should we follow her anyway?'

Abner shrugged. 'Because she's old, and clever, and because if she thinks you're moving against her someone will stake you in the middle of the night.'

'They wouldn't dare.'

Abner met his eyes with a slight smile. 'We did. In fifty-six.'

Slake stared at him. 'You would, wouldn't you?'

'I don't see why you mind, really. None of you would be here if all those positions hadn't opened up.'

Slake sat down, shaking his head. Abner was the only oldster who paid much attention to them these days – the other old ones didn't seem to do much of anything besides sleep and feed, as far as he could tell. They'd totally forgotten to be excited about being vampires, for chrissakes. He still hoped he'd die before he got old.

But the younger ones he might still be able to reach. It was all a matter of playing to the audience, reminding them what they were there for. He rounded on the crowd by the TV.

'Look, why do we live like this? Because we're free. We don't have to live by anyone's rules. The only law we have is the law of the jungle. The hunt. That's freedom.' Listen to me, damn you! 'Isn't that worth standing up to her for?'

Spike looked vaguely at his shoes. The other five by the TV sat like waxworks. Abner just sighed, drenching the sound in so much condescension that Slake nearly broke his neck right there and then. 'Talk all you want, Edwin,' he said, 'You'll still have to do what Harris says.'

'We shouldn't have to do anything anyone says,' snapped Slake. 'That's the whole point of being vampires, isn't it?'

'Hey, keep it down,' called Rusty, 'Deborah's in this scene.'

'Cool,' said Spike, and plopped himself down at the foot of the couch between Shredder and Reaper. Even Abner deliberately turned his back on Slake and sauntered over to the idiot box. Slake watched them all, finally speechless with disbelief. None of them cared about making a stand, because they were all too busy watching Deborah Duchene vamp it up in a black evening dress.

'Ohhh man,' said Rusty. 'How come we never turned anyone like that?'

Abner said, 'An intelligent, sophisticated woman, faced with the prospect of a coven of overgrown adolescents drooling over her for eternity... If I were her, I'd stake myself in a heartbeat.'

Fine, thought Slake. They wanted entertainment? That was all they'd gone along with his other attacks for? Well that's what he'd give them. So what if they didn't care about the principle of it – they'd still follow him just for the sake of some good old-fashioned violence. All he had to do was pick a target.

After all, it was something for them to do.

She shouldn't have laughed so much, Sam thought; she could've pulled a stitch. Before all that, she'd been more than ready to take the Doctor's advice and zone out on the couch for a long while, but the laughing had given her just a tiny bit too much energy.

So now she was wandering the living room, somewhere between awake and asleep. Somewhere between staying and leaving.

It would actually be really easy. In real-time terms, they were now only a matter of weeks past the day she'd left with the Doctor. It would only take a plane ticket and she'd be right back in her old life. It felt so weird to see that as an option.

Oh well, whatever. She took a deep breath and went looking for the Doctor. He still needed help, and she wasn't going to leave him in the lurch. After the crisis was over... well, then she'd decide if she ever wanted to do this again.

He was waiting in the front hallway, hands clasped behind his back, gazing at the wall just to the side of the window. It was as if his eyes hadn't quite got up the nerve to look at the setting sun.

She sneaked up behind him and poked him in the side, to make him jump.

'Hey,' she said. 'You heading off to meet the vampires now?'

He looked startled. 'No, not quite yet.'

'Right,' she said. Her throat still felt a bit raspy. 'So when do we leave?'

'We?'

'Yeah.' She felt the words squeezing out of her throat, and they weren't what she'd thought she was going to say. 'I want to see them. I've got to see them.'

'What for?'

You know the answer. You just want to hear me say it. 'I want to see him.'

He reached out and held her arm gently. 'No, Sam. I know what you'll do.'

'Oh yeah? I wish you'd tell me, 'cause I certainly don't.'

He looked thoughtful for a moment, then answered honestly. 'Either crumple in a heap or tear him to bits, I'm not sure which. Either way it won't be good.'

Sam stared at him, but couldn't get a single word out of her mouth. It was as if all her words had formed a logjam in her throat, right below her stitches. 'He...' She made incoherent gestures towards her neck.

'Sam, Sam, I know... I don't want you to have to face him again.'

Oh, you don't, do you? She felt herself shaking with disbelief as she looked up at the Doctor. It was as if, after all that, he didn't want her along. She'd spent this time rallying her strength, getting ready to help him face them, and he didn't want her help. And the blue pill must be wearing off, because her throat was tightening up and there was a burning feeling in her eyes.

'I'm gonna have to,' she forced out.

He put a gentle hand on her shoulder. 'Not yet. When you're more ready.'

It didn't feel like she ever would be. What did she really think she could do? If she had to face him, she'd be helpless all over again (with his teeth in her throat).

The Doctor was watching her in bewildered distress. 'The one you're after wasn't even there last night. He might be in hiding.'

'Can you find out from Joanna?'

'Perhaps.'

'Right, then. You can go do that...' Sam leaned against the wall, giving a tiny shrug to get his hand off. She wasn't feeling a thing any more. 'I think maybe I'll go and lie down.'

He took his hand away. He looked scared, as though he didn't know what to say or do for once. 'Sam. I want you here, really I do. I just don't want you to be hurt any more than you have been.'

'Fine.' She collapsed on to the sofa. 'Look, how do you want me to feel about this?'

He just looked at her, shaking his head sadly. 'I want you to feel alive.'

Harris awoke like a flashbulb.

Instinct and reflex kicked in first: tighten up, defensive position. Look around – no one attacking. Door – undisturbed. No one sneaking in to kill her. Alone, therefore safe.

Slowly she sat up in the hammock, letting the fear poisons drain from her body. Her conscious mind, still quivering from the adrenaline blast, dragged itself into coherence.

Every evening she woke up like this. No one had tried to stake her in the day for about forty years now. Old habits died hard, she thought, and clambered out of the hammock.

Before anything else, she sat down at the computer and logged on. Instinct and reflex again, she thought fuzzily. When she was in no fit state to put up with dealing with the others, which seemed to be most of the time actually, logging on and switching off was the most comfortable thing to do.

And more than that, it gave her time to learn. To keep up. In the old days, it had just been her and a stack of books she'd borrowed from the library, centuries of afternoons shutting the others out and just reading. But now, thanks to the dedicated ISDN line Rusty had run into the basement of the theatre a few years back, the sky was the limit. Finally, after nine hundred odd years, they were producing information as fast as, or even faster than, she could learn it.

It was a blissful trancelike state to get into, just paging through all the bio and genetics groups her news server could find. She'd once spent thirty-six straight hours like this, sitting slack-jawed in front of the screen, only one finger moving to hit 'n' or 'q' or the space bar. Sucking information off the net without needing to stop for food or rest or any of the other tedious interruptions of the outside world. Geek heaven.

But pulling an all-dayer was the last thing on her mind right now. Everything was coming to a head at once. First the Doctor, who had turned up at just the right time. Now that the bloodfasting appeared fairly stable – all she could see from his mind at this point was a ghost image, clearer if she closed her eyes – she could get down to some serious work with him. He could supply the breakthrough she'd been plodding towards for centuries – and before the coven became any more strained.

Then there was Shackle, who finally seemed to be about ready after months of patient preparation. And she would have to get down to the warehouse tonight, to see if the project was ready for the next step…

'Am I intruding?' asked the Doctor politely.

She jumped up so hard she knocked her chair over, hissing at him, eyes flaring red. He was standing right behind her and she hadn't seen or heard him approach. Behind her the door was unlocked and she hadn't heard that either.

She took a breath and let her eyes go back to normal. 'How'd you find me?' she snapped.

He tapped his temple. 'How do you think?' he said blithely.

'I could have torn you in half,' said Harris.

'That's an original way to commit suicide.'

'Just don't do it again, all right?'

The Doctor was playing with a Venus' finger-trap, poking his fingertip into its bell-shaped, hungry leaves, pulling away just before it snapped shut on him. The tiny fanglike spines on the upper leaf strained to reach him, but missed. His eyes were wide with fascination.

'I've been studying the effect of the V factor on other species,' said Joanna. She had brought him to her bestiary, a long dark room filled with cages and the smell of animals and fertiliser.

'The V factor?'

'Ahem. It's something genetic, obviously, but I haven't been able to isolate it. It could be one gene, it could be several. Whatever it is, it's completely dominant. Add it to a rat, and you have a vampire rat. It's transformed rhesus monkeys and chickens. I've created vampire amoebas which engulf red blood cells at an incredible rate.'

'Good grief,' said the Doctor.

'I'd love to show you what we did with the cats, if we could find them. And then there was Fred the Eternal Snail.'

'You're joking.'

Joanna gave him a look that suggested she hadn't joked in centuries. 'We kept him as a mascot, until Slake stepped on him. He was still alive even then, but so badly mangled that he couldn't even slither. We had to stake him with a toothpick to put him out of his misery.'

'Good grief,' said the Doctor again.

'Of course I've always wanted to know what makes us what we are. But there was simply no way to find out, not until this past century or so, when genetics became a science. Hell, I had to wait for them to invent science.'

The Doctor had been peering at a row of test tubes. Now he looked up at her. 'You're looking for a cure,' he breathed.

'No,' said Harris. 'Lose the V factor and we lose immortality. We're not victims, Doctor: each of us chose to be what we are.'

He shook his head. 'Then why?'

'I have other, more important projects. The first step is to discover why we're dependent on human blood.' Harris flicked her ponytail back over her shoulder. 'My problem is that I'm entirely self-taught. I've made a tremendous amount of progress, but I need expert help to complete the project. Now's the time.'

'Indeed.'

'With Time Lord technology –'

The Doctor raised a finger. 'Which I'll have to keep to myself,

I'm afraid. But I have a couple of experts whom I think I can persuade to help.'

'Oh yes?'

'A biochemist and a medical doctor. Both very experienced.'

'Good. When can you bring them here?'

The Doctor looked around at Joanna's monstrous zoo. 'I rather think it might be a good idea if they worked somewhere else,' he said.

The vampire frowned. 'There's everything they need right here.'

'Yes, except perhaps for a general sense of not being in mortal peril.'

'Oh.' She blinked. 'I see what you mean.. I'll have to trust you with my notes, then. They're extensive. I have other projects to attend to.'

'That sounds interesting,' said the Doctor.

'Yes,' said Joanna. 'Doesn't it. Come through here, I'm going to give you about a kilogram of diskettes and samples…'

Carolyn opened her eyes. 'I've had it,' she said.

The Doctor startled. He was peeking around the doorway of her darkened bedroom. 'I didn't mean to wake you,' he said, face creasing in concern.

'No. Come in,' she said.

He hesitated, arms full of notebooks and diskette boxes. He looked around for a moment, abandoned them on to her dresser in a heap, and sat down on the edge of her bed. The red numbers on the alarm clock said 7.35 p.m.

'Carolyn, you don't have to keep dealing with this.' He took her hand, fingers curling around hers. 'If you want to go with James, I'll understand.'

She shook her head wearily. 'No, that's not what I mean. That's part of what I've had it with. I've been trying so hard to get all the weird stuff to go away, and then when it comes down to it it's James who goes away, you know? I've had it with the job and the boyfriend and being old and settled and ordinary. And the whole damn world, in fact. I want out of it.'

She looked up, into his green eyes, and said it. 'I want to go with you.'

He didn't answer. God, she thought, he must have heard this so many times in his life. Lives. Whatever. So many people must have trailed after him looking for their freedom, must have begged this magician to include them in his disappearing act. There was no way he could say yes.

'Are you sure, Carolyn?' he asked quietly. She shivered, wondering for a moment if he was leading her on just to let her down gently. 'I want you to think about it. It's not a small step, leaving your entire life behind...'

'I don't care,' she said. Why was she smiling? 'It's all blown to bits anyway.'

'I can't promise that things would be any better. Just different. You've seen what can happen.'

'I know. I've lived for twenty years getting glimpses of what your kind of world is like, all the weirdness. I still want to be a part of it. Because the things you do matter. Because it's right.'

'The last time I offered, you said no.'

She shrugged. 'So I was wrong. I don't care.'

He met her eyes. 'Would you really rather have given up the years you've had here since then?'

She couldn't bring herself to nod or shake her head. He squeezed her hand gently and went on. 'Be honest. What do you want?'

'I want you to take me. Uh, with you. Oh jeez. I mean...' She buried her face in her hands. 'Wait. Cut. Print. Start again.'

He waited till her nervous laughter died down before asking more. 'And what about James?'

'James can go...' She'd thought the words would be easy to say, but she suddenly found her throat closing around them. 'He...' All his things were still here. The other half of the bed was still wrinkled from where he'd slept, still smelled faintly of him. 'He left me,' she said in a tiny voice, and felt her whole body wrench.

She didn't cry. There weren't any tears left to come out. The Doctor held her by the shoulders, speaking quietly, insistently. 'No. Carolyn. He said you knew where to find him. He's waiting for you. He wants you with him. It's only… my kind of life he doesn't want.'

'But I do,' she said. God, he did have cute eyebrows. And eyes that were trying to look right into her brain, into her soul, and she felt tiny hairs standing up on the back of her neck.

'So did Sam,' said the Doctor quietly. 'And look what's happened to her now because of it… You don't have to decide now,' he told her.

'I have decided.'

'I'm not going anywhere for a while. We've got quite a bit to deal with here. See how this goes, all right? Then you can be sure.'

'I am sure,' she sighed.

'You've had a trying few days. Get some sleep first.'

'No way can I sleep.'

'Just rest, then. Shh.' And he was laying her back down into her bed, gently running his hand through her hair, his fingertips brushing against her temple, her vision becoming blessedly fuzzy as her head sank back on to the pillow. She hadn't been this sleepy a few seconds ago. He stood up and moved away from her, but she didn't mind, because for the first time in days she really felt certain of something.

He'd still be there when she woke up.

Abner was the youngest of the old, barely out of his first century. None of the others was younger than three hundred years. Abner thought about his future, tracing the development of the vampire through its deathspan by glancing around the room.

Around the four-hundred-year mark, you stopped moving unnecessarily; Mr Chadwick and Gregorio had once been inclined to conversation, but these last few decades… They sat still in their chairs, as though exhausted. Or waiting. No more stories of sixteenth-century metalworking, or of the search for El Dorado. Perhaps after four centuries you'd had every dialogue you were ever likely to.

The five- and six-hundred-year-olds were followers. They were bewildered by anything new, whether it was some advance in mortal technology or some change in the environment. He had seen one of them lose a life five hundred and eighty-seven years long because she had been fascinated and confused by a cigarette lighter.

At first, Abner supposed their brains were simply full. Later he had realised that the routines they had established, the certainties they had, were what had kept them unalive for so long.

Curiously, there didn't seem to be anyone who fell into the seven- or eight-hundred-year-old bracket. Abner's theory was that there had been another plot, another purge, similar to the one that had exterminated most of the youngest members of the coven in 1956.

And then there was Miss Harris. Born just before the end of the first millennium. And clever and determined enough to have survived into these last years of the second.

He couldn't help smiling, remembering when she had turned him. 'I can find any number of violent men,' she'd told him, 'but a good accountant is another matter.' He'd been so squeamish that she'd eventually spiked his ale with her blood. He'd known what he was drinking from the first mouthful. An eternity of creative bookkeeping. But he'd kept drinking.

Miss Harris said, 'It's time I let you know about the bargain I've struck with the Doctor. It's a temporary measure, meant to give us and him time to reorganise to avoid a war.'

She let that sink in for a moment. 'I've entered into a bloodfasting with the Time Lord,' she said.

Abner felt his jaw drop. He hadn't thought that was possible. Even the really old vampires reacted, turning their pale gazes on her.

Gregorio said, 'Is that wise? I want to hear your reasons.'

'We could have killed him,' said Harris. 'But then his people might take revenge. I know now the Time Lords are very real. We must escape their notice. And to do that, we'll have to work with this one.'

'If we had killed him,' said Kahnawake, 'there'd be no chance of his informing them.'

'There's more,' said Miss Harris. 'You know I've been working to free us from dependency on mortals as a source of food. I'm very close to accomplishing that goal. And the Time Lord will help me. Imagine it. Permanent security.'

The oldsters' eyes were dull again, reassured. Harris had got them through the centuries.

Only Abner still felt nervous. 'You've got to keep this from the youngsters, Miss Harris,' he said. 'Especially young Edwin. They're looking for a vulnerability to exploit.'

'Yes, indeed,' she said. 'Sound them out for me, Abner. Find out what they think of the idea of a permanent food source. Tell them, no more struggling with drunken men in dirty alleys.'

'I will,' promised Abner.

The others had sunk back into their semi-aware state, waiting for the next stimulus. Abner promised himself he'd never become like that. He wondered if they'd all made themselves the same promise.

A nurse held the phone up to Shackle's ear as he started pulling off his gloves. 'Really, Doctor, I'm sure this is all most interesting,' said Shackle over the phone, 'But at the moment I honestly don't care.'

The Doctor's face creased in puzzlement. 'Is there something wrong?'

'No, not especially. I just… don't.'

Shackle leaned back against the wall, bending his neck to hold the phone in place. The nurse went to help the others. 'I'm sorry I haven't been in touch,' he said, 'a couple of gangs have decided to increase their tawdry little war a few notches. I've just been operating on a fifteen-year-old with multiple shotgun wounds.'

'Don't worry about us,' the Doctor's voice buzzed in his ear. 'You have enough to do.' Shackle watched as the nurses and a paramedic started taking tubes out of the boy, unhooking the fat bags of plasma from their stands. 'But let us know when we can talk to you again.'

Shackle decided he would sit down, now. He slid down the wall, holding the mobile phone in one hand, raking his hair with the other. 'Look. I just feel really really tired, all right? I'll let you know when I can be bothered to get up again. All right?'

'Are you sure you're OK?'

Shackle closed up the mobile phone. He didn't have the strength to answer.

In a little while he'd get up off the floor; they'd need the room again soon.

He watched the nurses lifting the dead boy off the table and wheel him out of the emergency room. What he really wanted was to go and find Joanna Harris and talk to her.

It had been a snap to get them on-side, Slake thought. At last he'd realised that all he had to do was to sell it to them the right way. If they didn't care about the principle of the thing, let 'em ignore it. In a way, that was the principle of the thing anyway – that they didn't need a principle.

'We'll wait until midnight,' he told the others. 'Then we strike. Harris wants to·change things? Well, after midnight, everything changes.' He grinned, and the others oh-yeahed.

Spike was shaking his head. 'Harris is gonna have our throats, man.'

'Harris can go suck a goat,' said Slake. 'We act now, she won't have a chance to get to us before the humans and the Doctor come after her.'

And if she did come after them… what the hell, they might as well have it out with her. Live like you had nothing to lose, that was the way to do it. He'd got six of them on his side: him, Rusty, Elvis, Shredder, Reaper, Spike, and Fang. The post-'56 gang, united against the mustydusties. If it was going to come to a showdown, he couldn't imagine a better way to play it. Maybe they could have a big comic-book battle with all sorts of cool people and things getting caught in the crossfire. Now that would be a way to go.

Course, winning would be nice too.

He turned to the others and spread his arms wide. 'All right. You ready to go?'

'I dunno,' said Shredder, the thinner of the twins. 'What are we doing this for?'

Slake suppressed a scream. What now? 'If we don't hunt now, then we never hunt again. It's that simple.'

'No, I mean why something so big? I mean, it's a cool idea, but what does it get us? Why are we doing it?'

Slake turned and paced in front of them, like a general reviewing his troops, making them wait for the answer.

He could tell them that it was a blow at all the mouldy oldies, all the ones who refused to take them as seriously as they should.

He could remind them that they were the un-fricking-dead, a bunch of immortal badasses who put the Hell's Angels to shame. He could tell them this whole attack would be a great barbaric yawp of defiance, their claiming of the forbidden pleasures, their absolute unchained freedom written in their victims' blood.

He could tell them lots of things.

'Why shouldn't we?' he said, and bared his fangs just for the hell of it.

CHAPTER 11
CROSSING OVER

'It's getting darker,' said Shackle.

He lay slumped face first on Harris's desk at Angel Labs, the corner of her in-tray poking into his temple. He didn't move. People talked a lot about feeling hollow, but this was literal: it felt like everything in his chest was shrivelling down to a single flickering point, leaving nothing but a numb space where it had been.

She sat across the desk from him, leaning back in her chair, observing him. 'So I take it this isn't the usual, then.'

He shook his head, just a fraction. 'No one-liners. Too much effort to think them up.'

'Well?'

'It's been one day too many,' he said. 'People passing through the clinic, getting hurt or killed for the least of reasons – oh hell, you know the story. Maybe that is the usual. But this time I can't just brush it off. I can't.'

He could have gone to the Doctor, but the Doctor wouldn't understand. He couldn't: he was so gratingly optimistic there was no way he could ever have seen the world the way Shackle did. But Harris knew – she said things he could believe.

He rambled on. 'The jokes, the extravagance, they're an easy way to cope. Easy to be amusingly cynical about it all. But after a while you get to the point where you really do believe what you're saying.' That's where he was now, he thought – on the threshold, just short of crossing into believing it was hopeless. 'I don't feel like I can win any more.'

'You can't,' she said plainly.

He felt the little flicker within him contract even further.

She looked down at him from her seat. 'People die. People die stupidly. Hasn't changed in nine hundred years, and it's not going to change in another nine hundred. They can say all they want about every little bit helping, but that doesn't mean a thing to the ones who are dead.'

'But?' he asked, almost pleadingly. There had to be a 'but'.

'But what?' she said, and waited for him to come up with the answer. He couldn't find it, he couldn't.

This was wrong. He'd come here to feel better and it was only feeling worse. He was drowning, and she was throwing him a brick.

But everything she was saying felt so true.

The Doctor paused on the threshold, his key in the lock. 'You're sure about this?'

'You said you needed me here,' said Carolyn. 'Whatever you need me to do.' She leaned nonchalantly on the police box door and waited for him.

A little distance away, disconnected from the pair of them, Sam stood holding a black metal case. Carolyn tried to puzzle out her expression for a moment, then gave up. She wasn't giving any clues how she felt about the Doctor letting Carolyn into her home.

Of course, it wasn't clear whether she was being an unreadable distant teenager because she didn't want Carolyn to know how she felt about it, or whether she was being an unreadable distant teenager because she herself didn't know how she felt about it. Or whether she was just doing it out of habit.

'You don't have to,' the Doctor was saying. 'We can manage on our own if you don't feel up to it…'

'Open the door, already!'

'All right,' said the Doctor with a shake of his head, and opened the door. Carolyn took a deep breath and stepped into his home.

The TARDIS was huge. It was a museum. It was a cathedral. The ceiling soared away, the air hung still and cold, but you could hear the living vibration of the machine. Feel the age in the air, centuries of travel imprinting themselves on stone and wood and wire.

'Cool,' breathed Carolyn. 'It's…'

'Bigger on the inside,' completed the Doctor with a grin.

'… just like Sam described it,' Carolyn finished, and watched the Doctor's double-take. Yes! He must have been expecting her jaw to hit the floor. Not this time. If she was going to be a part of this world, of his world, she was going to make damn sure of what she was getting into ahead of time.

That way he'd know she was taking this seriously.

Sam was still hovering behind them, inscrutable. Carolyn hoped she wasn't regretting giving this stranger advance warning, wishing she wasn't quite so relaxed in her home. The teenager was looking around like a tourist, too, as though seeing everything for the first time.

'Yes, well.' The Doctor brushed a speck of dust off his coat. 'How about the ten-cent tour?' When Carolyn nodded, he set off on a brisk walk, leaving her and Sam to trail along behind him. 'Excellent. Over here we have the library, down that corridor are the guest facilities, don't go through that door, and down that hall, first door on your left, is the lab you'll be using.'

'Using for what?' she asked. 'You still haven't –'

'I'll explain as we go,' he said as he hurried in the opposite direction from the lab door. 'The lab equipment won't be quite the type you're used to, but I'm sure it'll puzzle out how to work with you. For your purposes it should be quite straightforward. There's the food machine.' He gestured at a huge brass-and-piping contraption which suggested what would have resulted had M.C. Escher and Rube Goldberg collaborated to build an espresso machine.

She couldn't wait to tell James all about this. Then she caught herself, and remembered she wasn't supposed to be thinking about James.

It didn't really feel like he was crying. No sobs, no tight clenching feeling in his chest, just his eyes steadily streaming like melting ice cubes.

Harris was watching him, impassively, not reaching out or saying a word as he lay there. Just waiting for the last of the tears to leave him dry.

It didn't surprise him that she wasn't doing anything. The more he thought about it, the more it sank in what a wonder it would have been if anyone cared at all about someone like him. But there weren't any wonders in the world.

He'd given up expecting anything more. Nothing disappointed him, nothing amazed him, and now he didn't even feel any of it.

He could get used to not feeling.

The Doctor led them down a huge arched hallway. Carolyn half expected that the moment they turned their backs, all sorts of bizarre and amazing things would start dashing across the hallway just out of their view, like a deranged clip-art collection straight out of *Yellow Submarine*.

'And here we have the music room.'

Carolyn looked around. There wasn't an instrument or a record player to be seen, just some odd green boxes and about three thousand clocks. In a corner, a sprawling model train layout chuffed happily to itself, switching trains on its own in a never-ending dance.

'And through here, the lab.'

Carolyn was inside the wood-panelled room before she realised. 'Wait a minute,' she said. 'Didn't you say this was down that other corridor?'

The Doctor looked at her as though she'd just asked him how many heads she had. 'It is,' he said.

OK... 'So, what did you bring me here for?'

'I need you,' said the Doctor as he took the case out of Sam's hands, 'to help me put a jigsaw together. Harris has been gathering data on vampirism for centuries. You know at least as much about biochemistry as she does. I brought you here to my lab –'

'To find a cure?' said Carolyn disbelievingly. 'Or a weapon?'

'No such luck,' muttered Sam.

The Doctor was shaking his head. 'No no, to find an alternative food.' He sat the case down on the table and opened it, revealing thermal containers and notebooks. 'These are samples Harris has given me, her notes, all that sort of thing. With the technology in the TARDIS, it should be easy to isolate what compounds they're using for nutrition. And then we mix up a batch, and all's well that ends well.'

Carolyn took the case slowly, as if grabbing it too suddenly would make her wake up. Then she shook her head sharply and started looking over the samples with a clinical eye, each box labelled in neat handwriting. 'Use alien technology to analyse vampire blood. No problem.'

The Doctor came back to life and hurried off across the chamber, the tails of his coat flapping behind him. 'Anyway. There's much more I need to show you. So little to do and so much time – no wait, strike that, reverse it.' Carolyn shut the case and followed him. 'Ah, the library…'

Carolyn and Sam caught up with him again by the overstuffed easy chair. 'We're back in the console room,' said Carolyn. The Bug sat parked at the edge of the library area, just to the side of the Persian carpet. She looked back towards the police box doors, and decided not to even think about how it fitted through.

'All the manuals for the lab equipment are in here,' the Doctor continued. 'Somewhere. And there's a collection of data on vampires tucked away as well – I've made a bit of a study of it these past few hundred years. Not that there was much to study – mostly mythology.'

'So where are the ones I need?' she asked, looking at the masses of books.

He shook his head. 'No no no, they're not here, these are just A to C. The Vs are through there.' He pointed to a portal in the corner, and Carolyn risked a peek through it into the next chamber. The far ends of the shelves were lost in darkness, but as far as she could tell the library didn't have a far wall, just a horizon line.

'Just take anything you need. And that's the console,' he concluded as the control panel in the centre of the room let out a vaguely annoyed-sounding chime. He hurried off to adjust something, leaving her alone with Sam.

Sam was gripping the back of the chair. She had an abstracted look on her face as her fingers ran over the coarse fabric, like they were trying to memorise the feel of it. 'You OK?' Carolyn asked.

'It feels like home already,' Sam whispered.

Oh, of course, Carolyn realised. Sam wasn't looking at everything for the first time. She was trying to take it all in because she thought it might be the last time.

'So,' said Carolyn, 'you think you want out.'

'So,' said Sam, 'you think you want in.'

A pause. 'Which one of us is nuts?' asked Carolyn, and Sam chuckled thinly.

'I dunno,' said Sam. 'Maybe he'd be better off with someone like you. I think maybe he'd rather be a kid himself, instead of having to look after one.'

Carolyn glanced at the Doctor, who was happily fiddling with the switches on the console. She remembered the model train set.

Sam said, 'One day he dropped me off at a rally, and when I got back he told me he'd just popped off in the TARDIS for a while. A pretty long while, actually – like a year.'

'My God.' Carolyn sat down on the edge of the chair. 'What did he do all that time?'

Sam shrugged. 'Not much,' he said. 'He had a bunch of things to take care of, and one thing led to another… Then he brought the TARDIS right back to the moment he'd left.' She leaned on the back of the chair, speaking quietly. 'But it was like when your mum is an hour late picking you up from a dance. He got distracted. He just forgot.'

'That's awful. I hope you told him where to get off!'

She smiled, just a bit. 'I couldn't – he was too busy apologising from the moment he turned up. I wouldn't've even known if he hadn't told me… There are other things I've found, too. He's always got someone with him – it didn't have to be me. Even my room used to belong to someone else.' She looked at Carolyn with the full force of teenage mournfulness, crouching beside the chair. 'I'm just a boarder. I could leave at any time.'

Carolyn thought about all the rooms the Doctor had shown her, glanced around at the vast console room, with its archaic furnishings and its cold stone walls. There was precious little evidence that a teenager lived here.

'Maybe,' said Sam, 'we're going to change places. Maybe.'

Carolyn couldn't help it: she hugged the teenager, feeling her tense and then relax and then hug her back. She wondered if the Doctor noticed.

'Death wins.'

'I know,' Shackle mumbled sleepily. That little nagging sense in the back of his mind had said this all along. All she was doing was echoing it. 'All these huge things, and I can't change any of them. Not at all.'

When he'd been a kid, being grown up had looked like an endless field of possibilities, a chance to do whatever you wanted and have it work. He wondered where all the choices had gone.

'Would you want to try something different?' she asked him quietly.

He shook his head as it rested on his arm. 'Nothing else I can do. It's what I spent all those years training for. Got to work to eat, got to eat to live.' He raised his head and looked at her. 'Either I keep living this life, or I die and there's nothing, there's nothing in between. No way out.'

'There is another option,' said Harris.

'Sam, Carolyn, over here,' the Doctor called. He was down at the far end of the room, waving his arms over his head so they could find him. 'Want to see my butterfly collection?'

Carolyn frowned. The Doctor was a butterfly collector? Fixing dead things in a display case hardly seemed his style at all. But then, she'd never pictured him living in a museum like this place either.

She and Sam hurried after him, through a doorway she hadn't noticed before, into a short stone tunnel. The Doctor had already disappeared through the door at the other end. Carolyn turned to Sam, got a blank look in response, and opened the door.

The butterflies blew through the air like leaves in a windstorm. They formed swirls in the sky ahead, clouds made up of uncountable flecks of colour. They ranged from tiny checked moths to fluorescent Lepidoptera as big as two hand spans. Thousands and thousands of them, covering the hillside (hillside?) and scattering the sunlight *(sunlight?)* in all directions. The grass and flowers were carpeted with them where they rested. She could hear them all, a million tiny sounds at once, a fluttering rush which barely rose above a whisper.

She couldn't help it. Her heart flooded with awe.

The Doctor stood on the hill, his arms spread wide, a huge grin on his face as the butterflies swarmed around him. They alighted on his fingertips, got tangled in his hair, formed garlands down his chest and clung to him as if he were made of nectar.

'Well don't just stand there, come on in. Careful, don't step on any of them.'

'Temporal paradoxes and all that again, right?' asked Sam, treading carefully. Carolyn shuffled through the grass, somehow feeling like she was floating towards him.

He shook his head. 'No, I just don't think they'd like it very much. Oh, and mind the flutterwing,' he said, with a glance upward at a huge rippling shape which Carolyn had taken for a cloud.

As they reached him, many of the creatures scattered; only a few of the braver ones ventured up to her and Sam. A great green rainwing settled in Sam's hair, like a comb.

'This is where I come to get away from it all.' There was a yellow moth clinging to the tip of the Doctor's nose.

'Peace and quiet, huh?' Carolyn said, listening to the whispering of a million wings.

'Hardly.' He waved a hand at the furious rushing motion surrounding them. 'I can watch all this for hours and not get bored. And then I'm always on the lookout for a hurricane developing. It hasn't happened yet, but you never know...'

'Better close your mouth before any of them fly in,' Sam said coolly. Carolyn realised her jaw had dropped. And she found she didn't really mind.

She still had her feet up on the desktop. There wasn't any more glamour or mystery in the way she slouched now. Joanna Harris was still just the same dishevelled figure she'd been before she told him who she was, and somehow that made it horribly easy to believe.

She'd even showed him her fangs, pulling her lips back to point them out. The sharp canines were there, very subtle and unshowy, just slightly more pointed teeth than normal.

'So it's you,' he mumbled. 'You're one of the ones I've been looking for, you're one of the killers...'

'When I have to be,' she said, playing with her pencil. 'I just do it to live, it's not like I do it for fun. Unlike certain other people in our group' – she rolled her eyes like a put-upon teenager – 'whose positions in the coven are probably going to be open suddenly in the very near future.'

'So that's why you came out of the coffin, mm?' Chuckling felt like too much work. 'To seduce me to the dark side of the moon?'

He saw her frown; there wasn't any seduction in that face. 'It's just an offer. A new life instead of the one you're fed up with.' Her voice was quiet, methodical, a cold certainty working its way up from the back of his mind. 'Unlimited lifespan. A body that doesn't age. More strength, more endurance, more time… Sounds useful, doesn't it?'

'If you can't be part of the solution, be part of the problem?'

Her voice was going on, calm and practical. 'All that stuff you're giving up on anyway, you wouldn't need to worry about it any more. You can do what you want to. If you don't want to work for a living, you won't starve. Doesn't sound bad at all, does it?'

He almost wanted to believe in it simply because it was so different, just because he needed different right now.

It was almost a wonder.

'But the killing,' whispered Shackle.

'Funny you should mention that,' said Harris. 'Do you have any idea how sick of the whole hunting thing I am? I've got better things to do with my time. I've been working on a different way of feeding for a while now. And with an MD to help me out…' She let the invitation hang in the air.

'Wouldn't hurt anyone, would it?' he said.

'Not at all.' He closed his eyes, contracting even further inside himself. Her voice kept coming from a long way away. 'It's your life, it's your body… The only one it affects is you yourself…'

He knew something should be stopping him, there should be some barrier in his mind to keep him from even thinking about this. He couldn't find the reasons why he shouldn't, not any reasons he could believe. He was feeling in the dark for the fence at the cliff edge, but it wasn't there.

There was nothing here left to feel.

* * *

163

When they got back, Shackle's car was parked in the driveway. Carolyn tooted her horn at him. 'Come on, Dr Shackle, let the nice oncologist put her car away!' she said.

They could see Shackle sitting in the driver's seat, but he didn't respond. Carolyn looked at the Doctor. 'Hey, you don't think –'

'Stay here,' he told Carolyn and Sam.

He walked up to the driver's window and knocked on it. Shackle was inside, alive, staring through the windscreen. His eyes were red-rimmed. He blinked, and a moment later, he wound down the window.

The Doctor crouched down, leaning his arms on the windowsill. Shackle held a hip flask, the sharp scent of whisky filling the car. 'What's the matter, David?' he said.

'I think I'm in trouble,' said Shackle. He glanced at the Doctor. 'I think I'm in a lot of trouble.'

'Can I help?'

Shackle smiled for a moment, but then it was gone. 'You see,' he said, 'all of those things I said about life not being worth living... Well, they're all true.'

'What brings you to that conclusion?'

'Joanna Harris,' said Shackle. The Doctor stared. 'You know her?'

'I'm bloodfasted to her,' said the Doctor. Shackle blinked at him. 'What did she do?'

Shackle took a mouthful from his hip flask. 'Nothing. We were talking. She works at Angel Labs, they do a lot of path work for us. She wants to turn me.' He ran his free hand over his face, and his voice shook. 'She wants to turn me into a vampire.'

'She won't,' said the Doctor. 'I promise you.'

'I want her to,' whispered Shackle. A tear meandered down his cheek. ''Cept I'm scared. I want you to talk me out of it.'

'What's your favourite flavour of ice cream?' said the Doctor.

Shackle looked at him. 'What?'

'Chocolate? Rocky road? Spider swirl?'

'I don't – it's strawberry,' said Shackle. 'With those little pieces of actual strawberry frozen into it.'

'Good. David, I want you to come inside the house. We'll talk in there. All right?'

Shackle nodded. 'Hell's bells, I'm tanked,' he said.

'Just a moment,' said the Doctor.

Carolyn and Sam had got out of the Lexus, leaning against it, watching and waiting. 'What's up?' said Sam. 'Is he OK?'

'No,' said the Doctor. 'He's just been made an offer he can't refuse.'

'I had a Goth friend in school,' Sam told Carolyn as they drove up to the Seven Eleven. 'Annette.'

'You should send her a postcard,' said Carolyn, switching off the engine. 'Imagine how jealous she'd be.'

'She'd think these vampires were full of it,' said Sam. 'Along with half the creeps in the Other Place. I wish she was here now – she was great at puncturing people with attitude problems.'

'We could set her on Dr Shackle,' said Carolyn.

Sam grinned. 'You know, she once talked another Goth out of killing herself? Really talked him out of it. She said that being a Goth was about accepting the world's sadness, not about destroying yourself to get away from it. She said it was bad manners to kill yourself. Like dropping in on Death without phoning first.'

Carolyn leaned over the freezer, looking at the vast array of ice creams on sale, searching for the strawberry. 'I wish I could meet your friend. Maybe we'll come and visit,' she said, and mentally bit her tongue.

'Maybe you will,' said Sam. 'Or not.' She reached into the freezer. 'Let's see if we can get one without gelatine.'

'There's an old Buddhist story about a doctor,' said the Doctor.

'No doubt,' said Shackle. He lay on the bed in the guest bedroom, arms flung over his eyes.

'He worked in the middle of a war that went on and on. All the wounded he treated went right back to the front lines to be injured all over again, or killed. And this doctor couldn't see the point in it any more.'

'It just doesn't matter,' said Shackle. 'Death wins.'

'No matter what he did, a lot of good people died. And he didn't know what to do about it. He tried withdrawing from the world, but that didn't make it any better. He tried to be cynical and heartless, but despite his best efforts at giving up hope he couldn't quite manage it completely. He even tried to take control of the people around him, and manipulate them into changing things, but no matter what he did he could never control things enough to change everything that needed changing.'

'Why shouldn't I choose how? And when?' Shackle murmured. 'Better than catching a stray bullet or a needlestick.'

'So this doctor started looking for enlightenment,' persisted the Doctor. 'He went on a long journey, and he met many people and did many things. I won't bore you with the details of everything he found on the way. But eventually, after many years, there came a moment when he finally *understood*.

'And then he knew he had to put into practice what he'd learnt.

'And he went back to the front lines, to tend to the wounded and heal the sick. Of course it didn't make any more sense than it did before, he didn't have any more control over the world than he'd ever had, but that wouldn't stop him from holding back death whenever he could.

'It's what Doctors do.'

Shackle shifted his arm slightly. A bleary eye looked out at the Doctor. 'And the moral of the story is?'

The Doctor looked at him.

'Oh, it was very nice.' Shackle's last word was a twist of the knife. 'Naive and simplistic, but ever so sincere.'

The Doctor sighed in defeat. He got up from the rocking chair. 'Get some sleep,' he said.

Shackle said, 'I thought you were going to try to talk me out of it.'

'Only you can talk yourself out of it,' said the Doctor.

Carolyn and Sam sat at the kitchen table. They'd put the strawberry ice cream in the freezer, and were eating the other tub they'd bought, alternating spoonfuls.

'You should tell Shackle about your Goth friend,' said Carolyn.

'What do you say to someone who wants to die?' said Sam. 'What if I say the wrong thing? Push him in the wrong direction?'

The Doctor said, 'I'm going out, and I may be some time.'

166

They jumped. Carolyn said, 'How's Dr Shackle?'

'Beyond my help,' said the Doctor simply. 'When he wakes up, take him two aspirin and a bowl of strawberry ice cream. Don't wait up.'

They were partners in crime now, supposed the Doctor. Joanna had simply pushed the door until the deadbolt had snapped, and the Doctor had disabled the alarm with a bit of wire from his pocket. He'd slip a few notes under the till to pay for a new lock, leaving the shop owner with the mystery of who would want a haircut at 10 p.m.

'I haven't done this for decades.' Joanna was positively... animated wasn't the right word, was it? She certainly seemed to be enjoying herself, rummaging in the tray of equipment. 'I had this bizarre job for five years, giving haircuts and manicures at all hours of the night in a very, very expensive hotel.'

Breaking in had been her idea, and he'd decided to indulge her, for the moment. 'The best thing about eternal life,' she'd said. 'You can do whatever you want, whenever you like – what's it going to matter in a hundred years?' He wanted her to be in a good mood before they started the serious negotiations.

The Doctor sat in the swivel chair. 'I can see you in the mirror,' he said.

'Of course. Did you expect to see a floating pair of scissors?' She fingered his hair. 'Look at these split ends. You need a wash and some conditioner first. When did you last have a haircut?'

He thought about it as she led him over to the basins. 'I don't think I have had one. Not in this life.'

'That long, hmm?' She sat him down, leaning him back. His neck slotted into the oddly shaped basin. She switched on the water.

'Why did you give up your job?' said the Doctor.

'You know how it is,' she said. Warm water flowed over his scalp. 'I got bored. I think there's an inverse ratio between how long you've been around, and how long you can keep your interest in any given thing. Have you found that?'

'Not quite,' said the Doctor. 'Sometimes... Sometimes it does seem that nothing's ever going to change again. That I can't imagine the future being any different from the present or the past. But then somehow… there's always something new.' There were squelchy noises as Joanna squeezed shampoo into her hand. 'The thing that throws me is how many memories you build up, so that wherever you go, you get déjà vu. Even if you haven't been there before. Everywhere begins to look familiar.'

'I know just what you mean!' said the vampire. 'I'm always checking through my journals to see why someone or some place rings a bell.'

'Precisely how old are you?'

'You tell me,' she said, working the cold stuff into his hair.

'No, thank you,' he said. 'I prefer the bond between us as it is now. Quiescent.'

'Mmm. It does make thinking a lot easier. You travel a great deal – that's one way to avoid boredom.'

'I'd never thought of it that way before,' said the Doctor. 'As avoiding something…'

'That's what unlife is all about. Avoiding the sun and the stake. As far as we know, we can live forever, barring accidents.'

'But you're the eldest. There must be a lot of accidents.'

'Hold still,' she told him. 'And relax, this isn't going to hurt.'

He sank into the chair, obediently, as she massaged his scalp, pushing her knuckles gently but firmly into his forehead, gradually backwards to every part of his skull. 'Relax,' she said again.

The memories came up without his searching for them, without effort or difficulty. Her memories. Vampires waiting for the sunrise to burn them because it was the only interesting thing they could think of to do. Vampires simply curling up and dying because they could see no reason to climb out of their coffins and go on. Vampires dying of boredom.

She thought of it, half joking, as the mid-death crisis. She'd come through it hanging on to that single pounding beat, the need to survive. It was all she needed.

She had been born in Canterbury the day William the Conqueror died. She was slightly younger than he was.

'All right,' she said. She was squeezing the water gently from his hair, a warm towel pressing against his scalp. He realised he'd almost fallen asleep. 'Over to the mirrors with you.'

'Just a little off the ends,' he said, as she tied a plastic cloak around his neck.

She should have taken him seriously.

Carolyn knocked on the door, realising her heart was hammering. What if she should have come up five minutes earlier, clutching the little bowl of strawberry ice cream, just in time to stop him from slashing his wrists or hanging himself with his belt or something?

She knocked again, loudly. 'Come in,' he said, at last.

Shackle wasn't asleep. He was sitting up on the bed, long legs stretched out, three pillows propping up his head. He didn't look up at her.

She hadn't taken it seriously. He'd been too much in love with the sheer melodrama of being alive and miserable. Now all his broad hand gestures and theatrical line readings had been scraped away. He was just sitting there, unmoving, his eyes fixed on nothing in particular.

No wonder Sam hadn't wanted to come up here.

'I brought you this,' said Carolyn. She sat down in the rocking chair. When Dr Shackle didn't move to take the bowl, she put it on the bedside table.

He didn't say anything, just kept staring, as though he was seeing something at the foot of the bed that she couldn't.

'Do you want to talk?' she said. He didn't answer. 'Do you want me to go?'

'It just sort of hit me.' His voice was quiet and empty. 'No, "hit" is the wrong word. It reached me. Dying really isn't a big thing. It's very small – just a moment. Nothing to be afraid of. You can do it any time.'

Carolyn grabbed and hugged him. She felt herself shaking with all the fear he didn't have.

She couldn't feel anything move in him. His hand patted her vaguely on the back, as if acknowledging and dismissing her concern. Thanks but no thanks, you still don't understand.

'Why?' she whispered into his ear. He smelled of booze and despair.

'Why what?' he said blankly.

'You know what I mean,' she hissed, and instantly hated herself with a passion for snapping at him. 'Why doesn't it matter any more? What made you stop caring about being alive?'

He shrugged and disentangled himself from her. 'I have no idea. I could quote from *Hamlet*, or tell you some story from the medical centre which would rend your heart, but the truth is none of that really matters either.' He still sounded like Shackle, and that only made the emptiness behind the words sound even worse. 'There's nothing to hold me here. I'm not hoping for anything here any more.'

'You save lives,' she said.

'That doesn't save my life,' he said. 'I don't know them. They come into the ER, and they go out alive or they go out dead. Either way, they all just go away.'

'They all do,' she said, thinking of James. 'Yeah,' she said. 'All the things I've been caring about here, they've just fallen away.'

'Like you're moving on to something new,' he said. 'Time to make a change. Like spring-cleaning your life. You do understand.'

She really wished she didn't.

'You said you urgently needed to talk me to about something.' Joanna picked up a particularly sharp-looking pair of scissors. The Doctor was limp in the chair, letting her measure and snip, measure and snip. 'What was it?'

'You tell me,' he said.

She didn't answer, entirely concentrated on his damp hair.

'Doctor Shackle,' said the Doctor. 'He told us about your offer. I'd like you to leave him alone.'

Measure, snip. 'Not likely,' said Joanna.

The Doctor looked at her in the mirror. 'He was almost begging for help this afternoon.' The horrible realisation dawned on him. 'You've been working on him for some time, haven't you?'

'Months,' said Joanna.

The Doctor sat up in the chair. The corner of her mouth twitched in irritation. 'He seemed like the perfect opportunity,' she

170

said. 'I'd been hoping to find someone like him. That's why I took the job in the first place. You know I analysed Sam's blood sample?'

'You did?'

'Relax, she's clean. The bite doesn't carry the V factor. Anyway, Shackle. He's perfect - a guy from the neighbourhood who's trying to track us down, who can accept that we exist, and who's just enough in love with the idea of dying that he might be able to see our point of view. If you don't want them to beat you, have them join you.'

The Doctor pulled away as she tried to go on cutting his hair. 'So you're willing to destroy him?' he said, outraged. 'Shatter what little faith he's got, just so you can have him pass you test tubes and tell you how brilliant you are?'

'Well, I don't need him now,' said Joanna. Her free hand stroked his wet hair. 'I have you.'

The Doctor jumped out of the chair, tearing the cloak from around his neck. 'You're destroying a man, crushing his desire to live, just because it was convenient!'

'It's not as though I've broken our deal,' she insisted. 'I've been keeping my side of the bargain. We've called off the hunting.'

'You're still killing him,' he said flatly.

'Turning him.'

'I've seen his face. You're killing him.'

'I'm giving him a choice.'

'A choice? He's as likely to slit his wrists as to join you.'

'I'm just trying to talk him into it. I'm convincing him.'

'You honestly don't understand, do you?' he asked, shaking his head in disbelief. 'You really have no idea.'

'No, I don't,' she said. 'What's the problem?'

The Doctor grabbed her hand. The scissors clattered to the floor. 'Don't turn him. Don't do it under any circumstances. If you do, our deal is over.'

Harris didn't even blink. Her hand was reptile cold, and he could feel the enhanced strength of her arm. She could easily have pulled away, but she didn't. 'And then what?' she asked. 'You can't kill me, remember.'

'Oh, I don't have to kill you,' said the Doctor quietly. 'I can still break your coven. I can drive you from this city. I can tear down everything you care for, leave you alone and hunted, and all the while make sure that they never kill you.'

She believed him. He saw it and he felt it.

'And if you destroy David Shackle, I will do this. I will not let you harm him.'

'OK, OK,' said Harris, 'Don't get your Gallifreyan knickers in a twist.'

The Doctor let go of her hand.

'Sit down,' said Joanna, picking up her scissors.

'I don't think so,' said the Doctor.

She sighed. 'I was just about finished with you, anyway.'

Carolyn stood under the street lamp, watching the road down which Shackle's car had driven off fifteen minutes before.

The Doctor puttered up in the Bug. He leapt out and hugged her, and she just let him hold on to her. Now it felt like too much effort for her to move too.

'So,' he said quietly.

'I tried to stop him,' she said. 'He listened to everything I said, and he just patted me on the hand, like I was the one with the problem.' She realised she was crying. 'H-he didn't even want any ice cream.'

He just held her tighter. She wondered what the neighbours thought.

When he let her go, looking at her with intense concern, she said, 'Why didn't you show him the things you showed me? Why didn't you show him your butterfly collection?'

The Doctor shook his head. 'He wouldn't have believed in it.'

They were quiet together, watching the clouded sky.

'Still feel like running away with me?' he asked.

Shackle walked into the lab and stood behind Joanna Harris. He looked limp, like a scarecrow with its stuffing pulled out.

'I'm ready,' he said.

She looked up at him. 'There's been a change of plan,' she said. 'I can't turn you.'

172

'You can't,' he repeated.

She made a wry face and shrugged. 'Nope.'

He stood there. There weren't any words that would come. That one point of purpose left in his chest contracted further and vanished, leaving nothing but the hollow behind.

'So what do I do now?' he asked.

'You've got me there,' she said, and turned back to the microscope.

CHAPTER 12
RAISING THE STAKES

'You're going to do something stupid, aren't you?' said Abner. 'No, wrong word. You're going to do something *mindless*.'

'It's gonna be glorious,' said Slake with a flash of his fangs. The six other youngsters were backing him up in the TV cave, dressed to kill, fidgeting with that pre-party energy. Ready to unleash some serious random violence whenever he gave the word. 'So come with us. Let's put all this bickering behind us, and do some real damage for once. Think about it.'

Abner thought about it. 'No thanks,' he said. 'I have some old issues of *California Law Review* to read tonight.'

Someone snickered. Slake barely restrained the urge to hit Abner, to see those little glasses fly in pieces across the room. 'Right, just get him the hell out of here,' he snapped.

None of them moved against Abner. Slake looked from one to another of them, his face turning apoplectic. Abner just shrugged. 'Maybe they find me more entertaining than you.'

Slake put his mouth right next to the accountant's ear. 'Not after midnight tonight, they won't. Now get out, before I punch open your ribcage and twist out your heart with my bare fingers.'

Abner jerked back, staring at him. 'I was just leaving anyway,' he said.

Sam lay on the sofa, channel-surfing.

She could hear Kramer galumphing around upstairs, freshly awake after the afternoon sleep the Doctor had told her to grab. Sam wished she'd had enough time to do the same, but little things like trying to keep Shackle alive had eaten up her spare moments.

The naps she'd been stealing were enough to keep her going for a while longer, but they weren't enough to get her past the jet-lagged feeling. In a way she was glad of the sleep deprivation, though: it gave her something she could blame her general sense of dislocation on.

Her throat still hurt.

The Doctor was there. She wondered how long he'd been sitting on the seat opposite her, watching her with that worried-daddy look on his face.

'I spoke to Joanna,' he said.

'Any luck?'

The Doctor shook his head. 'She honestly doesn't understand what's wrong with deliberately making someone miserable. I thought that was so basic and fundamental that every being in the universe had some concept of that.'

'Doctor,' said Sam, slowly. 'Read my lips. They're – vam – pires. Savvy?'

'Yes, yes, yes, but… I had hoped that even after centuries of killing, there might still be something left in Joanna. Something… Perhaps I hoped a little of me would rub off on her.' He put a hand to his face, wearily. 'Arrogant.'

Sam shrugged. 'Worth a try.'

'She hasn't had to live by human rules for nine hundred years. Think of a wild child brought up by wolves – you have to teach them what it means to be civilised.'

'And then do we get to throw her in jail with six hundred consecutive life sentences for murder?'

The Doctor looked at her. 'I won't give up on her. On any of them. Not yet.'

Sam just settled back down on the sofa, changing channels. I'm more worried about how much of her is going to rub off on you. She didn't say it.

Harris looked up from her Angel Labs microscope, the small hairs on the back of her neck standing on end. 'Well, if it isn't Life's Champion,' she muttered.

'Sorry I'm a bit late,' the Doctor said as he breezed into the lab. His grin was like fingernails down a blackboard. 'I took a detour through Golden Gate Park. You wouldn't believe what the sky can look like through those trees…'

'Look,' sighed Harris, turning down the radio, 'can we just take the glory-of-being-alive stuff as read?'

'You've just tried to talk a man into dying,' said the Doctor. 'I think it's only fair you have to put up with me trying to talk you into living.'

His smile was just as broad as always, but she realised it had stopped reaching his eyes quite some time ago.

He looked around the lab. 'In fact,' he said, 'I suppose this is where you did most of your work on him. How long have you been working here?'

'Oh, years,' said Harris impatiently. 'Is there something you want?'

'I wanted to see how Dr Shackle was.'

'I told him I wasn't going to turn him.'

He looked at her for a long moment. 'Don't try so hard,' she said quietly. 'You don't have to try and read my mind. You know I'm telling the truth.'

His expression softened. She almost jumped when he reached out and took her hand. His fingers had that feverish tingling common to all mortal skin, but there was a coolness to the touch which reminded her of her own.

'Joanna,' he said, 'we have to make this work. For everyone's sake. Of all of them, Kramer, Slake, all of them, we're the only ones who can trust one another.'

'I had no idea you'd object,' she said. 'They live such a short time. It's a blink of our eyes. After a few hundred years, they stop mattering.'

He shook his head. She wasn't getting through to him. 'I want this to work too,' she told him. 'Sometimes you have to see things the way I see them. Close your eyes.'

He looked at her. Then he closed his eyes.

She moved closer to him, squeezing his hand gently. 'Can you see yourself? Can you see how I see you?'

He tensed for a moment, as she slid up to him, her eyes wide. 'Do you see it?' she whispered.

She bumped up against him, but he didn't startle. 'Yes,' he said.

'How do you look?' she murmured.

'I look…' He opened his eyes.'This is terribly difficult for you, isn't it?'

She could only nod. *Youkali* was playing on the radio, a distant voice singing in mournful German.

'A blink of our eyes,' said the Doctor. 'Everyone you've ever been close to, in any way, is long dead.'

'Only the coven goes on,' said Harris, voice soft as she listened to the tango. 'And even the coven doesn't go on. Whenever the humans find us, they kill us. We had to kill seven of the youngest vampires ourselves, in 1956.'

'So you become totally alone,' said the Doctor. 'You shut down everything. Affection. Compassion. Anything that could tie you to another person.'

'Imagine a compassionate vampire,' said Joanna. They stood very still, not dancing at all. 'They'd starve in a week.'

'Joanna –'

The phone screeched. The Doctor took a step back, embarrassed, as if the telephone had caught them in a compromising position. Harris hit the speaker button. 'Joanna Harris.'

A dry voice came from the speaker. 'Miss Harris, it's Abner. I thought you might like to know. Slake and some of the young ones are planning an open hunt.'

'What!' gasped the Doctor. 'What for?'

'Shock value,' said Harris. 'It'll keep the humans from trusting us.'

'But why?' the Doctor was insisting. 'Why doesn't he want them to trust you? Doesn't he realise how delicate the situation is?'

Abner sighed. 'Young Master Slake has a glorious vision of clan warfare among the vampires. His "posse" against the world.'

'I knew I shouldn't have let him play that *Masquerade* card game so much,' sighed Harris.

'No,' said the Doctor. 'I've got a better idea. General Kramer. Where's her number –'

'Are you insane?' Harris grabbed his wrist, tight. He tried to pull away, and couldn't. 'They'll slaughter us all the first chance they get.'

'We need a show of unity,' said the Doctor. 'Let him know he can't play us against one another. I'll cover the human military, you cover the –'

She pushed his rushing words away from her. 'Hold on, hold on, let's think this through.'

'That's what I was doing!'

'One step at a time.' She turned to the phone. 'When?'

'Midnight. When else?'

'Where?'

He thought. 'I'm afraid I didn't get that bit, sorry.'

'Follow them,' ordered Harris. 'Let us know the moment you find out.'

Abner agreed and hung up. The Doctor had already turned away, muttering to himself at high speed. 'It'll be too late by then. We've got to figure it out ahead of time.' He started pacing. 'It would have to be something showy. Grandiose. Self-aggrandising. Something fundamentally vampiric. Well?'

She stared into space for a moment. 'He's being daring, hitting targets that would call the most attention to us. That's part of it.' He made hurry-up gestures at her. 'I suppose,' she said slowly, 'it's possible he might want to hit something close to home.'

By now he was almost hopping with impatience at the way she was thinking in complete sentences. 'Near the theatre then.'

She continued, undeterred. 'Or it could be something that would be associated with us. Something that would tip people off, the way the other killings did –'

'The Other Place!' cried the Doctor. 'Of course! Come on!' He spun around and charged for the door, leaving her looking after him in utter irritation.

'I was about to say that,' she muttered.

'We'll need as many troops as you can spare, Adrienne, at the nightclub, within an hour. Harris is rallying her forces as well. They'll all be there.'

'Just what we need,' said Sam. She stayed out of the way, watching him bustle around Carolyn's kitchen. It was like he was so wound up he couldn't stop doing something.

'So this is it,' said Kramer. 'They move to break the truce, we stake them all. Except for Harris, of course.'

'No. No no no no no no no. No.' The Doctor didn't skip a beat in his loading of the dishwasher. 'The whole point of this is to keep there from being any more bloodshed.'

'But they'll all be in one place. We could deal with the whole problem at once –'

He went on shoving dishes away. 'No, Adrienne. And that's final.'

Kramer just stopped. Very slowly, she turned to look at him. Sam felt the sudden need to duck and cover.

'Of course,' said Kramer, in a perfectly level voice. 'I wouldn't want to get out of my place. 'Cause we all know UNIT's just your unpaid military advisers –'

'Adrienne –'

'Hold it!' she exploded, and the Doctor jumped.

Kramer went on, icy calm. 'Look. UNIT assigned me to deal with threats to humanity. And unless there's something you're not telling me, this is the perfect chance to take care of this one. With me so far?'

'Oh, please don't tell me you're only following orders,' muttered the Doctor.

'No, I'm giving the orders,' said Kramer. 'My responsibility, my decision. And I want to keep the civilians alive. You got a problem with that?'

'So do I, so do I,' said the Doctor, trying to calm her with waves of his hands. 'But you can't just kill all the vampires. Right now, Harris's followers are working with us. But if you start killing their comrades, they might well defend them. Do you think the survivors will ever trust us again?'

'I'm more concerned about our survivors than theirs. The moment they look like they're going to grab someone, we attack them.'

'And the moment they see a drawn stake, Slake will attack.' He came to rest in front of her, and looked straight into her eyes. 'They want a bloodbath. Please, just give me a chance to avoid it. Don't give them what they want.'

That settled it, thought Sam. He was giving Kramer his sincere look, and she'd never seen anyone resist that.

Kramer met his eyes and sighed. 'I'm sorry.' She shrugged and headed for the door. 'But I'll give you as much leeway as I can…'

'So you'll hold off on the attack? Promise?' he said.

She stopped in the doorway and looked back. 'Doctor, you know I don't break promises. So I try not to make 'em. We'll see what happens.' She drew her mobile phone and left the room. The Doctor spun on his heel and stared desperately at the heavens.

Sam tried to make it out of the kitchen before the Doctor could buttonhole her. She didn't want to have to tell him she thought Kramer was right.

He caught her right at the door. 'Sam,' he said, 'would you please go back to the TARDIS and tell Carolyn to look up Joanna's notes on what she's flippantly termed the V factor –'

'Nope,' Sam said casually.

The Doctor skidded to a conversational halt. He blinked at Sam, his mouth hanging open. 'I'm sorry?'

'Nope,' she repeated. 'I don't chase wild geese. You can't just send me off there to keep me out of the way so I won't get to face the vampires. Now, I'd be glad to do it if it was part of your real plan, but –'

'This is my real plan,' said the Doctor. Sam blinked. 'I need the data to give Slake something to think about.'

'What do you mean? How's that going to help?'

His shoulders slumped. 'I'm not entirely sure yet.'

'And you weren't just trying to keep me safe out of the action.'

'Well, I admit, that's not a bad idea. I'm sure I would have thought of that in a few minutes as well.'

Sam found a kitchen chair and sat down heavily.

'You really have been making this all up as you go along,' she said. 'All of it. Letting Harris drink your blood in exchange for setting James free – that was all you'd thought of. You weren't up to anything else.'

He shrugged. 'It worked, didn't it?'

She shook her head slightly, still staring at him. 'That was the one thing I was sure of, that you had something up your sleeve.'

'I did,' he answered, and with a flick of his wrist produced a jelly baby. In a daze, she popped it in her mouth.

'So this really is your real plan.'

'Mm-hm.'

'You've got it all under control.'

'Exactly.'

A pause. 'We're screwed, aren't we?'

Carolyn looked at her watch: 11.39 p.m.

Her eyes kept searching the crowd in the club, watching for more of the vampires. Sam stood next to her, her gaze fixed on the Doctor's table. She'd told Carolyn she was coming along, in that ever so cool and restrained tone that didn't leave you any room to disagree. It was only when Kramer said she'd be better off somewhere safe that she'd become spiky.

The general had managed the best compromise she could, keeping the two of them at her table near the exit. Up here, the music was just loud enough that you could have a conversation without shouting.

The Doctor had spoken to them only briefly, flipping through the stack of notes Carolyn had brought from the TARDIS and murmuring strategy with Kramer, before he'd settled at a table with the short hawk-nosed vampire he'd called Abner. Since then they'd been left to wait and watch.

Her heart was pounding. Something was happening at last. Was going to happen.

She looked down around at the crowd, the bobbing heads and swinging arms of the dancers, costumes and coffee in the booths, pale faces at the bar. Imagined the music stopping, all those lives ending in an explosion of screaming and panic.

She was terribly, terribly glad that James wasn't here.

'Eighteen minutes,' said Abner.

The Doctor was feverishly intent on the top button on his waistcoat. It had come halfway off, and his struggle to weave the loose threads into something that would hold together seemed to be consuming all his attention. 'Have any others turned up yet?' he asked.

Abner scanned the club. The place was packed, wall-to-wall velvet and lace. 'Just Slake and the other two at his table, so far.'

'Well, we'll see how many more make it soon enough.' The Doctor took his hands away from the button, noted that it stayed on, and instantly it was gone from his mind. He sat back up and shifted his gaze to Abner. 'By the way, I've been wondering. Why do you run this place? The club, I mean.'

'Money,' said Abner, surprised. 'We still have to buy things just like anyone else – especially Miss Harris, with all her expensive hobbies. Also, it's a good recruiting ground… although we haven't turned anyone since we replaced Eva in seventy-seven. In fifty-seven this used to be a variety of Bohemian coffeehouse, and that's where we found Edwin and most of his little clique.'

'Edwin?' asked the Doctor.

'Slake. His real name is Edwin Pratt. Local boy. Sad, isn't it?' The Doctor made vague sympathetic noises. 'Born in thirty-five, turned in fifty-seven, and a dreary little thorn in my side ever since.' Abner chuckled. 'He's still outraged at me for the time in 1983 when I shot him six times in front of a bunch of mortals. The poor sop started to run after me – and you should have seen the look on his face when he realised he'd forgotten to fall down!'

The Doctor couldn't help it. He laughed.

Sam gripped the railing. 'I don't believe it,' she said, her breathing harsh. 'He's making conversation with them.'

Carolyn put a hand on the teenager's shoulder. God, she was tense.

Kramer sat at the table, ignoring the Kahlúa Sombrero she'd ordered. 'I dunno,' she said. 'It must be a relief for him to get to talk to someone his own age.'

Carolyn glanced at her. 'What do you mean?'

'They're probably swapping anecdotes about the Renaissance,' said Kramer drily. Carolyn smiled. Sam didn't even relax a bit. Her whole body was wound so tight she must be in physical pain.

'Come and sit down,' Kramer said, but Sam just ignored her, eyes riveted to the Doctor.

'I think we've got two more,' said Kramer. 'The two guys heading up to the bar.' She pointed only with her eyes, as subtly as possible.

'Yeah.' Sam's voice shook with tension. 'The one on the left is one of the twins.'

Kramer and Carolyn exchanged glances. 'Look, Sam,' said the General hesitantly, 'If you want, UNIT's got counselling services. We've got a whole SETSO programme – Survivors of Extra-Terrestrial/Supernatural Occurrences. I've been told it helps a lot. We can get you into it, if you want to stick around.'

'Later,' said Sam, letting her breath hiss out between her teeth.

'And another two,' said the Doctor, craning his neck to watch the entrance. 'Elvis and Fang, I think.'

'That makes all seven of the young ones.' Abner sighed and shook his head. 'I was hoping some of them would have enough sense this time.'

'This time?'

'As opposed to the upstarts. The ones in 1956.'

'Ah.' The Doctor was once again intent on splicing the loose button with another thread which had come loose from his waistcoat. 'We've caught Fang's eye. They know we're here.'

Abner pursed his lips thoughtfully. 'Which begs the question, since we've spoilt our surprise that we're planning to spoil his surprise, is he going to come up with another surprise of his own?'

'I wouldn't be surprised if he did.' He gave the threads a final twist and took his hands away from the button. It stayed on. He straightened up and smiled. 'Either way, I think we've got it under control.'

The button fell loose again.

'Twelve minutes.'

'How many?' asked Slake.

'Maybe two dozen,' said Reaper. He swept his eyes across the rest of the room one more time. 'Bunch of plain clothes. McConnell. The girl we got last time. And *him* and Abner.'

'Three-to-one odds,' smirked Slake. 'Hardly seems fair, they're so outnumbered. Even if they've got one of us with them.' He picked up the Bleeding Heart he'd bought at the bar and studied the cocktail languidly. Of course he hadn't bought it to drink it, just to add to the impression of realism. It gave him something dramatic to do with his hands when he talked.

He put it down emphatically and addressed the other two. 'Remember, don't bother with anyone who's not an easy mark. We're going for quantity here, quantity and chaos. And if the soldiers come after you, keep a civilian in front of your heart. It's the best insurance you've got.'

'I dunno, maybe we should call it off, man,' said Spike. 'Abner must've figured it all out and told them –'

'Abner's a dead man,' Slake said, and swirled the ice in his glass.

Carolyn sighed. 'Look, why can't you just believe what he says is going on?' She could feel the look Kramer was giving her, but she ploughed on regardless. 'He's told us everything he's done, and why, and every word of it's been true. If anything, he's been telling us more than we need to know.'

'Yeah, he has, hasn't he?' said Kramer pointedly.

'What's that supposed to mean?'

'Think about it,' said Kramer. 'You want to hide a tree, the best place to put it is in a forest, right? He may be telling you everything, but that means he's throwing so much information at you that you don't have time to think about everything he's told you. And so you still miss what's really going on.'

'Hey, if you can't keep up with everything he's telling you, is that his fault?' Carolyn asked. 'Things just happen fast when he's around.'

'He makes things happen fast,' Sam pointed out. 'That's his game. Misdirection. Sleight of hand. Remember?'

'Now maybe he's not planning everything he does,' said Kramer. 'But if he pulls something off, it's not magic, it's 'cause he's fooling everyone somehow. And I'm not fond of being fooled.' She looked at her watch. 'Five minutes, folks.'

Shredder reached into his mouth and removed the plastic stage fangs he wore to hide his real ones, then turned back to look at Slake.

Slake licked his lips. His followers were ready for their cue, and the soldiers in their plain-clothes outfits were growing edgier by the second. If this was a Western, the piano player would be closing the lid and fleeing the saloon right about now.

And the kids on the dance floor still hadn't noticed a thing.

'Three minutes,' Abner told the Doctor.

Slake looked from one of the vampires at his table to the other. He nodded, and they passed the nods on to the other tables. Moving as one, the vampires across the club got to their feet. Two of them moved to block the exit, while the other five began to converge on the dance floor.

Abner looked worried. 'I think his watch is fast.'

Kramer's troops were closing on the vampires. The vampires were closing on the dancers.

The Doctor stood up and waved to Kramer, who motioned to a carefully nondescript man sitting near the wall, who jumped up and dashed over to the DJ as Slake and the others closed in on the dancers. The circle tightened.

The nondescript man reached over and cut the sound system off.

'All right,' said the Doctor from the centre of the room, 'Would everyone who is neither a vampire nor a heavily armed member of the military please leave the room at this point?'

Slake glared at the Doctor. The bastard was trying to upstage him. Well, let him see what that got him. 'Right,' he yelled. 'Now!'

'One question,' said the Doctor. He didn't sound like he was yelling, but somehow his voice drowned Slake's out. None of the vampires moved. 'The V factor. What do you know about it?'

'What are you talking about?' snapped Slake.

The Doctor stepped forward, and the crowd on the dance floor parted around him. Already the confused murmurings of the mortals were getting louder, ripples of movement heading towards the exits.

'The genetic coding that makes you a vampire.' Slowly the

Doctor circled around him, just out of reach. Slake turned to follow him. 'Some sort of rogue gene with a particularly virulent vector. And do you know the secret of how it works?'

'Why should I care?'

The Doctor had almost turned him in a complete circle by now, his eyes holding on to him, his voice relentless. 'Do you know?'

'No, already!'

'Oh well,' shrugged the Doctor, 'I thought I might as well ask.'

And now that Slake could see the dance floor again, all the dancers were gone. While the Doctor had him turned away from them, the troops had cleared the floor and were guiding the mortals' stampede to safety. They'd formed a wall between his followers and their victims.

Slake's face twisted. No easy pickings, no innocent blood to revel in.

There was only the Doctor left.

He took slow, furious steps towards him.

Sam hustled the last of the clubbers out of the corner near their table. The moment the Doctor got up, the UNIT troops had slid into action, escorting potential victims out of the building. She and Carolyn had joined in, but Kramer had done a good job keeping them away from the real action, keeping them safe.

Which would have been fine, except that being safe was the last thing she needed right now.

She still hadn't spotted him. There was no way he couldn't be here – she had to face him. She had to finish it, this once, and then she'd know if she'd ever want to do anything like this again.

Over on the dance floor the Doctor was smiling. She could see the confusion on Slake's face, as it flared into rage. Now Slake was advancing on him, his hands twisting into claws, and he was backing the Doctor towards the others, and if they turned on him –

Kramer levelled her gun. Her soldiers matched the movement, ready to fire the first shots.

'No,' said the Doctor calmly, without turning around. 'Not on my account.'

'Think about it,' gloated Slake. 'I'm gonna be the one who killed a Time Lord.'

'Oh, you're just shameless, aren't you?' said the Doctor. 'You'd do anything for your moment in the sun. As it were.' Somehow the Time Lord was managing to look down his nose at Slake, despite the fact that Slake was a good three inches taller than he was. 'Don't you have anything better to do?'

'I don't need anything better to do,' said Slake. He lunged towards the Doctor and grabbed his lapels. Guns clicked in anticipation. Slake leaned in close, and ever so slowly he bared his fangs. 'This is what it's all about.'

The Doctor gave him a withering look. 'Now there's a sign of a man with a limited imagination.' He took a step backward, and Slake nearly overbalanced trying to hold on to him. 'How many years has it been since you died? Forty or so, isn't that it? And in all that time you haven't been able to think of anything better to do than terrorise people. Any street gang could do that.'

'Not as well as I can.'

'But you don't know any other tricks, do you?' The Doctor swung an arm wide, indicating the last of the patrons being herded out by Kramer's troops. 'In forty years even the most mundane of these people can raise a family, get new jobs, do things they've never done before – and you're still doing just what you did back in your gang in 1956. Talk about arrested development. All these years and you're still a teenager.'

'That's me,' said Slake, 'Forever young.'

'Oh, *please,*' said the Doctor. 'You're forty years out of date. You still think you're a real gone cat, don't you, daddy-o?'

Slake simply reached up and wrapped an arm around the Doctor's shoulders, gathering him up. The Time Lord tensed, finally, finally realising how close to death he was.

'That's enough,' Slake breathed, his mouth just below the Doctor's ear.

'No!' ordered a voice from behind him.

None of his followers moved. They all seemed to be staring fixedly over his shoulder.

He spun around, keeping his grip on the Doctor. Harris was standing by the swinging kitchen doors. Behind her were Gregorio, Chadwick, Kahnawake – all of the old ones, all moving inexorably towards them. Abner had stepped through the line of soldiers to join them.

The one who bit her was missing. Sam had counted the vampires twice, and still come up with only thirteen.

She didn't know what she'd had in mind – half-formed visions of confronting him with a circle of UNIT soldiers backing her up, standing over him with a stake and challenging him, telling him he had no right to do the things to her that still made her stomach twist to think about them… The more she thought about what she'd been going to do, the more she realised that she hadn't had any idea.

Slake's vampires and the soldiers stood on opposite sides of the floor, like boys and girls at a school dance. Harris and her bunch stayed on the sidelines, keeping their distance from the soldiers even more than Slake's mob.

And the Doctor stood between all of them.

In a moment of cold clarity Sam knew she'd never have the nerve to do that.

'You've done enough,' said Harris.

Slake looked at her over the Doctor's shoulder. 'Why should I listen to you? Why should any of us?'

'Because she's stronger than you,' said the Doctor. 'Welcome to the second link of the food chain, so to speak.'

And Slake was backing away, his eyes flicking from the Doctor to Harris to the soldiers. His fight-or-flight reflex welling up when flight wasn't an option. His followers hanging on his word, waiting for the order to attack.

And the Doctor, still facing him, utterly calm. He smoothed down his coat and put his hands in his pockets.

'Seven on six,' said the Doctor quietly. 'Even odds. Perhaps a bit in your favour. You've got a pretty good chance of winning. But what does it mean if you lose?'

Slake was listening. The Doctor turned his back on the vampire and walked towards the soldiers. 'Oh, it won't be a heroic struggle against the mundanes,' he said out loud. 'It just means that there's someone out there who's better at your game than you are. It just means that you lost.'

Then he nudged the nearest soldier, who inched over, leaving a break in the line. Slake stared in astonishment. The Doctor gestured towards the gap, towards the open door beyond.

'Or,' said the Doctor, 'you can walk away.'

Slake quivered. It was all up to him.

Slowly, he straightened up.

'Fine,' he said with a dramatic curl of his lip. 'We've got better things to do.' He turned to address the old ones, the soldiers, everyone around. 'Don't imagine this is a victory. You can't even begin to comprehend us. And there are pleasures even you won't have the will to deny us.'

And he motioned to his followers and sauntered through the break in the line. They followed him, not hurrying in the slightest.

Sam stood by the gap, her eyes locking on each of them in turn. Slake smirked at her. One of the twins looked away uncomfortably. None of the others paid any attention to her.

She felt a tightness in her chest, a scream or a leap at them struggling to burst out, and suddenly she knew how Slake had been feeling just a moment ago. But there was no way she was going to ruin it now.

'Keep an eye on them,' said Harris. Wordlessly Chadwick, Kahnawake, and Smith separated themselves from Harris and followed the young ones. Abner and Gregorio stayed by her side.

Slake turned back in the doorway to face them, standing in silhouette. 'There will be a reckoning, Time Lord.'

'Yes, yes, all right,' said the Doctor. 'Now run along home.'

And the vampires were gone. Sam could see the Doctor standing alone on the dance floor, as if about to take a bow. The soldiers were looking around, not quite sure if they should relax yet. Harris and the other two stood like mannequins in the corner. Kramer stared at the Doctor with something that looked like awe.

'Well,' said the Doctor. 'Anyone for a cup of tea?'

'They are always the same,' said Gregorio in his thick Spanish accent. 'A century ago they would have thrown bombs in the name of anarchy. Eight hundred years ago they would have smashed up Moorish settlements on the way to the Holy Land. Always the same violence, nothing more.'

'Oh, yes,' said the Doctor. 'Can't you just imagine Slake as a ruffian trying to impress his way into the musketeers?'

Gregorio gave a dry laugh. 'Or a Regency fop, perpetually in search of a duel to fight.'

'Oh, I can just see that,' laughed the Doctor.

The conquistador smiled. 'You are not so different from us, Doctor.'

The Doctor stopped laughing. He looked at the old vampire. 'What makes you say that?'

'Perspective,' said Gregorio. 'We have seen enough of history that we can step back from it. See the patterns and repetitions.'

'Ah,' said the Doctor.

Joanna was watching Kramer debrief and dismiss her troops, talking with Lieutenant Forrester about the details of the cover story. 'You dealt with the situation remarkably well,' she said. 'We're indebted to you.'

'Well,' said the Doctor modestly. 'I have been doing this for a very long time.'

The Doctor looked around the empty nightclub. Sam and Carolyn were still at their table upstairs, talking. John Seavey was complaining to Kramer about the disruption to his establishment. Kramer was just standing there, not saying a word yet, her smile growing more and more taut.

'What now?' Gregorio asked.

Joanna said, 'We need a more permanent solution to our problem.'

'During the day?' asked Gregorio.

'During the day,' said Harris.

'It's a shame,' said Abner. 'I'm almost going to miss the little bugger.'

'What's Slake doing this for?' said the Doctor. 'There must be an underlying reason. What's it all about?'

'This whole hunting thing,' said Joanna, 'stalk, kill, feed, stalk, kill, feed, yadda yadda yadda… It gets numbing after a while. After a few hundred years –'

'Miss Harris,' said Gregorio, glancing at the Doctor.

'– after a few hundred years,' she went on, 'you hit a midlife crisis. Either you find something else to live for, or you off yourself. Usually in some spectacularly self-destructive way.'

'Perhaps that's what this is all for,' said the Doctor. 'Slake's got an undeath wish.'

'Maybe,' said Harris. 'Or the other way you can go is if the hunting really becomes everything in your life. Your ambitions and imagination don't go beyond where your next meal is coming from. And then you're just one step above an animal. I couldn't live like that.'

'They don't last long when that happens,' said Gregorio. 'The humans quickly find them out and kill them.'

'How do you survive this midlife crisis?' said the Doctor. 'How do you survive knowing you'll live for ever?'

Abner said, 'We all have to find something to do with our time. Myself, I've been working on a law degree since nineteen, ah, sixty-eight.'

'I'm so sorry,' said the Doctor, getting up. 'No sentient being should have to endure law school for that long.'

The corners of Abner's mouth curled in the direction of a smile. 'What do you expect when you can only take night classes?'

The Doctor beamed. 'We did it.' He gave a joyful hug first to Kramer, then to Sam, and finally to Carolyn. 'I think we really did it.'

'Like hell,' said Sam. The force of the words nearly knocked the Doctor backwards. 'Nothing's over. We didn't accomplish a thing.'

'You mean, besides saving the lives of a few hundred people?' said the Doctor. He was still holding on to Carolyn. Sam wasn't sure about the way Carolyn was leaning her head on his shoulder.

'Give the vampires six months, they'll have killed 'em all one at a time anyway,' she said. 'I suppose Vampirella will be wanting her notebook back now.' She tossed it on to the table. 'What was all that business about the V factor anyway?'

'Pure distraction.' The Doctor grinned. 'He could have started killing those civilians at any moment. The more he's thinking about biotechnology, the less chance he has to remember that he wanted to go out in a blaze of glory.'

'And every word of it was true,' said Kramer pointedly.

'Of course,' said the Doctor, bending to collect the notebook, and completely missing the looks Kramer, Carolyn, and Sam shot back and forth over his head. 'They'll handle the problem from here. You can go put all your soldiers away.' He started to dash off after Harris.

Kramer stepped in front of him. The immovable object had just plopped itself in the path of the irresistible force, thought Sam. 'So what's going on?' asked the general. 'How exactly do they plan to handle it?'

'Joanna thinks Slake isn't going to listen to reason.' He took a breath. 'I think she thinks he might need to be destroyed.'

Kramer looked over to Harris, and pulled a face. 'Now she decides this. We could've saved her the trouble.'

'Somehow I don't think it would have been quite the same,' said the Doctor. 'You see, they recognise their own authority, but not yours. They'd rather take care of the problem themselves.'

'Great,' muttered Kramer. 'Suddenly I'm back in the Gaza Strip.'

'So we've got three different problems to worry about right now,' said Carolyn. 'Shackle, Harris, and Slake.'

'Sounds like a vampire law firm,' put in Kramer. Everyone else ignored her.

'Four, actually,' said the Doctor. 'But don't worry, I think I can handle the fourth one on my own. You don't need to worry about it.'

'Uh-huh,' said Kramer, looking at him suspiciously.

The Doctor stroked Carolyn's hair. 'I'd better go and sort a couple of things out with Joanna,' he said. She stepped back, giving him a sort of glowing look which Sam didn't like one bit.

He covered the notebook with his other hand for a moment, and suddenly it wasn't there. 'I'll see you in a moment,' he smiled, and bustled off to speak to Harris.

Kramer squinted in confusion at where the notebook had been. 'How'd he do that?'

'It's magic,' said Sam in her best Doug Henning voice.

Kramer shook her head. 'No, wait, you don't understand. I know that trick. My nephew's a stage magician – he taught me how to do it. See?' Deftly she unscrewed the top of the salt shaker, and palmed and unpalmed it several times. 'But you can't do it on an object that big. It's not physically possible. So how'd he do it?'

Carolyn just smiled and turned away.

Now, this was more like it.

They ran, through the alleyways and down the streets. They didn't need to run, but it felt good.

The young ones ran in front. There were still crowds, this late at night, and they pushed through them or jumped the curb and ran on the street, dodging the cars, laughing.

They spread out a little. They could feel one another like beacons in the blackness, the older ones like hot lights, watching over them.

Keep running. Find someone, someone alone, someone vulnerable, someone who no one will care about. Find the forgotten. The forgotten belong to you.

The adrenaline in Sam's system was slowly fermenting, making her feel giddy and exhausted. But she wanted to talk to the Doctor. Now.

She caught up with him before he reached Harris. 'It's not fair,' she said. 'It isn't right, they shouldn't get to do what they've done and just walk away laughing.'

'I let them keep their dignity,' said the Doctor. 'It's all they have.'

'Remind me again why we're keeping them alive.'

He blinked in confusion. 'You mean aside from the idea that massacring your enemies just isn't the thing to do?'

'That's not good enough,' said Sam.

'All life has its place,' he said softly.

'They're not alive!'

194

'Joanna Harris is one of the most advanced biochemists in this century. Gregorio could give you first-hand reports from European history over the past four hundred years.'

'And Slake could tell you how to be a street punk?'

'They're not all the same, Sam.'

'Yes, they are. They're all killers. I don't see why they should live.'

'Oh, Sam,' he said, and his voice was heavy with sadness.

She stood there, feeling like she was going to cry. He looked so – he looked disappointed in her. It wasn't fair, why couldn't he just understand?

'I thought you didn't believe in the death penalty,' he said.

She thought for a moment. 'I dunno. Maybe I'm against mass murderers more.'

'Yes, well, welcome to the second link of the food chain.' Sam's mouth gaped open. Quickly the Doctor started placating her. 'I know, I know, that doesn't make it any less horrible. But now we can put an end to the hunting. That's why we're working with Joanna, remember? She's the only one with enough authority to deny them – Oh no.' She could see something dawning behind his eyes. Without another word, he turned and ran.

'Joanna!' The Doctor dashed up to Harris, his eyes wide with tension. 'What Slake said about pleasures we don't have the will to deny him – they're hunting. They're hunting now.'

'And?'

It sank in further. 'They're all hunting. The old ones and the young ones.'

She was surprised that he was so startled. 'That's why I sent them. To keep the young ones from getting up to anything else. Keep them out of trouble.'

'This *is* trouble. Stop them.'

'What can I do?' she said. 'They still need to eat. I've cut them down as much as I can – one mortal for twelve of them. Any less and they'll start going catatonic.'

'I don't care!' He grabbed her shoulders. 'Stop them now.'

'It's too late. If it's going to happen, it's happened.'

The Doctor just stood there, his face crumpling. His hands slid down her arms, and then he stepped back, as though he couldn't bear to touch her. 'What have I done?' he said.

'I'm not going with them,' she said. She touched him on the arm, feeling the fabric of his coat, not sure what to do. 'If I did, you'd see it through my eyes. I wouldn't do it, even if I was starving. I don't want to put you through it like that.'

'I'm touched,' he said bleakly, and turned away.

Slake slipped into the alley. He took a deep breath of the air through his nose. He couldn't smell perfume, or cooking food, or at least he didn't care if he did smell them.

But here, he could smell loneliness and alcohol.

Abner was right behind him, walking calmly into the alley and following him.

They walked until they saw the man, asleep under a pile of cardboard and newspaper. Slake crouched down, an angular shape in black velvet. He could feel the others zeroing in on their location, coming into the alleyway, one by one.

'It's a shame he's not awake,' breathed Slake.

'Like a bit of a chase, don't you?' said Abner. He leaned a palm against the alley wall, looking down at the man.

'Like a bit of a struggle,' said Slake. He leaned right down, bared his fangs, and shouted into the man's ear. 'Hey, you!'

The man woke up, just for a moment. Just for a moment, he saw Slake, saw the half-inch fangs, saw the hungry eyes.

Abner bent down and bit into his carotid before he could scream.

'You're no fun,' said Slake, good-naturedly.

Abner didn't answer, pushing a hand into the man's mouth to silence him, holding on to his throat until his struggles stopped. He let go with his mouth, wiping the blood gingerly from his bottom lip, and handed the limp corpse to Slake.

He looked up at the assembled vampires, watching with hot eyes in the cold city night.

'Plenty for everyone,' he said.

CHAPTER 13
UNDEATH WISH

He kept his hand wrapped tight around the stake in his coat pocket. As he paced down the hallway of Angel Labs, looking for Harris's door, he found himself rehearsing in his head what he was going to do.

How should he play this? Slow, implacable, and vengeful, letting her know exactly why he was doing it? Or should he just charge in and take her out before she knew what hit her? Surprise or suspense? Whatever, it didn't damn well matter in the end – there wasn't any audience to see it, and whether she died or he did no one would be there to really appreciate the moment.

Either way, he might as well get it over with. Slake eased the door open and stood in the doorway. He drew the stake from his pocket and prepared to launch himself at her.

She wasn't there. There was a man sprawled in her chair, a gaunt man staring at the ceiling. He lay there like a puppet with his strings cut.

'Where is she?' demanded Slake.

The man gave a tiny wave of his hand. 'Gone. Not here. Months of working on me, and then suddenly she decides I'm not worth any more attention.' His voice was a cracked ruin, with barely a flicker of life in it.

Figures, thought Slake. After all the trouble he'd gone to to sneak away from the old ones on the hunt and confront her, now she was blowing off her work. 'What are you talking about?'

The man rambled on. 'None of it was real. It wasn't me she cared about. She just wanted to turn me into one of them.' He raised his head and looked at Slake. 'One of you.'

'Ah,' said Slake. 'Miss Harris has been talking to you.'

'Oh yes.' Shackle nodded. 'For months. When I look back now, I can remember everything she said, how soothing it all was… She was leading me to the cliff. Making sure I wouldn't be afraid to plummet over the edge.'

'She manipulated you,' said Slake. 'The same way she jerks us all around.'

'No,' said Shackle. 'Everything she said was true.' He drew a hand across his brow. 'And now she's changed her mind. Or the Doctor's changed it for her. She's left me teetering here, at the edge, not sure which way to tumble…'

Doctor, huh. That bastard's real name was probably something even worse than goddam Edwin. He looked at Shackle. 'What're you going to do if she won't turn you, ever?'

'Slash my wrists,' said Shackle. 'Hurl myself from the Golden Gate Bridge. I don't know.'

'You know,' said the vampire. 'I think we might just be able to come to an arrangement.'

'You're one of them, aren't you?' asked Shackle, his voice tiny. 'Not just a vampire: you're one of the ones I was tracking. The killers.'

'And?' asked Slake.

Shackle said nothing. Finally a broken chuckle escaped his lips. 'It's just poetic justice. Poetic injustice. Further proof that irony is the fifth fundamental force of the universe.'

'I like you,' said Slake. 'You talk my kind of language.'

The human looked up at him, a lost, almost pleading look on his face. 'You're not afraid of falling, are you?' he said.

Slake smiled, showing his fangs. 'Hell, I'd rather jump.'

'I have a problem,' said the Doctor.

Mina, Carolyn's cat, was meandering the living room, secure in the knowledge that this whole territory was hers and that she could visit any portion of it on her slightest whim. Right now she seemed most interested in the few square inches where the Doctor was standing. She wandered up and brushed her cheek against his trouser legs.

'Yes, I think you've got a pretty good idea what it is, haven't you?' He reached down and let the cat wander back and forth under his fingers.

He'd brought Sam back here, after dropping Carolyn off in the TARDIS lab. Sam had been clearly in need of a bit more sleep, but for reasons he couldn't puzzle out she seemed ill at ease at the idea of staying in her room. So Carolyn had volunteered her guest room.

He'd gone to tuck Sam in, but she'd just curled up in a ball on top of the covers and dropped off instantly. So he'd wandered down here, at a loss for what to do next.

'Do you ever give Carolyn a present of a dead mouse?' He smiled. 'Yes, I just bet you do. There's nothing wrong with that, is there? It's just what you do. Doesn't mean you should be put to sleep…' He sighed and gazed at the light from the street lamps shining in through the bay windows. 'But then, of course, there's always the mouse's point of view.'

He picked Mina up and carried her over to the couch. She twisted in his grasp, but once he sat down she settled herself in his lap. He stroked her gently as she curled into a circle.

'You must be enjoying it,' he said. 'Everyone's asleep. The house is your own again. All the kittens are tucked in for the night.' He turned and looked out of the window, watching the moonlight. 'It must be such a relief to have a few moments where you don't have to keep them from fighting.'

None of them could understand why he still had hope for them. At the moment, he had a hard enough time believing in it himself. Sam saw no more inherent reason to let Joanna live than Joanna did to spare that last victim, and yet he still saw such potential in them both. It was the kind of hope Shackle had dismissed as naive, as if a glib cynicism was somehow more sophisticated than a hard-won optimism. As if it somehow took more insight to catalogue each defeat and disappointment than to notice all the successes, small and large, and draw as much joy as possible from them.

Mina began to purr. 'It's much easier from your point of view, you know,' murmured the Doctor. 'I could succeed in many things, fail in many more, but as long as I've petted the cat I've done everything that really matters.'

He sat quietly for a while, just letting his head droop.

'Would you really think it was worth it?' he asked. 'Even if you can't do everything, even if you can't save them all? Even if all you can do is keep trying?'

The cat stretched out across his legs and arched her back, her eyes narrowing into half-open slits. She rubbed the side of her head against his belly, as if petting him right back. He looked at her, his eyes slowly widening. Now he could feel the little quivers of aliveness running through her body, her breath rising and falling beneath her fur, the thrum of a tiny heartbeat keeping the life flowing through her.

He sat there, feeling the warm purring mass in his lap, and he was smiling quietly again, as if none of the evening's events had ever happened. 'Yes,' he said, 'I do believe you would.'

Shackle kept his coat wrapped tight around him. The abandoned theatre had been cold enough, and down here in Slake's apartment it felt like it was sucking the heat straight out of his bones. Maybe it was just the onset of a hangover.

The vampire walked back in the door, carrying a small medical case. 'I swiped this from Harris's lab,' he said. 'It should be all we need.' He set it down on the table in front of Shackle, who opened it.

Inside were a 10 c.c. syringe, a bottle of rubbing alcohol and a few cotton balls.

'Remind me again why you can't just bite me,' said Shackle.

'Doesn't work that way,' said Slake. 'It's my blood you need to get turned. And I can't open a vein in the usual way – Harris or someone could notice the scar. We don't want her to know, do we?'

'Not after the way she treated me.' Methodically Shackle rubbed the vampire's arm with an alcohol-soaked cotton ball. Not that either of them would have to worry about infection – it was just force of habit. 'Is this what they had to do for that bloodfasting thing?'

Slake gave him a sharp look. 'What? Who?'

'Harris and the Doctor. He said they'd been bloodfasted. Whatever that means.'

'Well,' said Slake. 'Well well well.' He brought his hand up to his chin, stroking it theatrically. 'Now that opens up all sorts of possibilities.'

'Do you mind?'

'Oh, sorry.' Slake put his arm back, and Shackle inserted the needle.

The blood came out slowly, thick and dark. It had a distinctly blackish-purple hue, like a bruise. Shackle wondered how their metabolisms worked, if they had metabolisms. Did they somehow convert their victim's blood into their own, or had this stuff been sitting around inside Slake, coagulating, for the last few decades?

Slake was watching, smiling. Shackle wondered if he looked as green in the face as he felt. He withdrew the needle. 'You want a band-aid?' he mumbled.

A single drop of the dark stuff lingered on Slake's arm. The vampire lifted it to his mouth, awkwardly, and rasped his tongue over the tiny wound. In a moment, it healed over.

'I've got a lot to learn,' said Shackle hoarsely.

'But all the time you need to learn it,' said Slake. 'Do it.'

An injection was positively routine. Shackle had never injected anything into himself, but it was surprisingly easy to do. He tied his belt around his arm and pulled tight, closing and opening his fist to make the blood vessels sit up. A deep breath later, he was sitting there with the needle in his vein.

He should be feeling something. At a moment like this he should have something thoughtful going on in his head, some kind of insight on what he was doing.

All he felt was tired, all he wanted was a way out. He was giving up things he couldn't even remember now.

It should be a big dramatic moment, but it was so small.

With a smooth slow motion he pushed the plunger in.

It was only afterwards that he felt his whole body tighten up, and the frantic irrational thoughts surge into his mind – pull the plunger back it'll suck it all back out it'll all go away.

There was a spot of numbness around the tip of the needle, slowly spreading up his arm. He could feel the stuff soaking into his tissues. A hint of the pins-and-needles of an arm having gone to sleep, but even that dissipated.

He pulled the needle out carefully, pressed a cotton swab

against the punctured vein, and tried to lift his arm to put pressure on the tiny wound. His arm flopped down loose at his side, refusing to cooperate. When he grabbed it with his other hand, it was like holding a slab of meat. He couldn't feel where his fingers were digging into his own skin.

The dead arm slipped through his fingers. There were tremors running through his whole body, and he didn't know whether that was Slake's blood attacking his nerves or just the first ripples of the huge wave of panic that was about to crash down over him. The numbness was in his shoulder, now, spreading across to his neck and his chest.

His throat wasn't working right. 'What's happening to me?' he managed.

Slake leaned on the table, examining his fingernails. 'Just wait till rigor mortis hits.'

Shackle heard a strangled gasp come from his own throat.

'Oh, it'll pass,' Slake said casually. He leaned back in his chair, just out of Shackle's reach, watching the show with an amused leer. 'You'll figure out how to control your body again – it'll just take a little while. Maybe an hour.' Shackle wanted to grab him and shake him for not telling him but he couldn't lift his hands. 'In the meantime, you might want to head to the men's room. While you can still walk.'

CHAPTER 14
AMORAL OF THE STORY

Carolyn dug through the books piled on the TARDIS library shelves, trying not to think about the rustling noises coming from somewhere behind her. The text she was looking for had to be here somewhere.

The books and scrolls and CD ROMs and data crystals were all catalogued on an impossibly sophisticated flat-screen computer disguised as a leather-bound book. The lab manuals hadn't been under L, or M, or even B for biology, but under H, presumably standing for *How does this thing work anyway?*

Not that it would be fair to complain, considering that the Doctor had to maintain this collection all by himself. Just alphabetising books in all these different languages must have been a nightmare – did you put the !Xs before or after the Xs, and how about the Πs and the Δs and the letters she didn't even recognise?

The cure for cancer could be on one of these shelves. So could the realisation of any dream she'd ever had. She almost started opening books at random, just to see what miracles she could come across. But somehow that felt like cheating, like peeking at the answers in the back of the book.

The rustling was getting louder.

If she just stumbled across that cure in one of these dusty, alien books, would that mean the last two decades of her life had been a waste of time? But if the answer was here, how could she let people keep dying?

She pulled out the next book and saw a bat staring at her.

It leapt and she yelped and the bat was in her face. It must have been sneaking up on her on the back side of the shelf. She banged up against the shelves behind her and lost her balance, screaming, falling sideways as the creature thrashed through the air around her head.

And the Doctor was charging through the stacks towards her, calling out for her and – Jesus Christ, he'd just caught the bat in his bare hands. She stared up at him in disbelief, her heart still pounding.

'Awww,' said the Doctor, scratching the bat under the chin, 'Did the big mean owd wady fwighten you?'

Carolyn gaped. 'What the –'

'Oh, I'm sorry, you haven't been introduced,' said the Doctor. He continued to pet the terrified bat, soothing it till it stopped wriggling in his grasp. 'This is Jasper, and that one' – he pointed at a shape hanging from a nearby girder – 'is Stewart. They've lived here for a long time. We're old friends now.'

'Oh. Sure,' said Carolyn shakily. He let Jasper flap off towards the rafters, and reached out a hand to help her to her feet. She picked up the book she'd dropped – it figured, it was the one she'd been looking for all along – and followed him as he paced back out of the library into the console room.

'So how far have you got?' he asked her.

'Well, I can't feed 'em, but I can kill 'em,' she said.

'It's always easier that way, isn't it?' sighed the Doctor.

'I've been synthesising samples of each of the individual proteins found in human blood, trying to see what they need for nutrition. It should be just a process of elimination, what with all this Time Lord technology.' She grabbed her notebooks from the table at the entrance to the library.

'So it's just a matter of time.'

'Yeah, suppose so,' she said with a shrug. Using all the gadgets in the Doctor's lab wasn't just like looking up the answers in the back of the book: it was like having the book sit you down and explain step by step what needed to be done.

He must have caught the sigh in her voice, because he turned around and looked at her. 'Carolyn, be proud. You've accomplished more today than Harris has in centuries.'

She started to dismiss that, but then it sank in what it meant. It really was still the same day, the day that had begun with their rescuing James. She couldn't remember the last time she'd felt a day be this endless and unbounded.

When she was a kid, each day had been infinitely long – a half-hour TV show was an epic adventure, and she could do more in an afternoon than an adult could all day. Kids actually experienced time differently, she was sure of it. Maybe that explained the Doctor.

For no reason whatsoever, she hugged him. He was like a spot of heat in the vast coldness of the console room. She could feel him breathing in her grip, his chest rising and falling against hers.

Gently, he disentangled himself from her. 'So what else have you found out?'

She started to pull up a chair next to his, but he just sat down on the carpet at her feet. She sat down next to him and spread her notes out all around, feeling like a kid working on a science project. 'Well, I've found out what's toxic to them. I started growing cultures of vampiric cells to use in the experiments, but I needed a way to keep them from growing out of control. They're virulent, just like cancers, they'll grow right over the edge of the Petri dish if you leave them.'

She tapped her finger on some Polaroids she'd taken of the cultures. 'They seem to be immune to most cytotoxins, but I've mixed up a sort of silver nitrate and taxol cocktail, with a few additional herbs and spices. The taxol slows them down long enough for the other chemicals to kill them.' She looked at him. 'It could come in handy.'

'I'm afraid that's not what I'm trying to do here,' he said.

'Pity.'

He made a mournful face. 'Not you too…'

She flipped through the pages of the book she'd found. 'I'm not saying we should go on a vampire hunt, it's just nice to know we have another weapon. The stuff is toxic to humans as well, though.' Something fell out of the book.

He reached for it, but she beat him to it. It was a greetings card, faded with age. She opened it. 'Happy birthday…' She raised an eyebrow at him. '*Grandfather?*'

He looked away from her, and drew his knees up towards him, curling all his loose limbs inwards. 'Yes, well. It's a bit of a long story.'

'I should have known.' It figured, something like this was bound to turn up. It was such a cliché, after all – falling for the mysterious stranger whose dark past was overly cluttered with melodrama. 'It's an alien thing, huh?'

'Yes, as a matter of fact it *is* an alien thing.' He looked so bewildered, like he had no idea why it bothered her at all. It sure bothered him, though, his words were pouring out in one big rush to try and wash the subject away. 'And it's not like you need to worry very much. I hardly have any dealings with them –'

'It wouldn't have hurt if I'd at least known you had kids.' She waved the card in an exasperated flourish.

He held up his hands as if trying to hold off her flow of words. 'Carolyn, that was many lifetimes of mine ago. I was a different person then. Literally.'

'Well, I don't know who he was. I'm still not sure I know who you are.' He moved as if to get up, and she reached out to his shoulder to keep him there. 'There are all these basic little things you still haven't told me yet. I mean – how old are you?'

He thought for a moment, counting back through the months. 'Three.'

'What?' She sat up and stared at him. 'Three what? Centuries? Three oogleplexes? What?'

He shook his head. 'No no, three years. I'm sure I overhead Sam lecturing you about regeneration.'

'Well, yeah, but –'

'It's all perfectly simple. That's how long it's been since my last fatal accident. That's when this body was born.'

'No no no, I mean how old are you really? All your lives together.' Good grief, she thought irritatedly, it sounds like you're interviewing Shirley MacLaine.

'Well, I'm not really sure, there's some question of whether I lost count…'

'Round it off, at least.'

He started frantically counting on his fingers. 'Um, about…'

'Come on, it can't take that long to –'

'… one thousand and twelve.'

Silence.

'Carolyn?'

This was sensible, it was logical, when someone's lived a bunch of lives in succession it's reasonable for them to go past a normal human lifespan. She really should have thought about this before – it was obvious really. There was absolutely no reason for her suddenly to be feeling cold.

He moved over until he was sitting next to her. 'It's a big number, isn't it?' he said quietly.

She nodded without a word.

He smiled gently, and the corners of his eyes crinkled up. 'I know. That's why I prefer three.'

'At least that was the last time I ever have to go through that,' Shackle said weakly. He lay flat on the table in Slake's room. 'I can handle an eternity of never having to run to the bathroom again.'

Slake smirked. 'What, you think all that blood we drink, we never have to get rid of it? A couple of decades of holding it all in, and you'd end up as bloated as Elvis. You can't get around the call of nature.' His smirk grew broader as he patted Shackle on the shoulder. 'It's just a bit different now, that's all.'

'Oh God,' said Shackle.

He felt numb all over. Not the sudden numbness that had been so frightening before, the total loss of feeling and movement. More of a distant feeling. He rubbed his hands together, experimentally. It felt as though he was holding a sponge between them, absorbing the feeling of skin on skin. His body was an ungainly collection of pieces, his mind operating them from a distance.

'I'm going to leave you for a while,' said Slake. 'Don't worry, you're past the worst of it now. I'll introduce you to your new brothers soon. But first, we have some things we need to take care of.'

The vampire plucked one of the lilies from the vase on his mantelpiece. 'Hold on to this,' he said.

Shackle's fingers closed around wire and cloth. 'Why?'

'It suits you,' said Slake.

Shackle looked at the lily. 'I'm dead...' he said. 'The occasion really calls for more panic than I'm feeling.'

'As I said,' Slake smiled, 'you're past the worst of it.' He went out.

'Doctor,' said Sam, as she walked into Carolyn's living room, 'a word.'

He looked at her, and then looked at her properly. She'd been waiting for him. 'How are you feeling, Sam? Better?'

'Fine,' said Sam. 'Disgusted. We both know the vampires killed some innocent person because you insisted on keeping them alive.'

He sagged against the wall, suddenly, as though all the energy had gone out of him.

Sam pressed the attack. 'They're killers. It's mass murder in slow motion.'

He stepped forward, but she blocked his path. 'We've been over this,' he said.

'No we have not! We started to talk about it last night, and you suddenly realised what they were doing. So you went running to your vampire girlfriend –'

'My what?'

'– but she was the one who sent them out in the first place.' She tapped the side of her head. 'When's it going to sink in? They're monsters. They kill humans for food.'

'So do lions and tigers, but I don't see you campaigning for their extermination. Quite the reverse, in fact.'

'You don't let a tiger run around loose in the middle of a city!'

'Exactly.' He smiled, and she nearly throttled him. 'You tame them or you move them away. You don't just massacre them.'

'These are people's lives we're talking about!'

'Precisely,' said the Doctor. 'They're just another form of life.'

'They're not any form of life,' shouted Sam. 'They're dead. They don't feel, they don't care, they don't –'

'Think about it. What makes them dead?' he asked. 'What's the definition of life? They eat, they reproduce themselves, you can have a conversation with them...'

Sam felt a scream building up, far beneath the surface. It was all reasonable and thoughtful and a real interesting philosophical question.

But she didn't want him to be reasonable. He should be outraged by these creatures. He should see she wasn't just upset and angry. Well all right she was upset and angry: every time her mind felt those teeth in her throat she got closer to an absolute fricking rage, but that didn't mean she wasn't thinking about things too. It wasn't just anger – he should see that what they did was *wrong*.

'It's 'cause they don't put anything back into the world.' She halted for a moment, feeling the thought crystallising in her head even as she blurted it out. 'Ferchrissake, when they die you can't even use 'em as worm food. They don't make the world a better place: they just take things away.' She swallowed hard, feeling a sting in the corner of her eyes. 'If that's not death, what is?'

He actually had the decency to look surprised. Even impressed. 'Interesting thought.'

'I thought I learnt it from you,' she said.

Her voice was choking. He moved up next to her and put an arm around her. She grabbed the hug from him, suddenly needing it desperately.

Then he just went right on.

'But now you see, I've got a chance to get them to give something back to the world. Their understanding, their knowledge about new kinds of life… They can share that, and they won't need to take the blood. They don't have to be trapped, living the way they always have. They can put that behind them.'

Couldn't he tell how her whole body was tightening up? Couldn't he feel it?

He looked down at her and ruffled her hair. 'They're not dead. Not while there's still hope for them.'

She didn't say a word.

'Sam?' He looked at her, worriedly. 'Please, Sam, say something.'

She took a deep breath. 'I was waiting till I could say this calmly.' She stepped away from him and stared him in the eye. 'This is wrong. They're still killers.' One more shuddering breath. A pause. 'And this can all go to hell.'

She turned and ran out of the door. 'Sam – wait –' he called, but he could hear the front door slam.

* * *

By the time General Kramer got to the Doctor she'd already alerted her troops to be on the lookout for Sam, but the chances of their finding her in a city the size of San Francisco were ridiculous. She had a twenty-minute head start in the Bug, and they had no idea where she was going.

The Doctor sat at the kitchen table, chin propped on his folded arms, the mobile phone inches away. He looked as though he hadn't moved an inch since he'd called her. Carolyn's cat was brushing against his legs, unnoticed.

'I'm not handling Sam very well,' he admitted. 'Adrienne, you're a parent. Why do they do it? Why do they keep running off and putting themselves in danger?'

Kramer looked around the kitchen. It was a mess, the plates from hurried meals and a dozen coffee cups lying about.

'It's the same thing that makes 'em run off with you in the first place. You know full well what it is. It's the reason you pick them, isn't it?'

'Pick them?' asked the Doctor. 'They pick me. Sam picked me.'

'They keep putting themselves in trouble for you,' insisted Kramer. 'Now, I don't know what you're up to with Sam, but –'

'Adrienne,' he sighed sharply, and turned to stare her in the eyes. 'Do I look as though I had any of this in mind?'

She could see something in his eyes that she'd never seen before. Hell, she'd never been able to see anything in his eyes before – the last Doctor would never have dropped his guard enough for her to make out what he was thinking. That look of worry, it was real.

'No,' she admitted at last, 'you don't.'

She could believe him. Either that, or he was a better liar than he'd ever been before, and she'd have no hope of telling if he ever was lying… What the hell, she might as well just grit her teeth and trust him anyway.

'You have a teenage daughter,' he said. 'How do you deal with her?'

'Is that how you see yourself?' said Kramer. 'As her father?'

'Oh heavens no. But I can hardly ask you for advice on how to be an older brother, can I? She has a perfectly good father of her own at home.'

'Yeah, but you have to look after her, to teach her…'

'It's so difficult,' he said. 'She wants so much to know that we're doing the right thing. She wants to be involved in everything.'

Kramer put down the mugs she was carrying. 'Give her something useful and safe to do. Tell her a few white lies to keep her out of the worst of it.'

'No,' he said. 'Not Sam. She trusts me. Real trust is as rare and precious as having a cat pay attention to you. She didn't storm out of here because I'd lost her trust: she left because she disagreed with what I was doing. She shouldn't be alone out there…'

Kramer sat down. 'Typical, isn't it? You put in all the effort to keep them safe, and then they go off and put themselves right back in danger.'

The Doctor began to smile. 'If anything it's got worse these past few years. I just thought it would be a good idea to talk to someone who didn't have inexplicable urges to run off with me.'

Kramer snorted. 'They're hardly inexplicable,' she said, and went back to stacking the dishes. When she registered the confused expression on his face, she put them all down. 'Look. You want my honest opinion?'

'Whatever gave you that idea?' muttered the Doctor.

'You should get used to it,' she said. 'As far as anyone can tell, you're a young single male with a mysterious past and a life of adventure. Of course they're gonna flock to you. They don't see the thousand years, or what a job saving the Earth all the time is.' She shrugged. 'And besides, chicks dig the time machine.'

'It was never like this before,' he said.

'You never exactly gave 'em the same kind of invitation before,' she said. 'Your last regeneration, you didn't act so… uh, approachable.'

'I was so much older then,' he said. 'I think there were things I made a point of forgetting when I stopped being so old.'

'No, it's more than that.' Kramer cast around for the words. 'Lemme put it this way. You weren't so much of a hands-on kind of guy.'

'Oh.'

'That makes a difference – you gotta be able to see that. The way you look, the way you act, the way you're so touchy-feely all of a sudden… It gives you a kind of power over people.'

He looked blank. 'What do you mean?'

Kramer shook her head. I don't believe it, she thought. 'Look at Carolyn. You really didn't see what you just hugging her was doing to her?'

He looked surprised. 'I thought she was enjoying it.'

'Ohh boy,' said Kramer, shaking her head again. 'You're a danger to yourself and others, you know that?'

'No, I really don't understand. Where does power enter into it?'

'Look at her. She's having a rough time with her boyfriend. Along comes another unattached male who can take her away from it all – and who's acting all cuddly and approachable.'

'And who has cute eyebrows,' he said, incomprehensibly.

'And then she's willing to put herself in harm's way for him.' Kramer smiled out of the corner of her mouth. 'You really think she'd be doing that so easily if you looked like me?'

'Oh dear,' said the Doctor. Kramer couldn't help smiling outright.

'You should smile more often,' he said. 'It looks lovely.'

Kramer raised an eyebrow at that. 'I'm a *general*.' She abandoned the washing-up. 'C'mon, I promised you a ride back to your TARDIS.'

'No no,' he said. 'I've changed my mind.' His attention had landed on a note Carolyn had stuck to the refrigerator, an address and phone number. 'I want you to drop me at the, ah, the Regents Park Hotel, there's something else I need to take care of.'

Angel Labs, Shackle had said. Where Harris worked. If there was any way she was ever going to find out what was really going on, this was where to start.

So Sam sat in the Bug, in the car park lot behind Angel Laboratories. The building was locked, but the lights in what must be Harris's lab were still on, so all she could do was wait till Harris came out. She passed the time by flipping through the radio stations, idly trying to find any halfway decent music by someone who wasn't on heroin.

All these problems, the way the Doctor was acting so strange – it had to be something Harris was up to. There wasn't any other explanation. It was only since the bloodfasting that he'd been acting so… well, so old, wasn't it? Like he was more like one of them than like her. The Doctor who was calmly defending those murderers couldn't be the same one who had stood in the TARDIS with butterflies in his hair, could he?

It just didn't make sense for him to be acting so dead. He was the most alive person she knew.

So that was the plan. She'd find out whatever it was that was going on, bring it to the Doctor, and solve the whole mess. Get it done with style. And after that… well, then she'd know if those holes in her throat had really healed or not.

Let's see, now. She could probably figure out which one of the few cars in the car park was Harris's. And then it would help if she had one of those tracking devices like she'd stuck on to Eva's car back in seventy-six. It would make it easier to follow Harris – but getting one would mean going back to the TARDIS, and that meant facing Carolyn, and maybe him too.

She shouldn't be feeling so shaky about that. It was like she was more scared of dealing with him than with the vampires.

Oh, sod it. She thumped her head against the vinyl steering wheel. What was she doing, sitting in a car in a bad part of town at quarter to two in the morning? This wasn't daring risk-taking, this was just stupid. She was trying to be the Doctor, and instead she'd end up like Shackle in the alleyway. No way was she cut out for this sort of thing –

But the light in the lab had gone out.

'Ladies and gentlemen, Miss Harris has left the building.'

Sam scrunched down in the driver's seat, wishing the Bug wasn't so cramped. She heard Harris's footsteps echoing across the car park. After a few heart-thumping moments, Sam saw the headlights snap on, heard the engine start. Heard Harris's car reach the gate and go through.

She made herself count to ten before she followed that car.

She spent the next twenty minutes tensed all the way up to her eyeballs, her gaze locked on the pair of tail lights half a block ahead.

This alone left any of those stunts with the billboard in the dust.

Mr Selby back at school was always big on asking kids who their role models were. Part of his continuing search to find someone else to blame for why his students turned out so rotten. The last time he'd asked, she'd said, 'Lisa Simpson.'

But next time she'd be able to tell him that her role model was a man who staked vampires through the heart and double-talked killers into walking away from their victims.

If she ever made it back to school.

Harris drove straight to a warehouse, a few minutes away in the late-night traffic. Sam carefully doubled back, parked a couple of blocks away, and walked down to the big, dark building. She found herself trying to look in every direction at once. It would be terribly embarrassing to get mugged at this point.

Sam had rummaged in the trunk of the Bug earlier on, looking for useful stuff. It was a typical Doctorish mishmash of junk, from a tin of toffees to an ancient-looking urn to the crowbar she was holding in her hand.

She walked around the warehouse, listening hard, wondering if Harris could walk silently. There were weeds growing in cracks in the pavement, and the gates and chicken-wire fence were rusting. No one had come here for a long time. She could smell machine oil and salt water.

The vampire's car was parked around the front, so presumably she'd used a key to go in through the front door. Sam walked down the side, round the back – there, a door at the top of a short flight of concrete stairs.

Sam looked around. The warehouse backed on to another warehouse – there was no one around to notice her. She shrugged, wedged the crowbar's tip into the door, and pulled with all her might.

The door cracked open with surprising ease. It hadn't been

opened for a lot of years – the wood was soft, splintering around the crowbar, the deadbolt tearing right through it. It didn't even make all that much noise, the echo deadened by the walls on either side.

No alarms were going off. Christ, she was in. Sam got a good grip on the crowbar, switched on her flashlight, and crept inside.

She was in a narrow hallway with a couple of doors heading off it. It smelled of dust and urine.

The hallway led to a sort of balcony running right around the inside of the warehouse, a huge rectangular space. The air was cold and musty. She couldn't make out the ceiling or the floor, and she didn't dare shine her torch beam down there.

So instead, she listened.

She kept listening for a few minutes, trying to think. What would Harris keep in here? Why would she need so much space? Were there coffins down there somewhere? Chemicals?

Enough, she told herself. Get your behind out of here, and get back to the Doctor and tell him about this place. Maybe he'll bring you back here with him when he comes to investigate.

She heard a baby crying.

She froze, feeling her hands grip the torch and the crowbar so tight that it hurt.

There! The sound came again, echoing distantly through the warehouse's dark shape. She was sure that was a baby crying.

God, she couldn't leave. Harris had a baby down there and she was going to kill it.

Sam looked for a way down to the warehouse floor, heart racing. The vampires probably had a whole bunch of babies stored here, or even kids and maybe adults, like a giant larder.

Stairs! Metal stairs. Noisy. Didn't matter, just get down there, the flashlight clenched between her teeth. The crowbar was a hard, cold weight, sliding around in her palm. What you going to do with it? You can't kill her, you can't kill her without killing the Doctor too. Have to think of something. Should have gone for help? No time, got to get that baby.

She jumped down to the warehouse floor, shining the torch around. Empty in every direction. A doorway across the floor. She started heading for it.

She heard the baby crying again. It sounded wrong, distorted. Too deep, too loud, right behind her.

She swung around. Her heart was beating so hard it felt like it should hurt. Another door, behind the stair, that's where the noise is coming from.

There was some kind of high-tech keypad next to the door. She wished the Doctor was there – he'd open the thing in thirty seconds with a toothpick and a paperclip. She had to get in. What was she going to do?

'What's your lucky number?' she muttered, and punched a random number, four digits. The keypad went beep, the lock went clunk and the door opened slightly. Had she hit the combination? Impossible. No time to think about it. She pushed it open.

The cry was so loud she nearly dropped the torch. It wasn't a baby crying. What the hell was it? A vampire baby? Some chimera Harris had cooked up in her lab, something she was keeping here, feeding it as it grew, what?

Her torch found a cage, like a circus cage. Something was moving inside there. She moved forward. The cage was a cube, maybe three metres tall, pushed back against the opposite wall.

Her head said right NOW is the time to GO, SAM! Her hand kept the torch moving, over the thing at the back of the cage squealing at the touch of the light.

It was human. It looked human. It was crying like a baby. It was bigger than she was, naked and pink, a grown-up man, scared to death.

She turned to run.

Harris grabbed her by the throat.

CHAPTER 15
OVER THE EDGE

'Oh God,' said James.

'No, not quite, but some say I'll do in a pinch,' said the Doctor cheerfully. James was too paralysed to shut the hotel room door in the Doctor's face. And then it was too late: the Doctor was inside.

'So how've you been keeping?' he asked as he fluttered through James's room. 'Have a good day back at work? Keeping yourself busy, managing to fill the evenings on your own? No nightmares?'

'Look, what do you want?' asked James. He hadn't meant his voice to sound that high and thin. God, suddenly he was shaking all over again. 'It's after two in the morning –'

The Doctor smiled engagingly. 'You work in the theatre. If anyone would be used to being up at this hour it would be you.'

He had a point. James had been sitting up, trying to think of something useful to do, at an hour when the TV had run out of interesting shows.

This hotel room was just what he'd needed. Normal wallpaper, a normal bed, identical to every other hotel room he'd ever been in right down to the tasteful painting at the head of the bed. He could believe in it. It wasn't going to sink its teeth into him when he wasn't looking.

What in hell was the Doctor doing in a place like this?

'Carolyn needs you,' said the Doctor. 'She's trying her best not to, but she does.'

'She hasn't been answering her phone,' he said.

'She hasn't been home very much.'

'What's she been up to –' James began, then blanched. 'No wait, I don't want to know.'

The Doctor ignored his protest. 'Oh, all sorts of interesting things,' he said. 'We've stopped the vampires from raiding the nightclub, we're in the middle of trying to deal with a schism in their ranks, and we're about halfway to finding an alternative food for them.'

James just stared. 'So you've got all this to deal with, and you take the time to come over to talk to me?'

'Of course,' said the Doctor. 'Why not?'

'Look, what do you want me involved in all that for?' A penny dropped. 'You don't want me to –'

'Oh no no no. This is just about you and Carolyn.'

James looked at the man sitting on the corner of his bed. Even his outfit clashed with the decor. 'We'll be fine,' he said. 'We'll be back to normal. Just as soon as all this goes away.'

'What if she doesn't want it to go away?' asked the Doctor quietly.

'You mean, what if she'd rather be doing things like that, than things with me?'

'It's possible,' said the Doctor gently.

'No.' James shook his head, barely more than a quiver. 'She's not like that.'

'Are you sure?'

'I know her,' said James. 'I know her. Listen, I've eaten breakfast with her every morning for months now. Every so often she gets bored with the usual stuff, the French toast, things like that… She starts trying a bunch of new recipes. Some of them she keeps, some she doesn't. But she never stops making the French toast. She doesn't want to lose the comfort of knowing that some things will always be there. You know?'

The Doctor shook his head slowly, and his face looked strangely melancholy. How do you get through to a guy from space? 'Look,' said James. 'I already feel lousy for leaving her alone like that.' He bent forward, pushing his fingers into his hair. 'But I mean… You know what they did to me,' he whispered. 'You really think there's anything wrong with me not wanting to have anything to do with them, ever?'

'No. But she wants to deal with them.'

'But they're not what really matters to her life. They're not real.' And here in this hotel room, surrounded by maid service and complimentary newspapers, he could almost believe it literally.

'What do you think is real?' asked the Doctor, his eyes suddenly distracted.

James shrugged. 'Me and Carolyn having dinner over at the Tiffts' house. The things she's spent her whole life trying to figure out. Her research, my job, our trips to Angel Island – wait, what is it?' The Doctor had his hand to his forehead, and his face was tightening up in pain.

'Oh, don't worry, it's just the bloodfasting acting up a bit,' he said.

James still had to fight the urge to back out the door. 'The what?'

'A psychic connection between me and the leader of the vampires. It's a long story. When Joanna gets excited about something it's hard to block it out. Now, you were saying?'

'Well, that I – that Carolyn and I can have a meaningful life even if I'm not some kind of vampire hunter.' James was alarmed by the sound of his own laugh. 'It's just not on my agenda, you know? I look at what you guys are doing. I don't see any real emotion behind it. Kramer's just doing her job, you're not even human… No offence.'

The Doctor shook his head. 'Go on.'

'That's why it's not real. I can't believe in it. Even the vampires, like Slake, they don't care, they're just doing it all for a performance. They're just acting, really.'

'I think Sam would beg to differ,' the Doctor murmured.

'I mean, maybe they're old, maybe they drink blood. And they may act like they're big mythical horrors or something, but when it comes down to it they're just people. Just… really screwed-up people, the kind the police deal with all the time. That's why we have police, isn't it? So people like me and Carolyn can just live our lives without having to handle these things ourselves. Nothing wrong with that. We don't have to do it all.'

The Doctor didn't say anything.

'Doctor?'

The Doctor was slowly rocking back and forth on the edge of the bed, eyes screwed shut, a hand raised to his temple. 'Sorry,' he said. 'I. The blood.'

'You OK?' stammered James.

The Doctor ignored him, hunching even further over, bringing up his knees into a foetal position.

Then he exploded outward, leaping to his feet and screaming. 'No! Let go of her!'

Sam's neck was between Harris's thumb and forefinger. Sam could feel her leaning in, positioning her teeth for just the right incision. No time left to feel anything else.

Then Harris froze, a sudden current running through her. Sam kneed her in the guts and ran for the door.

The Doctor crumpled, landing on his knees on the carpet. He looked like something invisible was attacking him. James grabbed his arm and tried to drag him back to his feet. The Doctor's hand landed on his shoulder, grasping so tightly that James gasped with surprise and pain. 'Hey!' he said, panicking. 'Let go!'

Sam collided with the door – shut tight, locked, by Harris, silently, after Sam had come in. And there wasn't any time to do anything with the keypad because Harris was right there grabbing for her again, fingers like metal biting into her shoulder.

James stared, keeping well back. The Doctor was screaming at the skies. Oh jeez, he was going to wake everyone in the hotel – was he terrified or was he angry? 'Don't! I'll –' He looked wildly around him, trying to find anything he could use to stop whoever he was yelling at.

And then the Doctor was dashing to the old-style window in the corner of the room and shoving it open, and he was wriggling out through the gap, and there was nothing out that window but an eight-storey drop.

Harris lifted Sam up by her collar. Sam twisted in her grasp, kicking and yelling, but she couldn't get loose. Harris slammed her against the door. She grabbed Sam's wrist and squeezed until the crowbar fell out of her fingers, clattering on the floor.

The room was huge, full of cages, and the smell like the animals' cages at the zoo. The naked people in them were staring at her and Harris, watching, scared.

Harris had fangs, and her eyes were glowing, red, or were they reflecting like cats' eyes? Her knuckles were pushing into Sam's throat. It hurt. Harris's teeth were peeling back from her lips, showing off those long canines. They looked sharp, the way the one's in the nightclub had looked sharp, and her stitches were tearing and it was going to happen again!

By the time James got his head out of the window the Doctor was clinging to the brickwork, his heels balanced on the corner of the sill, his eyes stared fixedly at something James couldn't see. 'Joanna! I'll jump! You know I will!'

'No!' screamed Harris. She was trembling, as if about to fall over, her grip loosening. Sam just stared at her in shock.

'Oh God,' gasped James. What were you supposed to say to a suicide? 'Come inside. Just come back inside.'

The Doctor kept on shouting. Lights were going on across the street. 'The bloodfasting's too strong to block out. If you bite her, I'll lose my concentration, I'll lose my balance! Let her go!'

'Who are you talking to?' said James, reaching out a hand. He didn't dare touch the Doctor in case he startled him. Beneath them, eight floors down, cars were chunky shapes moving up and down the street. 'Come in here, please, please come inside.'

'I will not let you kill her!' roared the Doctor.

And in a moment of terror and wonder James believed him.

Sam couldn't take her eyes off Harris. The woman's face was twisting, as if she was the one in pain. As if she was the one pinned to the wall.

Finally Harris let out a wail and sank to her knees. What was going on? Who cares? Sam grabbed for the door handle.

Then a hand caught her leg from behind, and her shoulder was hitting the floor.

She rolled as best she could, dragged herself up, and had a couple of seconds' head start at stumbling before Harris caught her again. She felt the vampire grab her, scary-strong arm sliding under her armpit, clamp fingers in her hair, and manhandle her towards the cage door. The naked people crawled back from the door, making fearful lowing sounds.

Harris gave her a shove, and she hit the floor face first inside the cage. By the time she rolled over, Harris had slammed the cage shut.

Sam backed into a dark corner and huddled there, trying to remember how to breathe. The grunts and whimpers from the people in the cage were slowly subsiding. They stared at her, curious hands reaching for her. 'Back off!' she shouted, and they startled and flinched away.

She fell back against the bars, noticing the throbbing in her shoulder, the way the whole right side of her chest spiked with pain when she moved.

Harris had slumped down against the far wall, next to the door, holding herself to stop her shivers.

There were bloody tears in the corners of her eyes.

'Oh Jesus,' said James. He was trembling violently. 'That was real. That was all real.'

'Yes. Quite,' said the Doctor. Now that the energy had gone from him, he was clutching on to the brickwork with every spare inch of his body. His eyes were riveted on the ground far below, as if he'd only just noticed it was there. 'Now could you give me a hand getting back inside?' His voice almost squeaked. 'Please?'

'Oh, not again,' moaned Abner.

Slake was pacing the TV room, a feverish energy in his steps. 'We've got to strike now. Before they expect another attack. Otherwise we'll never get out from under their thumbs.'

'No doubt,' said the accountant, leaning against the wall and filing his nails, 'you have another cunning plan.'

'Simple. First we go after the old ones, one at a time. Get 'em when they're alone, before they can warn anyone. Get as many of them out of the way as we can. Then when Harris finally figures out we're after her… we leave her and take out the Doctor.'

'Huh?' said Reaper.

'Guess what,' said Slake, and grinned. 'They're bloodfasted. They've been keeping that little bit of information from us.'

'So if we take him out –' said Elvis.

'Then we've taken out Harris, and we don't even need to go near her. We've got nothing to worry about.'

'Except for the other old ones,' said Shredder.

'And the Doctor,' said Reaper.

Slake curled his lip dramatically. 'I don't fear the Time Lord.'

'What if he's got a pointed stick?' said Abner with a smirk.

'Just shut up,' hissed Slake. His face had turned a furious red. He turned back to the others and paced even harder, spoke even louder. 'The Doctor's got no stomach for a real war. He won't stand against us once we've tasted his allies' blood –'

'There you go again. Talk about your one-track mind,' Abner sighed. 'It's always blood, blood, blood, war, war, war. You'd think after forty years you'd have come up with some other topic of conversa–'

Slake swung around and staked him to the wall.

He hadn't even known he was going to do it, but the stake was right there in his pocket and Abner was in just the right place, and now Abner was screaming a long drawn-out human scream of pain, curling around the stake, hands clasping Slake's, too weak to pull the lethal chunk of wood out of his body.

He'd never seen one of them die before.

He hadn't expected a scream like that. He wanted to wipe the splatters off his face but his hands were soaking too, and Abner was still holding them. He stared down at his ruined shirt.

The others were still frozen, their minds slowly realising in utter disbelief that Slake had actually *done* something. They were waiting for him to speak, to say something which would snap their minds into understanding what had happened.

Abner let go of him. The stake couldn't hold his weight. He fell to the ground, exploding in a shower of broken ash. The stake rolled out of the grey flakes and across the floor. It touched

Reaper's foot, and he flinched, staring at Abner's remains.

Slake looked the other vampires over, and then pulled himself up straight, getting his own breathing back under control.

'Now they're going to come after me,' he said quietly. 'And then they're going to come after all you, 'cause they think you're on my side. Doesn't matter if you're not, really – you're not worth the risk of keeping you alive.' He looked at each of them, and in his eyes there was an odd calm certainty, the clarity of knowing there was no longer any choice. 'So what's it gonna be?'

The red haze was back. The Doctor just managed to stammer out the address he'd glimpsed in Harris's mind to the taxi driver before it overwhelmed him again, and he couldn't see the inside of the cab any more. He was back in the warehouse with Harris.

But Harris wasn't in the warehouse. She was outside, somewhere, under the same cold sky, looking for someone. There – a lone figure sleeping in a doorway, mostly covered by pages of the *San Francisco Chronicle*.

'You OK, mister?' asked the taxi driver. The balding guy looked in his rear-view mirror, worried.

The Doctor couldn't answer. He had to stop her, he couldn't let this happen, he had to do something, but there was no time, no time, no time.

'Please don't,' he pleaded.

Joanna drew an arm around the chest of the shaking human. She pushed a hand over his mouth, drawing his head back. He was wiry and thin, smelling of sweat and illness, the way they always did. It had been decades since she had killed anyone clean and whole and loved.

This one would be a live kill. Give him the full sensory experience. She rasped her tongue on the man's neck, tasting dirt and skin. He whimpered, bewildered.

I can't make you feel what you just made me feel, Doctor. But this will hurt you.

The taxi had stopped. The driver had pulled open the passenger door. 'Jesus, mister! You need a doctor!'

'You don't have to do this,' the Doctor was pleading. 'Please don't, you don't have to do this.'

Joanna clamped her mouth over the man's neck. He went limp in her grip, giving up, too frightened to fight any more. She paused, for just a moment, feeling the red haze filling her up.

The Doctor exploded out of the taxi. 'Hey, mister!' The driver stood by his car, watching the strange man running up the street, panicked, slowing, finally standing still.

The driver jogged up to him. The man was shaking, fists clenched, staring into the night. The driver took one look at his expression and backed off. Whatever he was seeing, whatever hallucination this one was having, he just didn't want to know.

The man fell to his knees, covering his eyes with his hands. 'Stop it!' he shouted. The taxi driver backed further away. 'Stop it, stop it, stop it!'

But whatever it was, it didn't stop.

THIRD BITE

CHAPTER 16
BLOOD WAR

Sam woke up with a violent start, banging her head on the bars behind her.

The…people in the cage were keeping their distance from her, gazing at something over her shoulder.

She hadn't had much of a chance to look at them before. They were soft-looking, no muscles. Kept in these cages their whole lives, Sam bet. Their faces were blank, curious, but listless and afraid. Vegetables, she thought. No – animals. They couldn't talk, they were like big caged monkeys.

She turned around. Harris had come back in, silently, and was standing at her lab bench. That wasn't what had woken Sam up.

The Doctor was standing in the doorway. He was glaring at Harris like the wrath of – well, like the wrath of the Doctor, which was the most wonderfully frightening thing Sam could imagine at the moment.

'How dare you?' he breathed. He advanced on Harris. To Sam's surprise, she backed away from the bench. He kept on coming, and she kept backing, until her back was against the wall and he was leaning right in.

Sam leaned against the bars, watching, ignored by both of them. The caged people were watching, too, arms raised as though to ward off the voices.

'How dare *you*?' Harris asked, her voice tight. 'After all you've said about how important it was to keep the peace between us?'

'Keeping the peace?' exclaimed the Doctor. He was so close to her, not touching, just taking up all her air. 'You just took another life!'

'So you could feel it,' she hissed. 'I wanted you to know what you've done to me.'

'What *I've* done? You went off and killed a man in a fit of pique. All that trust we'd built up, you shattered, just like that. Why?

Why why why why why?'

'You were going to kill me!' Harris shrieked. 'I could feel it, you were going to jump. You would have killed yourself and me if you didn't get your way.'

Sam's heart clenched in her chest.

Harris stared at the Doctor, breathing hard, her glasses askew. Then she swallowed, forced her voice back into a whisper. 'I put my life in your hands by getting bloodfasted to you. A bond like that is the closest thing my people have to something sacred. And you were going to use it to kill me. And you talk about *me* breaking a trust?' Her voice began to crack around the edges again. 'How could you do that? How could you?'

'I had to save Sam,' he said quietly.

That did it. Sam started sobbing like a baby.

Both of them looked at her, but she couldn't help it.

Harris unlocked the cage, and Sam clambered out into the Doctor's arms. She buried her face in his coat, feeling all her fear just pouring out. Just for this moment she didn't have to be cool and in control, she didn't have to be the grown-up, because the Doctor was being the most grown up she'd ever seen him.

Gregorio was remembering Tenochtitlán. A wide, straight road that aimed like an arrow for the great city, so crowded with travellers and sightseers they could barely get through. People watching the strangers from the lake, the water choked with canoes.

He was just one of the soldiers, then, barely four hundred of them, warned by the enemies of the Mexica that they'd be killed the instant they reached the tyrants' city. But when they got to Tenochtitlán, the chiefs kissed the ground before them as a sign of peace, and Montezuma himself was waiting to meet them, wearing sandals made of gold.

The stake had not quite missed his heart. There was a lethal tear in the tissue. Gregorio could feel his life leaking forth into his chest, a little with each heartbeat.

The young ones had been too afraid of him to finish him. He remembered the fear in their eyes as he had roared and stumbled about the stage, knocking over dozens of cold candles. The arrogance, too, like the Aztecs' pride, proud to the end as they died in their thousands.

They'd left him, after a while, that infant Slake saying, 'This is getting boring, let's go and find someone more interesting.'

And they were right. He was finished. But they didn't flee because he was boring them. They fled because they couldn't bear to watch him die. Now that they had begun their war, they knew that this would be their fate, too.

Sam was sitting on a stool at the bench. The Doctor had taken a spare lab coat from a peg and put it on her. It made her a bit warmer.

They were still arguing, quieter now, leaning side by side on the bench.

If they started any mushy stuff, she would scream.

'Try to imagine it,' Harris was saying, softly. 'You spend nine hundred years knowing that anyone who finds out anything about you will kill you, or expose you, which means you'll be dead anyway. Unless you kill them first.'

Her voice grew more ragged. 'And then along comes someone who says he wants to help you. And somehow, in spite of everything, you end up trusting him. You begin to think he might understand. And then he turns around and tries to kill you.'

'When you tried to kill his friend.'

'I thought she was just some intruder. She set off a silent alarm when she broke in. I didn't know she was one of yours,' Harris insisted. 'Think about it. You've built up a life somewhere, then some stranger blunders into your most secret hideaway... Would you just let them walk away?'

The Doctor paused before responding. 'No, I didn't,' he admitted. 'It took me a long time to learn. That's the only reason I still think there's any hope for you. I could let you off with a slap on the wrist and a "no more Janis thorns", but I think it's gone a bit beyond that.'

'It's a matter of survival –'

'Not for the man in the alleyway.'

Harris opened her mouth to dispute him, but then stopped herself. 'You're right,' she said quietly. 'I wasn't thinking clearly. I... I was hurt.'

'So was he,' put in Sam. The Doctor turned slightly, put a shushing hand on her arm.

Harris continued, swallowing her words. 'I was so shaken, so furious with you, so... scared, I didn't know what I was doing. That's not like me. I don't kill just because I'm angry. I don't get angry. I don't think I've done anything like that before in my life.'

'We might both get off on temporary insanity,' he murmured. 'Though I doubt it.'

Harris looked down. 'I'm sorry.'

'Like that just sweeps it away,' said Sam. They looked at her. She bristled, and pointed at the cages, where the monkey people were watching them with glittering eyes. Silent, empty faces. 'What's all this for?'

'Food substitute.'

The Doctor shook his head, his eyes icy. 'It's hardly a substitute.'

'No, you see, I've been growing these clones with substantial genetic manipulation. No higher brain functions. They're not self-aware: they're less conscious than your average cow. And their blood's one hundred per cent compatible with us.' She smiled. 'It's an elegant solution. All I need to do now is find out how to make them grow fast enough to keep up with the demand.'

'No,' said the Doctor.

'What?' said Harris.

'No,' he said again.

He knelt down by one of the cages, reaching his fingers through the bars. One of the frightened creatures curiously shuffled forward, keeping its distance, looking at him.

'There's far more brain activity going on in there than you imagine,' said the Doctor.

'They're animals,' said Harris flatly. 'They just look like humans.'

'And you propose to grow them in pens, and drain the blood from them throughout their lives, until they're too anaemic for further use?'

'Veal calves,' said Sam. 'My God, you've invented battery humans.'

'Actually,' said Harris, 'I wasn't planning to drain them. Just take one out of the cage when it's time for the fourteen to feed.'

'You've created a new species, Joanna,' said the Doctor. The dirty woman in the cage was moving closer, shoulders hunched, reaching out a curious hand towards him. 'I thought you would be developing some kind of artificial blood. Not a slave race – created solely so you can kill them.'

'And what about the ones who go for the joy of the hunt?' said Harris. 'They can't get that with a beaker of fake blood. We've got to keep Slake's kind happy. Otherwise they'll start the trouble all over again.'

'No,' said the Doctor. Somehow he managed to squeeze certainty, conviction, and utter bewilderment that she'd even think that way into the one syllable. 'Right now the happiness of your people is the last thing that matters to me.'

'If we don't throw them a bone once in a while we'll have open warfare all over again.'

'Will this be enough for them?' The hunched woman was stroking his coat through the bars. 'Slake and his friends won't be kept happy by something like this. They're too in love with the hunt.'

Joanna closed her eyes, standing perfectly still for a moment. She slammed her hand down on the bench, knocking over a retort stand. 'Slake will do as he's told.'

'Will he?' said the Doctor.

Gregorio stumbled as he tried to climb down the stairs, almost fell. The stake jarred inside him, sending great blue explosions of pain through his chest. He gasped, but caught the rail, and staggered down to the backstage area.

There was a telephone in the desk drawer. He pulled it out with fingers that were rapidly growing numb and pressed it to his ear. Silence.

He was about to drop it in despair when he saw that the cord had fallen from the wall.

He lowered himself to the floor as gently as he could, keeping his grip on the phone. He pushed the plug back into its socket. It seemed so difficult to move it, to force it into place. Perhaps it was damaged somewhere inside.

He had memorised her number, but his mind was full of the smell of blood on the steps of the Great Temple, the scent of flowers in the capital, and the glistening of the gold they had been presented by Montezuma himself.

His fingers found the buttons without his help. 'Gregorio?' said Miss Harris's voice.

'I am dead,' he said. It hurt to speak. 'We are all destroyed. Beware the young ones. Farewell.'

Six hundred thousand pesos of gold, and the gems, and the exotic plumes, and the smoke from the temples...

The line went dead.

Harris held on to the phone, as if not hanging it up would mean that the call hadn't happened.

The Doctor stepped up behind her, and whispered in her ear. 'It's started.'

When you hear a noise in the night, you freeze, listening hard, waiting for the strange sound to resolve itself into something you recognise. A cat, or a car door, or the garbage collectors.

John Seavey was in his bedroom when he heard the screams.

He sat perfectly still at the first scream, pen in his hand. Ash fell from his cigarette on to the night's paperwork. He'd taken it upstairs along with a nightcap. The place was closed for the night, just a few staff left clearing up.

At the second scream, he jerked back in his chair, listening. It was coming from somewhere in the building, downstairs in the empty nightclub, maybe the kitchen. It didn't sound like a laugh, or someone playing around.

He was just getting up when the door of his room slammed open.

A tall, lanky Goth stood there. Seavey stared at him. With a deliberate gesture, the Goth wiped the blood off his face.

'Did you know,' he said, licking his fingers, 'that most murders happen in the home?'

* * *

'What?' yelped Harris.

'You lost your head?' shouted Sam.

'Please,' said the Doctor. 'Sam, I need you to stay here.'

'It's like a bad joke!' protested Sam. 'Locking a vampire and a vegetarian in a room together!'

'If I have to put up with one more rant about factory-farming, I'm going for her throat –'

'Please, please, please,' said the Doctor, shushing them with his hands. 'I've got something for you both to do.' With a flip of his fingers he produced a plastic vial, filled with a silvery-brown liquid. 'This is a little cocktail Carolyn used in my lab. It's lethal to vampire cells. Unfortunately it's none too kind to ordinary human cells either, so be careful with it. She gave me a few samples – and the formula.' He dug a few mangled sheets of notebook paper from an inside coat pocket, and set them down on the counter. 'Now, if the pair of you can brew up a few batches of this, you'll have a weapon.'

'Cool,' said Sam. 'Vamp-Away.'

He barely paused for a breath as he circled Harris's lab bench. 'Now, I'm going to tell Carolyn to start synthesising some more. Then we'll arrange a chance for us to stage a counterattack.'

'I thought that was what you wanted to avoid,' muttered Harris.

The Doctor stopped short. 'I've seen Slake and the others now. They don't deserve to be kept alive. Not at the cost of others' suffering and death.'

Sam's mouth fell open. 'Isn't that my line?'

'Of course. You were right.'

Sam blinked. And this after he'd almost had her convinced! 'But what about all that stuff you were saying, about everyone having a right to live –'

'Oh, that's right as well.'

'But they completely contradict each other,' put in Harris.

The Doctor half smiled. 'You're right too. Now all you need to do is figure out how we can all be right at the same time, then you'll have it.'

He should have licked Abner's blood off his fingers when he gave the speech. It would have been the perfect touch. But hey, the performance had still been good enough, it had got them to follow him, and now everything was different and it was all down to him.

Slake swaggered back into his apartment, his mind awash in all the new things they could try now. There'd have to be new recruits first, to swell their numbers back to a full coven, and that presented possibilities he could barely imagine. Forget going for two-bit street punks – he was going to make San Francisco the home of the classiest gang of nightstalkers in the history of mankind. Hell, he'd turn Anne Rice herself.

Then the fun would really begin. No one to hold them back, no one caring about drawing attention to themselves... They were gonna be legendary.

How many could they kill in a night? Could they pick off every resident in an apartment building one by one? Or maybe a block of row houses – the atmosphere would be better there. No one would admit they heard the screams, even if they heard them. Oh man, imagine the face of the last person they came for – they'd have to make sure he realised that they'd offed all his friends and neighbours and he hadn't noticed a goddam thing. Now that would be drama. This was gonna be like starring in a new slasher movie every night.

And then there were the Heights, with all the rich people living above it all, in the neighbourhoods where it could never ever happen. The ones who figured they'd be safe as long as they never met anyone's eye when they walked down the street. They could just take a night and hit half a dozen places, grab folks as they got out of their cars to go inside, and just spend the next month watching everyone panic. Yeah, that would be a joy, just to watch those pampered mothers go out of their heads afterwards with the fear that it could happen again, any time, anywhere.

Move over Charlie Manson – he was an amateur, he'd wasted time justifying it with ritual doubletalk. He didn't kill just because he felt like killing, just because he could, just because he was so much stronger and sharper than the people he wanted to kill. Imagine if he'd done it every night, all night, if he'd had decades to practice...

They just needed to finish the overture. Then the show could really get started.

The ex-mortal, Shackle, was sitting on the sofa feeling sorry for himself. He seemed to be running his thumb over the points developing on his teeth, trying to get used to the feel. 'Where've you been?' he mumbled.

'I told you,' said Slake. 'Taking care of deadwood.'

Shackle shook his head wearily. 'I don't want to know. Just tell me you're ready to get me some of that synthetic blood of Harris's. I think it's getting to be time.'

'Oh, we're just about ready,' said Slake. 'But I got one question for you. You know where the Doctor would be. Don't you, Dr Shackle?'

The Doctor found a public phone, found a quarter, and dialled Kramer's mobile phone.

'Yup,' she said.

'It's war,' he said.

'I want that in writing,' said Kramer.

'The young ones have gone berserk. There's no way to forge any kind of peace with the vampires while they're on the rampage. I need to talk to your soldiers. Where can we meet?'

'Let's you and I meet first and have a little talk. They've killed Seavey, and three of the staff at the Other Place. I've been trying to find you all this time.'

'Oh, I've been all over the place. James is all right, by the way.'

'That's good news. My troops are on alert at the Coast Guard station at Yerba Buena Island, I can have them wherever they're needed within thirty minutes.'

'All right,' said the Doctor. 'I'll see you at Carolyn's house within' – he took out his pocket watch – 'within the hour.'

'Yessir. What were you doing at James's place anyway?' asked Kramer.

'Trying to solve the fourth problem,' said the Doctor. 'I'll see you shortly.'

Driving the Bug was relaxing, even in the evening traffic. It gave him a moment of silence, no one to explain to or cajole, alone with his thoughts.

He hoped he had been right to leave Sam with Joanna. Sam was no scientist, but she'd helped him once or twice in the TARDIS lab. More importantly, she'd be safe with Joanna, as long as Slake didn't know where the warehouse labs were. Very safe. Joanna wouldn't dare jeopardise her own existence by threatening Sam's.

Kramer had beaten him there, sitting on the front steps and bullying a sergeant over her mobile phone. She waved to him, tucking the phone away. 'Carolyn's home,' she said. 'She looks wiped.'

Carolyn sat in the living room downstairs, frowning at the blank screen of the television.

'You ought to be resting,' he chided her, putting a hand on her forehead.

'Mmm,' she said. 'The work's going well, everything's set up in the TARDIS. We can make as little or as much of the anti-vampire stuff as we need.'

The Doctor nodded. 'I've got Sam and Joanna making some Vamp-Away the hard way. We're going to need it.'

'Are we going to kill all of them, then?' said Carolyn.

'No,' said the Doctor. 'But Slake and his followers have to be stopped. The only reason they haven't started slaughtering the population at random is that they want to kill all the older vampires first.'

'Apparently the Time Lords have a long and honourable tradition of genocide when they think the stakes are high enough,' said Kramer. 'Timelooping whole races, going back in time to prevent them from ever being created... Even fighting that last war against the vampires till they were all wiped out.'

'I told you those were means of last resort,' said the Doctor. 'I'm still hoping for something with a bit more finesse than that. Come on, Carolyn. You need to sleep.'

Carolyn got up. 'Oh,' she said.

She was facing the front windows.

One of the vampires was leering in through the white slats, his grin huge. He punched his first through the window, spraying them with glass and splinters.

'Everybody out!' yelled Kramer, drawing her gun.

'Mina!' shouted Carolyn. She ran for the kitchen.

'Come back!' yelled Kramer.

The Doctor squeezed past Carolyn. 'I'll get them,' he said. There was an almighty crash from upstairs. Another window. 'Follow Kramer. Right now.'

Carolyn turned wordlessly and ran out through the front door.

Kramer stood on the front step, her gun trained on one of the vampires, a black kid. He bared his fangs and hissed. Without hesitating, Kramer pumped three shots into him. Carolyn slapped her hands over her ears.

The vampire fell over, but he wasn't dying. 'Ow!' he said. 'You said that wouldn't hurt!'

The other black kid was still clinging to the front window. 'So sue me,' he said, jumping down into the begonias.

Kramer turned around and emptied the rest of her clip into him.

There was a vampire sitting on top of the Bug, grinning at the two struggling to their feet in the garden. A skinny kid with red hair. Kramer was reloading her gun.

Carolyn pulled one of the tomato stakes out of the front garden and screamed at the monster, 'Get your ass off that car!'

'Whoah,' said the vampire. He got his ass off the car.

The Doctor came running out of the front door, Mina in his arms.

'The kittens!' screamed Carolyn.

'Get in the car!' ordered the Doctor. 'Now!'

'Hey, Slake! They're down here!'

Kramer put four bullets into the red-headed vampire. 'Hey!' he said from the pavement. 'I got off the car, dude...'

The Doctor pushed Carolyn into the back of the Bug while Kramer got into the driver's seat. He put Carolyn's belt on. Mina was clawing her, trying to hold on as Kramer floored it.

'The kittens,' shrieked Carolyn. 'What about the kittens?'

CHAPTER 17
ALL RIGHT ON THE NIGHT

Thursday

The sun was only just up when James got back to his hotel room. He dropped the dozen long-stemmed roses on the desk and headed straight to the bathroom to splash some water on his face. He couldn't quite bring himself to shut the bathroom door.

It wasn't surprising that he looked like hell, considering he'd got three, maybe four hours of sleep. Still, it was for a good cause, one he should have paid more attention to before, and once he'd freshened up a bit he'd be ready to go back out again.

He heard a frantic knocking at the door. It had to be Carolyn – somehow he could recognise her knock. He hurried to the door and pulled it open.

The Doctor was the first through, scattering apologies as he barged in. Next came Kramer, hot on his heels. After they'd nearly run him down, he was left with Carolyn standing at the door, holding Mina and looking like she was about to fall apart.

'What happened?' he stammered.

'They tore up the house. We had to find somewhere to go.' Her eyes were wide, and her voice flat and disconnected. She didn't even hug him, and he felt a sudden knife in his gut until he decided it was probably because her arms were full of cat.

'We've been crammed into the back of the Bug for the past couple of hours,' said Kramer. 'We kept moving so they couldn't track us.'

'Uh-huh,' said James absently. He eased Carolyn over to the corner of the bed and took the groggy cat from her arms. 'Oh, jeez, Carolyn, you look like you've been through hell. Did you get any sleep at all?'

'Sleep, as the Doctor is fond of saying, is for tortoises,' said Kramer. 'Happy well-rested tortoises, but tortoises nonetheless.'

The Doctor was unloading the kittens from assorted coat pockets, piling them on the hotel desk. They started clambering all over the roses, investigating each petal with a child's fascination for detail. Kramer hurried back to the doorway, checking the hallway one more time before locking the door.

James just let all the action swirl around him. So the weirdness wasn't going away, so it had burst into his hotel room and taken over, fine, he didn't care, he'd just ignore it all and stay in a corner with Carolyn. Was that really too much to ask?

'Nice roses,' she said.

'Oh. Yeah.' He glanced at the flowers on the desk. 'You won't believe what I had to go through to find an all-night florist. I was going to stop by around breakfast and try to catch you...'

'Thanks,' she said. She tried to smile, but didn't move any closer to him.

'You were right,' he said. 'That is, I mean, I was right that I shouldn't have to deal with them, not after everything, but I still should've stayed around, for you...'

She squeezed his hand, briefly, and let it go again.

'Ah. James.' The Doctor plopped down on to the bed next to the pair of them, nearly sitting on Mina. 'Hope the lifestyle's coming together a bit. Listen, I've just had an idea. We need to set a trap for them, and we're going to need your help.'

James started shaking his head. 'All right,' said Kramer. 'So what are we going to need him for?'

'Think about it, Adrienne. They know we can counterattack during the daylight, so they won't want us to find them then. So where's the one place they won't be?'

'The theatre,' concluded Kramer. The Doctor shook her hand and dashed off.

'You did what?'

'We went to kill the Doctor. You got a problem with that? Now?'

Shackle just stared at Slake, at the dingy hotel room they were sharing for the night. He hadn't imagined eternal life would have quite so many cigarette burns in the carpet. 'But what has he done to harm you –'

'Just shut up,' snapped Slake, 'You don't even know. What do you care, anyway?'

'I seem to vaguely remember something about the Hippocratic Oath,' muttered Shackle. 'I know, I know, but Joanna kept telling me about food substitutes…'

'You can forget about that. Harris is dead, she just hasn't figured it out yet.' Slake flopped on his twin bed and turned away.

Shackle sat down on the edge of the other bed. Everything that was going on was so remote from him, as distant as his own body felt now. He only wanted to sit down, to sit back and see where events swept him.

Slake had swept him out of the apartment under the theatre an hour or so before sunrise, saying they had to find someplace else to stay for the day, and that he knew just the place. So they ended up in this dive.

Wait, it was eight thirty, he was running late, he had to call the medical centre and –

– oh.

'Slake,' said Shackle, and his voice was shaking, 'I think I'm very hungry.'

'Shut up and go to sleep.'

'It's all right,' said Shackle. 'It's all right, I'm more tired than hungry.' And he was, the bed dragging him down. He curled on top of the rough cover, facing Slake's indifferent back. 'Did you actually kill the Doctor?' he asked, his voice drained.

Slake grunted and shook his head.

'Oh. So that's why you rousted me out of your apartment. You were afraid they'd come back to the theatre and repay you in kind.'

Slake rolled on to his back. 'Oh, they can try,' he said, tilting his head back languidly. 'If they do, my servants will take care of them.'

'Your servants?' said Shackle weakly. 'You mean vampire bats? In San Francisco?'

'Not quite,' Slake muttered.

'Then what?' Slake preferred a mysterious silence. 'Look,' said Shackle, 'you brought me into this, I've got a right to know...'

'All right,' grumbled Slake, 'They're squirrels. But they work.'

James had never seen the Orpheum in daylight. They'd kept him in a back room at the club till it was dark enough for them to move him, and then he'd only got a glimpse of what the theatre looked like.

There were an awful lot of steps leading up to those doors. And then it was an even longer way back down inside.

The rest of Kramer's troops were going around to the side entrance, driving their Land Rovers filled with the equipment he'd borrowed from work. But someone had to descend into the Orpheum first, to open the big sliding equipment doors. Someone who could find his way around in a theatre, someone who had the experience to know what to look for, someone willing to face whatever was lurking in that building away from the daylight.

'There'll be a small pair of buttons mounted on the wall opposite the loading door,' he told the Doctor. 'You can't miss it.'

The Doctor nodded and hurried over to the steps, where he started making plans with General Kramer. James shivered and turned away, then jumped. Carolyn was standing just behind him. She was staring at him in that fixed way that meant she was absolutely furious.

'What?' he sighed.

'He went down there for you,' she said flatly. 'He risked his life to go down into that hellhole and bring you back out.'

'I *said* thank you...'

'I don't care.' He could see how bloodshot her eyes were, how she was leaning heavily on the corner of the Bug, but that didn't blunt the edge of her words at all.

He turned away, hunching over a bit, his body instinctively going into a protective crouch. 'Look, I'm not running out on them. I'll do everything I have to. But that, I don't have to. They're soldiers, they're trained to deal with this...'

'No, that's not it, it's nothing like that. It's...' She stumbled, groping for the words. He could see the sleep dragging at her. 'I understand it now. The butterflies.'

It scared him to see her standing there, speaking gibberish with absolute conviction. God, she must be so tired, he could barely imagine what she'd been through.

'He went down there to get you out. That's what he does. That's who he is.'

'Carolyn,' said James. 'Honey darling dear love of my life.'

'What?' she snapped.

'You're exhausted. You need sleep. Seriously, I mean it…'

She shot him a furious look and stormed off towards the Doctor and Kramer.

Then he saw she was climbing the steps with them. It took just a moment for it to penetrate his brain, and then he ran after them.

The Doctor was the first through the door. He stood on the threshold and looked back at James. 'Are you sure?' he said.

No of course not, let me out of here. 'Are you?'

'Of course,' he said, surprised, and stepped inside.

Kramer and the Doctor switched on their torches, pale beams picking out small circles of the water-stained walls.

James trailed behind them. The Doctor walked through the ruined foyer with confidence, trusting in fate or time or whatever that nothing was going to try to kill him. But at the same time his head was turning from side to side, watching for anything that would threaten the people following him.

James stayed close to Kramer and Carolyn, well behind the Doctor, with all of them talking sotto voce as he led them onward.

'Don't you see?' said Carolyn. She was still trying to explain whatever that insight of hers was. 'That's why they hate him so much, that's why they're so scared of him. It's because he's so alive. Everything he touches just gets filled with life.'

'Fertility symbol, huh?' said Kramer.

Carolyn blushed. 'I'm not sure I like where this is going,' muttered James.

Kramer peered into the darkness ahead of them. 'You ain't seen nothing yet.'

Ahead lay a stairway, curving down and away from the last trickles of sunlight. They followed the Doctor down the steps, staying as close to the magic circle around him as they could.

'Before we go any further,' whispered Carolyn, 'Have some Vamp-Away.' She opened her handbag and passed them each a couple of vials of that anti-vampire solution she'd been brewing up.

James couldn't quite bring himself to think of it as 'Vamp-Away' – he just wasn't ready to be silly about this sort of thing. 'What do we do with it?' he whispered.

The Doctor held up a hand, shushing them.

There was a rushing, pattering sound, coming from somewhere farther down the staircase. Like rain falling, or…

'Rats,' said James. 'That's all.'

'Those aren't rats!' said Kramer.

The creatures came up the stairs a few at a time, pausing to sit up and sniff the air. Their eyes glinted in the darkness. They were a foot long. They were covered in moth-eaten grey fur and they had enormous fangs and big bushy tails, and there were maybe twenty of them, chittering from all around.

Vampire crack squirrels, thought James, and wished he hadn't.

Things were happening so fast around her and she was moving as if mired in a dream.

She fumbled the cap off the vial but her fingers felt huge and clumsy and she heard the vial shatter against the floor and only then could she tell it was gone from her hand.

All the fatigue toxins building up in her body, curdled by yet another blast of adrenaline, were flooding her brain till she couldn't figure out how to move at all any more.

And the creature on her neck was moving so fast.

James grabbed the monster that had run right up Carolyn's body and was gibbering in her face, trying to get its massive teeth into her throat. She wasn't even screaming, just lurching about. Another lurch, and the creature had to let go of her. Suddenly James's arms were full of angry undead rodent.

He threw it at the floor, aiming for the puddle of Vamp-Away. It hit hard, slipping in the foul-smelling stuff and the broken glass. It didn't seem to bother the little monster.

Around him, the Doctor and Kramer were staking squirrels left, right and centre. James didn't have any stakes. He wasn't even supposed to be here.

He booted the squirrel as it came for him, hearing the satisfying sound of bones breaking. Carolyn had fallen down, her back to the wall, and another one of the little critters was going for her.

'James!' shouted the Doctor.

James somehow caught the stake he was thrown, and shoved it through the giant squirrel just before it got its fangs into Carolyn's leg.

'They're retreating!' shouted Kramer. 'Watch your backs!'

The staked squirrel exploded in a puff of ashes, as though it had suddenly burnt up from inside. James grabbed the stake and finished off the one that was struggling in the pool of Vamp-Away.

The last of the creatures scurried away.

James sat down, heavily. 'Watch out for that stuff,' said Carolyn. 'Don't get it on you.'

The Doctor crouched beside the puddle. 'It looks as though it doesn't work as a contact poison,' he said. 'They heal too quickly. Probably only toxic enough if they drink it, or get it into their bloodstream.'

'Now you tell us,' said James shakily.

The Doctor shrugged. 'Now we know.'

'Hypodermics,' suggested Kramer. 'Either that or we could mix it with something corrosive.' The thought was enough to make James cringe.

He turned to Carolyn. She was still slumped against the wall, staring fuzzily at the scratches on her arm, as if she couldn't believe they were really there. God, she must have been about to pass out even before any of this. 'You OK?' he asked, and helped her clamber to her feet.

She nodded, murmuring half to herself. 'They could have killed me. They really could have killed me.'

Guess that means I saved your life, he thought. He let out a high-pitched chuckle. All hail James Court, Squirrel-Killer.

They opened the loading-dock doors, letting light into the backstage for the first time in years, and Lieutenant Forrester tracked down the fuse box. Kramer dispatched a detail to mop up the rest of the squirrels. Once the lights came back on, the Doctor escorted the dazed Carolyn away, letting her lean heavily on him. She needed a little rest, he said.

Kramer motioned to her two dozen troops, and they assembled around her. 'Right,' she said. 'Now we get into the fun stuff. Far as you're concerned, I'm transferring command to this man.' She clapped a hand on James's shoulder, and he looked at his makeshift crew with no idea where to begin.

He cast his eyes at the grid above him for inspiration, then turned to the nearest private. 'All right, gimme a big blank sheet of paper, I'll see what I can do.'

The next time he looked up was four hours later. It occurred to him as he lugged a beam projector across centre stage that he'd completely forgotten to think about any of the big things that had been weighing him down.

The soldiers were all bustling around him on the stage, carrying equipment and clambering up ladders to the electric grid, their movements part of a complex order which couldn't really be distinguished from chaos. What with keeping them all moving, dealing with all the snags, and dashing back to the booth at every opportunity, he'd managed to avoid any reminders of what he was doing all this for.

Theatre stress was positively therapeutic.

Kramer approached from the wings, and James rolled his eyes exhaustedly. 'If they've dropped another Leko, I don't want to hear about it.'

Kramer shook her head. 'Just wanted to tell you I've posted lookouts. When the vampires get back here, you'll get about three minutes' warning.'

'Lovely,' said James. Just the kind of reminder he didn't need.

'So,' said Kramer. 'Will it be ready by sundown?'

He shrugged. 'Something will be. We could still take six more

248

hours, if we have 'em.' He went back to circling the stage, trying to anticipate what would go wrong next. There was a forlorn look on his face as he watched two of the soldiers try to stretch a cable to reach an outlet six inches too far away.

'Oh well,' said Kramer. 'Break a leg.'

'Just as long as they don't break any more of my lights.'

Kramer didn't see the Doctor again for another hour, till she stumbled across him in the theatre shop. He was hidden away in a corner, making arrangements with someone over a cell phone. With a start, she realised it was *her* cell phone, and made a mental note to keep a closer eye on her belongings when the Doctor was around.

'The sun's nearly down,' she told him. 'If you're going to get the rest of that Vamp-Away, you'd better do it now.'

'I'm handling that now,' he said, waggling the phone at her. 'I'm arranging where to meet Joanna.'

'And then you've still got to figure out how you're getting the vampires here.'

He held up his free hand. 'Please, please. I can only handle seven things at one time.'

'About Carolyn…'

'Yes?'

'You seen the way she was looking at you when we came in here? She'll follow you anywhere. I think she thinks you're the only thing she can still trust.'

'I won't let her down,' he said. 'I won't let her be hurt.'

Kramer shook her head. 'That's not what I mean. She's only got one life, you know? And it's here. She goes off with you, she'll miss out on it.'

The Doctor pointed out into the auditorium. Kramer followed his finger to where James was making yet another trip back to the lighting booth.

'You know, I do believe it's all falling into place quite nicely,' he said, and breezed out of the door.

* * *

She remembered the Doctor leading her off somewhere, following muzzily in his footsteps. She remembered him laying her down on a couch in a small dark room, and her eyes almost instantly giving up their battle to stay open. She knew he'd be there when she woke up.

When she opened her eyes, it was James who was there. He was bent over a small console beside her, adjusting knobs by the light of a desk lamp.

'Hey,' she said.

'Hey.' He held out his hand. She took it. He gave her hand a gentle squeeze.

It took her a moment to realise she was in the lighting control booth. 'What's up?' she said.

'Oh, you won't believe what's been going on,' said James. 'All the hardware here is seventy years out of date. I had to send a runner to a rental place to get this control board. Nothing's compatible with anything, and the crew is great at following orders but doesn't know an ERS from their elbow…'

'All in a day's work, huh?' she said. He put his head in his hand and groaned. It was the healthiest sound she'd heard him make in ages, because it was so familiar.

'Where's the Doctor?' she asked.

She saw him tense up, as if he'd just been hit. 'He had some errands to run,' he said. 'I came up here to keep an eye on you.'

'Thanks,' she said, and meant it.

'He has got to be the worst director I've ever worked for. Half the things he wants to do all by himself, all at the same time. And the other half he expects everyone to do without any kind of decent explanation.' He sighed and rolled his eyes. 'At least he's nice about it all…'

'Jealous,' she said, and tried to smile with it. She saw him shrivel at the word, and instantly wondered why she'd said it. This was James – she didn't want to hurt him. 'Sorry. Thanks for the squirrels… I just fell over.'

'I'm not surprised. You've been asleep all day long, you were whacked.'

'It could have killed me.' It still didn't feel real.

He shrugged. 'Yeah, well, give 'em a little time, they still could.'

They were quiet for a moment together. She looked around the cramped lighting booth, the foxhole they'd both ended up in.

'Sun's just gone down,' he said. 'They could come through that door any minute, I guess.'

'Yeah.' She was still holding on to his hand.

She hadn't given herself a chance to think or breathe or sleep. She'd pushed herself so far so hard that she'd almost lost her life. Even if the squirrels hadn't got her, she'd almost lost James and her job and everything she had here, just because she was so willing to run off with the Doctor.

Twenty years she'd tried to keep one foot in some other world, keeping an eye out for adventures that could have been and lovers that never were. Waiting for the Doctor. She'd built a life here, but she'd still been so willing to toss it all away. And while she'd been wondering what adventures she'd been missing out on out there, God only knew what she'd almost missed out on right here.

'I don't want to die,' she mumbled. 'I haven't finished my research.'

'Lots of things we haven't done yet, huh?' said James. 'I've still been meaning to get you to that Indian place for dinner, Maharani or whatever it was – we've been talking about it for weeks…'

'I couldn't miss out on that.'

Lots of reasons to live. To live here.

James was quietly scared out of his skull, and she could understand that. She understood him. But the Doctor cheerfully refused to be understood – he was a piece of sleight-of-hand on legs, who acted so young when he had a thousand years hidden up his sleeve. He was a hero, a trickster, a dazzling figure who'd risk his life for you and still pick your pocket without a second thought. Who may or may not have looked Eva in the eye and deliberately stabbed her in the heart. She'd wondered about him for twenty years. But no matter how amazing he was, there was something to be said for being certain.

She turned to James, and they smiled at each other for a moment. 'So what would you do if a vampire came up here?' she asked.

His response was instantaneous. 'Turn out the lights and pretend we're not here – you think I'm crazy?'

Carolyn smiled.

CHAPTER 18
REALITY BITE

The cemetery staff had set up work lights around the gravesite, to accommodate the unusual night funeral. It wasn't a big affair. Actually, it was a tiny affair: six mourners, no flowers except for a single, vast bouquet of carnations and babies' breath.

Harris stood next to the Doctor in the front row, by the casket, trying to puzzle it out. When the Doctor had phoned her and told her to meet him here at the cemetery, to pick up the anti-vampire toxin, she'd thought he was just showing a macabre sense of humour. She hadn't figured on his leading her right into a private ceremony and taking up residence with the mourners.

Only one of them got up to speak: the deceased's sister, a weary, rake-thin woman in an ancient black dress. She had a beautiful, soft voice, talking about their childhood. Harris listened for a while, trying to puzzle out who the guy in the casket was. The other mourners were a man in a blue suit that had seen better days and a couple of bearded, unkempt men sitting a little distance away. She could taste their poor health from across the chapel.

The woman began to sing. A hymn, her voice weak but pretty.

'Remind me who this is,' Harris whispered out of the corner of her mouth.

'Albert Brennan,' answered the Doctor.

'Don't know him.'

'You knew him very well indeed for thirty seconds last night.'

Very slowly Harris felt her skin turn even colder. Now she could feel every pair of eyes fixed on her, knowing somehow. 'You know what they'd do to me, if they knew?'

'Oh yes, quite.' He was still barely moving his mouth as he spoke, but she saw it curl into something resembling a smile. 'I wanted you to get to look at them.'

Harris looked. The guys with beards were derelicts, the family members were white trash. Hey –

'Who's paying for this?'

'You are,' said the Doctor, casually.

Harris felt a jolt of pure fear.

Then he produced a credit card from up his sleeve and handed it back to her. 'You should watch your handbag more closely.'

She made herself relax. 'And you arranged for them to have it at night. Just to prove a point to me.' It was just so typical of him – all those traps they were setting up for Slake, all those details he should be taking care of, and instead he spent his time off on a frivolous little tangent like this.

He shook his head. 'Oh, not just you. I did it for them.' He nodded in the direction of the other scattered mourners. 'They could never have afforded this otherwise. And I suppose I did it for me as well. I missed Grant Oxwell's funeral, I missed Ben-Zvi's, I thought I should make at least one.'

The service was over quickly, the priest running through the standard prayers. After the talking was over, they followed the casket out to the freshly dug grave. They always made Harris feel claustrophobic.

'So what were you hoping for?' she asked the Doctor, as they walked.

He sighed. 'Well, I certainly wouldn't have minded a tearful realisation of the harm you've wreaked. But I'll settle for reminding you that maybe you shouldn't do things like this just because they could do it to you.'

Harris looked around at the non-crowd.

'Might have been a more effective lesson,' she murmured, 'if more people actually cared.'

'I called in sick today.'

Slake said nothing, preferring to dig through the folders full of papers in Harris's desk drawer.

'Maria said this was the last of my leave for the year. It's like the old joke, isn't it? I've used up all my sick days, so now I've got to call in dead.'

Now that the Doctor had gone to ground, Slake had figured they had about as much chance of finding Harris instead. She had to have another place where she conducted the other experiments she kept hinting about, but she hadn't left a single clue to where it was. Not at the theatre, and it looked like not here, either. Cautious to the point of paranoia, as always.

'She must have called in sick too,' Shackle went on. 'I wonder what story she told them. She couldn't have said you were going to kill her.' He said the words like he couldn't quite believe in them.

Shackle had led him to her office at the medical lab, and here they were searching for any sign of where she could have run to. Or rather, Slake was searching, he reminded himself with venomous self-satisfaction, while Shackle was riffling through a few stacks of papers and rambling on about his feelings.

'Perhaps this really is for the best,' muttered Shackle. 'I never was a morning person.'

Slake tossed the files on the floor. 'Nothing!'

'Maybe I could switch to the night shift. Keep borrowing plasma from the blood bank.'

'Why would you bother?' said Slake. That shut him up.

Slake looked at the scrap of paper in his hand: a bill, one of many. A delivery of a low-speed centrifuge to an address less than a mile from here.

'I've got it,' he said abruptly.

'So where do we go now?'

'First, to the Other Place,' said Slake. 'I think it's time you met our secret weapon.'

'What's that?'

'Who's that,' Slake corrected with a smirk.

Now this could be a lot of fun, he thought. If anything could shake Harris up, the 'secret weapon' would do it. And if they couldn't find Harris after all, well, maybe he should just feed Shackle to him.

If nothing else it would keep him from having to put up with any more of that tedious self-absorbed prattling.

You know who you're beginning to sound like? the back of his mind taunted him. You must be getting old, Edwin.

Slake turned away, twisting up his face as if that would make it go away. You little turd. I killed you already. Aren't you ever going to lay off me?

'I know your kind,' said Harris.

'Yeah,' said Sam. 'Another tasty mortal, right?'

'That's not what I mean. Gimme that test-tube rack. I run into people like you all the time on the net. More concerned about using the right words than doing anything real.' Harris put down the pipette and glared at Sam. 'Lemme guess. We're not undead, we're living-impaired, right? Biologically challenged?'

Sam's mouth leapt open, but she carefully shut it before anything could escape. Deep breath, best polished pose. Don't let her bait you. 'I call people what they want to be called,' she said without blinking. She did have a few ideas of her own about what to call Harris, but the Doctor had said to keep things from getting violent.

'At least you're not lecturing me any more. If you've got to feel morally superior, for God's sake keep it to yourself.'

'You know what I think?' said Sam.

'Yeah, I know what you think. It doesn't matter that I'm trying to help the good guys. I'm still politically incorrect.'

Sam rolled her eyes. 'Oh yeah, and I'm so politically correct because I think ripping someone's throat out in an alley is kind of slightly wrong. Just like I'm oh so PC because I think mowing down every rainforest on the planet might be a bad idea, or because I think spitting on Asians in the street could be considered just a tad impolite. Believe me, I hear that rubbish all the time.'

'Sounds like you believe in lots of things,' said Harris. 'But if you're so sure of it, how come you haven't killed me?'

'What?'

Harris gestured with a hypodermic at the equipment around her. 'All this lethal stuff I've been working on… It would've been easy for you to shoot me full of it when I wasn't looking. So if you really think we don't deserve to live, how come I'm still alive?'

'Well, 'cause…' Because I can't. ''Cause we need your help to beat Slake and his bunch. Because I've never killed anyone before. Because you could kill me.''Cause it's not right to just stab someone in the back like that…'

She was fumbling for an answer, for a justification for what she knew was right. 'And 'cause it'd kill the Doctor.' D'oh! Why didn't she think of that in the first place?

Harris smirked. 'It's always something, isn't it? Now if you were serious about what you believed…'

'Look, don't even bother with it!' Sam exploded. 'I've heard the whole routine enough times, I can do it for you, save you the trouble. I'm a fake, right, a rich kid with too much time on her hands. List of causes a mile long and an inch deep. No way I could really care about things. I couldn't possibly have thought about any of it for myself, I'm too young. I gotta be just following the crowd, right?'

'Talk's cheap,' said Harris.

The words just kept pouring out. 'Yeah, they all say that too. That I can't know what the real world is like, 'cause I'm just in school and don't have to really live for real yet. And you know what? They're *right*. I've had it easy. I haven't had to prove myself yet. Why the hell do you think I'm *here*?'

Harris raised an eyebrow at her.

'It's to keep from being the kind of person you think I am. That's why I went to a real school instead of a farm for upper-class twits. That's why I ran off with the Doctor. It's cause I want to make a difference. It's 'cause I want to be real.'

Then why, asked a voice in her head, are you thinking about leaving?

'I don't believe it,' said Harris. 'You just used how many words trying to convince me you're not all talk?'

With a flourish Sam handed the completed beakerful to Harris, a gotcha smile on her face. Through the whole argument, she hadn't missed a step in the work. 'This is real, isn't it?' She allowed herself a moment of pride – ten out of ten for style, twenty out of ten for substance.

Then they heard the scraping at the door.

All sorts of horror legends leapt into Sam's mind. Then she figured it was probably someone trying to pick the lock. Harris was already heading towards a monitor screen in the corner, which switched between views from the security cameras over the four doors.

Three figures were clustered around the front door of the warehouse, one crouched at the lock. Others waited at the other entrances. Sam swallowed hard. They were surrounded.

Harris shrugged with resignation. 'Oh well. Looks like we might have to fight our way out.' She started back towards the workbench. 'We'll try the back side door. It's near my car and there's only two of them there…'

'Hang on,' said Sam. 'There are two too many of them.'

She pointed, and Harris looked. The high-angle cameras couldn't show very much of their faces, but there were definitely at least nine dark-clad figures in the shadows outside.

Harris squinted at them. 'They can't have had time to find two recruits yet. Unless…' She stopped. Her eyes didn't move from the screen, but Sam could see a slow frozen horror spreading across Harris's face. That must be how her own face looked right now.

Suddenly Harris spun around and stared her in the eye. 'Give me a description of who bit you.'

'The Doctor never told you?'

'We've had a few other things to worry about,' snapped Harris. 'Come on.'

'Skinny guy. Glassy stare. No hair. Walked like he didn't quite know how his body worked. Hung on to my neck like he was starving – wait, what, what?' Harris had turned away, her hands gripping the countertop, her eyes widening at some horror which Sam couldn't even imagine.

'*Shītan*,' said Harris. 'They've been letting out Weird Harold.'

The hollow-eyed vampire stood beside Slake at the doorway.

Food. There would be food. They never let him out unless they wanted him to catch some food.

Maybe this time it would be enough.

'We don't know his real name,' said Harris. 'Neither did he when we found him. He can't even remember how to speak. He'd snapped, his mind had been gone for ages. He'd gone underground.'

Not even the Doctor had left Harris this off-kilter – she was stumbling around the lab, digging through drawers and rambling. Seeing Harris rattled was making Sam feel even more rattled.

Harris's shaking hands ransacked another drawer. 'It's the vampire equivalent of a healing coma – if you're badly injured, you bury yourself for a few years, and when your body's recovered enough you regain consciousness and dig your way to the surface.'

'So that's what he did?' asked Sam.

Harris nodded. 'Trouble is, while he was underground, someone put a building on top of him.' Just telling the story was making her shiver. 'He must have been awake for years, trying to dig through the concrete. Starving. Panicking the whole time. We discovered him after the oh six quake brought the building down, and by then he'd worn all the flesh off his fingertips.'

'Oh God,' whispered Sam. 'So what did you do?'

'We took him in, tried to nurse him back to health, had people bring back leftovers from the hunts to feed to him –'

'You took care of him?' asked Sam

'Of course,' said Harris. 'He was in no state to hunt himself – and he never has been. He's too far gone. He doesn't have the social skills to lure any prey, and he's not cunning enough to street-hunt. We bring back whatever blood we can from the hunts – but there's never enough.' She stared Sam in the eye. 'He's been hungry for over a hundred years.'

'Oh Jesus,' said Sam.

'Do you know what that does to someone? I was with the others when we found him, and since I'd just eaten I offered to let him drink from me. He grabbed my throat and held me down and wouldn't let go even when I was completely dry.' Harris looked up at Sam, and Sam could see the trauma still in her eyes.

Harris opened another equipment drawer and found what she'd been hunting for, a set of outsized hypodermics. She grabbed them and ran to the workbench. 'That's what malnutrition does to us. Animal blood, or no blood at all… Eventually, the brain just goes. All that's left of him is the appetite.' She filled the first syringe from the beaker of Vamp-Away, trying to keep her hands from trembling. 'I wonder if that happens to you anyway, if you get old enough, that's all that's left of you.'

So that's what vampires have nightmares about, thought Sam.

'We keep him locked away in a room beneath the Other Place, as far away from us as we can. I didn't believe they'd ever let him out. I didn't think even Slake was that crazy…'

Then all the lights went out.

Sam's eyes couldn't cope with the complete blackness. No light sources, no windows, nothing at all – it was like having a blindfold slapped over her eyes.

A cacophony of startled whimpers and growls came from the people in the cage. Harris swore loudly, just a couple of feet away from Sam's ear. 'Rusty cut the power line.'

With a clunk the front door unlocked. All she could see were silhouettes outside, two of them shoving a single shambling figure into the warehouse with them, and slamming the door behind him.

Sam caught just a glimpse of Harris in the moment of light. She was staring in terror at the one who had just been locked in with them. 'The bastards. The sick bastards.'

Now Sam could hear the slow, awkward gait of the vampire coming towards them.

She didn't even need to see him, she knew every detail of the face. She could feel those sunken eyes staring at the two of them. Did he remember how she tasted? Did he remember her at all?

Sam reached out into the darkness and grabbed for Harris's arm. She felt Harris jerk, brought back to her senses, and start dragging her by the hand towards the back side door. 'This way.' Of course, night vision, thought Sam. Must've made it easy when she was the one stalking me.

She stumbled after Harris, letting that hand lead her around the obstacles in the warehouse, trying not to think about how close he was behind her.

This isn't me, she thought. This isn't my life and I'm nuts if I think it is. What is my life? Some kind of safe little suburban activist who believes from a safe distance. I might as well be dead. I may be dead anyway. I can't keep doing this. For God's sake, I'm a high school kid. I'm a high school kid who someone's trying to kill.

The hand stopped leading her. Sam reached out and felt the wall, the edge of the door. 'Wait. No power. Electronic locks. How do we open the doors?'

'One of these.' Sam heard the jingle of far too many keys in the dark. 'Can't see which. Too dark even for me.'

'No time.'

'I know.'

Sam groped for Harris's hand again, and when she found it she felt the loaded syringe in Harris's grip.

'If he gets you –'

'He drains me, I'm helpless, they kill me.'

'No. I'll do it. Just work on the door.'

What the hell did I just say? she thought.

'You're crazy,' said Harris. 'He'll rip you –'

'You'll have more time.'

'The Doctor'll have my head –'

'Look, will you get out of here?' Sam yelled. ''Cause if you die the Doctor dies, and I'm not gonna let that happen.'

Harris started to protest, then stopped. She felt Harris's hands grab her shoulders and turn her around. Aiming her towards the vampire she couldn't see. 'I'll say when.' The syringe was pressed into her hand, and then she heard Harris turn away and the keys jingling and scraping against the lock.

She couldn't see a thing and the vampire had to be maybe ten feet in front of her. Her mind could already feel the two points of enamel digging into her neck.

Ah, sod it, she couldn't back down now anyway. And if she gave up she'd be just what Harris said she was. Just a scared little girl who didn't have the guts to go through with what she said she stood for.

Pop quiz, hotshot. What do you believe in?

The Doctor wouldn't back away. He'd put himself on the line

for James, for Harris, for anyone and anything. If anyone deserved to live, it was him. If anyone was worth killing or dying for it was him, 'cause he was as close as she was ever gonna get to someone else who believed in everything.

'Now.'

Sam lowered her head and charged.

Her head and shoulders connected with Weird Harold's gut. She stabbed upward with the needle but she and he were already falling and she had to throw out an arm to catch herself. She kept her balance but he hadn't and he was somewhere at her feet. Somewhere. She'd missed with the syringe and now she couldn't find him.

No, don't run. Stay right there, be a target, cause if you're not there he'll go after Harris again.

She heard the fumbling as he picked himself up. Slowly she backed away, slowly, making sure the noises were following her. Feeling behind her with her heel on each step, praying to whoever was listening that she wasn't backing into a corner.

A hand from the darkness grabbed at her. She twisted away from it, but he was right there and she still couldn't see him.

Then there was light, a little of it, as the door flew open and Harris charged out. Weird Harold was a silhouette in front of her, too close. Beyond him she heard Harris shouting something loud and threatening as she ran, the exclamations of the two startled vamps guarding the door.

Weird Harold was between her and the light. She turned and ran.

She could see just enough to make it through the stacks of junk, running deeper into the warehouse. At a sprint she left him behind, but there was no way to lose him. All she could do was buy a few more seconds.

The food storage bin. She swung round the side, opposite Harris's workbench, and pressed herself against it. She raised the syringe high and tried to remember how to breathe.

From behind her she heard the sound of a struggle, of someone being slammed against the outside wall of the warehouse. A pair of running footsteps, a couple more in pursuit. A door slamming, a car starting, men's voices shouting back and forth.

She'd done it. Well, part of it. Harris and the Doctor were safe – now it was just her.

She had to do this.

She wanted to do this.

She could hear the footsteps. He was moving a lot faster now – he must have realised there was food ahead of him. This was it. She raised the syringe, feeling her lungs rattling in her chest, ready to bring it crashing down on him.

No, wait, you're behind the only scrap of cover in sight, he knows you're there. Do the unexpected, remember? Attack from some other direction. Find something. Look around. You're in a laboratory.

She leapt across the pathway to the lab bench. Twist the gas tap. Box of matches, got to be some there, found them. Weird Harold's rounded the corner now, run like hell, get the workbench between you and him.

She was face to face with him across the bench. His chest was just out of her range, but that was good, he couldn't reach her either. Stall him. Keep the bench between you and him. He goes left, you go right, he goes right, you go left.

Strike the match.

Raise the syringe.

You can do it. You can do this. He goes right, you go right. Towards him. Towards the gas tap. You've got him.

Sam dropped the match into the gas jet.

The fireball lasted just a moment, just long enough to make him cry out and throw up his arms to protect his eyes. He howled and she was screaming, a great scream of defiance as she grabbed on to him and sank her own fang into him and he was never going to hurt her again, more than that, never going to hurt anyone again. She could feel the skeletal body writhe and collapse against her, the muscles turning to ash, the bones to powder.

When he slipped through her fingers and trickled to the floor, she still didn't let go. She stayed there, swaying slightly on her feet, the empty syringe still clutched in her hand. Feeling relief and joy in each shaking breath.

She'd done it.

She was alive.

Slowly she let the tension melt out of her shoulders. She turned off the gas, put the spilled beaker of Vamp-Away back on the workbench, and started for the door. All she had to do now was get to the Doctor, and they could finish this.

'Well, if it isn't Buffy the Vampire Slayer.'

Slake filled the doorway. Instantly Sam raised the empty syringe, wielding it like a knife fighter.

'I have to say I'm impressed,' said Slake, strutting towards her. 'You seemed to enjoy that tremendously. I think you could even get a taste for it.' He advanced on her, the other vampires following his lead.

She backed away a bit, towards the workbench. 'You offering me a position or something?'

'Why not?' He smirked knowingly. 'We could always use new recruits. Particularly ones with enthusiasm for the kill.'

'Why the hell would I want to join you?'

'So I wouldn't kill you,' he said.

'I've got a better reason for you not to do that.'

'Oh?'

'So you won't piss off the Doctor.'

Slake just raised an eyebrow, then lowered his voice to a murmur. 'Surely you must be curious. There's so much I could teach you, about taking the source of life and bending it to your pleasure.' His hand reached out as if to caress her cheek. 'To indulge in the forbidden desires you've always hidden…'

'Oh, shut up!' Sam yelled. She raised the syringe and took a step towards Slake. 'Maybe they're not forbidden desires, maybe I just bloody well don't desire them!'

He grabbed her by the throat. Her stitches screamed as his fingernails dug into them. The pain blotted out any smart remarks, let the syringe slip out of her hand before she even knew what her fingers had done. Oh well, if this was it at least she'd gone out on a high note.

'Fine, then,' pouted Slake. 'You don't want to join us, we've still got one other use for you first.'

* * *

The Doctor hustled across the stage, trailing a cable in his wake and talking to everyone around him at once. 'No no no, you can't put the downstage units out there – run them from the first electric. Yes, I know it'll take another hour to set it up, but we've got to keep the side aisles clear for the soldiers. Put that one on circuit three, circuit two's at maximum load. Hello, yes?' The last words were directed into his borrowed cell phone as it rang.

'Uh, Doctor?' said Sam's voice. 'They got me.'

The Doctor stopped.

'I got one of them, though.'

The soldiers near him were beginning to notice he'd stopped, slowing their work, freezing in place. 'Sam, are you all right?'

'Yeah, she is for now,' said Slake's voice in her place. 'We want to talk to you. Now.'

The Doctor stared at the phone, his mouth working up and down, completely at a loss.

'Oh. Ah. I…' He sounded as flustered as he could. 'At the theatre?'

'We'll be there. Twenty minutes,' said Slake, and broke the connection. The Doctor looked up from the phone, listening to the silence which had fallen. Looking at the stage full of soldiers, all hanging on his next word.

'Well,' he said. 'Twenty minutes to showtime.'

CHAPTER 19
MATTER OF DEATH AND LIFE

'How could you do this?'

Dr Shackle looked down at Sam. 'What else was there to do?'

They were sitting in the back of a big, cold van. The vampires were ignoring them, mostly because Reaper had insisted on playing Faith No More at about twelve thousand decibels.

'Oh right,' said Sam. 'What are my options for today? See that new film, do a bit of shopping, turn to the dark side and grow one-inch canines.'

'Once,' said Shackle, 'once I worked for three days straight. There was a fire and a gang war. I didn't sleep. I ate crackers. I fainted twice, but I kept going. Kids your age were being wheeled in, burnt or shot. There were bodies on the floor in the morgue.'

'You were a hero,' said Sam. 'How could you give that up?'

'After the first twenty-four hours or so,' said Shackle, 'I kept imagining cutting my wrists. I think it started because one of the first patients that Friday was an attempted suicide. She was all right... all right for someone who wanted to be dead. But all weekend I saw those cuts on her wrists.'

'It wasn't like that every day, was it?' said Sam.

'I kept telling myself that,' said Shackle. 'I knew there was no reason for me to kill myself. I just didn't believe it.' He clutched his heart. 'I didn't believe it.'

'Is this what you want?' said Sam. She looked at the van full of losers. 'Is this really what you want?'

'If you'll pardon my change of metaphor,' said Shackle, 'it's a bit late to change your mind five storeys from the pavement.'

Harris ran into the theatre and almost ran into Kramer. 'Miss Harris,' said the soldier.

'They've got Sam,' said the vampire.

'We know. They're on their way here.'

'They want me,' said Harris. 'I'm the last of the old ones left alive. When I get my hands on Slake –'

'No,' said Kramer. 'We'll keep you out of the action. Hidden.'

'What are you planning?'

'Oh, all sorts of surprises,' said the soldier. 'This way.'

'So,' asked Sam. 'You tasted blood yet?'

'Why?' muttered Shackle. 'Do you think there's still hope for my immortal soul if I haven't?'

'It's just that you're gonna be having the same thing for every meal now. For ever. You could have anything you wanted for breakfast when you were alive, think of all the different things you tried, all the different tastes… Better forget about that now.'

Now that was just twisting the knife. He wanted to look at her, see what was in her eyes, but she'd pointedly turned her back towards him. The van rounded another corner, pushing them both against the wall.

'I never really had breakfast,' he said. 'Never enough time.'

'Always the way,' she said coolly.

His taste buds felt just as remote as the rest of the body he was rattling around in. 'What a con,' he said quietly. 'The whole vampire thing was always supposed to be the great sensual experience. Dark romance and a new exotic taste.' He looked at her, almost pleading. 'Don't tell me you never saw the attraction there.'

'Why?' She turned to him with a look of surprise. 'Who needs blood when you've got chocolate?'

The van jerked to a halt. Slake turned off the motor, then swung round to look at the others. 'OK boys, let's knock 'em dead.'

The Doctor stood on the stage, alone, illuminated by a single spotlight.

He clasped his hands behind his back. A dozen UNIT soldiers were crouched in the aisles at the sides of the theatre, waiting silently.

The doors at the back of the theatre opened.

Slake led the young ones down the aisle. He had his hands on

Sam's shoulders, propelling her in front of them. They got halfway down when he called out, 'Get the soldiers out of here, or I'll rip out her throat right now.'

'All right,' said the Doctor. 'Lieutenant, take your people out of here. I'll handle this.'

'We'll handle you,' jeered Rusty.

Lieutenant Forrester stood up and saluted the Doctor. The soldiers filed out, carefully, keeping their eyes on the vampires.

The Doctor had hoped Slake would be brash enough to attack him right away, giving Kramer's people a chance to deal with some of the others. That was one line crossed off the list of options.

'Now,' he told Slake, 'let her go.'

'Make me,' said Slake. He started moving towards the stage again.

'What?' said the Doctor cheerfully. 'Not even a pretence of negotiation? That won't do at all, you know.'

'I don't see why we should waste any time on formalities,' sneered Slake. 'What've you got to negotiate with, anyway? All you could scrape up was a handful of soldiers, and now they're gone too. It's just you, and your little BBC girlie, and me and my boys.'

'Survival of the cynical-est?' said the Doctor, as the vampires jumped up on to the stage. Slake twisted his fingers in Sam's hair and pulled her after him. 'And the bleak shall inherit the earth?'

The vampires were circling the Doctor. 'I know why you're here,' said the Doctor quietly. 'You don't need her, you've got me now.'

'You'll keep,' Slake told Sam. He gave her a shove, and suddenly she was outside the circle of killers.

'Doctor, I'm sorry,' she said.

'Don't worry,' said the Doctor, keeping his eyes on Slake. 'If this one's foolish enough to attack me, he'll regret it.'

Slake snorted with laughter. 'Do you know what we're going to do with you?'

'The foxtrot?'

'Doctor,' said Shackle, from somewhere among the dark seats, 'I'm sorry.'

'You've made your decision,' said the Doctor. 'I wish I could say you had to live with it. Last chance, Edwin.'

'Rip him apart,' said Slake.

'Sam!' shouted the Doctor. 'Hide your eyes!'

Cue zero, thought James, and pushed the master slider on the light board up to full.

Dawn came up inside the Orpheum.

It had taken an hour to plan and four hours to set it up. The whole lighting rig, every available light at full strength. The perfect mix and balance of gels, fluoros, and a dozen blacklights, burning down on to the stage in just the right spectrum.

Artificial sunlight.

The vampires started screaming.

Slake flung his arm over his face. The Doctor could see his fingers blistering in the hot light. Sam had stumbled back, both hands covering her eyes.

Reaper and Shredder ran off, stage right. 'Jeez, Slake, this hurts!' cried Rusty, heading for the auditorium.

'Stay here!' roared Slake. 'Don't let him get away! Don't break the circle!'

The vampires obeyed him, trying to protect their faces.

The Doctor was darting back and forth, the vampires staying in any patch of shadow they could find, Shredder behind a ladder, Elvis behind the proscenium. 'Come on, Slake!' called the Doctor. 'This is the best chance you've had to work on your tan in half a century!'

Slake roared and rushed into the light. The Doctor jumped to one side, hands catching the rungs of a ladder, and started climbing.

'Where's he going?' said Carolyn.

'Into the lighting rig,' said James. 'To one of the catwalks up there.'

'The light isn't killing them,' said Carolyn. 'It's hurting them, but it's not killing them. Can't you do something?'

'I can't do anything else,' said James. 'If we could have installed some vari-lites, but there wasn't time…'

Slake snatched at the Doctor's ankles, snarled, and started climbing up after him. Fine smoke was rising from the vampire's skin.

'Why are you even bothering?' yelled Slake. 'When I catch you –'

'I'm busy right now,' shouted the Doctor, 'but perhaps I could pencil you in for next Thursday.'

Slake lunged upward, catching the Doctor's ankle. The Doctor lashed out with his other foot, gripping the ladder hard. His toe caught the vampire under the chin. Slake yelled and let go.

Rusty ran out to the exposed ladder and hopped back, yelping as his skin started to smoke. Elvis darted out from behind the proscenium and grabbed the ladder. With a single, violent wrench, he pulled it loose, bolts wrenching free at the top and the bottom. The Doctor was six feet below the safety of the catwalk. He made a desperate lunge for the lighting rig over the stage.

There was another ladder on the other side, in the shadow of the curtain. Shredder started climbing up, and then hand-over-hand on to the lighting rigging. But he couldn't get near the Doctor to reach him without emerging into the light.

The Doctor was laughing. 'Six to one, and you still can't catch me!' Keep your eyes on me, Slake, give Sam her chance.

'We'll catch you, Doctor,' said Slake. 'You'll wish you'd held your tongue when I bite it out of your mouth.'

Shredder swung on the lighting rig, trying to shake the Doctor loose. The Doctor clung on to the metal for dear life. 'That's the problem with you, Slake! You're dependent!'

'I'm what?' the vampire snarled, his shout filling the theatre.

'Dependent. Without someone to scare, someone to hurt, someone to kill, someone to feel superior to – what are you? Nothing!' He laughed. 'You're nothing, Slake!'

'You come down here and say that!'

The Doctor looked down, past his dangling feet. His hearts convulsed. He must be forty, fifty feet from the stage and his hands were chafing on the lighting grid.

Never mind that, he told himself, grinning.

He reached out and grabbed one of the lights, turning it until the spot passed over Shredder's face. The moment before the vampire realised it was a green gel and not another of the blacklights, he instinctively let go of the rig.

He crashed into the stage, and for a moment everyone was looking at him, and Sam ran for the auditorium.

'Rusty! Grab her!' shouted Slake.

The vampires were suddenly lunging for Sam as she ran, jumping over Shredder's groaning form and running to the edge of the stage. They were going to catch her. 'Slake!' shouted the Doctor. 'Slake!' The vampire didn't look up.

Plan B, thought the Doctor, and opened his hands.

At thirty-two feet per second squared acceleration due to gravity, starting from a height of about forty or forty-five feet, he figured he had approximately one and a half seconds to work out the details of what Plan B was before –

'Doctor!' screamed Sam.

'Get him!' screamed Slake.

Elvis was the first one to reach the Doctor. The Time Lord had landed wrong, and was trying to get up, clutching his side. Elvis grabbed his collar and dragged him, struggling, into the shadow.

Sam started to run back. The vampires had gathered around the Doctor, crouching down. She couldn't help him. There was nothing she could do to help him.

'Kramer!' shouted Sam. 'For God's sake!'

She ran up the aisle, towards the doors. If the soldiers wouldn't come she'd get one of their guns herself.

Shackle was in her way. She was about to punch him in the stomach when she saw he was watching the stage in horror.

She turned. She saw Slake grab the Doctor's head and smack it against the stage, and again, the Time Lord's fingers tangled desperately in Slake's hair, trying to keep his mouth away from his throat.

She pushed Shackle out of the way and kept running, tears blurring her vision.

Behind her, the Doctor roared in agony as Slake sank his fangs into his throat.

Kramer stared at Harris, out in the foyer. The vampire raised her hands, slowly. Blood was running down her arms from her wrists, blood was trickling down her throat. As Kramer watched, a bright red stain spread through Harris's shirt.

'Hurt,' whimpered the vampire. 'He hurts.'

Kramer exploded in through the doors as Sam reached them. 'They're killing him!' screamed Sam.

Kramer looked. 'Jesus Christ,' she said. 'We're too late.'

Harris stumbled blindly down towards the stage. The young ones didn't care, didn't care about anything, attached to the Doctor. Elvis had one of his wrists and Rusty had the other and Slake had torn open his shirt and was biting into his chest, for God's sake; the Doctor was still struggling, still fighting, but Shredder had his throat, and Fang had grabbed his arm, and Reaper was actually biting his ankle, desperate to share in the kill.

Kramer was running towards the stage, and Sam and Harris with her, but they weren't going to be able to save him.

There was a terrible scream, stopping everyone in their tracks. It echoed through the theatre, through the sudden silence.

Slake raised his head up from the Doctor's chest and screamed again. He let go of the Time Lord and crawled away from him, gasping in agony.

He exploded in a shower of grey, his body spreading out on the stage in a human shape made of ash.

The others sat back from their victim, staring at Slake.

Harris swayed, and Sam caught her. 'Let me go,' slurred the vampire.

'No, stay out of the light,' said Sam, grabbing her arm. 'It must be a delayed reaction to the light. Look at them!'

Rusty was shrieking, little piping sounds of panic, and then he fell over and disintegrated into ash. Fang just fell on to his back and exploded. Shredder and Reaper got up and tried to run and made it a few steps before they fell and burst in puffs of grey powder.

Elvis was the last to go. He died with his mouth still clasped to the Doctor's wrist, gulping down one last mouthful before he died.

The others jumped on to the stage. 'The lights!' shouted Sam. 'James, kill the lights!'

Sudden darkness. Then the house lights came up, soft after the glare of the artificial sunlight.

Harris fell to her knees beside the Doctor.

He lay in the centre of a pile of ashes. He was breathing fast, in shallow gasps, his eyes tightly clenched shut.

'He's dying,' said Harris, thickly.

'No way.' Sam lifted the Doctor's head, gently, holding it in her lap. 'What would you know about it? You don't know anything about it, shut up!' Harris didn't reply.

Carolyn was suddenly there, too. Everyone was standing or kneeling around the Doctor. Sam wanted to scream at them to do something, but there wasn't time, there wasn't anything they could do. Carolyn was weeping, James standing behind her. He knelt down and put his arms around her.

The Doctor was white as a sheet, his forehead icy cold. Sam gently felt for his pulse. It was racing, weak. How much blood had he lost? Enough, she thought. The end. The end of her big adventure, the end of their travels together, the end of the magic.

Something rolled out of his coat pocket. Sam picked it up. It was –

The Doctor's eyelids flickered. He tried to lift one hand. It trembled. Sam reached for it.

The Doctor reached out and grasped Joanna Harris's hand.

She tried to pull away. He held on tight. 'Joanna,' he breathed.

'Oh my God!' said Carolyn, realising what he was asking. 'No, you can't!'

'Are you sure?' the vampire asked him. 'Are you completely sure?'

'Forget it,' said Sam.

'Look at him!' said Harris. 'I'm his only chance. Do you want him to die?'

Sam could still see him swinging from the grid, his long legs

274

kicking out in the air, the mad smile she'd spotted on his face. He'd known exactly the kind of horrible things people like Slake could do, and it hadn't stopped him from grinning.

She said, and her voice was completely calm, 'If you destroy what makes the Doctor the Doctor, I'll kill you.'

'Please,' gasped the Doctor.

'It's not your choice,' Harris told Sam. She took the Doctor away from Sam, gathered him up. 'First things first,' she murmured. 'We've got to stop that bleeding.'

She pressed her mouth to his throat, very gently. There were terrible bruises where the vampires had worried the flesh. In a moment she had sealed up the wound, the blue damage was fading into yellow.

Harris was lifting the Doctor's torn wrist to her lips when she stopped, eyes widening. 'The taste is wrong,' she said. 'He –'

She crumpled.

Sam glanced down at the vial in her hand. It was empty.

She looked around, at the piles of ash that had once been vampires. *If this one's foolish enough to attack me, he'll regret it.*

'It's over,' said Kramer.

'No,' said the Doctor. He was struggling to sit up. Sam grabbed his arm and helped him. 'Joanna, no,' he said.

The vampire lay where she'd fallen, eyes closed. She wasn't breathing.

The Doctor turned her on to her back and kissed her.

No, he wasn't kissing her – he was pinching her nose closed, puffing into her mouth, watching her chest rise. One, two, three, four.

'Come on, Joanna,' he said, pressing his fingers into her throat. 'You're not dying. You only think you're dying. Come on, you've got a pulse, I can feel it. Please. Concentrate. Live.'

He bent over her again. He breathed into her mouth, turned his head to listen and to watch her chest rise and fall, breathed, turned, breathed, turned, just like they'd been trained at school. Kiss of life, thought Sam.

And here I was feeling all proud 'cause I'd killed someone.

Harris coughed and gasped and spluttered, breathing hard. The

Doctor sat back. Sam held him up. 'There,' he said. 'I knew you could do it.'

'I'm breathing,' said Harris hoarsely. 'I'm *breathing* breathing.'

'I'm afraid you're going to have to get used to it,' said the Doctor. 'Again.' He took her hand. 'Life wins,' he said, with a gentle smile.

'You killed me,' she said, and started sobbing.

CHAPTER 20
GETTING A LIFE

'Pretty simple in the end, wasn't it?' said Kramer, taking a big bite from her fudge-ripple ice-cream cone. 'The good guys kill the bad guys. End of story.'

The Doctor shook his head. 'No no no. The bad guys killed themselves. All the good guys had to do was let them make the right mistakes.' He took a lick from his own cone and grinned, showing off a hint of a chocolate moustache.

Kramer shrugged. 'Even better that way.'

Sam watched Kramer from across the kitchen table. 'If you think this was simple, you're wrong,' she said quietly. She was still seeing Weird Harold exploding into a puff of grey death, all around her.

It had been the Doctor's idea to stop for ice cream. At the first sign of an all-night grocery store, he'd steered them straight into the frozen-foods section. He'd said something about having to restore his blood sugar, but from the look on his face it was clear he'd done it just because he enjoyed it. The drowsy clerk hadn't even noticed his bandaged wrists.

He'd made a great ceremony out of offering a huddled and withdrawn Harris her first meal in more than nine hundred years. She'd chosen strawberry, and after a few dubious licks Sam had caught a faint smile wandering on to her face. Sam had clinked her cone against the Doctor's in a mock toast.

Carolyn was saying, 'They were as good as dead either way. It didn't matter, all that stuff you said about how everything has its place, how they had a right to live too... The moment you decided they'd crossed that line, they were dead.'

'Yeah,' said Sam. 'Funny, y'know, that you had the Vamp-Away in your system before you knew the vampires would attack you.'

The Doctor shrugged it off. 'Yes, well, I drank it a little while before they arrived. It seemed reasonable.'

'I still can't believe it didn't kill you stone dead,' said Carolyn.

'Different biochemistry,' said the Doctor. 'Fortunately, I can metabolise chocolate.'

'But you must have drunk enough to kill an elephant.'

Harris said, 'That's right. To have the concentration you had in your bloodstream, you'd have to have drunk a lot more than that vial. And a lot more than a few minutes before the meeting. Probably even before we heard Slake had started the war.'

'All right then,' sighed the Doctor, 'I drank it a little *more* than a little while before they arrived. It still seemed like a reasonable precaution. Now, are you quite finished?'

'Oh, I dunno.' Sam had a satisfied grin on her face, like someone who had just filled in the last clue in a crossword puzzle. 'Funny that you found a way to slip Harris just enough of a dose to kill her as a vampire, while the bloodfasting was strong enough to keep her alive as a human.'

'Funny that you agreed to get bloodfasted,' put in Harris. 'I'd warned you you could get turned, but I never thought it could work the other way.'

'Yes,' said the Doctor casually. 'Worked out well, didn't it?'

'Almost like you'd planned it that way,' said Sam.

The Doctor shook his head in disbelief that they could even think that of him. 'That was luck,' he protested.

'Face it, Doctor,' Kramer said, and grinned. 'You've got a rep.'

'It very nearly didn't turn out well at all,' said the Doctor. 'Do you really want to believe that I'm the kind of person who would let things get as bad as they did, if I cleverly had it all under control?'

Kramer and Sam exchanged glances. Harris stole a spoonful of Sam's butterscotch ripple.

'Well, what do you want? What do you want me to be?' the Doctor asked. 'Someone who knows exactly what he's doing and has it all under control, or just some fellow who makes it up as he goes along, and still makes it happen?'

He met both their eyes, and they could see an honest question in them. 'Which do you want it to be? Magic tricks, or magic?'

* * *

'Green,' said Carolyn.

Kramer shook her head. 'No, they're blue.'

'Look, I'm telling you, they're green. Just ask him.'

Kramer stared at the Doctor, who was waiting on the streetcorner with Harris. The colour of his eyes was lost in the yellowish tinge of the streetlamp.

'Ah, don't even bother,' she muttered, and grinned. 'You think he'd ever be just one or the other? He'll tell us something and it'll make us both think we're right.'

The Doctor paid them no attention. His eyes were on Harris, who was looking shakily around her. 'I remember when this place was magic,' she said.

They stood at the corner of Haight and Ashbury Streets. 'Oh yes,' said the Doctor. 'I remember those days. In fact, I think at least three of me visited. The summer of love, before the autumn of disappointment and terrible hangovers. It was fun while it lasted.'

Kramer and Carolyn had rejoined James and Sam, looking at something in a shop window. 'Nothing left of it now, is there?' Harris said. 'Just some shops and some tourists. Nothing of what it used to be.' She was shaking. 'What am I going to do?'

'You're strong, Joanna.' He put his hands on her shoulders, held her still until she stopped trembling. 'You can survive anything.'

'Except dying,' she said.

'Yes, well,' said the Doctor. 'You don't have to worry about that for a long time to come.'

She flashed her old sarcastic smile. 'Maybe I'll just find another vampire somewhere, and get him to turn me all over again.'

The Doctor gave a sigh, part frustration and part bemusement. 'Joanna, I think you're somewhat missing the point here. You're alive. Go and walk in the park, feed the ducks, fall in love, read a book, do whatever it is that young humans do.'

'Oh,' said Harris flatly. 'That.'

He changed direction without missing a beat. 'All right, then. Find something else to do. Whatever you want – think of all your enthusiasm for finding out what makes vampires tick. Just to know, just to understand. Just for the joy of using your mind. For heaven's sake, you don't have to be dead to do that.'

She was shrinking, overwhelmed by his enthusiasm. 'It's been a long time. I don't think I remember.'

He squeezed her shoulder, gently. 'It's like riding a bicycle.' He smiled and started to turn away, then caught himself. 'At any rate,' he said sternly, 'you've still got a warehouse full of people to care for. That should keep you quite busy for the rest of your life and theirs.'

'I think UNIT might be interested in helping out with that,' put in Kramer, as she and Sam caught up. 'In exchange for the services of a biologist with hundreds of years' experience, of course.'

The TARDIS was another block down the street. They waited until some tourists had finished taking a photo of it.

The Doctor unlocked the door and turned to the others. 'Right,' he said. 'So who's coming with me?'

He took a step back, and nearly ploughed into Sam, who'd come to his side before he'd even realised she was there. She looked up at him and grinned, and he ruffled her hair. Then he looked at each of the others.

'What, are you kidding?' said Kramer. She grinned out of one side of her mouth.

'No thanks,' said James. 'Nothing personal, you understand.'

Harris's face was torn. She looked at the Doctor and the TARDIS with longing in her eyes, and Sam tensed. She hadn't realised the Doctor's offer extended even to the ex-vampire.

Then Harris shook her head. 'I can't. I've got things to take care of here.'

The Doctor nodded, pleased. Right answer, thought Sam.

'Carolyn?' he asked.

Carolyn looked at him, then slowly turned, walked over to James, and kissed him senseless.

As they walked away, Kramer said to Carolyn, 'Would you be interested in a position as a part-time scientific consultant to UNIT? Might as well collect 'em all.'

'We can work together,' said Harris. 'If you like. Don't worry, I don't bite.'

Carolyn said, 'I'll think about it.' She thought about it. 'James?'

'It's up to you,' he said bravely.

'OK,' said Carolyn. 'As long as I don't have to do any alien autopsies.'

There was a dreadful noise behind them. They all turned around.

Kramer said, 'Abracadabra!'

The civilians stared in astonishment as the TARDIS dematerialised.

A few seconds later, Carolyn burst into applause.

Sam buzzed around the console while the Doctor oiled a stuck control. 'I still want to know,' she said. 'When'd you plan it? When'd you take the Vamp-Away?'

He tried his best to look inscrutable, though the effect was somewhat spoiled by the smudge of chocolate next to his mouth. 'A good magician never reveals his secrets.'

She smiled softly. 'Not even to the sorcerer's apprentice?'

He grinned for a moment and patted her hand. 'I don't know how much I can really teach you. You seem to be picking it up just fine on your own.'

Epilogue

He should have gone with them.

They'd left the theatre and never known he was still alive. Probably they'd figured he'd died with the others, just another of the heaps of dust, to be swept away with all the other loose ends. Perhaps they hadn't even thought about him at all.

When the bloodbath had started, he'd hung back. Despite all the times he'd said he'd given up all hope, all the times he figured he'd lost any semblance of what he'd once believed, he still couldn't bring himself to join in with the others as they tore into the Doctor.

It had saved his life, such as it was.

When the dead had tried to kill the Doctor, he'd hung back in the shadows. When the living had tried to save the Doctor, he'd hung back again. He hadn't dared approach them, not after everything he'd said and done. He figured he'd burnt every bridge he'd ever had.

But even then at the end, they would have taken him back. He could see that now, after they had gone.

The Doctor had no fear of falling, because he knew he could always clamber back up, through the sheer force of who he was. Through the people he loved, through the things he believed in, through knowing with that childlike certainty just what he wanted to be.

Unfortunately, thought David Shackle as he stood alone on the Orpheum stage, not everyone had the Doctor's sense of clarity.

Still, if nothing else, at least whatever he did next would be his own decision. He'd almost forgotten what that felt like. There was no one to lead him any more, the way Harris or Slake had led him, no more path of least resistance to wander down. He could go after Harris, or Carolyn, or just go straight back to the clinic. Or wander out into the sunlight and burn himself to nothingness. For the first time in as long as he could remember, he could see all sorts of possibilities.

In fact, right now, he thought as he looked at the ruin surrounding him, possibilities were about all he had.

Outside the sun was rising.

Acknowledgements

First of all we owe a huge debt to the inventors of the Internet – while most of this book was written face-to-face, these last few months we've been e-mailing chapters from Washington DC to Sydney and back at a frantic pace.

Then there's all the other eighth-Doctor novelists, especially Paul Leonard and Mark Morris – we've been swapping lots of e-mail trying to make sure the new Doctor and companion really sparkle together. Plus Paul Cornell for inspiration, Andy Lane for making Jon think he really could write in the first place, r.a.dw, a.dw.c, Special K, and all the rest of the online community we're so glad to be a part of.

The all-new read-through crew – Melissa Boyle, Kevin Cherry, Cary Gordon, Beckie Hunter, Rachel Jacobs, Adam Korengold, Sadron Lampert, Neil Marsh, Greg McElhatton, Marsha Twitty, and Jeff Weiss – for laughing at all the bits that deserved to be laughed at.

Jennifer Tifft – who, in addition to being everything Kate said she was in the last book, is also a wealth of information about her home town.

David Carroll and Kyla Ward, for all the vampire flicks and neat little insights.

Special thanks to our respective families – the best sets of in-laws-to-be either of us could ever ask for.

And finally, a hearty thank-you to Phil Segal and everyone else who helped make the telemovie – you folks gave us all these neat new pieces to play with in the greatest Lego set ever invented.